# Guardian Spirit

## B. Ellen Gardner

**Front Cover Design:** Richard Trigilio

**ISBN – 13:** 9781796452693

*This book is dedicated to my two beautiful daughters, Laura and Sarah, who both love a good mystery. No bond is more powerful than the bond between a mother and a child.*

# FOREWORD

Zunis believe all things have spirits. These spirits are known as kachinas. A kachina might be an animal, plant, or a force of nature. Twice a year during July and December, the kachinas leave their homes in the sacred mountains to visit the villages. At this time, Zuni men dress as particular kachinas, becoming that kachina. They are known as kachina dancers. According to Zuni belief, the kachina dancer is able to see the spirit he imitates. The spirit in return gives the dancers certain powers that will empower the villages and their people.

A guardian spirit is a spirit that is connected to another spirit. There are times when humans are chosen to be guardian spirits. The guardian spirit protects its kindred spirit and is able to detect disharmony within its soul. A fetish, such as a ring or necklace, sometimes known as a power object, is used to connect the two spirits. The union of the two spirits is deemed sacred and can never be broken.

# PROLOGUE

Toby Garcia cut the lights, and the neon sign that flashed outside of the *Blue Horse Bar* went out.

"Closing time," he called out to the handful of people seated randomly around the bar.

Billy Nehah, a forty-year-old Zuni artist, who sometimes stopped by the *Blue Horse* when he came to Gallup selling his paintings and jewelry to local merchants, got up first. He stood around five-ten, stocky build, wearing dark pants and a white shirt with buttons trimmed in turquoise. He liked to display his livelihood and was wearing the earrings, belt, and rings he had designed and made. His long black hair was knotted in the back with a woven ribbon and a red bandana swept around his forehead.

Before leaving, he laid a tip on the counter for Toby and waved goodbye to Lee Flanks, a fifty-year-old regular, who more times than not lagged around until closing time.

"See ya, Billy," Toby said and started clearing out his register.

A smart looking blonde around twenty and her companion, a rugged type around thirty with tattoos and a full beard, were sitting on one side of a booth near the back of the bar. On the other side of the booth, a small girl around four or five was sleeping. Toby heard her call the blonde mamma. He didn't recall the child ever speaking to the man, but overheard the woman call him Jack.

The child was a shy sort. Smart too, Toby guessed. She knew when to sit quietly and when to talk. She had sad hollow eyes that stabbed at his heart. Billy had noticed them as well. Earlier, they had tried to speak to her, but she had hidden behind her mother. Billy tucked a small necklace he had made inside her hand, a fetish used to protect against evil.

"This is a spirit necklace," he told her. "The spirits, the Kachinas, will always be with you so long as you keep it near your heart."

The child held the necklace, made of shell beads and dyed eagle feathers on a braided strap. She constantly rubbed the soft feathers back and forth as if this movement was somehow soothing her troubled spirit. She never thought to place the necklace around her neck, but clutched it tightly in her hand. Even when she later fell asleep in the booth, she held onto the braided strap that weaved in and out of her small fingers.

Toby casually watched the scene taking place in the booth. He wondered how a classy looking gal like her mama had gotten mixed up with such a low life. All night, this scum had been feeling her up, indecently exposing her to everyone in the bar. Not that Toby blamed the guy for having a good time with her. She was a looker for sure, with silky blonde hair and deep brown eyes and a body that made him wish for younger days. It just seemed to Toby that he was having a better time than she was.

Toby was sure that if it hadn't been for the booze and if she hadn't been so tipsy, she would have been downright embarrassed at the way he was handling her. Ordinarily, he would have stopped such behavior, but let it go tonight since it was a Monday and there weren't many customers. Besides, the smart ass was laying some good tips on the table.

The couple got up and the punk shook the sleeping baby until she woke up. As if she had done this every day of her life, the small girl got up and followed him. She had one hand wrapped around her mother's leg and the other hand was clutching her necklace. She shuffled her tiny feet forward still half asleep. Her long brown hair flopped in her face.

When they reached the register to pay their tab, the man

called Jack pinned the blonde against the counter just in front of Toby and started kissing her and rubbing his hands up and down her breasts. He lifted her T-shirt in order to fondle her for Toby's benefit. His steely eyes spoke volumes. The young woman blushed when she caught Toby's eye, but her cocky boyfriend only grinned and handed him a fifty.

"Christ," Toby muttered as the man led the woman out. He watched the three walk down the sidewalk into the dark night and locked the door behind them.

"Slime," he muttered. Guys like that gave him the creeps.

He grabbed the money bag hidden under the register and tucked it in his jeans. Toby was a large man; almost six feet and weighed nearly three hundred pounds. The bulk from the bag was well disguised by his large frame. He turned to see that Lee Flanks had passed out at the counter. He made one final walk-through the bar and then nudged the old-timer.

"Come on pal. Time to go home."

Flanks pulled his head up slightly trying to stand up. Toby steadied him, wiping the sweat off his brow on his way towards the back.

"Christ, for a little guy you sure are heavy," Toby mumbled dragging Flanks outside. Flanks was a thin man, slightly balding, with eyes that had dark wrinkles below them—a tribute to a lifestyle of daily drinking and smoking three packs of cigarettes a day. A retired Army sergeant, he was a likable sort, who told a good story and kept the customers entertained.

It was two a.m. when Toby locked the back door of the bar. Like clockwork, he closed the bar the same time each day, except Sunday, when he closed at eleven. If he hurried, he could be home by two-thirty. He reached into his pocket and pulled out a shiny turquoise ring he had bought from Billy. It was for his wife, Sue. Next week was her birthday. She always liked Billy's jewelry and Toby had this piece specially made in the shape of a rose, her favorite. On the inside, her name was engraved. Toby slid the ring on his pinky so he wouldn't lose it.

He had inherited the *Blue Horse* when he married Sue. Her

daddy, Tom Berry, owned the joint and gave it to them as their wedding gift. Toby was an illegal immigrant from Mexico and had no means to support his wife. Before he had come to Gallup, he had been a wanderer, drifting from town to town after leaving his home in Juarez. Tom forced Toby to marry Sue when he caught the two in the supply room after closing hours.

When the bar ran good, Toby would brag how he banged the boss's daughter to get his niche in this world. On nights like tonight, when he barely scraped by, he cursed his sleazy father-in-law, now deceased, for trapping him into a marriage with a gal who had humped half of Gallup. Then he cursed himself for being stupid enough to get caught.

The *Blue Horse* wasn't much to look at, just a rundown hole-in-the-wall type establishment. Toby kept its prices low, attracting a lower social-economic crowd. Toby knew most of the people who came inside the bar, by name if not by face. Occasionally, drifters he didn't know came in, like the couple that just left. That didn't happen too often since his bar was near the edge of town and miles away from the main highway.

Most of his customers were men around forty-five or fifty, who came to the *Blue Horse* to get cheap booze and escape the humdrum of everyday life. The young fellows usually brought their girls with them or sought out local prostitutes who sometimes made their way to Toby's bar looking for an easy John.

As he left the *Blue Horse*, Toby saw the headlights of a '72 Chevy truck near the edge of the alley but didn't think much of it. Often cars drove down the alley, even at this late hour. It was a shortcut from Main Street to the south side of Gallup, which led past the Wingate Depot and eventually into the desert toward Arizona. Flanks grabbed Toby's arm for support as Toby struggled to prop up the semi-conscious Flanks on the passenger side of the truck.

"Edna ain't gonna be happy with you tonight," he puffed heavily.

Flanks didn't hear him having passed out once again.

4

"Shit. Just once I wish you'd make it home without passing out. Now, I'll have to tuck your sorry ass in bed again."

Toby opened the door to the driver's side, but before he could step inside he felt a sharp pain thrust his side. He heard the backfire of what he thought to be a car, probably the Chevy in the alley. When he felt another blow, he knew he had been shot. He couldn't move to see who shot him. The third shot hit his right shoulder, causing him to fall to the ground and lose consciousness.

The gunman felt of Toby's faint pulse and realized he was near death. Flanks moaned, shifting and sliding around and the attacker pointed at him, ready to fire. Realizing Flanks was still out cold; he slipped the gun inside his belt and reached for Toby's money bag. He impulsively began to count money.

"Damn. There ain't much here."

When the gunman reached to search Toby's pockets a drubbed Toby stunned him by grabbing hold of his leg, knocking him to the ground. He drew his gun and shot Toby square between the eyes killing him. The killer rummaged through Toby's pockets only finding a few dollars and small change. He went through Flanks' pockets. Nothing. The moonlight shone on the bloody scene and the ring on Toby's finger caught his killer's eye. Thinking it might be worth a few dollars, he tucked it into his pocket and ran to the truck.

****

Billy Nehah couldn't find rest. The old motel room didn't have an air-conditioner and the night was unusually hot for a June night in Gallup. His watch read 3:47. He lit up a cigarette, a habit he only indulged in when he was away from his family. Even then, he could make a pack of cigarettes last a whole week. Tonight he was on his second pack. He couldn't shake his restlessness.

He thought maybe this strangeness was due to the fact that he and his wife, Sadie, had fought before he left. After seventeen years, he should know better than to fight with Sadie. She wanted to take their goods to Albuquerque, but he insisted on Gallup since he had made the ring special for Toby's wife. Sadie was so ticked she refused to go with him. Billy liked taking his family with him. He liked teaching his eight-year-old son, Jess, the ropes of his trade. After all, it would be his someday. It would all belong to him and his baby sister, Nellie.

The image of his three-year-old daughter filled his mind. She was such a delight, so full of life. Billy thought of the little girl at Toby's tonight, so opposite of Nellie. A sudden chill invaded him and he jumped upright. He walked toward the window and stared into the darkness. He decided to leave Gallup in the morning even though he hadn't sold all of his merchandise. He'd go home and pick up Sadie and the kids. The four of them would go to Albuquerque. He found peace in his decision and lay back down. At last, sleep came to him.

****

Some two hours after Toby was shot, Flanks was awakened by the lights of two Gallup police cars shining on Toby's truck. Still hungover, Flanks abruptly sat tall when Ed Berry, a local cop, shook him.

"What the hell happened tonight?" Ed asked Flanks.

Flanks looked over his left shoulder to see Toby's lifeless body lying on a stretcher and watched as the two paramedics lifted the stretcher, moving Toby toward an ambulance that was parked in the middle of the alley. He looked at Ed Berry and his face registered his confusion. Ed grabbed him by the arm and led him to the police car.

"Gonna have to take you in for questioning."

Flanks tried to speak, but his mouth was like cotton — bone dry. The words wouldn't come out. A paramedic rode with Flanks and Ed to the station. He checked Flanks over. He was unharmed. When they pulled into the station, Flanks was finally able to speak.

"What's wrong with Toby?"

Ed Berry shook his head.

"I was hoping you could tell me."

"He sick?" Flanks continued to inquire.

"Sick?" Ed asked. "Shit, Flanks. He's dead. Shot four times."

Flanks slumped down in the seat.

"Dead?" He asked rhetorically.

"It was the shot to the head that killed him."

Flanks stared unbelieving at Ed.

"Last thing I remember was Toby lifting me up and carrying me to the back of the bar."

Ed led Flanks into the station. Inside, he poured Flanks and himself a cup of coffee.

"Here, drink this. Then go to the men's room and wake yourself up. You have to remember more than what you've told me. I'm going to find out who did this, and you're going to help me."

Ed paused to drink his coffee and reflect on Toby's murder. Tears filled his eye and Flanks was sober enough to notice.

"Ah, shit," Flanks spouted recalling Ed's relationship to Toby. "I forgot Toby was married to your sister."

Ed Berry let out a warning to the killer, more for himself than for Flanks.

"If it takes me the rest of my life, I'm gonna find out who did this to Toby. I swear to God I will."

\*\*\*\*

Billy was awakened by a nightmare. His baby girl was crying for him and he couldn't find her. A superstitious man, Billy was shaken. He kept hearing his baby's voice calling for her daddy. He was so shaken, he didn't hear the sirens of the ambulance and police cars as they passed. His body was soaked with perspiration. He checked his watch, 4:42. Only an hour had passed since the last time he checked the time. It wouldn't be long before morning came. He decided to get his things together and leave right then. What was the point of staying? He couldn't sleep. He slipped out of the motel about a half-hour later and headed home, about a forty-five-minute drive in his old truck. Figuring he'd be there by sunrise, he turned on the radio, lit a cigarette, and drove the dark road that led to the Zuni reservation.

The morning sunrise in the desert always brought a certain spiritual sensation to Billy's heart. As he approached the reservation, the early light was just peeking over the mesas, bringing a spectrum of rich colors. The summer morning brought with it a light rain adding to the beauty of the horizon. The red earth was like wet clay and Billy felt his old tires sliding, having little traction. He slowed down his speed. Through his open window, the desert air brushed across his face awakening his senses with its defined redolence.

Billy's spirits were lifting. He rubbed his eyes, bloodshot from lack of sleep and worry. How he loved that woman of his and was angry with himself for arguing with her. He'd make it up to her. His thoughts of Sadie were interrupted when he saw a small bulk lying in the middle of the road. His first thought was that it was a coyote or dog. As he got closer, he realized he was wrong.

He slowed the speed of his truck to a near stop. His heart was racing wildly. His stomach was churning. Then, he did stop. He sat frozen behind the wheel and stared at the tiny form spread out on the road in front of him. He was paralyzed with fear from the reality of what he knew he was seeing. Fighting the dread that invaded him, he willed his shaken body to get out of his truck.

He knew it was the little girl he had seen earlier at Toby's, even before he turned her frail body over and saw her face. She was wearing the same outfit she had worn when he last saw her, a light yellow sundress. Her feet were bare and her cold flesh was coated with wet earth. Billy brushed back her mass of brown hair and felt a wet clammy area at the back of her head,

8

probably the result of a blow or a fall. Billy's stomach tightened, tears filled his eyes, and he found he was unable to hold back the sickness that overpowered him. He turned from the child.

His hand rested on her neck slightly and in his bout of weakness, he felt the pulse of life touch his fingers; her life. It was a slight pulse and he turned abruptly toward her, checking to make certain his mind was not playing tricks on him. Then he felt of her skin. Though cold and clammy from the morning air, she was still warm with life. He gazed into her sunken eyes that had death written all over them. Her lips were blue, but she was still alive.

He reached to pick her up and dangling from her hand was the necklace he had given her. A peculiar breeze swept over them coming from the direction of the Kachina Village, the land of the dead. Billy knew the spirits were near and had saved her from certain death. There, in the middle of the road, Billy sought mercy from the spirits to restore her life and to erase from her mind the horror she had suffered. He removed the necklace from her clutched hands, kissed it reverently, and placed it around his own neck. Now her spirit will flow through him like blood, and if ever such evil should invade her spirit again, the necklace will warn him. He would never be free of their sacred bond, nor would she ever forget his offering. In the depth of devotion, she would receive from him her guardian spirit.

****

One week later, Sid Michaels left Denver, Colorado, on a flight to Albuquerque, New Mexico, to pick up his baby girl from protective custody, now known to the police and public simply as *Desert Baby*. He would also identify the body of a twenty-two-year-old woman found murdered near Gallup, New Mexico, as his wife, Kate Michaels. Her boyfriend, Jack Adams, had seemingly vanished into thin air leaving the authorities to question his involvement. Clutched in Sid's hand was a note Kate had written months earlier.

*Sid, I know about your affair. It's okay. I found someone, too. I'm leaving Denver with him and I'm taking Rebecca. How sad we had to end this way. I hope you find the happiness you are looking for. Kate.*

"Oh, Kate," his torn heart cried out. "I love you.  It was always just you."

Sid thought of Jack Adams. His blood ran cold.

"How could you have killed her, Jack?"  This is beneath even a man like you. Well … you may think you've gotten away with murder, but I assure you, no one can remain hidden forever. Someday I'll find you and when I do … God help you. God help me."

# Chapter 1

*Seventeen years later ...*

"Good morning, all you listeners. We're coming to you live from the Dallas Convention Center where already several hundred Native Americans from all walks of the United States are setting up displays filled with food, costumes, art, and a miscellany of Native American artifacts. This hopes to be the largest gathering of Native American tribes ever. So come join the excitement that kicks off today at noon and continues throughout the week, ending next Saturday with an encore of activities certain to be spectacular.

"Here's a song to set the mood of the convention. It's written and composed by a Southwest Native American artist named Jess Nehah. The song is titled *Spirit of the Desert*. I think you're gonna like it.

"For those of you still hugging your pillows this morning, the time is seven-fifteen ... time to get your morning blood pumping and your vegetating bodies out of bed. Come on now; shake off those Monday morning blues."

Bailey Carson rolled over in her bed to double-check the time on the clock. "Seven-fifteen! Damn, I'm going to be late."

She lay dreary-eyed for a moment, giving herself ten more minutes in the comfort of her bed, a well-deserved pampering after a night that consisted of only four hours of sleep. She haphazardly gave the many books and articles spread across her bedroom floor a quick glance, systemizing the details of their contents. At first, nothing came to mind, then her head was charged with facts and events that became as scattered as the upheaval on the floor.

She had stayed up half the night researching the Native American tribes of the southwest, primarily the Zuni tribe that lived in New Mexico. Later today, she would be meeting with a representative of the tribe and would interview him. Always wanting to appear professional, she gathered books and articles about the Zuni culture. The more she read, the more she realized how complex the Zuni mystique was. She knew her interview with Billy Nehah wasn't going to be an easy one because the Zunis were closed about principles concerning their religion and spiritual beliefs.

Bailey drug herself out of bed and stepped inside the shower, letting the steaming water massage her worn body. She heard the phone ring and then, seconds later, the answering machine kick on. It was her fiancé, Ron Baker. Before she could get to the phone, he had left a message and hung up. She rewound the machine and listened.

"Hey, Babe, it's me. I guess you're already gone. Shit. Really wanted to hear your voice. Looks like I won't make it home before Friday. That gives you five days to miss me. Don't worry. We'll make up for lost time. Are you still my baby? Miami is okay. It would be better if you were here. Miss you. Love you. Call you tonight."

Resuming her shower, her mind drifted into thoughts of Ron and their two-year relationship, which as of late, had become somewhat complacent. They had had little time to spend together. She could feel them drifting apart and it was no wonder, what with Ron in his second year of internship at Baylor Hospital in Dallas, and her pushing hard to balance going to school full-time at Texas Woman's University and working part-time for the *Dallas Morning News*.

Ron was presently in Florida attending a five-day medical conference and they had argued before he left. Though they had been engaged for one of their two years together, Ron was reluctant in committing to a specific date for them to get married. She wanted to marry in December when her parents would be visiting Dallas, an ideal time she rationalized since they lived in Barcelona, Spain and rarely found themselves in the States anymore.

The night before Ron left for Florida, she had planned a romantic evening to initiate the idea that they get married in December. Of course, she was nervous about approaching him. Still, she believed that after he heard her logic and understood the basis behind her sudden desire to plunge into matrimony, he would be agreeable and comply with her wishes. She had underestimated his unwillingness to marry right now. For the first time, she began to understand the differences in the way they saw their relationship. She wanted more than he was obviously willing to give.

Before he arrived that evening, she had changed her outfit three times, until finally deciding on a white, sheer dress. To ease her jitters she had downed two glasses of wine and was well into her third when she heard his car pull up in front of her apartment. Before he had a chance to step completely inside and notice the candles, the flowers, the soft music, or even the line of her silk dress, she had him in her embrace and was kissing him. When the kiss ended, his eyes rested on the rise of her full bosom. Her thick hair waved down her back and the glow from candlelight made her brown eyes glisten in shades of gold. Her full lips, moist and red, once again met his. She depicted a seasoned seducer for a girl who had not quite reached her twenty-first birthday.

Ron's voice was thick with lust. His sandy hair fell across his forehead just enough to tip his brow and draw attention to his blue eyes.

"Baby, what's this all about?"

"I just love you, that's all."

"Do you know what a helpless man I am in your arms? Always have been. From the first day I saw you, I knew we'd be together. I knew you'd be mine."

"Am I yours?"

"You have to ask?"

"Let's get married, Honey."

"We are, Baby. We are. See?" He rubbed his fingers over her engagement ring.

"When?" She asked impatiently.

"Shhh, quiet," he said. It was obvious to her that he had little interest in the conversation. Still, she did, and it had to be done before they got too carried away.

"I have to talk to you, Honey."

"Later," he said, moving his kiss down her neck. "God, you're beautiful."

"Ron!" She drew away." It's important."

Through passion-filled eyes, he watched her. His body was heated and fairly shook with the anticipation of what she so openly had planned for them tonight.

"What is it?" He asked rushed, as he brought her back to his embrace, barely hearing her words. Once again, his kiss found her neck.

"Mother and Daddy are planning a visit to the States."

"Oh, yeah," he said automatically, edging one hand up a long silky leg. "Mmm … sweet."

"They'll be here in December."

"That's nice." He pulled down the strap of her dress and exposed the top of her breasts.

"Christ, what you do to me."

She pulled away from him." You haven't heard a word I've said. Have you?"

"Sure I have, Baby. Daddy is planning a visit."

"Yes," she sighed heavily." In December. Ron, I was thinking…"

Something in her voice commanded him to grant her his full attention. His eyes were intent on her next words, sensing he already knew what those would be. Still, he had to hear them.

"What were you thinking?" he asked.

"Well," she said. "I was thinking … I was thinking we could get married while my parents are here."

The cold reality of her words cut through him and he was

suddenly aware of the music and the candlelight, her dress, everything. It all fit into place now. She had set out to seduce him into saying yes to marriage. Angered, he moved away from her. Turning his back completely to her, he spoke harshly.

"Bailey, how could you?" He could barely contain his anger. "Did you think you could seduce me into marrying you? God, I never thought you would stoop this low. But then again, you are Sid Carson's daughter."

"Don't be angry with me, Ron. I only thought…"

"I know damn well what you thought, and I won't be manipulated into marriage, Bailey."

Her hopes deflated, she looked at him. "Don't you…don't you want to be married to me?"

"Just don't rush me."

"I hardly think I've been rushing you."

"Christ, Bailey. Think about what you're asking. December is only three months away. That's a short time to plan for a wedding. Besides, I'll never be able to get off at Christmas. Shit. Christmas is peak season at the hospital."

"I'm only asking for a day. We don't need an elaborate ceremony. I just want my parents at our wedding and who knows when Daddy will be back in the States again."

"Daddy would come back for his little girl's wedding, no matter when it was."

Ron's sarcasm showed his contempt for Bailey's father. "Anyways, I don't live my life around Sid Carson's schedule."

"I'm not asking you to."

Ron sighed heavily and leaned in to kiss Bailey, hoping to rekindle her earlier mood. Yet when she drew away, he threw up his hands.

"You know, it's times like these when the differences in our ages and backgrounds are so obvious. You can be such a child and such a …"

"What? A brat?"

"No," he backtracked.

"I think you'd better leave, Ron."

"Yeah, you're probably right."

He fumbled for his keys and took a moment to glance at her defiant stance before walking toward the door. The heat from her kiss still burned his lips.

"We'll work this out when I get back from Florida," he said, and then added, "I hope."

He stood for some time at the door as if waiting for her to take him in her arms. She didn't. When he left, she stared at the closed door, and for the first time was able to admit to herself that their relationship was in real trouble. The ambiance of the room left her with a sudden loneliness. Already she missed him, but she began to wonder if he was worth missing.

****

Before moving to Dallas and meeting Ron, Bailey had lived a privileged but sheltered life with her parents in Europe. Though she loved both parents dearly, she was the first to admit that her father, Sid Carson, was her idol. Ever since she could remember, she had been her daddy's girl, and rarely as a young child growing up had she left his side. When she did, her daddy was quick to call her up or send her gifts until the next time they were together.

Daddy had been through all the teeming events of her life. Nothing but the best for his daughter would do. He sent her to private schools and scaled with the eyes of a hawk those who came in contact with her. He never lost sight of his little girl and was always careful to be only an arm's length away. In Europe, she studied art, music, and dance. But ballet was her passion, and like her education, her dancing revolved around an elite sect.

Ballet became her life, her social outlet – her only outlet from the protected world in which she lived. Physically, she fit the mold of a ballerina. She was tall and slim, bearing a style of elusive grace. Even when she wasn't dancing, she carried this pliancy with her, when she walked – when she played. She had deep brown eyes, hovered by a thick brow. Her skin was fair and a touch of natural rose hinted on her cheeks and lips. Her hair was deep brown with a touch of auburn. When she danced her mother, Mara Carson, would roll the long mass in an elegant twist, displaying the line of her slender neck.

Through the years, she became Mommy and Daddy's "Prima Dona," and they loved giving their daughter their full attention, stealing as many precious memories as they could. They dreaded the day when she would grow up and life would steal her away from them. That day came when she was eighteen and broke her leg in a skiing accident. This put her dancing on hiatus and to comfort her, Sid allowed her to visit her stepbrother, Sammy, and his wife, Diane, in Dallas, Texas. It was a grueling decision to let her leave his sight. It would prove to change the course of Bailey's life forever. During that visit, she began to see the world away from the sheltered clutches of Sid, and as fate would have it, she met a man who would become her mentor. He was a sixty-year-old historian named Byron Claiborne.

****

She was named after the town where she was born – Bailey, Texas. The story told by her parents was that they were traveling through the town of Bailey when Mara went into labor early. The small East Texas farming town was so small; the nearest hospital was an hour away. Mara was too far into her labor to travel any further. A local resident put Mara in touch with a midwife, who later delivered Bailey. Because of the unique situation surrounding her birth, they named her after the quaint town. When Bailey found out her birthplace was just an hour from her brother, Sammy's house, she had to visit.

The town of Bailey was much the way she had pictured it in her mind. Her first stop was at a local gas station, where an attendant named Cal, gave her info about the town and its people through small talk. He pointed out the only grocery store

17

and relayed that the town had no school, so the children were bused to the next town. In the course of their conversation, Bailey told him she was visiting her birthplace and filled him with a lot of questions. She asked him if he knew of a woman named Sarah Johnson. Sarah was the name given to her as the midwife who had delivered her.

"Don't know a Sarah Johnson," the attendant said. "Bet Miss Millie Claiborne would probably know. She's kind of the town busybody. Knows just about everyone and anyone who has stepped foot in Bailey. I'll get you her number."

Bailey never spoke with Millie Claiborne, but with her nephew, Seth Claiborne. He had no recollection of her story but vaguely remembered a Sarah Johnson. He thought she might have passed away some time ago.

"Sorry I can't be of more help," Seth said. "I'll give your information to Aunt Millie and maybe she knows more. Now, what did you say your father's and mother's names were?"

"I didn't. But, it's Carson, Sid and Mara Carson."

There was silence between them. Hers was disappointment. His was more conspicuous. Bailey noticed it right away.

"Something wrong, Sir?"

"Not wrong, just…well, you see, my dad is also a bit of a historian. In fact, he's writing a book about the history of this area and your story sounds unique. Any chance you can hang around until I get a hold of him?"

"How long would that be?"

"Don't rightly know. I'll give him a call now."

"I guess I could hang around for a little while. I have to get back to Dallas by five."

"There's a small café just up the road. Why not grab a bite to eat. I'll see if I can get a hold of my dad."

"All right," she said and then drove to *Bud's Café*.

\*\*\*\*

Just as Bailey was about to bite into a juicy hamburger, an

18

elderly man around sixty or so moved toward her booth. He was dressed casually, as if he had rushed to dress, with wrinkled pants and an unmatched shirt. He had silver hair and bore a sharp profile, and she suspected that in his earlier days he'd been quite handsome. He smiled down at her and he introduced himself as Byron Claiborne.

"I understand you are inquiring about Sarah Johnson."

Once again, she retold her story, later confessing she felt foolish driving all this way to see the town where she was born and meet the woman who had delivered her. He told her she wasn't silly at all, that folks were naturally curious about their roots. Said he was glad too, else he wouldn't have a job. He humored her with stories about Sarah Johnson and told her that Sarah had delivered his own daughter, Katherine. The gentlemen enchanted Bailey, and hours passed as he filled her head with stories of East Texas and the western U.S., as well as Mexico and even Africa.

"It must be fascinating to be a historian. Your son tells me you are writing a book about the history of East Texas."

He nodded. "It's been in the making for a while."

They laughed as he said he would have a great time telling the story of a European debutant who found her way to a small farming community in Texas to learn more about herself. She felt comfortable with him, telling him she didn't really remember much about her early life in the States. He teased her and said he couldn't remember much of his life before ten, but then admitted that he was an old man. She felt comfortable around him as if she'd known him all of her life. She recanted her accident that brought her to the States. She admitted she was beginning to feel good about it because she had started to resent dancing and only did it to please her parents. She disclosed she had always been fascinated with journalism. She told him she had worked on her school paper and later with an apprentice for an off-the-wall newsprint in Barcelona. She said that her dad rarely encouraged her efforts, but rather only humored. Byron told her she should seek out what her heart wanted to do.

"My parents are adamant that I study in Europe. I wouldn't mind studying in the States, perhaps even Texas. I love it. It's so big and I feel independent. And too, I would be near my brother."

What she didn't say was that she needed to begin life without her parents' watchful eyes. It didn't matter much anyway. Her father would never consider letting her live here permanently, especially to study journalism.

"Daddy thinks journalism is a man's occupation and that a woman would never be taken seriously. I told him maybe I could break the mold."

"We have a great journalism program at the university where I teach."

"You're a professor as well as a historian?"

"I am a man of many fascinations. I also help my son farm."

Bailey smiled. "You are quite the enigma."

She felt so at ease with him that she showed him some pictures of her family. There was a photo of Sid, Mara, and Bailey at her graduation. She showed him some of her dance photos. Another one was of her stepbrother, Sammy, and his wife, Diane. She divulged that he lived near Dallas. She didn't notice it, but Byron Claiborne's expression had changed as he viewed the photos. He was more subdued and serious. Without reason, he took her hand and held it a little longer than he probably should. Surprisingly, she didn't draw her hand away but studied his face.

For a long time, they talked of nothing at all and when two hours had passed, he seemed reluctant to let her leave. He watched her limp out on her walking cast and slide into the car. His protective nature wanted to say to her that she shouldn't be driving, but then hadn't she driven here? He held his hand to wave goodbye and she lent him a full-blown smile as she rolled down her window.

"Ever so nice to meet you, Miss Bailey Carson."

"You, too, Professor Claiborne."

As she drove away, she never saw the tears in his eyes.

****

Bailey did stay in Dallas to study and in her second semester at TWU, she took an Art History class taught by Dr. Byron Claiborne. To her delight, he was the historian she had met the past summer. He became more than a teacher to her, and even when she finished his course, she found herself turning to him in other areas of her life. He was not only her mentor, but was in fact, a stand-in-father in the absence of her own, and like her father, she placed him on a pedestal.

He encouraged her passion for journalism, pulling strings to get her a part-time job with the *Dallas Morning News*. She was so thrilled; she didn't mind the forty-five-minute drive from her new apartment in Denton. She was better at journalism than she realized, lacking the confidence only experience and maturity could bring. But, the determination was always there, pulling her, pushing her, directing her course.

With Professor Claiborne's coaxing, she found herself enrolled in another course under his direction. It was turning out to be the most challenging of her college career. It was also the most consuming. Each night as she cumbered over the work she was doing in his class, she questioned the wisdom of taking a class that didn't fit in her career plan. Yet when she was in class, she was transfixed. He was pure genius.

He had gotten her an interview with a New Mexico Zuni artist named Billy Nehah and today she was going to go over some ideas for the interview with Claiborne. Her boss at the *Morning News* told her that if it was a good interview, it would be printed in the following Sunday's paper. So today, even after her fight with Ron and waking up late, it wouldn't do for her to be late. She looked at the time on the clock once more.

"I can't be late." But even as she said it, she knew she would never make it to Claiborne's class by nine.

She rushed to dress, slipping on a saucy number Ron had recently bought for her. The red dress clung to her full form in such a way she questioned its appropriateness for an interview. Still, she didn't have time to change. She gave her plush hair a once over and slapped on a coat of crimson lipstick. Clutching her satchel, her hand barely reached the doorknob when the phone rang. It was Ron again. The answering machine clicked on. Ron's words left her speechless.

"Hey, Babe, it's me again. I've been thinking. I could get a couple of days off in December. Go ahead and reserve the church, Bailey. We're getting married. What the hell. I always wanted to play Santa Claus."

# Chapter 2

Bailey heard the police car's sirens behind her and looked into the rearview mirror to see the flashing red light.

"Great!" She slapped the steering wheel and moved her car to the side of the road. "A ticket is exactly what I need right now. It's just my luck to be stopped when I'm already so late."

After Ron's phone proposal, she called him back at his hotel and they talked for over thirty minutes before she managed to leave her apartment. And today of all days, she had to change her usual route because Dr. Claiborne was presenting a detailed slide presentation on Southwest Native American culture at North Texas State University. He was collaborating with Dr. Nathan Leighton, a contemporary of his who taught at the University. In an effort to accommodate both Leighton's and Claiborne's classes, the presentation was being held in the Liberal Arts Auditorium.

Because she was somewhat uncertain of her whereabouts, and because she was so preoccupied with Ron and school and her interview with Billy Nehah, she didn't notice the Denton police until it was too late. She knew she wasn't going to get out of this one, so before he had a chance to ask for them, she voluntarily handed him her registration and license.

"Guess I was speeding, huh?"

"Guess so," he said shortly.

He was a stout fellow, around forty with a protruding middle and hair clipped close to the head. His outdated black-rimmed glasses failed to hide the amusement in his eyes and his face drew a slight grin as he jotted down information from her license. She was jittery, thumping her dash thinking about how late she was going to be for class. The officer tapped her inspection sticker on her windshield with his pen.

"Did you know your inspection sticker has expired? It expired on the first. Today is the sixth."

"I didn't know," she said truthfully. "Ron – he's my fiancée, well … he takes care of these sorts of things."

"Not too well, he doesn't."

Bailey let out a nervous chuckle. The officer leaned toward her. His eyes were dancing merrily and she thought he found a little too much pleasure in her misery. She started to tell him so, but using her better judgment she stopped herself.

"Here's the deal, Ms. Carson. I'll let the inspection sticker go if you promise me to take care of it today."

"I appreciate that."

He tugged at her seatbelt.

"Were you wearing this when I stopped you?"

Somehow she couldn't make herself lie.

"I'm afraid I wasn't, Officer."

She gave him a shameful nod as if she had just been caught with her hand in the cookie jar.

"I'll tell you what. I'm willing to let it go if you promise me to wear your seatbelt from now on. You know, we wouldn't want anything to happen to such a nice lady."

She gave him a gentle smile. "I promise."

"For a pretty smile like that, I'd like to let your speeding violation go, but I can't. You see this is a twenty-mile-an-hour school zone and I clocked you driving forty-six. I'm afraid I'm going to have to write you up."

"Even if I promise not to do it again?"

"Is that a promise you can keep?"

"I'll try," she said apprehensively.

"A try is a start but I need your solemn oath."

"I guess you better write me up."

He smiled broadly." Well, you're an honest one."

He handed her the citation along with her license and registration. He yanked her seatbelt and remembering her promise, she dutifully fastened it. He gave her a wink and slapped the hood of the car, still holding on to his amusement.

"Let's get that sticker taken care of and try to keep that speed down."

"I will."

"I'll be watching to make sure you do."

He held out his hand for her to shake. She complied.

"I really do appreciate you not being too rough with me today, Officer … uhh …." She paused to glance at the name on his badge. "Officer Stanley. Thanks so much."

"I just didn't have the heart to completely destroy your Monday."

"You're very kind. Have a nice day, Officer Stanley."

"I'll try."

"A smile is a start, but I'd like to have your solemn oath," she teased using his very words.

He laughed outright.

"You've got it," he said and started back towards his car. Then, he turned abruptly around. "Say, tell that fiancé of yours to have your tires checked as soon as he can. From the looks of them, I'd say they were running on borrowed time already."

"I will. And, thanks again."

****

By the time she made her way to North Texas, she was already forty minutes late and the other students were engaged in casual, small-group conversations about the room. They were waiting for Dr. Claiborne to set up his slideshow presentation. The two-hundred seats that spanned downward toward the podium were almost filled to capacity. Bailey guessed that the speakers had already presented themselves and that the students were taking a break before the slide lecture. She was upset that she had missed the speakers, especially Billy Nehah. At least she hadn't missed Claiborne's lecture.

Hoping Claiborne hadn't noticed her late arrival, she slid into the room from a side entrance taking the nearest available seat. It also happened to be nearest the door. She pulled out her notebook and started fumbling through her purse for a pen. In an effort to reorganize her thoughts, she began to comprise a list of things she needed to do today. Her mind kept drifting back to thoughts of Ron and her soon-to-be wedding.

First on her list was to call her parents and tell them about the wedding. Then, she'd have to call the church. If things went as scheduled, she would be able to finish her interview with Billy Nehah, get her inspection sticker, and still have time to swing by Ron's place and check his mail before going to work. She looked at her watch, anxious for Dr. Claiborne to begin. During her wait, she began scribbling on her paper, Mrs. Ronald Baker, over and over.

"Ah," a tall, dark man whispered near her ear, as he sat down next to her, "a conscientious one."

She turned her notebook over and stared into the black eyes of the man sitting next to her. He was dressed casually, wearing jeans and a light blue denim shirt. His thick black shoulder-length hair was knotted in the back with a leather strap. His skin was roan colored and she impulsively compared it to hers, where she paled in comparison. Bailey couldn't recall his face, so she guessed he was a student of Dr. Leighton. He leaned his shoulders against the back of the chair and propped his right foot over his left leg. Unconsciously, he began jiggling his size eleven Nikes.

"So what did you think of the speakers?" He asked, knowing full well she had just arrived.

"Oh," she said. "I'm a little embarrassed. You see, I just now got here. Did Billy Nehah, from Zuni, New Mexico, speak?"

He shook his head." No. Billy Nehah didn't speak."

"Really? Oh good! That means I haven't missed him. I've been looking forward to hearing him talk for weeks."

The man lifted her arm slightly and rubbed over the face of her watch.

"Evidently."

Agitated, she tried to justify her tardiness.

26

"So I had a run of bad luck this morning and got pulled over for speeding."

"I see. A typical late Monday morning, huh?"

"Something like that, yeah."

"Did you get a ticket?"

"Only for speeding."

He grinned. "What other laws did you break?"

"Well – my inspection sticker has expired, and – now why am I telling you all this? I'm sure you could care less about my driving problems." She shuffled into a comfortable position and once again addressed the man sitting next to her. "Say, is Dr. Leighton as tough as I've heard?"

"Dr. Leighton?"

"Yeah, you are a student in his class, aren't you?"

"No, just an interested party, you might say." He held out his hand to shake hers. "I'm Jess."

Spread across his face was a warm expression and when he took her hand, he gave it a slight squeeze. His casual gesture was strangely arousing to her. His eyes were fixed on the way she brushed her brown hair away from her face and the way her eyes were coursing over him while she pretended to be watching the door. With every move she made, her tightly fitted dress perfectly detailed her form, and he had to force himself not to be obvious.

"Hi, Jess. I'm Bailey Carson."

"Nice to meet you, Bailey."

Just then, Dr. Claiborne and a man in a gray suit walked to the podium. She knew what Leighton looked like, so she naturally assumed this man was one of the guest speakers, maybe even Billy Nehah. She responded aloud.

"Why didn't he wear his regalia?"

"Who?" Jess asked.

"Billy Nehah. See the man standing next to Dr. Claiborne? The man in the gray suit? Was he one of the guest speakers? I was hoping to see him dressed in his native costume and jewelry. He definitely would have made a more interesting presentation wearing his regalia."

Jess smiled. "How do you know his presentation wasn't interesting? You didn't see it."

"Oh, I'm sure it was, but the Zunis have such magnificent ceremonial costumes and jewelry. It's just a shame he didn't share them with the audience."

"You know about the Zunis' celebrations and dress?"

"Only from books and facts that Dr. Claiborne has lectured on. The Zunis are really quite fascinating."

"I see. Bailey, I happen to know that the man next to Dr. Claiborne is not Billy Nehah."

"Are you sure?"

"Positive. Look closer. He's not even Indian. I should know, huh?"

Bailey studied the man sitting next to her, his dark skin, and black hair. She blushed slightly realizing that he was a Native American. She could just kick herself for her remarks about the regalia. How could she have been so thoughtless? So condescending? God, what he must think of her. Just then, the lights flashed off and on, a cue that the slide presentation was about to begin. Bailey turned a regretful eye towards Jess.

"Jess, I'm sorry. I..."

"For what?"

"The regalia remark. I just wasn't thinking."

"Forget it."

"Please accept my apology if I offended you."

"You haven't. Besides, I'm used to it. The Indian thing always manages to creep up in conversations I have with non-Indian people."

"You're upset. I can tell."

"I'm not upset, Bailey. Why should I be? I know you weren't disrespecting me. Maybe just a little misguided. That's all. I'm not offended because I understand where you're coming from. You have a picture in your mind about what Indians should look like and act like.

"Still, I'd like to pass on some friendly advice to you. We're people, Bailey, first and foremost. Most of the time we dress like everyone else. On special occasions, we get decked out – in our regalia. I agree with you. The speaker would've been much more impressive had he brought his native dress. Unfortunately, it's at the Dallas Convention Center on display."

The light in the auditorium went out. Professor Claiborne's first slide was titled "The Mesa of Taaiyalone."

"Corn Mountain," Bailey whispered to Jess, lost in the details from her studies last night. "The Zuni Pueblos fled to Corn Mountain in 1632 when they had a conflict with the Franciscans."

Jess looked at her with admiration. "I can see you've done your homework."

"I've heard it's sacred to the Zuni people."

"It's very near the Kachina village, a place the Zunis know as the *Land of the Dead*."

"A burial ground?"

He nodded. "That—and a spiritual commune."

"You seem to know a lot about the Zunis," she said.

He smiled broadly. She blushed once again.

"Let me guess," she whispered in his ear. "You know so much because you're Zuni."

He smiled, giving her a quick wink. She reached for his hand, squeezing it gently.

"Do you know Billy Nehah? I'm supposed to interview him later today for my newspaper."

"You're a reporter?"

"Only part-time. Actually, I'm more of an errand girl right now. I'm still pretty new at everything. Billy Nehah is going to be my first professional interview – you know, for the *Morning News*. I stayed up half the night reading about the Zunis and their culture."

Jess put his hand over hers.

"I'm sorry, Bailey, but you won't be able to interview Billy Nehah. He got sick before he was to leave New Mexico. His wife was afraid for him to make such a long trip, so he isn't here."

"No," she called out, so loudly the person in front of her turned around to sign for her to be quiet.

"I'm afraid so," said Jess. "Maybe—I mean if you wanted—you could interview his replacement."

"His replacement?"

"Yeah, his son. He spoke today in place of his father."

"Is his son an artist, too?"

"Yes and no."

"What do you mean, yes and no?"

"He works beside his father, but he has interests in other areas as well."

"How do you know so much about Mr. Nehah and his son?"

"I've known both all my life."

Bailey studied the man sitting next to her.

"You're Billy Nehah's son, aren't you, Jess?"

"You're not too disappointed, are you?"

"No. Embarrassed is more the word."

"Don't be. And if you don't mind second best, I'd be honored to give you an interview, Bailey."

He clutched her hand, intertwining his fingers within hers. He stopped when he felt of her engagement ring and gave her a disappointed look. "Lucky guy."

Bailey sat quietly. She stared into his dark eyes. She did little to remove his hand from hers.

"Jess, I would really love to interview you. When?"

"Tomorrow afternoon is good. About four?"

"Four is good for me, too. Afterward, we can have dinner."

Once again Jess played with her ring.

"He won't mind?"

"Ron? No. Why should he?"

Bailey looked at their clasped hands and suddenly felt uneasy, wondering what his intentions were.

"I know I would mind, Bailey, if I were him."

"Why, Jess? The interview is business. "

"And dinner?"

"Dinner is business, too."

Jess conceded. "I see. All business and no pleasure."

"That's the way it is, Jess."

"Too bad. Oh, well—some guys are just lucky."

He squeezed her hand, and before he stood up he leaned to whisper in her ear. "See you tomorrow, Bailey. Meet me at the north entrance of the convention center."

Then, he gave her cheek a quick pinch, got up and walked away.

# CHAPTER 3

Sid Carson hung up the phone after speaking with his daughter, first feeling alarmed, and then escalating into a silent rage. He looked at the panoramic view of Barcelona from his office window. This had been his home for six years. It had been Bailey's almost three; and before that, Paris. In Europe, he had kept Bailey under his watchful eye and had the assurance of always knowing where she was and what she was doing. He kept her safe and happy, guarded against the dangers of the outside world.

He had to. In his line of business, there was always someone out to get him—after revenge, or after a blessed buck. And there was no better way of seeking revenge or gaining wealth, than by preying on those things or people most valued to the hunted. A scam came in all forms, rich or poor, black or white, male or female, old or young.

Sid Carson knew this all too well because he was an ace con, knowing when to hold onto a deal and when to let go. He'd become a multi-millionaire buying and selling real estate. He acquired the upper hand by fully understanding his opponents' failings and by using his street smarts and proverbial charms. He knew that a scam artist had no conscience or soul and that his only motive was to achieve his desired goal. Sid looked at the picture of Bailey on his desk.

"I never should have let you out of my sight."

The phone rang. It was Mara, his wife. She was a small woman, and her soft voice matched her stature.

"Sid, did Bailey call you?"

"She did. I know all about her plans in December."

Mara brushed back her jet black hair and rubbed over her

dark eyes. Her skin was so pale in comparison, she looked fragile and years older than her thirty-nine years. Yet, when she smiled, her heart showed through.

"I can't help being happy for her, Sid. Besides, it's not like we didn't see this coming."

"The son of a bitch promised he'd wait until she graduated."

"I know what Ron promised, but Sid, this is what Bailey wants. Can't you try to be happy ... for her? Anyway, graduation is only a year and a half away."

"A hell of a lot can change in a year! Christ Mara, she's not even twenty-one."

"Sid, come home. We can discuss this better at home."

"Yeah, Yeah. I'll be there when I finish up things around here. I wouldn't wait dinner for me."

"Do I ever?"

**** 

Sid scanned his Rolodex for Sammy's new number, running his fingers through his mass of wavy black hair. His piercing black eyes seethed with disdain. He rubbed his chin, unconsciously tracing over a scar, a repercussion he had received when he was twelve years old by a local thug on the streets of Chicago. This minute scar was the only physical evidence he possessed that might hint to others he had had a jagged past. Otherwise, the dealings of his culprit lifestyle were well concealed, outwardly suggesting a man of sophistication and wealth. It was the kind of wealth associated with those born privileged. This was his first and predominate con, since he had been born dirt poor, squandering during his youth. Sid stretched his muscular legs across the top of his desk as he waited to hear Sammy's voice.

"Hello," Sammy answered.

Sammy Harmon was not the biological son of Sid Carson. Sammy's mother, Jean, married Sid when Sammy was two. Sid was the only father Sammy had ever known and he was proud to claim him as his father. Even when Sid and Jean's marriage broke up after three years, the two kept in contact with each other. Sammy spent every summer with Sid and he and Bailey became close. Eight years older than Bailey, Sammy became as protective of her as Sid, even when he got older and met Diane. They kept in contact through calls and letters. So, when Bailey wanted to move to Dallas, he convinced Sid it would be a good move. Sid was satisfied with the arrangement until Ron Baker came into the picture.

"How the hell could you let this happen?"

"Dad?"

"Bailey called. She says she and Ron are going to be married in December. Christ Sammy, I trusted you to protect your sister."

"Hell, Dad. I didn't know."

"Your job was to keep his ass away from her. Hell, I never would have let her stay in Texas if you hadn't promised to watch over her. I trusted you."

"I tried, Dad. But, Bailey has a mind of her own. She got pissed over my interfering. She quit coming by."

"I don't want to hear your excuses. Bailey will not marry Ron if I have to come to Texas and take care of his sorry ass myself."

"You really hate him, don't you Dad?"

"It's not that I hate him. I've just got other plans for Bailey."

"Bailey loves him, Dad. I think he loves her, too."

"If you believe that, you're a fool. Christ, he took my money, didn't he?"

"Yeah, he took your money."

"If he can be bought, he ain't worth shit."

"I guess."

"Look Sammy, I didn't mean to come down on you so hard. You know how I am about Bailey."

"Yeah, I know. What are you gonna do if Bailey doesn't

like the plans you have for her?"

"I've got to make sure she does and you're going to help me."

"How?"

"Rita."

"Ron's ex?"

"Yeah. I want you to find her. Convince her to start calling Ron and hassling Bailey again."

"How am I gonna do that?"

"Oh, I'd say five thousand dollars ought to do it."

"You're kidding me!"

"I'm serious as hell. I'm transferring the money to your account today."

"If you're serious, Dad, transfer it to Mom's account, not mine. I don't want Diane involved in this. She can't keep a thing from Bailey and she's already upset with me for the last time I interfered."

"Maybe you're right about Diane. Just tell your mom it was a gift from me to help you and Diane out and that you don't want Diane knowing about it. How is my girl anyway? Too damn good to be married to the likes of you, I know."

Sid's anger was fading. Sammy could always calm him down. Sid liked Diane. She was a little rough around the edges, having come from a broken home where her father drank and her mom slept around. Still, she was good for Sammy and she kept Bailey's head out of the clouds. She was the kind of woman Sid trusted because he always knew where she stood. Diane, on the other hand, found Sid overbearing and insensitive to Sammy. And too, she never felt like she could trust Sid completely.

"Diane's fine. You know, Dad, breaking Bailey and Ron up is really going to hurt her. And what if she finds out what we are up to? She won't forgive us, you know."

"She'll never find out, not if we are smart about things. Sure, she'll be hurt at first. But she'll see that things worked out for the best."

"I think you underestimate her, Dad."

"And I think you underestimate how much I don't want this marriage to take place. I can depend on you, can't I Sam?"

Sammy was silent.

"Well?" Sid repeated. "Need I remind you about a little girl from south Dallas? Sure would be a shame if Diane found out about her."

"Christ, you're heartless! You don't have to use blackmail to get my help. I'm not one of your thugs. I'll do this for you, Dad. I'll do this for Bailey."

"I'm sorry, Son. This wedding business has me on edge. You know you and Bailey are everything to me. I'd do anything to make things right for you two."

"Yeah, Dad, I know. Just sometimes your ways aren't so right."

"They got me where I am today, didn't they? Now listen, Sammy. Go to Bailey and tell her you talked with me and make like I'm as happy as she is about the wedding. That way, she'll come to me when things between her and Ron fall apart."

"You got this all figured out, don't you?"

"Just do what I ask."

"I will."

"Give Diane a kiss and tell your mom I just got her letter with the pictures from our wedding."

"Okay. Hey, Dad, what did you want pictures of yours and mom's wedding for? Mom was three wives ago."

"No reason really, just sentimental, I guess."

Sammy knew his dad always had a reason for the things he did. He also knew not to question those reasons.

"Anything else, Dad?"

"Just…"

"Just what, Dad?"

"Just make sure the job gets done."

"Consider it done already."

****

Rita McDonald worked at Baylor Hospital in Dallas as a surgical nurse. That's where Sammy found her. He lagged his stout legs down the corridors of Baylor's third floor, hating like hell what Sid had asked him to do. He liked Rita … a lot. He ran his hand through his black hair as he scoped the hall for signs of Rita. When he first caught sight of her, he almost didn't recognize her. She'd let her hair grow long and her eyes had lost that drawn look they had always possessed. When he asked if they could talk for a moment, she glared at him contemptuously, wondering what he could possibly want after all this time. He knew she'd be indifferent, but her reaction to him was much colder than he expected. She disliked him almost as much as she did Sid Carson. She led Sammy to a small waiting area at the end of the corridor. Wasting little time with niceties, she got right to the point.

"I know this isn't a friendly visit, Sammy. We aren't friends. Why don't you get right down to the reason you decided to ruin my day."

Sammy had to appreciate her brassy flair. He watched her flip back her strawberry blonde hair, that even when it fell limp like it did today, was sexy as hell. He understood Ron's attraction to her. She lit up the room just being in it.

"I will, Rita. You know, I've always admired your directness."

"Yeah? Well, I wish there was something I could admire about you."

"I can't blame you for not liking me."

Sammy pulled out a cigarette.

"Are you crazy? This is a hospital. You can't smoke here. You know that."

"I don't smoke anymore, Rita. I just like the feel of a cigarette in my hand. It calms my nerves."

She shrugged. "Whatever. Now, why are you here?"

"It's Ron," Sammy retorted.

"What about Ron? He's all right, isn't he? I mean, he isn't

hurt or anything?"

"He and Bailey are getting married," Sammy said directly.

"You came here to tell me that? Are you trying to humiliate me?"

"Not at all. You see, I'm not too happy about this wedding. I don't want him to marry my sister. I don't happen to think they are right for each other. I happen to think he's more suited – well, for you, Rita."

"You're crazy, you know it?"

"Tell me, Rita. Why do you think Ron's waited so long to marry her?"

"You tell me."

"It's obvious. He still loves you. Can't say I blame him. You could get him back if you wanted him."

"Well, I don't!"

"I've got five thousand dollars that says you do."

Rita looked at him at first shocked and then resigned. "You actually think you can pay me to get Ron out of Bailey's life? I've a good mind to tell Ron what you are up to."

"You could do that, Rita, but he'd say you were lying. Remember, you got a little crazy a while back. Surely, you haven't forgotten that."

"Get out of my sight, Sammy Harmon!"

"Think about it, Rita."

"I don't have to think about anything."

"The money's as good as in your account, Rita. Oh, in case you are thinking of telling my wife about this, don't. I won't hesitate to tell Ron that you're at it again. I can make things ugly for you."

She looked him squarely in the eyes, fearless. "Go to hell!"

As Sammy watched her stomp away, he couldn't help but to admire her virtue. Not many people would turn down five thousand dollars. Still, he wasn't discouraged. He knew Rita would change her mind. It wouldn't be for the money, but because she loves Ron. Too bad Ron wasn't as noble. For a year now, Sid had been giving Ron a hefty allotment in exchange for his promise not to marry Bailey until she graduated, a promise he evidently decided to break.

****

Sid Carson sat in the seclusion of his office. The Barcelona night lit up the sky with an array of stars shining through his window. He opened the letter from Jean and scanned over the words and pictures she had sent. They lent a haunting memory. These images combined with Bailey's news caused him to shiver. He drew from his desk a bottle of scotch. Once again, his eyes fell on the pictures from his past. They became fixed on the photo of him with his then best man. Hate consumed his heart as he stared at the man standing next to him in the photo. Sid took a swallow of scotch.

"Jack, you fiend, where are you hiding? Do you remember what today is? Think hard, my friend. You stood by my side at another wedding, too. Remember? Twenty-one years ago today, I married my beautiful Kate. God, how I loved her. She was young, just seventeen, and she was carrying my child, my beautiful Bailey.

"Oh, but you know her as Rebecca. You see, I had to change her name and mine, too. All because of you, Jack, old boy. I had to protect my Rebecca. I couldn't let you destroy her like you did Kate. What promises did you give my wife to make her leave with you? What lies did you tell? She wouldn't have gone with you otherwise.

"You probably think I've given up hope of ever finding you. Don't you, Jack? Oh, but you know me better than that. I will never give up hope of seeing you pay for what you did. I know you're out there. I know you think of me and Kate and that night. Does your heartbreak when you think of her? When you make love to another woman, do you see her face? I pray to God you think of her every minute of every day."

Sid tipped the bottle until he had consumed its entire contents. He tried to focus his eyes on the photo in his hand, but his mind was a blur. He heard the quiet laughter of a woman's voice. It was Kate's voice and he called out to her.

"Kate? Is that you?"

Then, the darkness haunted him. He saw her, his Kate, a bedraggled corpse lying on a stretcher in the morgue. Her skin was tattered with bullet holes and her sultry brown eyes expressed her fear as they bulged from her head. He couldn't look at her, but only from a distance. What had once been so beautiful was now a hideous paragon of death.

"Kate, forgive me for everything. Forgive me, my darling, for not being there for you."

# CHAPTER 4

Bailey waited at the north entrance of the Dallas Convention Center for Jess, arriving fifteen minutes early in an effort to show her competence. She was well prepared, carrying the leather satchel she had recently bought for her work at the paper, equipped with notes, a recorder, a camera, and all the necessary tools a reporter might need. For Jess, she had bought a framed photograph of the downtown Dallas skyline at night, a gift she thought he might like to remember his visit to Texas.

She was a striking picture, dressed in a tweed suit that set to perfection the line of her long narrow waistline and full hips. The front of her skirt buttoned up the right side and teased the eye with a tantalizing view of her sleek thigh as she walked. Her green silk blouse followed the v-line of her jacket, displaying a slight portion of her neckline. It was slight enough to be considered professional, yet daring enough to lend the eye an appreciation of her physical charms. The sides of her thick hair were pulled up and clipped at the back with a delicate clasp that complimented her gold jewelry. When she smiled, the brown of her eyes flittered in shades of green.

"Jess," she called out when she saw him moving toward the entrance, waving to get his attention. He nodded when he caught sight of her and was quickly at her side. He held out his hand to greet her and when they shook hands, both were stricken with a familiar attraction. It was so strong, it invited Jess to brush her forehead with a quick kiss, so quick neither one barely noticed.

"I'm on time," she laughed nervously.

"I had great faith that you would be," he smiled.

His smile teased her reserve, even more, when he held out

his strong arm for her and they moved toward the area where his father's work was displayed. She gripped his arm slightly, feeling his body heat permeate through his white starched shirt. Her eyes examined him intently, from the leather ribbon that held back his thick hair to the shine on his black boots.

"You look Texan," she teased.

He was garnished with articles that defined his trade. The buttons on his shirt were made of turquoise stones and on both wrists, he wore bracelets made from silver, with turquoise stones encased in a variety of sizes and shapes. His silver belt was a menagerie of desert animals etched within the fine silver. An eagle's head was carved within the buckle of his belt and its feathers were lined with a fine turquoise hand-chasing. Today, his brown skin was overpowering, cast against his white shirt and the flair of his silver and turquoise jewelry. Bailey found him handsome, more so than she had remembered.

He led her through a spectrum of timely art and history, representing nations of people who once dominated North America. She was surrounded by the familiar regalia and habiliments most associated with the Native Americans as well as those unfamiliar to her. As she walked through the footpaths of a history long past, she began to realize the narrowness of her world. She began to look at her own naivety at thinking such societies only existed in the past, never imagining until now their value in American society today.

Each booth was guarded by the convention's security and Jess handed a man standing next to his display a card specifying who he was. The guard nodded and pointed to a book where Bailey signed her name Bailey Carson – reporter—*Dallas Morning News*. He led her to a corner of his display room where a large oil painting spread across the entire back wall. Billy Nehah had painted it from the top of his pueblo home, depicting a widespread view of the Mesa of Taaiyalone outside of Zuni, New Mexico.

"Here's your Corn Mountain, Bailey. The Mesa of Taaiyalone."

"Oh, Jess, it's breathtaking. Your father's painting?"

"Yes, and one of his most popular. I guess he's painted this view a hundred times."

"Are all of his paintings originals? I mean are some reprints?"

"If you knew my father, you would know that he would never frame a reprint. Many art dealers have tried to have him duplicate his paintings and sell them. I suppose if he had, he'd be a rich man. But that's not Dad."

"I can see how proud you are of your father."

"I am. Unfortunately, I am not so sure I carry the same values on tradition as he does."

"You mean you would have sold out to the art dealers?"

"Probably not completely, Bailey. Maybe just enough to make a decent living."

"What do you mean?"

"What I mean is there were many times when we, my family, had little to eat and even less to wear. It's very difficult to maintain high virtues when your children are hungry. I probably would have commercialized some … but maybe not. Anyway, his ways have paid off. A painting like this is well worth the grand he receives."

"How long does it take him to paint such a picture?"

"This one? Four, maybe five weeks. That's if he works all day at it, which he doesn't usually. Most of the time he works with the younger Zuni men and women, teaching them the art of silversmithing. You see, Bailey, my mother, my sister, and I are his family, but only part of it. The Zunis are his family, too. They are his blood. And my father takes care of his own."

"Where did your father learn to paint?"

"He learned from his father. And too, it was a gift he was born with."

"And you learned from him?"

"I learned mainly from him, yes, but my mother as well. I also learned some in college."

"Where did you go to college?"

"In Albuquerque. I studied art and... "

"And what?"

"Music."

"Ah," she mused. "There lies your true passion."

"Hmmm…," he shrugged.

"It is, I know. Your eyes have the same look mine have when I speak of journalism."

Jess smiled.

"Tell me about your music, Jess."

"I like music, that's all."

"You want to break away from tradition, but you don't have the heart."

"I think we'd better continue our walk."

He led her to another wall that displayed photographs of different Zuni people. Bailey recognized one of Jess right away. She guessed him to be around sixteen or so, thinner and less assured than he was today, but still possessed the physical traits that at times left her confused.

"Did your father take these photographs?"

"I took most of them. I dabbled a bit with photography in college. It was fun."

"They are quite wonderful, Jess. Who took the one of you?"

"My sister, Nellie."

"Is she an artist, too?"

"Sometimes. You will see when you look at our jewelry where Nellie's talents lie."

Glancing at the photo again she asked, "What's that feather in your hair?"

"A turkey feather. It's worn on the side of the head for dancing."

"What kind of dancing?"

"The Zunis dance for ceremonial reasons mainly. There is always a purpose for our dancing. Most of the time we dance to celebrate or to invite the spirits to guide us."

"You still believe that? I mean, I thought some of these practices faded through the years."

"I am faithful, Bailey. Faith never fades."

She was fascinated by his culture that was in such contrast to hers.

"What are you holding in your hand?"

"That's a white kachina doll."

"I believe I read that kachinas are spirits."

"Yes, the spirits of those who have passed before us and the spirits of nature."

"I also read that Zuni men sometimes dress as different spirits. Why?"

"They are kachina dancers. The Zuni belief is that the dancer becomes one with the spirit and brings power to the dancer."

"Are you a kachina dancer, Jess?"

"To reveal this would take the power away from the dancer. The spirit will flee."

Part of Bailey thought his words were somewhere out of a voodoo book of spells, but the serious look on his face told her not to make light of what he was saying. She moved to a picture of an older Zuni man, around sixty, who stood next to a cage that held an eagle.

"Who is this?"

"He is Coyote, my kyamme, my uncle."

"What is he doing?"

"He guards the sacred eagle. The eagle will be used for many purposes."

"Such as?"

"Such as prayer sticks, dance masks, and medicine wands. Coyote uses the eagle for his medicine. You see, he is a medicine man. I think you would like my uncle, Bailey. He very much embraces the white race and sees them as valuable to our progress. His wife was a white woman he met when he visited California. She moved from her home to be with him."

"Did your people embrace her?"

"Most did. Some didn't."

"I see." She marveled at the strangeness of his culture. Her eyes trailed to a photograph of a man around fifty-five. His hair was long and black and like Jess, he wore it tied back. Like Jess, he was embellished with fine jewelry. Bailey looked at Jess and then back at the photo and realized this man was his father.

She stood staring at the picture, admiring the stance of this noble gentleman; long hair, thick brow, deep black eyes. There was a familiar look about him and for a moment she was sure she knew his kind smile. She studied this smile and her mind was lost in a mist of red earth that covered the mesas and the spirit of Jess's father seemed to soar through her. For a moment, she actually lost her balance, but then calmness prevailed. She looked at Jess confused.

"This is your father, I know."

"Yes," he answered more taken back by her reaction to his father's photo than the fact that she knew who he was.

"He wears a familiar smile, like I've seen it before. Of course, I know I haven't. I think maybe it's your smile I know."

Jess held her hand tightly, noticing that the color had gone from her face, even as she tried to reassure him otherwise.

"You look pale, Bailey. Do you need to sit down?"

"I'm fine, Jess. It's just that..."

"What, Bailey?"

She looked at him helplessly. "I don't know. I can't explain it." She looked at the face of Billy Nehah once more and her eyes trailed over a necklace he wore.

"Jess, what is your father wearing?"

"His spirit necklace. Some say when it is near your heart, the spirits are always near, protecting you. I wear one, see?" Jess pulled out a necklace strung on braided leather. Two eagle claws were adorned with beads and dyed eagle feathers.

"Do you believe in its power?"

"I believe in the power of the spirits."

Bailey reached to touch the finely decorated necklace, rubbing her fingers gently over its feathers. A strange sensation swept over her, much the same as when she saw Billy Nehah's photo. Her eyes sought Jess for understanding.

"The spirits are teasing you, Bailey. That is good. They like you."

"Jess, show me Nellie's jewelry now," she urged in an effort to cover up her uneasiness.

Bailey followed Jess down a small walkway that led to a group of tables encased in glass displaying the jewelry his family had made. There was a dazzling assortment of jewelry and accessories made from the finest silver and turquoise. It overpowered her with its beauty.

"Oh, Jess."

"You like?"

"I'm a woman, Jess. What do you think?"

"The Zunis' livelihood, Bailey."

A Zuni woman sat in a chair at the end of one of the glass tables and Bailey nodded to her. She responded by giving Bailey a broad smile. Jess led Bailey to her and introduced her as Nada, a Zuni silversmith. She spoke clipped English, so Jess did most of the talking. The woman honored Bailey by slipping a delicate silver and turquoise ring on her finger. Bailey looked at Jess.

"It's her gift to my Texas friend."

"Jess, I have nothing to give her."

"You are our guest. You have visited her."

"Thank you," Bailey said as she turned to Jess. "Does she understand me?"

"She understands."

Jess spoke to Nada for some time and then directed Bailey toward the entrance of their display room. As they moved toward the door, Bailey noticed a hallway filled with paintings of pueblo homes, mesas, buttes, desert animals, eagles, and kachinas.

"You've been holding out on me," she teased Jess. He smiled broadly.

"I was saving the best for last."

"Your father is so gifted, Jess."

At the edge of the hallway an obscure, almost ominous

painting caused Bailey to abruptly stop. It was a macabre of a woman roaming aimlessly amid the dark ravines of the desert. It was entitled: *The White Spirit Who Roams the Desert.*

"Jess, tell me about this painting."

"I know very little about the painting, Bailey. I just recently found it among some of my father's earlier works. He had it stored in the lower compartment of our pueblo. I was fascinated by the look of it and told my father I would like to display it.

"He said because I had come upon it after so many years, the spirits wanted it to be seen. When I asked him what the painting meant or about the title, he told me he could not speak of it."

"Look, Jess," she noted. "He painted the woman with no face. See how her long blonde hair drapes her like a mourning cloth. What are the dark illusions on the other side of the mesa?"

"They are Zuni spirits. They are calling her to join them, but she can't hear them. She is listening for another sound."

"What sound?"

He shrugged. "I can only speculate."

"What?"

"Well ... when I was a young boy, around seven, I remember hearing that my father had found a little girl in the desert. She was near death and there was much publicity about it in Gallup, a nearby town. My father said nothing to us at home, but I heard bits and pieces from other people. They talked about a white woman being found murdered near Corn Mountain. The same Corn Mountain that was shown on the slides yesterday."

"Jess, do you think the woman in your father's painting is the murdered woman?"

"Who else, Bailey?"

"What an incredible story, and such a sad one."

Jess watched her study the painting. He noticed her emotional attachment and he gently touched her shoulder.

"I think you will be a very good reporter, Bailey. You have a caring that wants to know the truth , not just to get a story. "

She put her hand over his. "Thank you for saying that and thank you for giving me a glimpse into your world."

His black eyes searched her face, so full of wonderment. He wanted to know everything he could about this amazing woman who had somehow managed to step into his life. The trouble was, she was from another world, so opposite his. And too, she was engaged, promised to another man. He couldn't send her away just yet, though. In his eyes, she was his at least for the rest of the night. She was his to spoil and admire. He gripped her tiny hand slightly, edging her away from his world and directing her back to hers.

"I'm glad you liked what you saw. Now - show me your world."

# CHAPTER 5

Jess wanted down-home Texas cooking, so Bailey took him to the *Texas Trail,* a swanky four-star restaurant and nightclub in North Dallas famous for its exceptional steaks and Texas-style atmosphere. Bailey ordered a bottle of Chablis but learned quickly that Jess wasn't a wine drinker after watching his face after several small sips.

"Something else to drink, Jess? A beer? Tea? Soda?"

"A beer would be great."

Bailey motioned for a waiter.

"What do you think of Texas so far, Jess? Do you like the country music playing in the background?"

"Texas is friendly, especially the women. And yeah, I like the music in the background. I like all music."

"What's your favorite kind?"

"People or music?"

"Music," she smiled." What kind do you like best?"

"I'm partial to jazz."

A tall muscular waiter, dressed in blue jeans and a red white and blue silk shirt approached the table. He tipped his hat at them and clanked together his shiny spurs.

"Two Lone Stars, please," Bailey said, holding up two fingers. He gave her a quick wink, took her order and headed for the bar.

"A live band is supposed to perform in about 40 minutes, the Dodge Boys, or something like that. Anyway, I hear they're very good."

"Let me guess?" Jess winked. "You're not a country and western fan."

"I like it okay, but if you promise not to think I'm too square

50

or anything like that, when I have a choice, I listen to classical music. I suppose it's because my entire life Mother only allowed me to listen to classical music. She played it for me, too, on the piano. When she was young, before she married Daddy, she traveled with a small company from New York. She could have played professionally. She's that good."

"Why didn't she?"

"I don't really know, Jess. My guess is Daddy and me. We were her life. I think it's a little sad, don't you? I mean to have such a dream and never see it through."

"Everything comes from experience, doesn't it?"

He gave her a weary smile and took a swallow from his beer.

"What about you, Bailey. Did you inherit your mother's ear for music?"

She gave a short laugh. "Not hardly, although Mother did try her best to encourage me."

"What happened?"

"It was awful. I mean, I was awful. You see, I'm completely tone-deaf. After years of agonizing lessons and even more tears, Mother finally put all of her energy into my dancing. It nearly broke her heart when I stopped."

"Why did you stop?"

"I danced mainly for Mother and Daddy. Journalism is where my heart is. My parents have a difficult time supporting my studies. So you see, Jess. I do understand your situation. I mean, you haven't really said, but I get the idea that your father doesn't approve of your music."

"You're wrong, Bailey. He does."

"Oh, well – I guess I'm confused."

"He approves of it, so long as I stay with tradition."

"By tradition, you mean the music of the Zuni."

"Yes. But don't get me wrong. The music of the Zuni is very beautiful. It's just that sometimes I feel like my people are lost in a time of the past and they keep themselves from growing, from prospering."

"There's much to be admired about people who don't conform, Jess."

"Yes, but those who are successful are those who are not afraid to take a chance, to change."

"Sometimes it takes more courage to stay the same and not to be led by outside forces."

Jess tipped his glass to her and smiled. "You and my father would get along well."

"I'm not saying you're wrong and your father is right, Jess. I'm just saying there is a certain peace knowing where you came from and where you're headed. Some people spend their whole life searching for such certainty. Take me, for example. I know very little about my family, other than my father and mother and brother. I never knew any of my grandparents or uncles or aunts except through stories."

"Why is that?"

"Daddy's work kept us moving and took us away from the States. When I came back to the States, I decided to look up some of my relatives from the information that he had given me. I couldn't find anybody who knew anything about my family. After a while, I gave up. It's so strange, Jess, to have no trace of the past, no memories of a family."

"You must have memories, Bailey."

"Oh, sure, of Mother and Daddy and Sammy. Still, there's an emptiness I can't explain. Anyway, when I marry, I'm going to have lots of children and I'm going to bring them up in one place. I want them to have a place they can call home. I've never had that. Even in Europe, we moved from house to house. The longest I ever stayed in one place was three years."

She looked at Jess who was studying her intently. His thoughts went back to his own home in New Mexico, his ever constant, never changing home. He thought of his grandfather and grandmother and aunts and uncles and all the people in his village. Yes, he sometimes longed to break free from the ever binding ties that so defined him. But she, this tiny woman, so outwardly confident was inwardly lost. She was searching for

52

something that perhaps only existed in her mind. Jess held her hand tightly.

"I'm sure your fiancé will be a fine husband and father."

"Yes," she wavered. This was the first time she had thought of Ron in hours, a matter that confused her considering his recent consent to marry her in December. Even more confusing was her reaction to his decision. For years, this was what she wanted, what she had prayed for. And now, she held a certain resentment that he had been the one to once again control the happenings of her life. Sadness was written on her face. Jess as quick to change the subject.

"I'd like to let you in on a little secret, so long as it remains between us. I mean, if this is off the record."

"A secret? What is it?"

"I've been offered a job as a backup guitar player for the jazz performer Jimmy Lee, Jr."

"Jess! How did you meet him? Are you going to accept his offer?"

"I met him through a friend of mine whose uncle traveled with him. He's giving up the road. Jimmy Lee heard me play at a lounge in Albuquerque. He offered me the gig."

"I've never known anyone who worked with a famous band before."

"Well," he smiled, "if I take the job, you'll know me."

"Oh, Jess, you have to take the job!"

"Only moments ago, you were telling me I needed to stick with tradition."

"What I was saying, Jess, was that you can't forget who you are and the things that are of value to you. I would be willing to bet that when you tell your father, he will say, go for it, Jess. He'll be pulling for you."

"Could I take you back to New Mexico and let you tell my father? You make everything sound so simple, so certain."

"The fact is, an offer like this doesn't happen to just anyone. It comes along once in a lifetime and that's if you're lucky. Jimmy Lee! My God, Jess, you have to take the job!"

"It seems the footpaths of our lives have unfolded before us and we only have to follow them. We both have been given a chance to see our dreams through. You have your upcoming marriage and I have my work. Things seem to be working out as it should for us."

Jess lifted his beer to toast their futures.

"To you, Bailey. May you have a house full of children as beautiful as you. May you find the happiness you deserve."

"And you, Jess. I want to open up the paper and see your name printed next to Jimmy Lee's. I want to tell everyone I knew him when he first got started. Just promise me that when you're famous, you won't forget me. And when you're in Dallas, you'll give me a call."

"I could call, if I had your number."

"Oh, here," she fumbled through her purse. "Here's my business card. It has my business number and my cell phone number. Now you have no excuse not to call."

Jess traced over a small photograph of her printed on the card, bringing life to the beauty of her kind smile. He tucked the card in his wallet and reached to unfasten the necklace he had hanging from his neck.

"Here, Bailey. You have given me your time and your hospitality. You have shown me your Texas and made me feel welcome in your city. Thanks for the photograph of Dallas. And now, I want to give you something, my spirit necklace. When you wear it, think of me."

"Jess," she whispered, "put it on me."

She felt the soft feathers brush across her skin as he fastened the necklace around her. He rested his hand on her shoulder and brought his mouth to her ear.

"Had we met at another time, perhaps this would not be goodbye, but a new beginning. If you ever need me, call me."

She put her hand over his and turned to face him, where their lips barely met. Both hearts were racing wildly. Had he tried to kiss her, she doubted she would have stopped him, could have stopped him. But, he didn't kiss her. He laid a tip on the table and led her away from this moment of fate, a moment neither one would ever forget. They were silent as she drove him to his hotel and by the time they reached the lobby, they couldn't look at each other—regretful that they had to say good night—fearful that they might not be able to say good night. Jess reached for her hand and kissed it softly.

"Goodbye, Bailey Carson."

She swallowed hard. "Goodbye, Jess."

She watched his dark form move inside the lobby and then down the hall, watching him until he faded into the shadows of the night. She edged slowly away from the Hyatt, down the murky road, just six blocks to Stemmons Freeway that led to her home in Denton. Her mind was whirling, lost in thoughts of Jess and his touch, and the realization that she might never see him again.

Before she had much time to dwell on it, she heard a thunderous bang and then felt herself losing control of her car. Without having to wonder what happened, she knew. She knew her tire had blown out. She fought to gain control of her car, stopping short of hitting a light post. When her car stopped, she was straddled up over a grassy knoll.

Shaken, she was unharmed, with only a slight bruise on her forehead. She looked around to find the night bleak and unattended. She knew the area well, and also the dangers of a young woman being out in the night alone. Spontaneously, she locked her doors and reached for her cell. Fear crept over her when she realized she'd left it at home.

"Damn!" She cursed her negligence. She thought of the other things she had neglected to do, like keeping her promise to get her car inspected. Had she kept her promise, she would have no doubt been forced to get new tires and wouldn't be deliberating on the side of a pitch-black road. She thought of Ron and the anger she felt toward herself shifted toward him. Why hadn't he seen to her tires before he left? She sat bitter, wallowing in her predicament.

"You can sit here and feel sorry for yourself all night, but that won't get you home," she said aloud.

She contemplated walking back to the hotel, and the thought of Jess's strong assurance comforted her, but the hotel was over four blocks away. Looking at the dark streets, she thought of a less risky option. There was a convenience store just a block or so away. She decided to walk the short block and use the phone there to call Sammy to come get her. She reached for her purse and willed her shaken body out of the car and into the still October night.

As she walked, she felt vulnerable. She heard something moving behind her and at first thought it was her imagination playing tricks on her. But as the sounds became more pronounced, she felt her adrenaline kick into gear. She recognized the slight brush of footsteps, but there was another sound, a more intrusive sound that prevailed. It was almost like the sound of a large branch tapping against a house on a windy night. The tapping became more vivid the closer it got to her. Instinctively, she picked up her pace.

She reached into her purse and scrambled in the dark for something she could use to protect herself. The only thing she found was a small can of hairspray. She popped the lid and reached for the nozzle, ready to spray, but when she turned around she didn't see anything or anyone. Ahead, she saw the lights from the service station and she began to run.

When she reached the station, the doors were locked, but the attendant let her use the phone to call Sammy. She breathed easier realizing help was on its way. Once again, she heard the tapping she had heard just moments earlier. From the shadows emerged a small figure. It was an elderly woman, sixty or so, dressed only in a thin robe and slippers. The tapping sound had been her cane. Her tiny body humped forward and when she moved under the stream of the lights Bailey could see her face. It was one of absolute confusion.

"What the hell?" the attendant remarked.

"She must be lost, "Bailey said. "I think we should call the police."

56

"Yeah, I think you're right."

As the attendant made the call, Bailey watched the tiny woman stroll unconcerned toward the busy intersection.

"No! No!" Bailey screamed to her, but the woman moved aimlessly, oblivious to her calls. Bailey saw the headlights of the cars moving down the access road, just off the freeway. Without thinking, she moved toward the woman. Then, a horn's noise alerted her. It was a deafening sound and before she knew what she was doing, Bailey was gripping the woman and pushing her out of harm's way. In her rescue, Bailey forced both she and the woman against the hard pavement. She had saved their lives but had knocked them both out cold.

# CHAPTER 6

Bailey awoke to find she was lying in a hospital bed surrounded by flowers and get-well greetings, filling the private room of Parkland Hospital to its capacity. Muddled, she tried to assess the details that put her in the hospital. The last thing she remembered was the sound of a car horn and feeling the impact of her body being jolted against the street. She heard the door to the room open and saw a woman moving toward her. As she got closer, Bailey recognized her sister-in-law, Diane, a sassy bleach blonde beauty, who was wearing a skimpy skirt and tight sweater.

Diane began fussing with Bailey's blanket and then moved about the room to water the plants and arrange the flowers Bailey had received during her two-day convalescence. Bailey tried several times to speak, but her mouth was so parched, no words would come out. She saw a glass of water on the table beside her bed, but when she reached for it, she could barely lift her hand. Diane jumped and let out a slight yelp. Instantly, Diane called for a nurse and then moved to hold Bailey, brushing her forehead with a gentle kiss.

"Honey, you're awake! You sure gave us a scare! The doctors say you'll be fine. Just need some rest, that's all. Here, Honey, want some water?"

Diane brought the glass to Bailey's lips and she drank every drop. Diane went to the window and opened the blinds, bringing day to the dreary room.

"God, Bailey," she commented. "Ron's in a state cause you're at Parkland and not Baylor. The doctors refused to let him move you. He's been such a doll. He cut his Miami trip short to be with you."

An aide came in with another floral arrangement. Dr. Benjamin Klistner followed her.

"How's our celebrity?" Klistner asked.

"She's awake," Diane reported, "but not saying anything."

He flashed a light into Bailey's eyes and she followed its stream.

"You're looking good. With any luck, little lady, you'll be out of here in no time."

"Some more flowers came for you, Miss Carson," the aide said. "Do you want me to read who they are from?"

Bailey nodded.

"They are from Professor C. The card reads: *We miss you in class. Get well very soon.*"

Bailey smiled and once again, she tried to speak. Dr. Klistner touched her arm.

"Don't worry, Bailey. Your speech will come back to you. Your mind has been jumbled and needs time to sort things out, that's all. You have a bad concussion. You're lucky to make out as you did."

Diane sat in the chair next to her, fumbling through a magazine until Dr. Klistner finished his examination. When he and the aide left, Diane stood next to the bed.

"God, Bailey, so much has happened. I don't know where to begin. You know that little old lady, the one you pushed so she wouldn't be hit by the car?"

Bailey nodded.

"Well, it turns out she has Alzheimer's Disorder and had wandered away from her home and had been missing for over two days. By the way, Honey, she's just fine. She got by with a broken arm and some bruises. Well anyway, it turns out she is the mother of a prominent Dallas family, who appears to own half of Dallas.

"My God, Bailey, reporters have been in and out of this hospital the last couple of days. The lady's daughter says she's gonna see to it that you receive some kind of honorary medal or something for your heroism. Wow, your picture has been in every Texas paper and your story even made the national news – CBS, ABC, NBC, CNN, FOX – all of them. Guess it's not so much what you did as who you saved."

Again, Bailey's eyes trailed over the massive stream of get-well greetings.

"Here, Honey," Diane continued. She threw her a copy of the *Dallas Morning News*. "Read all about yourself. I'm gonna call Sam and Ron and let them know you are awake."

Bailey scanned the paper to read the events that led to her hospitalization. The headline in the paper read: *"DALLAS WOMAN BECOMES HERO."*

The article stated: "A Dallas woman became an unsuspecting hero when she plunged in front of a moving vehicle just off the corner of Reunion Boulevard and the access road of I-35 to save the life of an elderly woman who had gone missing several weeks ago. An amazing turn of events occurred when the identities of the two women were revealed.

"The hero has been identified as a twenty-one-year-old woman named Bailey Carson. Ms. Carson had by chance been placed at the scene of her heroic endeavor when her own car had been left abandoned several blocks away. As fate would continue to play a part in this amazing story, the vagrant woman in the hospital has been identified as Josephine Gordon, the mother-in-law of Dallas mogul, Raymond Pena.

"Josephine Gordon has been missing from her North Dallas home for two days prior to her rescue. Ms. Gordon is reportedly doing well and has been released in the custody of her family, suffering a small break in her right arm and minor contusions. Ms. Carson, Dallas's young heroine, is still being hospitalized. She is expected to make a complete recovery…"

Bailey let out a stunned sigh.

"I have a surprise for you," Diane said. "But, you have to promise me you won't let on you know. Promise?"

Bailey shook her head yes.

"Your parents are coming to the States in a couple of weeks. Sid wanted to catch the first flight when he heard about the accident."

"Mother and Daddy," Bailey tried to say, but it came out in a jumbled utter. She was surprised by what she had just heard. She gave Diane a confused look.

"Yes, they were going to leave right away, but when Sam told them you were all right, just a little banged up, Sid decided to settle some affairs before coming. Now remember, you have to promise not to tell or let on that I told you. Hell, you and Ron should go ahead and get married while they are here, instead of waiting until December."

At the mention of his name, Bailey instinctively felt for her engagement ring and became panicked when she discovered it missing.

"Don't worry," Diane said. "They, the hospital staff, put all of your jewelry and stuff you had with you in a plastic bag. You know your purse and all. I locked it up in the suitcase I brought from your apartment. Want me to get it for you?"

Again, Bailey nodded. Diane handed her the bag and while Bailey hunted for her ring, she came upon the spirit necklace Jess had given her. She pulled the necklace from the bag and gently rubbed her fingers over its feathers. Diane studied the look on Bailey's face as she held the article close to her heart.

"Jess," was Bailey's first word. Her voice was soft and raspy, but his name was clear. Diane was quick to note that her first word was this Jess's name.

"Jess isn't here, Bailey. But he left you a note."

Bailey gave Diane a strange look, wondering what she might know about Jess.

"Don't look so baffled, Honey. It's just that this Indian guy came by to see you. He told me his name was Jess and that you had interviewed him and had dinner with him the night of the accident. He saw your name and picture on the news and came to the hospital to see how you were."

"Oh," Bailey sighed.

"Of course, the staff wouldn't allow any visitors, except family, you know. But, this Jess guy was pretty persistent. He finally cornered me in the lobby and gave me a note for you. He made me promise I would give it to you personally."

Bailey opened the note and saw Jess's name etched at the bottom. A picture of him filled her mind and a peculiar chill invaded her as she recalled his touch and her response to his touch. She remembered him fastening the necklace on her and whispering in her ear. Bailey clutched the note along with the necklace. Diane could see the effect both were having on her sister.

"A handsome lover you have tucked away?" she teased.

If Bailey heard her tease, she didn't let on, giving Diane more reason to speculate. Diane took the jewelry and note from Bailey's hand and tucked them in a drawer next to the bed. She took Bailey's engagement ring and put it on her finer, giving her a gentle pat.

"There. Now, let's get your hair brushed and some make-up put on. We need you beautiful for Ron."

****

Sid Carson had hired Bud Little, Sammy's stepfather and a self-made P.I., to keep watch over Bailey three years ago. Up until now, Sid's fears were minimal. With this recent publicity and with Bailey's photograph plastered in the newspapers and on television, Sid had reason to be concerned. Remembering the heinous details of Kate's death and the always present fear that somehow Jack Adams would find his little girl, Sid knew he had to nip the situation in the bud as soon as possible.

"Yeah, Sid," Bud reported. "Things are fine here. I've got a man watching her room around the clock. Not to worry. No son of a bitch is gonna come near Bailey unless he wants a shot up his ass."

"Good. I'm coming to Texas in a couple of weeks. I'm counting on you to protect her until I get there. I don't mind telling you, this situation has me scared as hell."

"I got it covered, man. Besides, you know I can smell a

louse like Jack a mile away. He's not here."

"You don't know him like I do. He's as low as a man can get, but he's smart as hell. He does his best work when challenged."

"Relax, Sid. Bailey's safe. Hell, if Adams is as good as you say, wouldn't he have found her years ago?"

"I'm not sure he hasn't. But then again, you might be right."

"Sure I am."

"Just don't let down your guard, not for anyone."

"I'm ready for him, Sid. If the bastard does come for her, he's gonna get one hell of a Texas welcome."

****

In Los Angeles, a reporter named Red Benning studied with keen interest the story of a young Dallas woman sited for her heroics at saving the life of a homeless woman. Red, long past his prime, was nearly sixty years of age and close to retirement. One of Los Angeles' top reporters, Red's area of expertise was homicide reporting. He is attracted to this particular story, not because of the national attention it is receiving, but because of the players involved. He is particularly interested in the young heroine, who bears an identical resemblance to a beautiful woman named Kate Michaels. Red had reported on Kate Michaels's murder some seventeen years ago when she was found executed in a New Mexico desert.

He scans through his old files to retrieve information about the seventeen-year-old murder, in particular, to look at photos of Kate Michaels. For the thousandth time, he reviews her unsolved killing. It had been an embarrassment to the Gallup Police, the FBI, and to Red himself. He always swore he'd solve the case. He never conceded to a perfect crime, but simply in perfect timing and luck for the criminal.

He reviews the details of a small child being found near death some fifty feet from the place where her mother's body was later found. The papers were only allowed to call her *Desert*

*Baby,* in an effort to protect her from the monster who had slaughtered her mother. The child was around four years of age. Today, she would be around the same age as Dallas's new heroine, Bailey Carson.

Red studies the photos of Kate and the ones of Bailey Carson in the news. The resemblance is uncanny. They were the same person, except for the color of hair. But, this was all he had to go on. In the past, he had hit so many walls trying to solve this case. This was more than likely another one. Still, it would be nice to retire with this one under his belt. A seasoned reporter, Red's gut feelings had helped him solve many cases. He had a strong gut feeling about the connection of this would-be heroine and Kate Michaels.

He decided he had to go to Dallas and speak with this Bailey Carson. He owed this much to himself and the work he had done on the Michaels's case. What if this Bailey Carson was the daughter of Kate Michaels? Surely, she has as many questions about her mother's death as he does, and maybe, some answers, too. It wouldn't be a bad end to his career to solve this mystery. Once again, he examined the physical similarities between the two women. They had the same eyes, the same nose, the same smile, the same cheekbones, but most convincing, were the eyes. He knew he'd never forget those eyes as long as he lived.

"It's like looking at a ghost," he remarks. "Bailey Carson is it possible that you are *Desert Baby*?"

****

Late that night when everyone had gone home, Bailey lay in her hospital bed thinking about the past three days. Her thoughts moved to Ron and how attentive he'd been all night, not letting her pick up even a glass without his help. And when she would talk, he would scold her saying she needed to rest her voice. Before leaving, he prayed over her and promised she'd be the most beautiful bride in Texas. He had been as gentle and loving as she had ever known him to be and she was reluctant to have him leave for the night.

So attentive was Ron, she didn't notice how quiet Sammy had been and the distance he had set between himself and Ron. Diane and Ron, on the other hand, were communal, acting up and carrying on for Bailey's benefit. Bailey thought of her mother and father and the fact that in less than two weeks, she would be seeing them again. Everything was happening so fast and thoughts of people and events shot in and out of her mind. She was thankful when the nurse came in to give her a sleeping pill. At last, she would be able to sleep.

She decided to read over her cards while she waited for the pill to kick in. There were so many of them, she didn't know where to begin. Then, she remembered Jess's note and opened the drawer next to the bed. She pulled out the note along with the necklace. As she began to read his words, once again her heart was charged with thoughts of him.

*Bailey, my friend, how frightened I was to hear of your accident. But, isn't it like you to place others before yourself? Your sister-in-law tells me you will recover nicely. I'm grateful for that. My heart is heavy with worry for you. I just wish I could hear your voice so that I can know for sure you are all right. Silly, huh? I leave for New Mexico Sunday. If you have an opportunity to call, I would appreciate it. Best to you always. I told you the spirits liked you. You must have a powerful connection with them. Perhaps even a guardian spirit. Love to you, Jess.*

Without thinking, Bailey picked up the phone, called the downtown Hyatt, and was connected to Jess's room. She heard his deep voice answer and felt the beat of her heart race at the sound of it.

Her own voice cracked. "Jess?"

"Bailey, I was hoping you would call me before I left. I heard you were doing well. I was so worried."

"I'm fine, Jess. That's why I'm calling, so you won't worry. I got your note. Thanks for coming by."

"I had to come to the hospital and see you. When do you go home?"

"The doctors say in a couple of days," Bailey answered.

"Then back to the old grindstone, huh?"

"Yeah" she giggled. "Jess, I want you to know that despite the accident, I had a wonderful time that night."

"I had a great time, too, Bailey."

She let a moment or two pass before speaking. "Jess, I know this might sound silly, except maybe to you, but I—well—I think your necklace saved my life. I think you were right when you said the spirits liked me."

She held tight to the necklace and was soothed by its soft touch. When she spoke again, her voice was a whisper. "Your face, Jess, was the first face my mind saw just after I woke up from the accident."

Jess felt his heart stir at the implications of her words. "Was it? That's probably because we had just been together."

"Maybe," her voice faded. "Jess?"

"Yeah?"

"Do you have your guitar with you?"

"I always have my guitar with me. Why?"

"I want to hear you play. Would you play for me? Now? Just for a while. Maybe a Zuni song, Jess."

Jess picked up his guitar and the soft notes floated through the receiver, connecting the two young people. When he stopped, she was mesmerized. She suddenly wished he were with her so she could see his smile and hold his hand.

"That was beautiful, Jess."

*You're beautiful*, he thought, but said aloud, "Thanks."

She dozed off for a moment. "Bailey?" he asked.

"Jess, I think the sleeping pill the nurse gave me is starting to work. I don't want to hang up, but I can barely keep my eyes open."

"Then, you'd better close them. At least now I know you are all right."

66

Still, they lingered.

"Do you think we will ever see each other again?" she asked him.

He sighed heavily. "Maybe – maybe our work will bring us together."

"I hope it does."

Again, they lingered. She drifted in and out of sleep. He was torn by what could never be. Then, she heard him say, "Goodnight, Bailey. I will never forget you."

Before she could reply, he had gently placed down his phone, disconnecting them. Her mind was filled with his image. His strong arms were holding her, rocking her to sleep. She felt gentle hands sweep through her hair and she called out into the dark night, "Jess?"

There was no response. She knew someone was there, but guessed it was probably a nurse or an aide checking in on her. Before she had further time to wonder, she fell into a deep sleep, unaware of the man hovering over her. Again, he swept a gentle hand through her hair. He moved to kiss her forehead, catching sight of her sleeping form. She was so peaceful, so angelic.

"My God, you're so beautiful, just like your mother. I'm here to take care of you, just like I promised Kate I would. Sleep tight, my baby. I'm here to protect you."

****

Billy Nehah awoke from a familiar nightmare. Though it was familiar, he hadn't had it for many years. Sadie shook him, for he was wrestling in his sleep.

"It's back, Sadie. The dream is back. The little girl's spirit is in trouble. She is in danger."

"Yes. I believe you are right. Many have said the *White Spirit Who Roams the Desert* is restless, too. She cries for justice."

"Come pray with me, Sadie. We must pray that the spirits will keep her from harm."

# CHAPTER 7

Jack Adams had been a hustler since he was able to walk. Even then, there was a raw cynosure about him, which attracted the attention of those he hustled. It wasn't until he made his final move, until it was too late for his victims to retreat did they recognize him for what he was, and he was the first to admit what he was. He was rhetoric of some dark evil. He was a fire out of control and cared little about those he hurt. As the years passed, his games became more dangerous and his stakes higher. What little conscience he had managed to salvage throughout his life seemed to vanish the moment Kate Michaels breathed her last.

At first sight, strangers were wise to be cautious of him and most were. Then, he would reel in his prey capturing the heart of them with his dark passion. His nature was generally opposite his opponents and it was easy to lure them to his side. He walked on the edge of life where few had the courage to walk. He skillfully bolstered their passage to his side. Once his prey had met him on his turf, he had them and used their weaknesses against them. In this respect, they lost all control and power to Jack.

While his ability to seduce the dark side of even the most righteous was by far his overriding talent, it didn't hurt that he possessed an offbeat charisma. It was the kind that threatened almost all men and one that few women were able to resist. By far, women were his most vulnerable prey and it wasn't by chance that they were his primary targets.

He baited their intrigue with his vernal grin, his erotic eye contact and his uncanny knowledge of knowing exactly what a woman needed. He used these needs to seduce them until they found themselves at his mercy.

He stood almost six feet and kept his muscular body in top condition by lifting weights and mastering the martial arts. He was a master at street war, too. It was as if he were able to see the entire scope of the world and could anticipate to almost perfection the moves those he targeted would make. He never stopped to live life, but rather watched it through keen eyes, waiting for an opportunity to come his way. When it did, he was always ready. At forty-six, he retained his early street prescience.

Jack slipped out of Bailey's hospital room without a hitch, giving a taut chuckle at the man posted to guard her. He considered himself lucky that Sid had stooped to such an amateur level. This green slug would only be a slight hindrance in his plans at getting close to Bailey. Still, he had to give Sid credit for keeping her hidden for all these years. But then Jack rethought his admiration for his once comrade.

"Had I not been incapacitated at the beginning, I would have found her long before now. Oh, well, fate and wit have ended my search."

He slid his oversized bulk inside the rented Ultima and lit a cigarette, giving a slight hack as the breeze from his open window swept through his thick brown hair, giving him welcomed relief from hours in a stuffy hospital. He set his sights on the road ahead and recalled the sweetness of Bailey's gentle touch. He was only able to get a slight glimpse of her face, but it was enough to see how beautiful she had grown to be. He fumbled through his pocket and retrieved a set of keys, Bailey's keys. He drove his car in the direction of her apartment, knowing Ron was already at his apartment in Dallas, knowing that Sammy and Diane were safely tucked in their home, knowing Bailey's apartment would be empty awaiting his arrival.

He parked several blocks away from her apartment complex and walked the dark blocks, grateful that the streetlight that lit up the complex was broken, a matter he had tended to earlier. He entered the dark apartment and stood for several minutes before moving toward the back. Satisfied that he hadn't been followed, he drew out his flashlight and found his way to her bedroom.

In the bedroom, he began evaluating the details of her life. In one quick sweep of his eyes, he was able to learn a great deal about the little girl his heart couldn't forget, Kate's little girl. On her end table, he saw photos of Bailey and Sid, Bailey and Ron, Sid and Mara, but none of Kate. This fact troubled Jack. He could only speculate about the reasons. He scaled his eyes over Sid and Mara's picture and noted the arrogance of Sid's smile and the regal air of his rich wife.

"It didn't take you long to forget Kate did it? Did you ever mourn her death?"

He reached for the photo of Bailey and Sid. Her portrait unnerved him. He wasn't seeing Bailey now, but Kate. He looked into her deep brown eyes. They were haunting and cried out to him. He held within his mind her image and fell weary upon her daughter's bed, mourning once again the loss of his beautiful lover. He breathed in Bailey's scent from her pillow and it recharged his spirit. It brought him back to the present and his purpose at hand. Within seconds, he was on his feet.

"I must not let love catch me off guard ever again."

He filled a bag with some of Bailey's clothing, the picture of her and Sid and copied down some valuable information, such as her checking account number, her social security number, student I.D., her phone number and credit card numbers. In her nightstand, he found a letter from Sid and Mara, noting their Barcelona address. Thumbing through her old phone bills, he obtained several listings for Spain and jotted them down.

"My sweet Rebecca, how easy you have made things for me. And Daddy thought he was so careful. Poor Sid. Did you forget the luck of my Irish blood?"

Unable to resist the impulse of hearing his former abettor's voice, Jack picked up his cell phone and called the first number on its list. Sid Carson, or Sid Michaels to him, answered on the

70

second ring. Jack stood immobile, halfway disbelieving even he had such good fortune, first finding Rebecca and now Sid. A flood of past memories charged him when he heard Sid's voice.

"Hello," Sid answered.

There was no answer.

"Who's there," he repeated.

There was only silence.

"Who is it, Honey?" Jack heard a female voice ask.

"Christ, I don't know. Hello," Sid said more sternly.

Then, the instincts that had brought him so far in the world surfaced and Sid clutched the phone in absolute terror. He reached for Mara, who could only stare confused.

"What is it, Sid?" He shook his head and held his hand over her mouth.

"Hello," Sid said alerted. Jack knew Sid was on to him or thought he was, but also knew he could never be sure. He hung up the phone. Sid immediately called Sammy.

"Yeah," a spent Sammy answered.

"The bastard is in Dallas," Sid warned.

"Dad? Who? Jack? How do you know?"

"I just do. Here's what I want you to do. As soon as we hang up, go to the hospital and check on Bailey. Stay with her all night. First thing in the morning, I want you to speak to her doctor and see if we can get her checked out. I want you to take her to our cabin near Taos, New Mexico. It's pretty secluded and not many people know about it. We have to be one step ahead of him. Mara and I will meet you there. We're leaving here tomorrow."

"What about Diane?"

"I hadn't thought that far. What do you think?"

"I think I should bring her, to help me with Bailey. I'm going to need her to help me persuade Bailey to leave."

"What will you tell her?"

"How about the truth, Dad?"

Sid was silent.

"In fact," Sammy continued, "I think it's time Bailey knew

the truth, too."

"Maybe. But not until I can tell her."

"Sure, Dad. You should be the one to tell her."

"Okay," Sid said, feeling somewhat in control again. "So Diane's in, Sam, but no one else can know our plans. Not your mom…not anyone. It's too risky."

"What about Ron?"

"Hell no! Not him. You'll have to give him some line why she has to go. I can't trust him, Sam. He's just not that loyal."

"Yeah, I think you might be right. Tell me, Dad. What makes you so sure Jack's in Dallas?"

"Sam, the bastard just called my house less than ten minutes ago. If he's not in Dallas, he's near."

"You positive?"

"I'd bet my life on it."

"What about the police, Dad? If he is this close, shouldn't they be notified? I mean, for Bailey's protection?"

"No police. Not yet anyway."

"You sure?"

"Maybe once we get to New Mexico. I don't know."

"Okay, but don't rule them out."

"I won't. Sam, I'm thinking Jack got to Bud's guy, maybe even Bud. So if Bud or his guy gets too nosy, just play along with our old plan. Don't let on we've changed things."

"This Jack Adams really has you scared, doesn't he?"

"I know what he's capable of, Sam. I'm just hoping that I'm wrong about things and that this whole nightmare turns into nothing but my imagination."

"Don't worry, Dad. I'm on my way to the hospital."

"Good. Oh, one more thing."

"Yeah?"

"Watch your back."

"My back? It's fine, Dad," he chuckled. "There are no knives or guns there, yet."

Though his words were said in jest, his tone was less assured.

72

****

Jack lingered for a short time after Sid's call, aroused at the sound of the fear in his voice. It was the same uncertainty he had heard seventeen years ago when Kate had called him from Albuquerque saying, she had left him for Jack. Once again, Jack's thoughts went back to Kate and a time when they had been so swept up by passion, they could do nothing but end up lovers, even at the betrayal of a husband and friend.

"Kate, do you remember our first kiss? You turned to me for comfort after your mother's death because your cheating husband had gone to his lover. Oh, but I was more than willing to lend you comfort. Do you remember that day? That night?"

Seventeen years ago seemed like yesterday to Jack. His mind went back to the time when his home, as well as Kate and Sid's home, had been Colorado. Kate and Sid had been married almost four years and once again, Sid had left her alone on a Sunday.

He was so predictable. He would leave at noon and return late into the evening. At this time, Kate would see her father's Lincoln pull up the driveway and park. Kate's mother would then have her weekly visit with her daughter and granddaughter. At exactly two-thirty, her father would return to pick up her mother, never entering Kate and Sid's home, but honking his horn to signify his arrival. Then, her mother would take Rebecca and join her father. The three would drive away, leaving Kate alone. This had been their Sunday arrangement since Kate, once the apple of her father's eye, went against his wishes and married Sid Michaels.

However, this Sunday was different. Her father wasn't to come this Sunday and perhaps he would never come again. He wouldn't be bringing her mother because the day before, he had buried her. Kate elected not to attend her mother's funeral, for fear that her father might stage a scene. She didn't want her mother's memory tarnished by their differences, not as her life had been. Sid had sent Rebecca to stay with his ex-wife so that Kate could have the proper time to mourn. Still, he felt no remorse for leaving her to face the loss of her mother alone. When Jack Adams just happened by their home that afternoon, it was his shoulder where Kate bore her grief. It was his arms where she sought and found comfort.

"Hold me," she sobbed. "Hold me."

"Kate," he soothed. "My arms are always here for you."

Kate thought it strange that she should find such peace within the arms of a man she generally felt uneasy around. The strong muscles of his arms were a powerful shield against her worn body, worn from the grief of her mother's death, worn from her contest with her father, and worn from a marriage that was falling apart. She indulged herself this comfort, gently stroking his strong arms, tracing the lines of his tattoos that so identified his personality. Vaguely, she wondered why he had come to their home when ordinarily he and Sid did their business elsewhere. She pulled away from his arms and stared at him through tear-filled eyes.

"Sid's not here, Jack. He's – he's away."

"I came to see you, Kate, and lend my respect for your mother's passing."

"Oh," she said, once again stunned that this man, usually unemotional, was now expressing with great skill more compassion than she had received from a man in years. Once again, she was back in his arms. She felt his mouth brush across the top of her head as he kissed it. He was rocking her in his arms, rocking away her tears and heartache. In his arms, she grieved.

"There, Darling. Let it all out."

"Jack, you are so kind to be here for me."

"I care for you, Kate. Don't you know?"

She smiled warmly at him and he returned the smile. His smile, cocked slightly to the side of his mouth was dangerously arousing. She stirred in his arms and laid her head on his chest, wondering why she hadn't noticed this gentle side of Jack

74

before now.

"Would you like some coffee? A beer? I think Sid has a beer or two in the fridge."

"Sure, Honey. A beer would be great."

Reluctantly, she moved from his warm hold and the two walked toward the kitchen. There were two beers and so she decided to have one too. She watched Jack gulp the contents of his drink in one raw, yet almost eloquent sweep. She took a few sips from hers and once again lent him a timid smile.

"Big drinker," he teased.

She giggled, more from the way her body was reacting to him than from his weak humor. She watched as his eyes trailed over her from head to toe, uncaring that she knew he was watching her, wanting her to know he was watching her. She topped her beer and drank its contents because her mouth had suddenly become dry from nervousness.

"Guess I was thirstier than I thought."

"Guess so," he winked.

"I'm sorry I can't offer you another beer, Jack. I'm out."

He shrugged. "No matter. Let's go sit down, maybe watch some TV."

"Okay."

Jack turned on the TV and the two sat down on the sofa. He propped his feet on the table nearby and spread his arms across the back of the sofa. Before she knew it, her head was resting on his chest with his fingers fumbling over it. She felt his breath escalating as he moved his hand up and down her back. She unconsciously pinched at the sleeve of his t-shirt in an effort to ease her nerves. After a few moments, he stood up abruptly.

"Come here, Honey," he directed.

Without questioning, she stood in front of him. He wrapped his arms around her gently and moved his hands up her arm until they found a resting place on her small shoulders.

"I'm really sorry about your mother, Kate. If I can ever do anything, please call me."

In the back of her mind, she was remembering something

Sid had once said. It was more of a warning actually, about Jack. Something about never becoming too close to him.

"I appreciate your kindness, Jack."

"You can have my kindness anytime you want."

His tone was seductive and raw.

"Are you flirting with me, Jack?"

"Do you want me to flirt with you?"

"No, I...," she blushed, lowering her head.

He lifted it up and stared at her darkly.

"I didn't think today would be an appropriate day for flirting, but if you want, well, I'm game."

"You're a strange man, Jack. Sometimes you frighten me."

"My advantage," he grinned.

"Do you always have to have the advantage?"

"With you, yeah."

"What do you mean?"

"Come on, Baby. Now, who's teasing?"

"Teasing?"

"I think I'd better go, Kate."

"Jack," she held his arm. "Tell me what you mean."

"Not now, Kate. Another day."

The phone rang and she reached for his hand.

"Stay," she commanded. "Let me answer this."

He nodded. The call was from Sid. He was going to be late, probably close to midnight. When she hung up the phone, she stared at Jack almost as if she was relinquishing herself to him.

"Sid's seeing another woman."

"What? No way, Baby."

She studied his face. This man standing before her captivated her. She'd known him for almost four years and yet, she really knew little about him.

"Why haven't you married, Jack?"

"Marriage isn't for me."

"Why?"

"What I mean is, I haven't found a woman worth giving up my soul for."

"That's sad, don't you think?"

"Maybe, but hey, I'm the consummate cynic."

"I believe in marriage, even when…"

"Kate, don't. You are right about marriage. Someone like you would make it all worth it."

"Like me, Jack?"

"Yeah" he mused. "I'd marry you in a heartbeat."

"Jack, I don't know what to say."

"Say you'll marry me."

"Have you forgotten? I'm already married," she teased.

"How could I? It still doesn't change how I…"

"What, Jack?"

"I care about you, Kate."

"You care about me? Then why…why are you so loyal to Sid? Why do you keep his secrets?"

"Kate…"

"You know where he's at tonight, don't you?"

"Kate, don't."

"Be my friend, Jack. Tell me this one secret."

He took hold of her hand and eased her once again toward the sofa. He brushed her forehead with a gentle kiss and then brought his kiss to her hands, holding them firmly in his strong ones. He was reeling in his prey, just as he had intended.

"Sid's a fool. Do you think I want to be the one to break your heart?"

"Who is she?"

"It doesn't matter who."

"Who?" she demanded.

"I haven't actually met her, but she's a little gal from New York. Sid met her through a client."

"New York? Does she live here now?"

"Yeah" he nodded. "Just recently moved here."

"To be near Sid?"

"Baby," he reeled.

She gripped his hands tightly and stared at him void of emotion. She moved her hand across his face, a face that already expressed the lines of a man who has led a hard life. She traced these lines until her fingers reached his mouth, his dangerous enticing mouth.

She edged nearer his face, boldly bringing a soft kiss on his lips. She wrapped her arms around his neck, gripping his hair. Again, she kissed him. She felt his chest heave forward and his arms jolt, trying desperately to control what he knew he would be unable to control if she continued.

"Jack, let me give you what my husband refuses."

"You're messing with fire, Kate. You don't even know it."

"I know it."

"And when you've gotten what you need, then what?"

"I don't know."

"I warn you, Kate. If we continue, I won't give you back."

He pressed her lips with a maddening kiss, jolting her in such a way; she began to question the wisdom of being with a man so dangerous, so completely over the edge.

"Do you want me to send you away, Jack?"

"Let me make myself clear. I never want you to send me away. By staying, I'll be breaking all my ties with Sid. You will have my loyalties. In return, I expect the same from you."

"Jack...," she began to protest, even as he continued his assault.

"Let me finish. I love you, Kate. I've dreamed of being with you, of you wanting me. But, I want you to know exactly what you're getting yourself into."

"You're scaring me, Jack."

"Am I? Good. I'm a devil, Kate. I'm a devil attracted to the beauty of an angel. I've done things, things you would hate me for. And I'll keep doing them, unless … unless you give me a reason to stop. Give me a reason to stop, Kate."

He drew her near. His mouth swept her eagerly. He moved his kiss up and down her throat. Before she knew it, she was in his arms moving toward the bedroom.

"Be mine, Kate."

She stared into his unbending eyes, so filled with desire, but there was also something else, something she could not define. Her practical mind told her to run away as fast as she could, but another part of her longed to reach into his soul. She matched his challenge with one of her own.

"Can you be faithful, Jack? Can you love just one woman? Can you love just me?"

He gave her a twisted grin, knowing he would always love her and be faithful to her.

"There is no other woman, Kate. No other woman will have me so long as one of us is still alive."

"I'm married, Jack … I..." He hushed her with his hand over her mouth.

"After tonight, you'll be married to me. I don't give a damn what any certificate says. You'll be mine, body and soul."

Years of being left alone and rejected had taken its toll on her. She studied this man whose only desire was to love her and be loved by her. She submitted to his appeal.

"Okay, Jack. As long as we both shall live."

\*\*\*\*

Jack broke away from his memories of Kate. He had wasted too much time in the past. Still, a day didn't go by when he didn't think of her. He turned his thoughts to her little girl. She possessed his soul as much as Kate did. They were both his babies. Not one who let fear get the best of him, he was suddenly haunted by it. He felt an urgent need to run to Rebecca and hold her in his arms.

"Stop!" he commanded to himself. "You must not be a slave to the mistakes of the past."

He left Bailey's apartment and drove to a nearby convenience store where he made another call. A woman answered.

"Hello," she said.

"It's me."

Not at all surprised to hear his voice, hers became a

whisper. She was mindful of her husband lying next to her. "I've been expecting your call, Jack."

She moved to another room.

"You've been a naughty girl. You've been holding out on me. How long have you known about Rebecca?"

"Call me tomorrow. Now's not a good time. My husband might hear us."

"Meet me at the corner of Houston and Elm. There's an off-the-wall coffee shop near the depository where the president was shot. Be there at nine a.m. tomorrow."

"I'll be there."

"You let Sid reel you in, didn't you? Even after everything you know, you took his side."

"I had to be nice to him, Jack, because of Sammy. But, I never told him where you were. I wouldn't do that."

"You'd better pray to God he never learns that you were ever loyal to me. Need I remind you, Jean? Sid Michaels shows no mercy to anyone who betrays him."

# CHAPTER 8

It was an unsettling nightmare. Bailey found herself amid a black night, where all her senses warned her to sit perfectly still, to be quiet. Cutting through the ominous blackness were the cries of a woman begging for her life, followed by a series of shots that subjected the woman's cries, reminisce of a chain of firecrackers. Bailey thought she should recognize the voice, but she didn't. Repeatedly, she heard her cries and then the crackling sounds. Yet, as wretched as these sounds were, they stopped. There was nothing but silence and Bailey found herself praying for the welcomed sounds of the woman's screams.

The silence was invaded by a sinister presence and she remained hidden in her corner of the darkness. She heard footsteps moving closer toward her and she felt her breath being sucked away by fear, a blessing, for the invader would not be able to trace her heartbeat. Still, the presence knew she was there because the raw scent of her fear was everywhere. Bailey heard a frenzy of footsteps, adamantly charged by the determination to find her.

Without reason, the footsteps were gone and the only thing that remained was the dense darkness, the awareness of being alone. Then, she heard the sound of a familiar form dragging nearer to her, one she knew she could trust. Thinking she should run toward the person, she remained frozen, remembering well a warning to stay hidden. The stealthy form stopped just short of discovering her and Bailey could hear the wheezing dissonance of its life near the threshold of death. And then, she heard nothing.

The next thing she remembered was being picked up by strong arms and being carried away. She opened her eyes and found herself face to face with a stranger. Or was he a stranger? She saw the tender smile of a trusting man, a dark man with long hair and caring eyes. She clung to him. In her dream, she knew who he was. He was Jess and he was carrying her to safety. She closed her eyes knowing she would not be harmed. When she opened them again, it was not Jess's face she saw, but the cold callous face of evil breathing down upon her. She turned to find Jess lying as if dead in his own blood, blood that blended within the red earth of the desert. She was awakened from her nightmare by the gentle arms of her brother and the soothing assurance of Diane's voice.

"Honey, it was only a dream," Diane eased, brushing back her wet hair, noting the fear in her eyes.

"Diane? Sammy? Are you really here?"

"Of course, Honey," Diane said.

"You were having some wild dream," Sammy reported.

"I know. It was awful and it seemed so real."

"It must have," Sammy agreed. "But it's over now."

Sammy looked down at his sister, still visibly shaken. His eyes met Diane's and it was as if they shared the same thought. They were wondering if perhaps Bailey was remembering things. Or, maybe she sensed some danger that lurked nearby. Sam brushed her forehead with a kiss and took her hand, squeezing it firmly.

"I'm glad you're here," Bailey said. "What time is it anyway?"

"Early," Sammy said. "Only six a.m."

Bailey stared at the two strangely.

"Why are you here?"

"Lucky for you we are, "Diane answered coolly.

"Yeah," she grinned nervously. She didn't care why but was just grateful they were there.

"Want a drink, Honey?"

Bailey nodded and Diane reached to pour her some water.

"And a shower, too," Bailey added.

A tall nurse entered the room, somewhat surprised that

Bailey had visitors already, but recognized the two as Bailey's family.

"Morning," she smiled warmly at Bailey. "Sorry I'm late with your medication, Honey. We've been busy this morning. A lot of things are happening around here. Guess you'll be happy to know that you won't be the center of excitement anymore."

"Oh?" Bailey asked curiously.

The nurse took Bailey's vitals and gave her some medication.

"What's the medication for?" Bailey asked.

"Just a little painkiller, that's all."

Satisfied, Diane went to Bailey's suitcase and picked her out a fresh change of clothes for the day. She looked out the window to see six police cars parked near the main entrance of the hospital.

"Why are there so many police cars outside?" she asked the nurse.

"That's what I started to say earlier," the nurse continued. "Some poor gal was found not too far from here, stuffed in a body bag and thrown in the trash just behind the *Morning Cup Café* on Greenville Avenue."

"Dead?" All three asked, already assuming she was.

"As a doornail. Word is the killer used her own clothing to tie her up and gag her. Then shot her like a coward in the back three times and once in the head, execution-style. Poor gal. No one knows her name yet? Police suspect she was working the streets and some bad John got hold of her."

"My God," Bailey said. "Did they bring her here?"

"Nope. She's at a downtown morgue, but the excitement seems to be here. You see, the police have been questioning everyone. They've been all over this hospital just like ants. The reason is that the body bag that the murdered woman was found in was one with our hospital's inscription. I don't think it really means much, though. I mean anyone can get a hold of one of those bags. It's still a little creepy to me thinking maybe the person who did this might be someone who works here or has worked here. Now, you didn't hear this from me. I could get in trouble for telling you and getting you upset."

Diane rubbed her arms to break the chill that had invaded her. She was remembering the details of the murder Sammy had told her about last night. Kate Michaels's death had been horrendous. Diane began to see this news as an omen. She moved toward the nurse and in a voice that clearly expressed her uneasiness, she asked about Bailey's discharge.

"Any chance we can see Dr. Klistner this morning? I mean, we were hoping Bailey might be able to come home today."

"Looks like I spooked you something good. Sorry about that. I guess we're all a little on edge this morning. I'll see if I can't locate Bailey's doctor and have him come speak with you. I'd say this child was more than ready to go home. Just so long as she promises to rest when she gets out of here."

"We would appreciate your finding the doctor as soon as you can."

"Sure thing. Now, don't you mind anything I just told you. You are safe here. We got half the Dallas police force right here in this hospital. Nothing is gonna happen to anyone so long as they're here."

"I know. I know," Diane remarked. "We're just anxious to get our sister home."

"Sure you are. I understand. I'll see what I can do."

When the nurse left and Bailey had found her way to the shower, Diane sat restlessly near Sammy.

"I'm beginning to understand your father's urgency. This girl's death is a sign."

"Diane, there's no connection."

"I know that, but still, it brings to light the fact that the man you spoke about last night might be in Dallas—could even be in this hospital. Everyone knows Bailey is in Parkland. I mean she's been in all the newspapers and on TV."

Diane thought of the murdered woman found in a trash dumpster and rhetorically replied.

"My God, Sammy, what kind of animal would gag and tie a

woman up and then shoot her in the back? She was so defenseless."

Unaware he even spoke, Sammy released a hidden piece of information concerning Kate Michaels's murder, information that only a handful of people knew.

"Kate Michaels was murdered execution-style."

"What did you say?" Diane asked alerted.

He shook his head, stunned by this related detail, so embedded in his memory. He stared at Diane, overcome by what he thought might be true.

"No Diane, that woman couldn't have been killed by Jack Adams. It's not possible."

"Of course not," Diane said unconvinced. Her heart was racing. Sammy squeezed her hand tighter.

"At last I understand," he spoke drawn.

"Understand what, Honey?"

"The agony my father has been through all of these years."

They were holding onto each other for support when Ron came into the room. He was somewhat surprised to see them.

"Diane, Sammy, no wonder I couldn't reach you at your home. Don't you answer your cells? Anyway, thank God I found you."

"Sammy had an early appointment downtown," Diane lied, easing away any suspicion. "I thought I'd come by and stay with Bailey today. She's bound to be going stir crazy, you know, from being in the hospital for so many days."

"I'm grateful you're here."

Ron sat on the bed despondent. His stare was a million miles away. His eyes were near tears. Both Sammy and Diane forgot their recent unrest as they questioned Ron.

"What is it, Ron? You look so...so sad."

"There's no easy way to say this."

"What?" Diane asked.

"Sid Carson called me about an hour ago."

"Dad? What did he say?" Sammy questioned strangely. Had Sid told him everything?

"It seems that Mara," Ron disclosed, "has had a heart attack and isn't expected to live. Sid wants Bailey to fly to Spain. That is if the doctors think she's able to fly. I don't know, Sammy. I think she is. Christ, she should be near her mother. I mean, what if she dies without Bailey seeing her again? She would never forgive herself if she weren't there."

"Mara?" Diane questioned. She turned to Sammy and she knew he was thinking what she was thinking. Was Mara really sick, or was this a scheme Sid had concocted to get Bailey out of Dallas?

"Christ," Ron continued. "Mara is so young, early forties."

"Listen, Ron," Sammy said. "We all know Mara hasn't been well for years."

"Yeah," Ron agreed. "I think Bailey should be with her, but…"

"But, what?" Diane asked.

"Hell, I can't take off to go with her. I am already behind as it is. And Bailey might need to stay in Spain for some time before she returns."

"You know, Ron," Sammy eased. "Mara means a lot to me, too. Maybe I could get some time off and go with Bailey."

"Oh, man, if you could do that, it would be great. I wouldn't worry so much about her then. Not if you're with her."

"Sammy," Diane said. "I think we need to call your father and let him know we're coming. We also need to check on our passports and hope they are valid."

Diane was very good at playing through this charade. Sammy played along.

"They are. I always keep them updated. What's this we business? "He smiled.

"Well, if you think you are going without me, you're crazy. Besides, Bailey might need me. You might need me if things go bad."

Sammy put his hand on Ron's shoulder.

"You're doing the right thing to let her go. We'll take good

86

care of her. Don't worry. Can you stay with her for a while? Diane and I want to call Dad and get things rolling."

"You bet," Ron said. "I took the morning off. I'm hoping to get her out of here within a couple of hours."

"Yeah, we had the same thought. Come on, Diane. Let's leave Ron and Bailey alone. Ron, we'll be back as soon as we can."

Diane looked confused as Sammy nudged her out of the room.

"Sammy, we can't leave her alone in this hospital, even with Ron. One of us needs to stay. Ron isn't aware of the danger and with this recent murder and..."

"Shhh. Do you think I'm going far? Let them have their time alone. Besides, Ron can do a better job talking to the doctors than me. I'm staying at the hospital, but I want you to go to Bailey's apartment, pack her bags, go to our house and do the same. As soon as I know what's going on, I'll call you. You got Bailey's keys?"

"They're in her purse. I'll go get them. Sammy, do you think Mara's dying?"

He shook his head.

"Not a chance. I spoke with her just hours ago. This is Dad's doing."

Diane smiled. In the past few hours, she had grown a new respect for a man she had always considered a self-serving control freak. Sammy whispered something to the man guarding Bailey's room, then turned to Diane.

"Do what you have to do quickly. Grab the passports and get all the cash the banks will let us have."

"We won't need a passport for New Mexico..."

He held his hand over her mouth.

"Get them anyway. Who knows what will happen. We must be prepared."

"Sammy," she almost cried, but then composed herself. "Do you think it's wrong for us not to include Ron? After all, he is Bailey's fiancé."

"I've debated this issue myself. Dad is adamant and I trust his judgment. He's a smart man, Diane. He's proven that to me time after time."

"I won't argue with you about this now, Honey. Besides, there's always time to tell him later. You know, this means Sid is going to have to tell Bailey the truth. I mean when she sees that Mara is ok?"

"I'm letting Dad handle all of that."

"Poor Bailey. What a shock this will be." She gave Sammy a loving kiss. He reached for her arm. "Well, I'd better go get her keys and then head out."

"Be careful. Remember, we are on our way to Spain. We have to be convincing to Ron and my mom and anyone else who might ask. And who knows, if this Jack character is watching, he just might get wind of our plans to go to Spain and be led on a wild goose chase."

"I get the feeling he isn't led astray too easily."

Sammy flinched. "Don't worry, Honey. Dad will take care of everything."

He pinched her cheek and moved down the hallway away from Bailey's room. Diane went inside to get her keys. Bailey was in Ron's arms and it was obvious Ron had told her the lie about Mara.

"Honey," Diane reached to comfort her. "I'm so sorry."

"Ron says that you and Sammy are going to Spain with me."

"That's right."

"I'm glad."

"Mara is going to be fine, Bailey. I just know it. You have to believe it."

"I will always believe that."

"I'm going to your apartment and get things ready for our trip. Sam is getting the tickets. Ron, you work on getting our girl out of here. My mom will come by and pick up all your flowers and plants. She'll take care of them while we are in Spain."

"What would we do without you?" Ron asked.

"Bailey is my family, Ron. I love her. Just like you do. Now, I need your keys, Honey. Are they still in that bag with your purse?"

Bailey nodded. Diane searched the purse, but couldn't find them.

"You sure they're here, Bailey?"

"I could have misplaced them, I don't know."

"Here," Ron said, handing Diane his keys to Bailey's apartment. "Use mine. I'll look for Bailey's later."

Diane gave a remorseful glance toward the two, who were cuddled on the bed. She was wondering when they might see each other again. When she saw their love for each other, she questioned the wisdom of not telling Ron everything.

"See you later, Honey. Bye, Ron." She waved and walked out of the door. At first, she walked slowly, overwhelmed by all she had to do. Then, she picked up her pace. No time to waste. Halfway down the hallway, she bumped into an orderly.

"I'm sorry," she said. "I guess I'm in a hurry."

"That's okay, pretty lady," he drawled.

Diane happened to notice a gathering of people at the end of the corridor.

"What's all the excitement?" she asked the orderly.

"Everyone's listening to the news. It's about the woman who was murdered last night. There's an update on her."

"An update?" Diane asked as she moved toward the crowd and the television broadcast. The orderly followed and stood with the gathering. Half a dozen or more people were watching as the news bulletin flashed a photograph of a twenty-two-year-old prostitute named Celia Johnson. The murdered woman had a name. She was blonde, with brown eyes. Diane dropped Bailey's suitcase and reached for the support of the orderly who was now standing next to her. Her face was crimson from the reality of what she was watching.

"You all right, Ma'am?" he asked.

Diane stared in disbelief. Again, he asked if she was ok.

"Do you know this lady?"

"Know?" Diane was clearly dazed.

The resemblance of Celia Johnson to Bailey was too coincidental. She wondered if anyone in the hospital who had been with Bailey these past days had noticed just how much this beautiful victim looked like her sister-in-law. Or, did she just notice it because of everything she knew about Bailey's mother? Diane had the impulse to run back to Bailey's room and take her out of the hospital right now. She realized that Bailey was probably more protected here than anywhere else. She knew she had to keep her cool.

"I'm sorry if you knew her," the orderly consoled.

"I didn't," Diane said. "I'm just shocked by her brutal death."

"Yeah, but it looks like they know who did it."

The newscast continued to report that there had been an arrest in the case. His name was Seymour Chavez, her former boyfriend and pimp. Witnesses said they had been quarreling just hours before her death and that he had threatened to kill her. It seems that Chavez had owned a gun, most likely that same caliber that was used to kill Celia Johnson.

"Her boyfriend did it?" Diane asked relieved. Dear God, she thought, this isn't the work of Jack Adams.

"Some boyfriend," a bystander remarked.

He was sitting in a wheelchair just feet behind her, also watching the newscast. Diane felt him stare intently in her direction. When she turned around, he gave her a slight nod and smiled. Still feeling uneasy from the events of the past night and from lack of sleep, Diane once again felt herself losing control. She picked up the suitcase and edged toward a nearby elevator. From the corner of her eye, she saw the man in the wheelchair move in her direction. She pushed the down button.

"Mind if I ride down with you?" his deep voice asked.

He looked at Bailey's suitcase.

"Taking someone home today?" he inquired.

Though he seemed harmless enough, with his leg in a cast and his neck in a brace, there was something precarious about the way his eyes riveted over her and through her. It was as if he knew what lay beneath her uncertainty. She couldn't explain why she lied to him, but her instincts told her not to trust this man.

"No," she said coolly, stepping inside the elevator and holding the door open for him to finagle his chair. "I'm afraid it will be a week or so before my sister is able to come home."

He slid his hand through his thick brown hair.

"Too bad," he grinned. "I mean to be laid up so long."

When the door to the elevator opened on the bottom floor, he motioned for her to exit before him.

"Ladies first."

"Thank you," she said, darting as fast as she could toward the main lobby and the main exit. When she turned to see if he was still watching her, he had vanished from sight. She let out a deep sigh of relief.

"Get a hold of yourself, Diane. He was just some guy in a wheelchair."

# CHAPTER 9

Jack watched as Diane left the hospital. Thinking Sammy had left earlier, he decided this would be his chance to get to Bailey. He was just about to call her room to see if she was alone when he saw two Dallas police officers ready to step on the elevator. Feeling cocksure about the recent news that an arrest had been made in the Celia Johnson murder, he thought he'd give them a casual but thorough once over. This was an extra precaution to ease away any misgivings.

"This is one they are not going to pin on Jack Adams."

He eased to the back of the elevator where two officers stood in front of him. A rookie officer named Jason Cort hit the button for the third floor, Bailey's floor. He turned to Jack.

"What floor, man?"

"The same," Jack said holding up three fingers. Where Jack usually kept a low profile from the law, today he was almost eager. "Heard the news say authorities caught the bastard who murdered that young girl. Some guy named Chavez. Is that right? A boyfriend alias pimp, huh? One with a record, I bet. Heard he was sending a message to his other girls."

The rookie fell into his trap.

"Yeah, well, it won't be long before we are sending him a message. This time he went too far. He's gonna pay for this one."

Jack was about to question him further when the elevator door opened on the second floor and a short, stocky man around sixty entered. He greeted the three men and stood between the two officers. Jack scaled his form like a hawk, noting the flamboyancy of this man. His bright red hair sprinkled with gray, dominated his appearance. A mass of freckles filled his roseate face and when he smiled to the officers, he exposed a shiny gold-capped smile. The man flashed his ID to the officers and introduced himself as Red Benning. Despite his cockiness earlier, Jack now felt cornered, defenseless, as the precognitions of his past alerted him.

"Christ!" Jack grunted to himself, listening as Red Benning talked to the officers. "So here stands the infamous Red Benning. At last! A face to go with a name. How long has it been? Five years? Aren't you tired of hassling me? Couldn't wait to crucify me on this one, could you Benning? Go hassle Chavez. Leave me out of this one."

"I'm here to see Captain Lou Steele, gentlemen," Red told them. "We're old friends. I worked with Lou some years back in Los Angeles. He told me to meet him on the third floor. You two seen him around?"

"Sure have," Cort said. "The captain's been here for hours. We're headed that way. We'll take you to him. You gonna do some investigating on the Johnson woman's murder?"

"What a bloodbath, huh? So they found the fellow who murdered her, huh?"

"Some pimp," Cort said all fired up. Ted Blair, his partner, nudged him as if to warn him not to disclose anything to the press. Cort was full of himself and ignored his warnings.

"Pretty cut and dry case, huh?" Red asked.

"They found his gun," Cort spilled. "We're ninety-nine percent sure it's his gun that killed her."

"Think I could look at the body?"

"She's at a downtown morgue. But the captain will most likely give his okay to an old buddy."

"Christ, it never gets easier," Benning said.

"Nope," both officers agreed.

"Not even with a gal like her." Benning snorted. When the elevator reached the third floor, the officers and Benning got off. Jack remained inside.

"Getting off?" Cort asked.

Jack shook his head and pressed the button for the first

floor. When the elevator door began to close, Jack by chance caught a glimpse of Red Benning as he flashed a smile at the two officers and thanked them for their help. And then, just as the door was almost closed, the rusty haired reporter caught a glance at Jack. Benning grimaced as they exchanged momentary looks. Benning stared at the closed door, semi-entranced by this seeming apparition from his past. He laughed aloud in an effort to calm his paranoia.

"Something wrong, Mr. Benning?" Cort asked.

"Damn," Benning said as he gave his shoulders a heavy shrug. "This little gal's murder has me reliving another murder I once investigated. Hell, now I'm seeing ghosts."

Lou Steele broke through his speculation, shouting Red's name across the busy corridor. "Red, over here!"

Red turned one more time toward the closed elevator before dismissing his uneasiness and turning his attention toward his friend.

"Red, how the heck are you?"

"Not bad," a shaken Red said.

"Well, you haven't changed much. Maybe added a few pounds." Steele gave a playful punch to Red's middle before noticing the swell of his lip and bruising on the right side of his face. "What happened to your face? You look like you've been in a dog fight."

Red unconsciously touched the tender bruising on his face. He gave a disgruntled grin. "Would you believe I fell in the shower at my hotel yesterday?"

Steele snickered. "Hell, with a face as ugly as yours, I'd say it was an improvement."

After a brief period of Steele harmlessly bashing Red, the two men filled in the years that had separated them with small talk. Then Lou led Benning to a secluded waiting room.

"I'm glad you got my message to meet me here, Red. This isn't exactly how I had planned to entertain you during your visit to Dallas. But, as you know, when duty calls, things like reunions and time off just go out the window."

"Sounds like you have a pretty nasty investigation on your hands." Red's eyes sparkled like shiny gold marbles.

"There's really not much to investigate. The gal crossed her pimp and he taught her a lesson and sent a message to his other girls. It's not unusual. Only most pimps don't kill their girls."

"Mind if I do a little reporting on this one?"

Steele sighed. "I knew you'd want this one, Red. But, this isn't Adams's doing. It's the little gal's pimp."

"You sure? I got a hunch, Lou. And what about the make of the gun and the fashion of the crime? She looks like the others, too."

"Damn press. You guys really like to kill an investigation."

"Who let out the facts?" Red asked. "It's all over the TV."

"I don't know, but when I find out..."

"As an old friend, Lou You really think this was Chavez?"

Lou shrugged his shoulders. "To be honest with you, Red, my first thought was Adams. But then, Chavez fell into our hands."

"What are you going to do when Chavez turns up clean?"

"I'm praying he won't. 'Cause if it is Adams, you can be sure he's long gone. Besides, Adams has been hidden for what, five, six years? He may even be dead, for all we know."

"He's alive, Lou. In any event, I'd like to see the body if it's possible, Lou."

"The autopsy's already underway."

"Geez, you didn't waste time."

"Well, I didn't want the press screwing up everything."

Red lent Lou a corky smile. "When you get the report, can I see it?"

"I'll call you."

Red held out his hand to Lou. "Care to wager?"

"No," Lou said disgruntled.

Red whispered in his ear. "It's Adams. You know it is. Chavez might be guilty of other crimes, but he didn't kill Celia Johnson."

Lou shot him a go-to-hell look. "Fix that tooth. Looks like

you chipped it when you fell."

****

It wasn't difficult for Red Benning to get past Harold Baxter, the brawny man Bud Little had hired to guard Bailey's room. When Baxter stopped Red near her door, he schemed his way inside by raising his already boisterous voice and causing such a disturbance Ron jolted open the door to see what the commotion was all about. Bailey stood next to Ron and Benning could do nothing but stare at her. Either he had found the daughter of Kate Michaels or someone that could be her twin. Her brown-eyed stare was the very same.

"What's going on out here?" Ron asked.

"This man wants to see Miss Carson. Says his name is Red Benning. He's a reporter. I told him I've been hired to keep all visitors away from her. He still insists on seeing her."

"Why in the world would anyone hire a guard for me?" Bailey asked.

"It was Sammy's idea," Ron explained. "You just don't realize the chaos there was after your accident. We couldn't keep the press out. People were trying to come in and get pictures. It was unbelievable. "

"Listen," Red interrupted. "I'm only asking for a few minutes of your time. Then, I'll be on my way."

"It's not a good time, Mr. Benning," Ron asserted. "Miss Carson has just received some grave news about her mother's health and I don't think she's in any condition to speak with you. You'll have to come back."

"I'm sorry, Miss Carson," Red said. "I do hope your mother's condition improves. When would be a better time for me to speak with you? Soon I hope. You see, I've traveled a long distance to talk to you and I don't know when I'll be back in Dallas."

"Just how far have you traveled?"

"I'm a reporter for the Los Angeles Times. I've come to ask

your help about a case I've been working on."

"Los Angeles! My goodness! Did you say your name is Red Benning? Surely, you're not the Red Benning! Not the noted criminal reporter? You say that you need my help on a case? How in the world can I help you, Mr. Benning?"

"Ah, so you've heard of me?" Red smiled confidently.

"Of course, I've heard of you. You're renowned, you know. I'm a reporter, too." Then she blushed by her presumed status. "Well...I'm nowhere close to being in your league but I'm working on it."

"Bailey," Ron interceded. "I'm not sure you're up to company. You really should be resting."

"It's okay, Ron. I feel fine. Maybe talking to Mr. Benning will get my mind off Mother. Besides, if I don't talk to him now, I may not get the chance."

"Well," Ron hesitated. "I guess a few minutes won't hurt. I'll go hunt down your doctor." He turned to Benning. "Fifteen minutes. No longer. I mean it."

Bailey kissed Ron "I promise. Now go find my doctor."

Ron left and Benning followed Bailey inside her room where he sat on a chair next to the bed. Like a small child in wonder, Bailey sat demurely on the edge of the bed and asked Red why he would seek her help.

"You have me curious, Mr. Benning. How can I help you?"

"Since I have so little time, I'll get right to the point."

He handed Bailey a picture of Kate Michaels. Bailey looked at him confused and then her eyes focused on the photo, worn and yellowed by age. When she spoke to Red, her eyes remained fixed on the woman's face. She dared to ask.

"Who is this woman?"

"Her name is Kate Michaels. Seventeen years ago, she was found murdered in the New Mexico desert. I was a freelance reporter then, hired to investigate the case. A case I might add that was never solved."

"You never found out who murdered her?"

"We knew who killed her. It was her low-life boyfriend.

The trouble was he ran off, vanished, and hasn't been seen since before her murder."

"Mr. Benning?" her small voice shook as much as her hand that held the picture. "What does this have to do with me?"

"Maybe nothing, Miss Carson. Maybe everything."

"What do you mean?"

"You see, Kate Michaels had a daughter. She was found in the desert, too."

"Dead?"

"Almost. But no, she lived."

Tears filled Bailey's eyes and her body already weak from her accident and the recent news of Mara fell limply across the bed with her back toward Red Benning.

"I still don't understand what this has to do with me."

"No?" he probed. "Well, you see, I had this hope you might recognize her."

She turned abruptly to face him.

"I've never seen this woman before."

"Are you sure?"

"Of course, I am."

"Ah, well, so the mystery continues. You see, I've been puzzled about this for seventeen years. I'm ready to solve it and call it quits on my career. You know how reporters are. They can't rest until the entire truth is told."

Red laid a legal envelope next to her. Inside of it were articles he had written about the murder. As Bailey randomly flipped through the articles, her mind was in a croon. She read a haunting headline about a little girl called *Desert Baby*. Kate Michaels's daughter had been found near her mother. As she continued to read, she came across a sentence that made her acutely aware of Red Benning's direction. Over and over, the sentence fixated in her mind. Red Benning was watching her every move.

The sentence beat like a drum in her mind. "Sid Michaels, the husband of the murdered Kate Michaels and the father of *Desert Baby* has recently flown to New Mexico to identify his wife's remains and to claim his daughter."

"Sid Michaels?" she thought. "He is the father of *Desert Baby*. It's not me. The fact that he and my father have the same first name is only a coincidence."

As Red observed the color drain from her face, he knew he had found Kate's daughter, even if she didn't know who she was. It was obvious to him that she wasn't aware of her past and that she had somehow managed to suppress what had happened to her so many years ago. He debated whether he should continue with his inquiry, wondering how much she was able to take. He'd try just a bit longer. He couldn't let his opportunity go.

"Miss Carson?" He asked. "After looking at these photos and glancing at the articles, does the name Kate Michaels ring any bells in your mind? Do you have any recollection of such a woman?"

"Nanny Kate," she spoke so low, even Red's keen ears could not decipher her words.

"What did you say?"

"I said, I remember I had a Nanny Kate. I can't remember her face. I just remember one day she was gone and that I used to cry for her."

"Dear God," Red said sitting down again. "Do you know what this could mean?"

Bailey's eyes emanated fear and her heart was beating out of her chest.

"Mr. Benning, you think I'm this Kate Michaels's daughter, this child called *Desert Baby*, don't you?"

"I think it's more than a coincidence that you had a 'Nanny Kate' and that her name was also Kate. But, it's more. It's..."

"What?"

"Bailey, I'm here because I saw your face on the news. When I saw your face, I thought I was looking at Kate's. Then I read somewhere or heard it somewhere that your father's name was Sid. First, it was your face and then your father's name and now you tell me about your Nanny Kate."

The fact that he addressed her by her first name and called Kate by her first name, as well as Sid, never registered in her mind. Red had crossed the line and become personally connected with her.

"If this is all true, why didn't my family tell me?" Bailey asked.

"Could be lots of reasons. The first that comes to my mind is that they were protecting you."

"You're wrong, Mr. Benning. Kate Michaels is not my mother. Mara Carson is my mother. She is the woman who has always been by my side. She's devoted her life to me. And right now, she needs me. She may even be dying. I must concentrate on her and not this Kate Michaels that you speak of."

"I'm sorry about Mara Carson and I'm not disputing that in your heart you believe her to be your mother. But, she is not the woman who gave birth to you. I'd bet my career on this fact."

"You're mistaken, Mr. Benning. I'm not this *Desert Baby*. If I were, wouldn't I have some memory of such a horrible ordeal?"

"I think deep down you do and that someday you will remember. But, it won't be today. You've been through enough today. Here, Bailey. Here's my hotel number and my cell number. I'll be in Dallas a week or so. We can talk tomorrow or the next day. I think we've done enough talking for today."

"I..." She was about to tell him she was leaving town and wouldn't be in Dallas to talk to him. Then, a nurse came into the room.

"That fiancé of yours is something else, Honey. He just charmed you right out of the hospital. Looks like you'll be out of here today."

Bailey turned to face Benning.

"I will call you, Mr. Benning. I really do want to talk to you again. It won't be tomorrow. Tomorrow I plan to be with my mother."

"Of course," he said. "That's where you should be."

"Mr. Benning? I'm curious about something."

"What's that?"

"The little girl has no name. There are no pictures of her. Why?"

"To protect her. Of course, later the press found out her identity, but by that time, her father had taken her into hiding. I myself never printed a picture of her. Just wasn't right. I'm sure if you wanted to find one, you could."

"Are there any pictures of her father, Sid Michaels, in your articles?"

"A few, I think."

Red scanned the many articles until he came upon one with a picture of Sid Michaels. It was dark and faded. Bailey studied it intently. Though younger and less imposing, it could be her own father – maybe – probably not. Another blow came when she noted the location Kate Michaels had been murdered. It was near the Zuni Reservation, by the sacred Corn Mountain. She thought of Jess and the story behind his father's painting, *The White Spirit Who Roams the Desert.* The peculiarities of this fate were almost too much for her to shake off as anything but truth.

"Dear God," she thought. "If I am this child, then it was Jess's father, Billy Nehah, who found me."

She turned to Benning to ask if he'd ever heard the Zunis tell the story of a white spirit, though she already suspected he had.

"Mr. Benning, have you ever heard the Zunis speak of a white spirit who roams the desert?"

He nodded precariously. He was thinking of Kate.

Bailey continued. "They say she is always searching for something. Do you think it's her little girl?"

"I'd say so, yeah."

"Do you think if she finds her, she'll be able to finally rest in peace?"

"That and knowing her little girl is safe."

"She fears for her safety?"

Red gripped Bailey's hand. "Bailey," he warned. "Why do you think your brother posted a guard outside your hospital room? It's to protect you. And, it isn't from self-serving reporters. I have a stake in the Kate Michaels's case. I've been trying to solve it for seventeen years. I found you by deriving a conclusion. Someone else has a stake in you, or should I say Kate's daughter, too. Someone whose intentions are less honorable than mine. That's why you must help me. In helping me, you help yourself."

"That is if I believe your theory."

"You believe it. I can see it in your eyes."

She closed her eyes demurely. "Mr. Benning, I must know. Who killed Kate Michaels? I mean, you said it was her boyfriend. What was his name?"

"There are multiple articles about him in that envelope. Read them all very carefully. His name is Jack Adams and he's pure evil, Bailey. Pure evil."

****

After his quick brush with Red Benning, Jack was rid of his wheelchair disguise and made a swift exit from the hospital. Jack was pretty sure Benning hadn't recognized him. At the very least Benning might be thinking how much this guy in the wheelchair resembled him. In reality, Jack was certain Benning would never in a million years believe it was him. Still, he didn't want to risk running into him again. Not just yet anyway. Now he had to wait a while longer before seeing Bailey. There was time. Diane had said she'd be in the hospital another week or so. Jack decided to lay low for a couple of days.

His mind drifted from thoughts of Benning to those of Celia Johnson. Her pictures on TV and those in the papers stunned him. She was an almost perfect match to Kate, with her long blonde hair flowing down her back and those deep brown eyes that cut through his psyche. And, she was just at that tender age, the exact age of Kate, and the exact age of Bailey.

After reading about her though, he knew she wasn't Kate. She was too well versed, knew too much. She was a woman who worked the streets much like all the others who had met her same fate. Jack recalled the trail of women who had been murdered in the same manner as Kate. Each resembled her physically. Each of their deaths were linked to him.

Jack drove to his motel and settled himself in for the night. He switched the channels on the TV trying to find out more information about Celia Johnson's murder. His mind drifted to thoughts of Bailey and then Red Benning again. What if by chance they should meet? What would he say to her? What did she already know? No doubt, Benning like Sid would fill her mind with lies about him. Did Bailey even remember he had once been a part of her life? Jack wanted her to know his side of the story. Regret and something like fear consumed him. He reached for the phone and called her room. He had to make certain she was still within his reach.

"Hello," she answered.

Jack sighed in relief. Just hearing her hello was enough. Bailey heard the phone click; disconnecting her from whoever had called.

"Strange," she sighed. "But then today has been nothing but strange."

She looked at the pile of articles spread across her bed. She found the yellowed photo of Kate Michaels. She traced it possessively. Vaguely she wondered if perhaps she was this woman's little girl. Again, the phone rang. It jolted her so that she accidentally tore the picture of Kate Michaels in half. Frantically, she brought the two halves together as if this was all that remained of a woman who just might be her mother. Nausea swept over her and she ran to the bathroom, stricken by a truth so compelling it could no longer stay hidden. The phone stopped ringing. Five minutes later, it rang again.

"Yes, hello," she answered weakly.

"Bailey, it's Dr. Claiborne."

"Dr. Claiborne," she cried. "How are you?"

"The question is how are you?"

"Better, much better."

"I've been worried about you, dear. At first, they wouldn't

let you have visitors, so I waited. Did you get my flowers?"

"I did. Thank you so much."

"When will I see your smile in my classroom? Soon I hope."

"I'm afraid not, Dr. Claiborne. I may have to drop out this semester."

"Oh?" he quizzed.

"You see, my mother's had a heart attack and I'm leaving today or tomorrow to be with her."

There was silence on the other line. "She's leaving me," he thought. "I'm losing her again..."

"Professor Claiborne?"

"I'm here. Bailey, I'm sorry about your mother. Of course, you must go to her. I...I want you to keep in touch, please. Promise me you'll keep in touch and that you won't forget us here in Texas."

"I promise to write you as soon as I can. I could never forget you. Why you've been more than a teacher and a mentor. You're more like..."

"Like what, Bailey?"

"Well, you're family."

"I'm glad you feel that way. Bailey?"

"Hmmm?"

He debated telling her that he was family, that he was her grandfather and that her real mother had not just had a heart attack. No, her real mother had been murdered when Bailey was four years old and that she herself had almost met the same fate. Claiborne thought of Sid. "He's doing what he has to do." All of the happenings of the past weeks hadn't escaped his notice. Sid has always seen to Bailey's safety. Somehow, he knew that's what was happening now.

"I'm not sure what I'll do if my mother dies, Dr. Claiborne. She and Daddy mean so much to me."

"A daughter's love for her mother can never die, Bailey. You must hold on to your memories."

"I will but losing her...well – it would be so painful."

"I know. I will pray for you and your mother."

"Thank you. Dr. Claiborne, would you do me a favor?"

"Anything, Child."

"I never wrote up my interview with Jess Nehah. Will you get in touch with him and explain my situation? Also, will you contact my boss at the paper? Tell him I'm sorry for deserting him like this."

"Consider it done, Bailey."

"I will write you. I promise. I may even have to call you to hear your voice." She was struggling to hold back her tears. "I miss you already, Professor Claiborne. Thank you for always being there for me."

"I wouldn't be anywhere else."

****

After midnight, Lou Steele read over the preliminary autopsy report on Celia Johnson. There had been three shots in her back and one in her head. The weapon was a 38 caliber. The perpetrator had stripped her naked. He used her panties to gag her and had tied her hands behind her back with her own blouse. He used the arm of her sleeve to blindfold her before he shot her in the back and head execution-style. This cowardly act of violence sent bouts of anger throughout him. This was calculated, not an act of passion...but a deliberate act of torture. Later the madman got his jollies raping her, probably as she was dying.

He really didn't have to examine the report to know how she'd been killed. He had investigated a case just like hers some five years ago in L.A., a coed named Jessica Framington. Before Jessica, he'd been aware of others killed in the same fashion, all linking back to a woman from Colorado named Kate Michaels. All leading him to one primary suspect, Jack Adams. Yet, unlike the others, Celia Johnson had put up one hell of a fight. She most likely caught him off guard, before he could set her up for the kill.

"Whoever did this is someone licking his wounds."

Lou deliberated what his next move should be. Should he wait until the reports on Chavez's gun were complete? Or, should he let his suspicions be known? He decided to call Detective Martin Gee to lead up the investigation. Gee was the best and Lou needed his fresh perspective. He'd confide his theory to Gee tomorrow.

With that thought, Lou laid down, worn from a long day's work. When he closed his eyes, visions of Jessica and Celia robbed him from sleep. Then, another thought took hold of him. It was of his former constituent, Red Benning, easing away from the other reporters at the hospital today to visit a patient named Bailey Carson. Thinking that it was odd he should be visiting her now, he found it disturbing.

"What's your interest in Bailey Carson, Red? There's no blood and gore in her story. Just a young woman who saved an old woman's life. So, what are you up to?"

# CHAPTER 10

Ron sat alone in his apartment, reliving the events of yesterday. He had managed to have Bailey released from the hospital with minimal difficulty by promising Dr. Klistner that she would have a physician in Barcelona reexamine her after she arrived there. Ron had hoped to spend a quiet evening with Bailey before she left, knowing he might not see her for some time. That hope was crushed when Sammy had managed to book them on a redeye flight leaving the Dallas/Fort Worth Airport just after midnight.

Maybe it was just as well because Bailey was not herself. She was distracted, worried about Mara. Ron was troubled that the stress from her worry over her mother might cause her to have a relapse. He was reluctant to let her go. It seemed, too, that she was clinging to him with the same unwillingness. Her mood almost frightened him.

Her wary stare led him to believe there was more to her mood than Mara's heart attack. He couldn't get her to open up and talk to him. She just held on to him as if she might never see him again. It wasn't until her plane had left the runway and he reached into his jacket and found a note, that he realized there was indeed more behind her strange mood. After reading her note Ron was left more confused than ever. It read:

*My darling Ron, I am leaving not knowing when we will see each other again. Everything is so uncertain. The one thing I know to be true is that I love you. Thank you for caring so much about my mother and her condition. I will be sure to have her know of your concern. Ron, there is another matter that weighs heavy on my heart. Just today, I learned something about my past. It has to do with a tragic event from my childhood.*

*This tragic event is so serious, I find I can do nothing but think about it and the only way I can deal with it is to find out more from my family. By now, you're probably wondering what in the world I'm talking about. I promise I will tell you everything when I find out everything.*

*Right now, I doubt I could find the words to explain what I have learned about my past. It is far too strange to explain or put into words. That's why I am asking for your patience and understanding. You know what you mean to me and how much I want you in my life. I want to be married to you. Still, I can't begin to think of marriage until I learn the whole truth about this secret in my past. For this reason, I find I must postpone our marriage.*

*I know this will come as a shock to you. It does to me, too. It is because I care so much for you that I must delay our wedding. It wouldn't be fair to marry you knowing there's a part of my past that is so uncertain.*

*Be patient with me and remember all the beautiful times we've shared. I care so much for you, Ron. I'll write you very soon. My heart is breaking from the pain I am putting you through. Please forgive me. Bailey.*

"Oh, Bailey," he cried out. "What event in your life could be so serious it has forced you to delay our wedding? Does it have to do with Mara and her illness? Is Sid behind this? Why couldn't you come to me? We could have talked about it. I'm your fiancé, for Christ's sake."

His speculating was interrupted by a knock at the door. When he opened it, Rita McDonald was standing in front of him. She was the last person he had expected to see, but as she began expressing her concern for Bailey's welfare, her warm smile became an inviting diversion to his drawn mood. Like always, she had a way with him. He didn't know why she was there, but he was glad that she was.

"What are you doing here, Rita?"

"I came by to see how Bailey was doing — and you. I've

thought about you so much. Well— you know how I feel, Ron. I hesitated about coming. I just wasn't sure it was right for me to come by and see you while Bailey was in the hospital."

"But you're here."

"Yeah," she said uneasily. "I'm here."

"Bailey's good," he said, moving away from the door. He didn't ask her inside, but he didn't tell her to leave either. She followed him to the sofa where he sat fatigued, stretching out his long legs on the coffee table. Rita looked around at his apartment and its upheaval, so opposite of Ron's usual tidy deportment. She sat next to him and gently rested her hand over his. He turned to face her, staring into her sultry blue eyes. She looked good and he began to remember a time when the two of them would sit together like this, so familiar, so comfortable. In response, he stroked her cheek.

"How do you always know?"

"Know what?" she asked.

He grinned. "You always know when I need you."

"What is it, Ron?"

"It's Bailey," his voice cracked.

"What about Bailey, Ron? She is okay, isn't she? I mean, she will be all right?"

"Bailey's been released from the hospital, Rita."

Rita was relieved. She had nothing personal against Bailey. In fact, had it not been for the fact that she had Ron, Rita thought that Bailey would be the kind of person that she'd like to be friends with. It was just that family of hers. They were insane.

"Well, that's good, Ron."

He turned a somber eye toward her.

"Her mother had a heart attack. She might not live. Bailey left for Spain last night."

"My goodness, is she well enough to travel?"

"Well or not, she's gone."

"You look worried."

"Sammy and Diane went with her - to take care of her."

"Sammy," Rita thought. "He's good at taking care of things."

She looked into Ron's tired eyes.

"When's the last time you slept?"

"Who knows," he shrugged.

"I bet it's been days. Come on, Ron. Let's get you into bed."

He lent her an unexpected proposal.

"That could be interesting. Will you be joining me?"

She let out a quick chuckle.

"Same old charmer, huh?"

Abruptly, Ron brushed over her mouth with a desperate kiss.

"Stop," she said pushing him away.

He laid his worn body across the sofa, propping his legs over her lap.

"You never used to turn my kiss away."

"What's going on here, Ron?"

"Nothing. I felt like kissing you. That's all."

"No, there's something more. Did you and Bailey have a disagreement before she left?"

"Fight?" he asked amused. "I guess you could say we had a fight, although we didn't say a word to each other."

"I don't understand."

"She left. That's what happened."

"She left to be with her mom, Ron. You act like she left you."

"Her mother, right. Sure, but she left me, too."

"You aren't making sense, Ron."

He swept his hand through his thick hair.

"She postponed our December wedding."

"Because of her mother, right?"

"That and…"

"What?"

"Christ, you go figure. Something about the past. I don't know."

"Ron? Did Bailey find out about us? I mean about last Christmas?"

An image of last Christmas filled his mind, as he recalled bumping into Rita at a party, where the two left and went to Rita's apartment. They were both feeling a buzz from overindulging in too much Christmas spirit. Old sparks began to fly. Bailey had flown to Spain to spend the holidays with her family and he was feeling somewhat cheated that she had chosen to spend Christmas with her parents instead of him. And too, he was angry at Sid Carson for so craftily dismissing an invitation for him to come to Spain with her. Ron's brief disclosure with Rita after the party was in retaliation to Sid's obvious dismissal of his place in Bailey's life. It was Bailey who stood to be hurt, not Sid. Ron shook his head emphatically at Rita.

"She couldn't have found out. No, something else is on her mind. Something about her childhood. I don't know."

Ron reached into his pocket and pulled out the letter Bailey had written him. He handed it to Rita.

"Here, you figure it out."

Rita read the intimate words Bailey had written to Ron. Her handwriting was jagged and in some places almost illegible. Rita soon understood Ron's confusion. She wondered what dire situation would cause Bailey to change her wedding plans. She thought of Sammy's recent visit to her. Had he convinced Bailey to rethink marrying Ron? Rita was certain Bailey's family was behind her sudden decision. She also knew how much Bailey cared for Ron. Even though her words were a parting of some sort, they certainly weren't a final farewell. This was a fact that stabbed at Rita's own heart, a heart torn by love for Ron Baker. Bailey's obvious torment rang bittersweet in Rita's mind as she read her note to Ron. She probed him for answers.

"Ron, do you have any idea what she might be talking about?"

"Not a clue," he said, hitting his fist into the back of the sofa. "Why couldn't she confide in me? Doesn't she trust me?"

"Maybe she doesn't know enough about this secret to tell you. That's what it sounds like to me. Maybe she will find out in Spain. I don't know. I only know that it's all so strange and that she sounds vulnerable."

"She's very close to her mother. I think this secret might have something to do with her mother and her illness. I think she believes she's going to die."

"Should you be with Bailey, Ron?"

"Yes, but I can't get off, Rita. Not if I want to finish my internship this year."

"Ron," she said flatly. "There's something about her family I just don't like or trust."

"If you mean they are very controlling. I know that. It just kills her daddy that he can't control me."

"What about Bailey? Could he control her?"

"Sid's been controlling her all of her life."

"I'm afraid for her, Ron. I'm afraid for you."

"Why me?"

She broke into tears.

"Rita, baby, what is it?"

His endearment calmed her somewhat as she told him about Sammy's recent proposal asking her to come between Bailey and Ron.

"Sammy came to me about a week or so ago. He offered me five thousand dollars to break the two of you up. Of course, I turned down the money. He said if I told you about his offer, he'd tell you I was lying and was back to my old tricks again."

Ron studied her face.

"And are you?"

"How can you ask such a thing?"

He gave her a slight grin, recalling the many times Rita had tried to come between him and Bailey.

"It's not like you haven't tried before. This would be just like you, Rita. And, this would be the perfect time to make a move. I mean, with Bailey away."

"I didn't know she was going to Spain."

112

"You knew she was in the hospital. You knew I'd be alone for a while."

"Look, Ron. I don't have to listen to this. I only came by to see how you were. You can believe what you want."

He rubbed his bloodshot eyes and once again found himself staring into hers.

"But then again, this is just like Sid Carson, too."

"So, you believe me? I mean about the money and Sammy coming to me?"

"Maybe."

Testing her, he drew her near, pressing his lips over her mouth that was eager to accept his kiss. As impulsively as he reached for her kiss, he pushed her aside.

"I believe you would do anything to break Bailey and me up."

She flung her hand across his face.

"To hell with you. And, good luck with Bailey. You're gonna need it. Whatever her family might dish out to you, it's no more than you deserve. Just don't say I didn't try to warn you."

She reached for her purse and darted toward the door. He was quick to go after her.

"You didn't let me finish. I was going to say that I believe you would do anything to break Bailey and me up, but I also believe you about the offer Sammy made you. He's made similar ones to me."

Ron failed to tell Rita that he had accepted Sammy's offers on many occasions.

"What are you going to do?" Rita asked.

"What I'm going to do isn't important. It's what you're going to do that's important."

"What are you talking about?"

"Sammy will be returning from Spain in a couple of weeks. When he does, I think you should give him a call."

"Why?"

"To accept his offer."

"You're as crazy as he is."

"Five thousand dollars is a hell of a lot of money to turn down."

"I don't want the money. I couldn't take it."

"Not even for me."

"For you? You would take it?"

"Why not? Sid Carson's loaded."

"You mean," she paused daring to hope. "You mean, you'd give up Bailey for five thousand dollars?"

"I intend to have the money and Bailey."

Rita's heart was bruised. At this moment, she understood Ron could never love her, not the way he loved Bailey.

"You're forgetting one thing," she snapped.

"What's that?"

"Sammy offered me the money. It would be mine."

"You'd share with a friend, wouldn't you?"

"Why would I, when I could have it all for myself?"

He swept her into his arms. She wielded little effort to draw him away before she submitted to his seduction. He held her kiss and could see this was going to be easy.

"I don't want the money, Ron."

"What do you want?"

"What I've always wanted, you."

"I won't marry you, Rita."

"I know," she conceded. "But, I think committing to such deceit entitles me to some sort of compensation."

"Such as?"

"A lesser consideration than being your wife."

"You would settle being my mistress?"

"For now."

"You know I love Bailey."

"I know."

"She comes first. She always will."

"Except…"

"No exceptions," he added.

"Oh yeah," she said. "When you are in my arms, then I

come first. You'll be mine, if only for a short while."

He pulled her closer, enticed by her desire.

"You may be worth the risk, just to put Sid Carson in his place."

"And," she thought. "Someday I'll put you in your place. Just when you can't live without me, that's when you'll get yours."

He saw her smug look of satisfaction and heeded a warning.

"If Bailey finds out about our arrangement from you, I swear to God that will be the last time you will ever see my face."

"She won't learn about us from me, Ron. Now, haven't we done enough talking?"

# CHAPTER 11

Exhausted and heavily sedated, Bailey never questioned why the flight they were on had taken them to Santa Fe. She vaguely guessed that this was just a pit stop on their way to Barcelona. She wasn't thinking clearly and she had little thought to worry over a trivial matter such as this. She never suspected that anything was amiss when Sammy told her that they were going to be laying over in Santa Fe and would have to spend the dark hours of the morning in a hotel. When the last sleeping pill that Diane had given her had taken effect, Bailey never realized she had fallen asleep, not in a hotel, but in the back seat of a rental that would take her from Santa Fe to Taos. Ten hours later when she awoke, she was staring into the eyes of Sid Carson.

"Daddy?" she questioned, reaching to touch her father's face in an effort to see if he was real or an illusion.

"It's me, Baby. It's Daddy."

She fell into his arms, holding on to him as if she had never held him before. His was the most welcomed touch she'd ever known. Finally, she could find peace for her troubled spirit. Daddy would make everything all right again.

"I don't remember coming home," she remarked dazed.

"You've been out a long time."

"How long? What time is it?"

"Texas time," he said looking at his watch. "It's just about two in the afternoon."

"I can't believe I've been out that long."

"A needed rest. You've been through a lot."

Once again, she reached for his embrace. His strong arms wrapped around her frail form, worn from the past week's

116

occurrences. She swept his face with tender kisses, reeling at the touch of her beloved father, her rock. Her happiness at seeing him again was clouded by the reason for her return home. She scanned her surroundings, so unfamiliar and realized she wasn't home. Confused, she wondered if perhaps her parents had purchased a new home. This was not out of the realm of possibility since Sid was in real estate. She thought of her mother and her confusion was put on hold as she questioned Sid about her health.

"How is she, Daddy? How's Mother?"

At that very moment, Bailey was painfully aware of her father's strained face. He looked years older than the last time she'd seen him. His eyes were red with dark, hollow circles. His clothing was unkempt and his hair tossed in no apparent direction. The strain of his recent struggle had taken its toll on him. Bailey believed that her mother's condition had become worse or that Mara had…

"No!" she cried out. "She can't be dead! She can't be gone!"

Sid held her tightly.

"No, darling, no. Your mother is not dead."

"Daddy," she cried. "Tell me she's better. Please tell me she is getting better."

"She is Darling, she is."

She fell into his arms once more, releasing the mountain of worry, she had generated over her mother's condition and what Red Benning had told her in the hospital. It was some time before she was able to compose herself enough to face her father again. When she did, his eyes were remorseful from what he had put her through.

"When can I see her?"

"Soon, Honey. Soon."

Sid drew out a cigarette from a pack that was lying on the end table.

"I thought you quit smoking, Daddy."

"I thought so, too."

Bailey studied her father. It broke her heart to see him this way.

"My poor Daddy. You've carried the burden for all of us."

He stared at her contrite, wondering how he was going to address the issue of why he had to tear her away from her everyday life and take her into hiding.

"It has indeed been a burden and I'm so tired."

"I'm here to help you, Daddy. I'm here as long as you need me."

He moved the chair next to the bed so that when he sat in it, his back faced her. He could confront any fierce competitor without flinching an eye, but he was unable to face the trusting eyes of his daughter as he prepared to tell her the truth about her life. He couldn't bear the disappointment she was sure to express. He couldn't bear falling off the white horse she had mounted him on.

"There's something I must tell you, Bailey. It's about you and something that happened many years ago. I always thought I was doing the right thing not telling you. I had hoped I would never have to tell you. Now I must."

"Is this about Mother?"

"This is about your mother, yes."

Bailey noted the conspicuous manner in which he said the word mother. She was suddenly stricken with fear. He was about to tell her something she already knew. She also understood that when he told her, she would have to face the truth of her past. She clutched the quilt that covered her until her knuckles turned white.

"What about Mother?"

"I haven't been honest with you, Bailey. Mother never had a heart attack. She was never sick."

"What are you saying?"

"Forgive me, for telling you such a lie. It was the only plausible excuse I could think of in this short of time to get you away from Dallas."

"I don't understand."

118

"I know you don't," he said, putting out his cigarette and lighting another one. "I had to get you out of Dallas very quickly and I knew you would argue with me for any other reason."

"Mother isn't sick?" she asked again, confused.

He shook his head.

"Bailey, we had our reasons."

"Mother!" she called out. "Mother!"

An astute Mara Carson ran into the room.

"I'm here, Sweetie. I'm here."

Within moments, Mara was sitting on the bed next to her daughter and was cradling her. The touch of Mara caressing her long hair soothed Bailey. She looked into her face and saw within her eyes the same dire expression she had seen in her father's eyes. She looked at Mara as if asking why.

"It was for your own protection," Mara said softly. "We had to make sure you were safe."

"Safe from what?"

Mara looked to Sid. He nodded, knowing he would have to be the one to explain things to her. He moved his tired body toward the window and stared into the dark afternoon sky that was threatening rain. Bailey watched his every move.

"Daddy," she said. "Please tell me this isn't about Ron. I mean about our decision to marry before you wanted us to."

Sid let out a short laugh.

"Christ, if it were only that simple. No, Bailey, this has nothing to do with Ron."

"Then...," she said, recalling what Red Benning had told her. "Then, this must be about her."

Mara and Sid looked at her searchingly.

"Her?" Sid asked.

"The woman Red Benning told me about."

"Red Benning?" Sid probed. "Who's that?"

"A reporter."

"What reporter? Where?"

"At the hospital, Daddy. He came to see me. He saw my

face on the news and said I reminded him of…"

"Christ," Sid blurted, balling his fists. "The bastard has seen you. What did he say, Bailey? He didn't try to hurt you, did he?"

"He was very kind. No, he didn't try to hurt me. Why would he?"

"Tell me what he said, Bailey."

"Why do you think he would hurt me?" she asked again.

Sid was thinking he was Jack Adams, a cold-blooded killer.

"Just tell me what he said," Sid said agitatedly.

She hesitated to tell him, but finally, she did. She let out a heavy sigh.

"He talked to me about her."

"Her? Who, Bailey?"

"Nanny Kate," she answered softly.

"Nanny Kate?" he asked. The color had drained from his face. He was by her side.

"How strange it is that I never remembered her before now. When he showed me her picture and started talking about her, I started to remember things about her."

"Oh," Mara said weakly, clutching Bailey for support. Both parents were clinging to her every word, wondering how much she knew.

"What things?" Sid asked coolly.

"Things like her smile and the way her hair would always smell like roses. She would always twist it around her finger you know, just like…I do."

Bailey read the torment in her parents' eyes and the looks on their faces told her that Red Benning had been right.

"It's true, isn't it? Red Benning was right, wasn't he?"

"What did he say?" Sid asked weakly.

"He said Nanny Kate was murdered."

"My God," he cried out.

"Was she?"

Sid nodded. Bailey was struck with panic by what this meant.

120

"He also said…"

"What, Honey? Just tell us."

"He said he believed me to be her daughter."

Mara's head fell despondent into Bailey's lap. Bailey caressed her mother's tiny shoulders, knowing at that very moment that the things Red Benning had told her were true. She was Kate Michaels's daughter. Bailey released her mother and edged out of the bed, putting a distance between her parents and herself. She turned a cynical eye toward Sid.

"And are you my true father?"

"Of course," he spoke drawn.

Bailey looked at the two people, her parents and her strength, and saw their broken spirits. They were broken by cruel fate and the burden they had been carrying all of these years. She also saw relief that the charade was now over and that the truth could finally be put to rest. No matter how dark and ugly it was. She ran toward them both, finding Mara first and held her tightly.

"I love you so. You are my mother. Nothing can ever change that."

Mara could not speak, but could only stare numbly at the child she had nurtured as her own, a child she loved more than life itself.

"My birth certificate," Bailey said aimlessly.

"What about it?" Mara asked.

"It has your name and father's name listed as my parents. And was I really born in Bailey like you said?"

"You were born in Denver, Colorado."

She looked at them defeated.

"Help me understand."

"I'll try," Sid choked, wondering where to begin. He decided to begin with what she knew.

"When your mother was killed…"

"You mean murdered, don't you?"

He looked into her cold eyes.

"Yeah," he continued. "Well, anyway, the man responsible

for her death hadn't been arrested. In fact, it seemed like he had vanished from the face of the earth."

"Jack Adams?" she asked.

"My, God," Sid said shaken. "You know about him, too?"

She nodded. "Mr. Benning said he was an evil man. He said he thought that Jack Adams might somehow try to come after me. I think you must believe this, too. But why? I mean, after all these years why would he come after me? Why would he risk such a thing, when he apparently already got away with murder?"

Sid was relieved that this Benning character wasn't Jack. Jack hadn't seen Bailey yet.

"There is no reason for Jack Adams's motives, Bailey." Sid turned to Mara. "Do you remember anything about this Red Benning reporter?"

"No, I don't. But there were so many reporters back then."

"He said," Bailey continued. "He said he was a freelance reporter and was hired to follow the case."

"By who?"

"He didn't say. Daddy?"

"Yeah," he said numbly.

"He also said that Kate Michaels's daughter, or should I say me, was found in the desert. I was nearly dead. Did Jack Adams try to kill me, too?"

"Your near-death came from your exposure to the desert and not by Jack Adams's hand."

"He left me to die? But I didn't die. And now he wants to make sure I do."

"He'll never find you. I won't let him near you."

"Oh, this is all so overwhelming. So very strange. Why can't I feel anything for this Kate woman? How could I not remember something as tragic as this?"

"You were very young, just a little over four years. The doctors said you managed to suppress what you had been through. At first you had nightmares, but then, they seemed to fade away quickly."

122

"I wonder if I'll ever remember."

"I pray you don't."

"Yes, but in forgetting the bad, I have also forgotten the good."

"The good?" Sid asked.

"The good about Kate Michaels," she clarified.

Mara broke into a sob and Sid was quick to comfort her.

"I think we've had enough revelations for today."

Submerged with confusion and questions, Bailey conceded to end the conversation for now. She had to have time to absorb what just transpired. She laid a gentle hand on Mara.

"Thank God you are well. My heart would break if I lost you."

Mara brushed Bailey's cheek and because she did not want to cry in front of her, she left. Sid was alone with his daughter and the truth. The two stared into each other's eyes as if each knew what the other was thinking. She lent him a tender smile when an image of Nanny Kate filled her mind. In response, he smiled back.

"You're thinking of her, aren't you?

Bailey nodded.

"She had a nickname for me. She used to play a game with me and my nickname."

"Yes," he said. "She would pinch your nose and say..."

"I know," Bailey finished. "She would pinch my nose and say, 'cute as a button you are.' She called me Buttons."

Sid now broke into tears. He stretched his worn body across the bed as he released his tears. They were tears for a child robbed of her mother. They were tears for a husband left without a wife. For the first time since he had laid Kate to rest, he was able to release his sorrow and he thought that quite remarkable. He actually believed he had long since dealt with this raw pain. Bailey lay next to him, brushing away his flow of tears, rocking him in her arms.

"My precious Daddy. I'm here for you."

"Oh, Bailey," he cried out. "I couldn't bear to lose you. My heart could not take losing you, too."

"You won't lose me. I promise. We'll get through this together."

He kissed her cheek and the two lay silent for some time before Bailey turned to speak to him.

"Daddy?"

"Yeah?"

"I know I was found by a Zuni man named Billy Nehah. Have you ever met him?"

"Only once. He made me promise to keep in touch with him, but it was too dangerous for me to keep that promise."

Bailey laid transfixed on her father's reply. An image of Billy Nehah swept through her mind as she recalled her dream and the strong arms that protected her. They were Billy's arms. She felt weak from this new bout of discovery. Then, she thought of Jess and their untimely meeting and how he was connected to her past. Was it as Jess's father had said about his painting? Were the spirits really asking for the truth about the woman in the painting? Was it time these truths were told? Bailey spoke to her father, but her voice was miles away amid an unfamiliar desert.

"I want to go to him. I must talk with Billy Nehah."

"Why must you talk to him, Honey?"

"So I can remember who I am."

****

Billy Nehah met Jess at the airport in Albuquerque. Jess was relieved to see his father looking well again. The cancer that had taken so much from his health four years ago had threatened to return. He'd been free of the colon cancer for almost four years but just before his scheduled trip to Dallas, Billy's doctors feared it had returned. Fortunately, no new cancer had been detected, but Sadie Nehah refused to let him travel. Jess held tight to his father. His grip was strong.

"Dad, you look good."

"I feel good. Just a little tired. Did you have a prosperous trip?"

"It was good. I met some interesting people."

"Yes? And did you meet with Byron Claiborne?"

"From the university?"

Billy nodded.

"Yes," Jess smiled, thinking of Bailey Carson. "I even spoke in place of you. Not as elegantly, I'm sure. But not bad for my first speaking event."

"I bet you did great. Byron Claiborne is a good man."

"Now, tell me again. How did you meet him, Dad?"

"He came to Zuni many years ago. He was doing some research about our culture."

"And you've kept in touch with this man all these years, Dad? That's cool."

"We have a common bond," Billy said, offering no more details. Jess was too uninterested to pursue the matter further. Still, he always found it amusing that the outside world was so fascinated by their culture. He never really understood the mystique.

"That's because you are an insider looking out," Billy would tell him. "Someday you will understand the significance of the Zunis' place on this earth."

"Dad," he said, easing his father away from the crowd at the airport and leading him to a secluded corner at a nearby food area. "We have to talk."

"What about?"

"I've been offered a job to play back up guitar with a notable jazz singer. I think you know him, Jimmy Lee, Jr."

If Billy was surprised, he didn't act it. Still, he kept silent.

"Of course," Jess continued. "I will still be able to help you with the business when I'm in town. I just don't know how often that will be. Anyway, Nellie is really the one most suited for our business, Dad. Eventually, she and Soll will run the trade when they marry."

"When will you go?" Billy asked.

Jess was hopeful because his father hadn't objected so far.

"In a couple of weeks or so."

"I see," was all he said. Jess noted the disappointment in his father's eyes and his silence was becoming far more unnerving than his usual lecture.

"Well?" Jess asked.

"You want me to say it's all right for you to go."

"I want you to be happy for me. I want you to be proud of me."

"I am proud of you."

"But you think I'm making a mistake, don't you?"

"You must follow your heart, Son."

Jess laid his hand over Billy's.

"I am, Dad. I am."

Billy gave a slight smile, but his eyes gave him away.

"Nellie is gifted, yes, but she has no head for business. It will be many years before she marries."

"Dad, this tour is only for a year. Then..."

"Then there will be another," Billy finished.

"Maybe. Maybe not."

"I know my son's heart."

"My family comes first, Dad. Never forget that."

"It is not for me to remember," Billy said. "Come on. Let's get home. Your mother is anxious to see you. We have to stop by the claims office and pick up our shipment. Do you have the claim's receipt?"

Jess reached into his wallet to pull out the receipt. When he did, Bailey Carson's business card fell on the ground. Billy picked it up. He stood frozen when he saw her picture. He kept staring at the card and then at Jess.

"Where did you get this?" Billy asked.

"From a girl I met. She was in Byron Claiborne's class. She works part-time for a Dallas paper and was going to interview you. Since you weren't there, she interviewed me."

"And this is her name, Bailey Carson? What do you know about her, Son?"

"I know very little about her."

"Yet I can see it in your eyes that you would like to know more."

"Dad, she's just a girl I met. Besides, she's engaged."

A vision of the small child he had once held in his arms, a child the spirits had so graciously saved from the clutches of death filled his mind. As sure as he knew his own children, he knew that Bailey Carson was this little girl. The sprits were leading her to him again, through Jess. He thought of Byron Claiborne and wondered how long he'd known her whereabouts. Billy traced over her picture and was overcome by a vision concerning her. Then, the mask of death consumed his mind and he cried out, grabbing Jess's arm.

"Dad?" Jess called out in alarm.

"Get me home, Son. I'm not well."

"Maybe we should stop by the hospital first."

"No," he said adamantly. "I must get home. I need to speak with Tahia."

"The priest of death?"

Billy saw the fear in Jess's eyes.

"It is not of my death that I must speak with him."

"Whose then?"

"Find her, Jess. She is in grave danger. The spirits have led her to me through you."

"Bailey?" Jess questioned.

Billy's stare answered his question.

"What danger, Dad?"

"Death is at her door."

"How do you know such a thing?"

"The mask of death tells me so."

"Why, Dad? Why would a Zuni spirit warn you of a white woman's impending death?"

"She is of my soul, Jess. I am her guardian spirit."

# CHAPTER 12

At first, Sid feared that Red Benning might be Jack, but he realized after reading the articles and talking with Bailey that this Red fellow was on the up and up and was indeed a legitimate reporter. Still, he made the necessary phone calls to confirm the facts. Red Benning was a renowned homicide investigator, who was employed primarily by private individuals or organizations to investigate the deaths of their loved ones. Sometimes insurance companies had employed him when sudden deaths left a beneficiary suspiciously wealthy. Sid couldn't help but wonder who had hired him to investigate Kate's death.

The many articles about her death left Sid understandably restless and his hatred for the man who had so abruptly put an end to her beautiful life once again haunted him. His heartache turned to anger as he remembered the sleepless days and nights just after Kate's death that he and his family had to endure. He feared that Jack might be near and ready to take his next victim, specifically, Bailey. Sid was convinced that Jack was nearby, charged by the idea of finding the daughter of the woman he had claimed to love so much.

Near midnight, the cabin was silent and everyone had long since gone to bed. Sid went into Bailey's room to reassure himself she was all right. He sat in a chair next to the window and watched her as the moonlight streamed over her sleeping form. She fought taking her medication this evening, but she was unsettled and could not find sleep. Reluctantly, she agreed to take it with Sid's coaxing and his promise that she could call Ron tomorrow.

She wanted to tell Ron everything. She wanted him to

leave Dallas to be near her. She needed his assurance, his love. An impossibility, Sid had told her and pointed out the danger she would be placing Ron in as well as herself. Bailey was still confused about why the police couldn't be involved, as were Diane and Sammy. When Sid told them stories about Jack Adams's connections with corrupt police officers they agreed to keep the law out of it, for now anyway.

Sid lit a cigarette and pulled out a pint of scotch he had nested under his shirt. He drank straight from the bottle, letting the warm brew ease away his edginess. The past began to run into the present, a usual occurrence when he sat up late at night with his bottle of scotch. As always, his thoughts were connected to Kate. Tonight she was seventeen years old walking down the streets of Bailey, Texas with her younger brother, Seth.

****

At seventeen, Kate Claiborne was a saucy beauty and had clearly captured the attention of the two old-timers who sat in front of City Hall watching the "goings-on" as if life in Bailey, Texas would cease to exist if they weren't there to supervise it. Kate's great uncle, Ned Claiborne, tipped his "Dallas Cowboys" cap to her and gave her a slight wink. Vail Michaels, Ned's collaborator on the daily activities in Bailey and his weekend drinking/poker buddy, gave her a short whistle just before he spat his favorite chew into a thin can placed near his mud-coated boots.

"Sid," Vail shouted to his grandson who was sitting in the air-conditioned City Hall, sipping on a coca-cola. "Come out here and see the prettiest sight in Texas."

Vail's twenty-four-year-old grandson, Sid, opened the door of the old wooden building that housed Bailey's City Hall. When he did, the Texas heat slapped him in the face and he nearly retreated to the cool building. Summers in Bailey were like a sauna, so close it felt at times like the air was a second skin. This summer was no different.

The three watched as Kate Marie Claiborne, the granddaughter of the late Ham Claiborne, who himself had been a former member of the old-timers' elite fellowship, sashayed before them. She looked like she had just stepped out of a summer bouquet, a beautiful flower to be admired over and over. From the moment she was born, Ham had spoiled and pampered his only granddaughter and for sixteen years, she was the light of his life. She was a remarkable sight. Ham wasn't wrong when he would brag she'd grow up to be the most beautiful gal in Fannin County.

Knowing her grandfather would have been sitting right there with Ned and Vail, Kate found comfort in seeing his old buddies. She often walked out of her way to see them, just so she might savor the memories of her grandfather and his buddies telling stories and making the world right.

Six-year-old Seth Claiborne ran to sit in Ned's lap, getting his uncle's full attention as he pulled out a stick of beef jerky for the boy to chew. Vail and Sid were intent on Kate, admiring the way she moved toward them. Her long blonde hair waved gently to one side and her summer dress rustled in the same direction, exposing a slight view of her shapely thigh.

It had been over six years since Sid had last seen her. Seeing her today, he realized she was no longer the little sister of his once best friend, John Claiborne. Back then, she was a scrawny tomboy, but now, she was like viewing an angel. She was a woman fully formed and fully aware of her charms.

"Morning there, Kate," Ned called out as she came within feet of them.

"Uncle," she drawled. "Seth, don't be a pest."

"Leave the boy be, Honey. He's sitting just right on my lap now. My, my, but don't you look the picture today."

"Thank you, Uncle." She turned toward Vail and Sid coyly batting her dark lashes. She curved her smile in such a way, it was clearly a gesture of allurement. "How are you boys today?"

"Can't complain, Lil' Darlin," Vail said, matching her smile with one of his own. "And I'm a heap better since I got a hold of your sweet Texas smile. Why, if I were just a few years younger, I'd carry you home with me."

"What a flirt you are, Mr. Michaels," she teased moving her smile toward Sid. "And you, Sid? How have you been all these years? Word is that you're home from the Marines."

Sid drew a cigarette from his pocket. She noticed the way his muscles danced as he moved his arms about. His flirting eyes moved over her expressing his pleasure at the woman she had become. She was as pleased with how he had changed and she nervously played along with his teasing. She turned to Vail Michaels.

"You know, just between you and me. Six years in the Marines has taken the boy out of your grandson. Don't you think?"

"This runt? Hell, darlin', I can still take him on and beat the piss out of him."

The three laughed at Sid's expense. He played along.

"Why Sid's not a fighter, Mr. Michaels," she continued. "I have it on good authority that he's more of a gentleman. If you know what I mean."

"A gentleman? Someone lied to you, Honey. Why this boy's as ornery as they come."

Both Sid and Vail were criminal handsome. And young Sid, like his granddad, could charm the skirt off any woman. Yet, he was more unscrupulous than his father was. What he wanted in life, he found a way to get it.

Sid had not been raised in Bailey. His mother, Sue Michaels, raised him on the streets of Chicago's south side. After his parents divorced, Sid learned about life the hard knocks way. When he was sixteen, his mother sent him to live in Bailey with his father. He had become too much for Sue to handle and was getting into trouble at school and around the neighborhood. His record in Bailey wasn't much better, but he did manage to graduate. When he was eighteen, he enlisted in the Marine Corps.

"I do things my way, Grandpa," Sid said.

Kate turned to face him. Her big brown eyes shot at him in such a way, he almost fell over. He sent her a forward gaze. She let out a nervous giggle.

"Why Sid Michaels, you stare at me as if you have nothing good on your mind."

"Could be," he said. "I could tell you what's on my mind if you care to listen."

He flung his cigarette into the street and swept his hand through his long black hair.

"I thought Marines had to keep their hair short."

"I'm not a Marine anymore."

"You aren't reenlisting?"

"No way."

"What are your plans?"

"I plan to get married."

"Oh, you're engaged?"

"Not yet."

"Have someone in mind?"

"Maybe."

"Anyone I know."

"Yeah, I plan to marry you, Baby."

Ned and Vail both laughed aloud. Kate stood startled and intrigued.

"When did you decide this?"

"The moment I saw you today."

"You're awfully sure of yourself."

"Yes, Ma'am."

"Why Mr. Michaels, I do believe your grandson has a thing or two to learn about charming a woman. What should I do? Should I let him talk to me this way?"

"If I were you, I'd turn and run in the opposite direction of my boy, here. I wouldn't let him near ten feet of me."

"That's not a very nice thing to say about your own grandson."

"Don't get me wrong. I love my boy. But a gal who looks

as good as you do puts all kinds of ideas into a boy like my Sid. Ain't no good ever comes from a man who's got just one thing on his mind."

Kate smiled. She liked how the boys always tried to lure her into kissing them, even sometimes going further than kissing. She always told them what they wanted to hear, knowing it really wasn't right to lead them on so. Deep down, she knew they knew she was just playing games. She had never known a boy like Sid, a man, and she wondered when he would try to kiss her. She only knew he wasn't like the schoolboys she had dated.

"You respect me, don't you Sid?"

"Yes, Ma'am. How about letting me drive you and Seth home?"

"Okay," she said, not batting an eye and not a bit surprised he had asked. She motioned to Seth that it was time to go.

"I'll get my keys," Sid said and went inside the building. Seth was saying his goodbyes.

Ned lent a serious tone to the afternoon.

"You know, little lady. Your daddy might not take kindly to Sid taking you home."

"Oh, Uncle, Daddy's buried that hatchet a long time ago. John's doing well now and Daddy knows it wasn't Sid's fault he got caught stealing that stuff from the Wal-Mart."

"Still, Sid put him up to it and John was the one who got caught."

"Daddy's fine, really," she assured, but as she watched Sid walk out with his keys, she wondered if this was wise. Her brother John's arrest had just about destroyed her daddy. Byron Claiborne told John he would only help him if he would promise to stay away from Sid and his thugs. That was six years ago, she thought. Surely, he couldn't stay angry with Sid for all of these years. Johnny and Sid were reckless back then. Sid was a grown man now. He had been a soldier in the United States Marines, after all.

Vail and Ned watched as Sid led Kate to his truck. He

made certain she was in the middle next to him.

"I'd be willing to wager," Vail said as he watched Sid's truck pull away. "Before that little darlin' gets home, she'll have him so riled, he won't know if he's going up or coming down."

Ned revealed to Vail some news about Kate's father.

"You know Byron sold all of Ham's land. He's moving his family to Colorado — Kate too. Johnny's out of jail now and Byron wants to give him a fresh start. Anyway, they are leaving at summer's end."

"I reckon he better move soon. Still, I don't suppose Byron will be able to keep those two from seeing each other if that's what they want. I mean both seemed willing. Don't suspect a couple of states are going to stop 'em either. When my Sid wants something or someone, he goes after it. And my guess is he wants that little darlin' something bad."

****

Byron Claiborne did move his family to Denver, Colorado, where he took a teaching position at the University of Colorado. Sid Michaels was quick to follow, landing a job as a loan manager at a Denver Collection Agency. On the side, he made a tidy bundle lending money at a high-interest rate to those would couldn't pay their bills. It was easy to find willing investors, so long as their cut was under the table. When the customers couldn't pay back the loans, Sid would send out his guy to collect.

Once he was established, he gave Kate a call. They started seeing each other and just six weeks shy of her eighteenth birthday, she told her mother, Becky, that she was in love with Sid. They were going to be married and they were going to have a child.

Becky Claiborne, against her husband's wishes, signed the consent papers for Kate to marry Sid. Present at their small wedding were only a handful of people. Attending were Kate's mother, her brother, John, Sid's mother, Sue, and Sid's best friend and best man, Jack Adams. They met each other when Sid first joined the Marines at Camp Lejune in North Carolina.

"Doesn't he ever talk?" Kate asked Sid about Jack when all the guests had gone.

"He's a man of few words."

"He's strange. He kept looking at me all night."

"Well, you are something to look at."

"Tell me that when I'm nine months pregnant."

He brought her near him and kissed her long and hard. He held his hand over her stomach.

"Can you believe it? I got the best looking woman in Texas and she's having my baby?"

"You're pretty charming yourself."

"No hard feelings about your daddy?"

"I'll never forgive him for not coming to our wedding and for treating you the way he did."

"I can handle it, Baby. I just know how it's hurting you. I know how close you and your daddy are. It doesn't have to be this way."

"I love you, Sid. Daddy will come around when he sees how much you care for the baby and me. Thank goodness Mama understands. I was thinking if the baby is a girl, I'd like to name her Rebecca, after my mom."

"Sure, Baby. And if it's a boy?"

"Sid Carson Michaels."

"Where did the Carson come from?"

"That was my Granddaddy's real name, not Ham."

"Yeah," said Sid. "I like that name."

Kate smiled. "Promise me, something."

"Anything."

"Promise me you'll always love me and never anyone else."

"That's a promise I can keep."

"One more promise, about our baby."

"What?"

"Promise you will always be there for her or him."

"I promise. Now, I have to tell you something. It's about

Jack Adams."

"What about Jack?"

"I'm thinking about leaving the savings and loan and going into business with Jack."

"Isn't that risky?"

"Going into business is always risky, but I've made some capital and connections at the savings and loan. Jack and I want to branch out – into real estate. I was thinking of including Johnny in on the deal."

"Sid, Jack scares me. Can we trust him?"

"In business, he's the best. None better. But that's as far as our relationship will go."

"He's your best friend."

"You're my best friend now. Jack and I will always be loyal to each other. We respect each other—in business. Starting today, any dealings I have with Jack will be strictly business. My hell-raising days are over. I have a wife and baby to think of now. Kate, I've made a lot of promises to you tonight. Now, you must promise me that you'll never get too close to Jack Adams."

"You make him sound so – I don't know – dangerous."

"He can be, Kate. I once saw him break a man's neck and not bat an eye. After it was all over, he made like nothing happened."

"My, God. Did he go to jail?"

"He killed him in self-defense. He wasn't arrested."

"Oh well, that's different."

Sid got silent and held her tight.

"Just remember. Don't go around him unless I'm with you. He's the only man I know who can charm a woman better than me."

"Sid?"

"Yeah?"

"Shut up and charm your wife."

He drew her near and as always, he was passionate and almost primitive with his lovemaking. She found herself

136

initiating moments to be with him, just so she could feel his raw passion. She was completely dedicated to Sid and vowed he would never desire the arms of another woman. He looked into her eyes.

"Kate, what would I do if I ever lost you?"

# CHAPTER 13

Rita stayed at Ron's until he left for his shift work. She cleaned up the place a little before leaving to go to her apartment. As always, when she and Ron had had one of their little indiscretions she felt empty and full of regret. When would she stop doing this to herself? He was never going to be with her, even if Bailey weren't in the picture. She didn't notice the car hidden near the corner of the complex pull away and follow her home. She was too oblivious as to what she had done and what she knew she had to do.

"I'll break it off," she thought, opening her apartment door. "There's nothing in it for me. I'm just going to get hurt again."

Thirty minutes later she was showered, dressed and out the door. She wasn't about to mope the night away. Ron wanted to play both sides. He wanted her and Bailey. She thought she could handle this, but after he left for work, she knew she couldn't be his second-best any longer. She called her girlfriend, Sandy, and they met at *Rendezvous,* a quaint sports bar for dinner and a few drinks. Rita thought it an appropriate name given her recent behavior.

"I'm done with him, Sandy. He's no good for me."

"Good. I've been trying to tell you this for years."

The waiter came to take their order. When he did, he pointed to a swarthy looking man at the bar.

"The gentleman at the bar told me to tell you drinks are on him."

The two women looked toward the bar. He tipped his glass to them. They giggled like schoolgirls to each other and waved to him as if to say "Thank you." Then, they saw him walk toward them.

"Oh, my gosh, he's coming over here," Sandy said. "He's kind of cute, a little old, but definitely a looker."

Rita flung back her strawberry blonde hair and gave him a quick smile. Immediately, her eyes drifted over him, over his agile form and his toned muscles, squeezed inside his jeans and t-shirt. He left little to the imagination. Older than most men she dated, she couldn't deny his overall appeal, nor the way his grin was causing her to take a second look and then another. When he reached their table, Rita understood well his effect on women. She knew because so many times she had the same effect on men.

"Ladies," he husked.

"Ah, thanks for the drinks," Sandy said. "You really didn't have to."

"How else was I going to meet you?"

By "you", Sandy knew he meant Rita for he was staring at her as if he couldn't get enough. He held out his hand.

"Carl Woods."

"Rita McDonald," Rita said, "and this is Sandy Mills. Nice to meet you."

"Likewise. Guess this is my lucky day. I mean, running into such beautiful women."

"Our boyfriends will be here any minute," Rita lied. She thought he was just way too sure of himself.

He held his heart as if he'd just been struck down.

"Damn," he said. "I just knew this was my lucky day."

Just the same, he sat down in the booth next to Rita.

"You don't mind if I hang out until they get here, do you?"

Sandy laughed. "Busted!"

"Really, Mr. Woods," Rita blushed. "We're just having a girls' night out. It's kind of a trash men night, if you know what I mean?"

"Okay," he said holding his hands up in concession. "You can't blame a fellow for trying. How about tomorrow for lunch? Will you be through trashing men tomorrow?"

He coyly slid his arms against hers and gave her a wink.

She jolted but didn't bother to move away. She smiled warmly at him.

"I'm sorry. I'm just not in the market right now."

"Does your boyfriend know how lucky he is?"

"I doubt it," Sandy blurted. "He's pretty much a jerk."

Rita kicked Sandy and when she did, her leg accidentally touched his leg.

"Come on Rita, one lunch, that's all."

His smile was irresistible.

"I'm working tomorrow."

"You have to eat, don't you?"

His determination weakened her. She let out a heavy sigh. The thought of having lunch with this stranger was out of the question, but she didn't think she could let this opportunity pass. He was charming and handsome and just what she needed to build up her confidence after so many rejections from Ron. What harm would it prove if she chose a safe meeting place?

"Meet me at twelve-thirty at *Fridays*, just a mile down the road."

He stood up abruptly. With more gentleness than she'd ever seen from a man, he took her hand and brought it to his mouth. He kissed it warmly. Then, he did the same to Sandy.

"It's been a pleasure meeting you, Ladies."

Turning back to Rita, he leaned to whisper in her ear.

"See you tomorrow, beautiful. Guess who I'll be dreaming about tonight?"

She gave him a wary smile. As she watched him move away from the table, she all but convinced herself she wouldn't meet him tomorrow. But then, he caught up with the waiter and not only paid for their drinks, but their dinners. There was something about him, something almost dangerous and yet he was gentle. A levelheaded woman, she knew she shouldn't meet him tomorrow. He was a stranger, a charming one, but a stranger nonetheless. He stopped before leaving the restaurant and waved at her. She trailed him through the window as he walked to his car.

"My God," she thought. "What just happened here?"

And then she knew. She would definitely be having lunch with him tomorrow and she couldn't explain why.

**** 

Jack Adams, aka Carl Woods, left the *Rendezvous* sports bar and thought of Ron's sidekick.

"What a looker," he thought. His contempt for Ron cooled somewhat. He doubted he could turn such a woman down. She was a beauty, no question about that. And with a body to match. He let out a quick whistle as he thought of tomorrow's lunch. "Hey, chum, who's in control here anyway?"

Jack drove to the hospital. He knew it probably wasn't wise to go inside and try to see Bailey, but he knew his window of opportunity was fading. She'd be leaving, Benning would be talking to her, and no doubt, Sid would be heavily involved in whatever transpired. He had to get close to her – and soon. He slid in a back door and walked the stairs to the third floor. He was surprised when he saw very little activity near her room — no press, no guard, and no police. He couldn't believe his luck when he walked inside her room with no resistance. That's when he knew she was gone. Without thinking about the consequences, he caught up with a floor nurse and asked about Bailey.

"Oh, she left yesterday. Gone home."

Jack bolted out and drove to her apartment. It was dark. Maybe she was sleeping, probably not. She was probably celebrating her release. He had to know where she was. Had to get close to her. Against his better judgment, he knocked on her apartment door. Stupid move, he knew. There was no answer. He went back to his car.

"What the hell are you doing? Do you want to get caught?"

He lit a cigarette to calm himself. The controlled, reserved Jack took over.

"You've got to stick to your plan."

He drove by Sammy's house. His Buick was parked in the garage, but it appeared that he and Diane weren't home. Wherever they were, they were most likely together. A nosy neighbor happened to see him snooping around Sammy's garage.

"Looking for something?" a plump middle-aged woman asked.

"Yeah," Jack lied. "I'm looking for Sammy. He's thinking of selling me his Buick. I came by to look at it. We had an appointment. Guess he forgot."

"They're out of town."

"Oh," he probed. "A weekend away, huh?"

"Couldn't say," she spoke apprehensively, realizing she'd already said too much. "Might just be for the day."

"He didn't leave a number to call, did he? I mean, I really would like to test drive that Buick."

She shrugged. "No, no number."

Jack was aware of her nervousness. He knew a liar when he saw one. When he drove away, he knew something wasn't right. His keen wit told him that. With his eyes on the road, he vaguely heard the news report on the radio. It was about Celia Johnson. He turned up the volume, but the bit was over. He decided to go to his motel and shower. He had to clear his mind and think about what to do. He didn't like the unknown. He'd been drowning in it for seventeen years. He had to find Bailey. He had to get her to safety.

****

At twelve-thirty Rita drove into the parking lot of *Fridays* Restaurant. She was nervous and drove around several times before parking. When she went inside, the man she knew as Carl Woods was already waiting at a table, wine served and a rose for the lady. He stood to greet her and kissed her forehead. She sat down and he was quick to sit right next to her. He

142

handed her the rose.

"Thank you," she said, sniffing the flower. "It's beautiful."

"You are."

She took a sip of water, jittery, unlike her usually cool demeanor.

"I almost didn't come."

"I know."

"How do you know?"

"It was a shot in the dark for me. A gal like you could have anyone."

He took her hand and kissed it. He took in every detail, polished nails, perfect hair, sexy jewelry, unforgettable smell. Yeah, she wanted this as much as he did. He smiled broadly.

"I thought about you all night," he seduced.

"Carl," she confessed. "I thought about you, too."

She took a drink of the wine he had ordered, even though she was on duty. He picked up an appetizer and fed her. She complied, thinking she'd never seen a man so sensual. A Queen song was playing in the background and he tapped his fingers on the table in rhythm.

"They don't make music like this anymore."

She was thinking, "And they don't make men like you anymore."

When their food came, they ate in silence, never taking their eyes off of each other. They barely got their meals eaten when Carl paid and they walked out the door. They met in her car and began a passionate interplay that lasted thirty minutes and eventually took them back to her apartment. She forgot her work and he temporarily forgot his reason for being in Dallas.

She fell asleep in his arms and he watched as she slept. In the course of four hours, he had learned a lot from this beautiful creature. He learned she was a nurse at the same hospital as Ron and that is where they met over four years ago. Ron had never been faithful to her and neither had he been with Bailey. He learned of her distaste for Bailey's family and Sid's recent offer to give her five thousand dollars to come between Bailey and Ron. Most importantly, he learned that Bailey and Sammy were in Spain, supposedly to be with Mara, who had suffered a heart attack.

"Smart move," Jack thought of Sid. "Getting Bailey out of Dallas."

Now, his plans would have to change. No point in hanging around Dallas anymore. He looked at Rita.

"Pity," he thought. "What a beautiful pity."

He released his hold on Rita and found the TV remote. A rebroadcast of the ten o'clock news came on. Celia Johnson's picture flashed across the screen. Jack grimaced when he heard that Chavez had been released from custody. The feed didn't say why, but Jack guessed he had paid his lawyer a hefty fee to bail him out. Of course, his lawyer said that the police had the wrong man and that the real killer was still at large. Jack turned off the TV.

"Enough. I'm outta here before they find a reason to pin this on me."

He returned to Rita. She nuzzled closer to him. He had to make his move now. He doubted she'd go along. It was too early. But, there wasn't time for a proper seduction. He kissed her fully on the mouth, long and hard. Within minutes, she was in his arms in full submission.

"What's wrong?" she husked. "Can't you sleep?"

"Not with a woman like you near."

"Oh, Carl, I've never met anyone like you."

He plucked at the ends of her hair.

"What about Ron?"

Her eyes flew open.

"What about him?"

"He called while you were sleeping."

Rita opened her eyes surprised.

"Did you talk to him?"

"Not really. But, I think he was shocked to hear a man's voice."

Her heart was pounding.

144

"Who did you say you were?"

"I didn't. He didn't ask either."

She let out a nervous laugh. "Serves him right."

"Do you love him, Rita?"

"I thought I did, until…"

"Until what?"

"Until you."

"Be honest, Rita. I might not like what you have to say, but I'll understand."

"I'm done with him, Carl. No matter what happens between us."

Jack let out a heavy sigh. He turned pointedly to face her and kissed her deeply.

"Come to Arizona with me."

"What?" she asked surprised.

"Arizona. I'm leaving for Arizona in a couple of days. Come with me."

"I don't know if I can get off. It's short notice. We have to give a couple of weeks before we take vacation."

He let out a hardy laugh.

"I don't want to go on vacation with you, Baby. I want to marry you."

"Marry me! Are you out of your mind?"

"I'm serious as hell, but before you give me your answer, there are some things you need to know about me."

# CHAPTER 14

The next morning after leaving Rita's, Jack went back to his motel. He gathered his things, making sure he didn't leave anything behind. He decided he would leave Dallas as soon as Rita made her decision. If she didn't make it within the next couple of days, he was gone. With the news of Bailey being in Spain, he'd have to rethink his plans. Except for Jean Little, Sammy's mom, Rita was his only connection to Bailey.

He felt edgy after checking out of the motel. He felt like the old days where he needed to pick up and run. Maybe he was feeling this way because running had become a way of life for him. He choked down a quick breakfast and decided to confirm Rita's story that Bailey was in Spain. It was always wise to double-check all facts.

He drove by Jean and Bud Little's house. Bud was still there, so he parked down a side road to wait until he left. He hoped it would be soon. Jean owed Jack a visit. She hadn't shown up a couple of days ago like she said she would. Jack was thinking maybe he couldn't rely on Jean anymore. He was wondering if she had talked to Bud about his contacting her. Probably she had. His speculations about Jean were interrupted when he stopped at a convenience store and grabbed the morning paper.

There was an article in the paper about the Celia Johnson case. The article along with several photos connected her murder to other unsolved murders. His heart stopped when he saw Kate's picture next to Celia Johnson's. Next to Kate's was a Tucson woman named Missy Dole, who had been murdered several years after Kate. Next to Missy's picture was Alana Greene, a Las Vegas hooker, who had been murdered ten years ago. And next to Alana's picture was Jessica Framington, a U.C.L.A. coed, killed some five years ago just outside of L.A.

Each woman was near the age of twenty-one. Each had long blonde hair and deeply set brown eyes. Each had been killed in the same manner—shot three times in the back after being gagged, tied, and blindfolded. An extra tidbit printed was that they had been raped after they had been murdered. An unconfirmed piece of information was that the killer had taken a prize from each of the girls as some kind of a sick trophy. The prize was undisclosed, but from previous articles, Jack knew the killer cut off most of the hair from his victim, as some sort of treasure. The article indicated that each woman had presumably been killed by a man named Jack Adams.

A composite of what Adams might look like was printed alongside the pictures of the victims. Jack slammed the paper down and instinctively headed back to Jean's house. He had to know the score between them. And too, she might know more than the papers were letting on. When he neared her house, Jack saw a most interesting scene.

Bud and Jean Little were standing outside their house conversing with a man Jack thought he recognized. He was the very man he had bypassed in the elevator at Parkland Hospital. It was the very man who had made him, Jack Adams, his personal crusade the past seventeen years. Jack watched Red Benning move inside the house with Jean and Bud following behind. Then Jack saw nothing but a closed door, leaving him to speculate their intentions.

"Benning!" He called out. "What would you do with your life if you didn't have me to hassle?"

Jack wondered if Benning had made the connection between Kate and Bailey. He had to guess that he had. Benning was sharp. He'd proven that time and time again. Jack was now positive that Jean told Bud about his call. She was probably telling Benning right now. This would give him something else to write about in his newspapers.

Jack thought of Jean and the history they once had. Hadn't

they once shared an intimate relationship and then later a friendship? For an inkling, he felt betrayed but then his heart hardened. Why shouldn't she deceive him? Hadn't everyone else? There wasn't one damn person he could trust – not completely anyway. Jack pulled away from the house, away from the "Brutus" crowd, and drove straight to Rita's. Her key was where she said it would be and he let himself inside. It was almost ten and he knew she would be on her morning break. He gave her a call.

"Working hard?" He asked.

"Not really. I'm too busy thinking of you."

Jack smiled.

"Well, that's encouraging. Have you thought about my offer?"

"That's all I've been thinking about."

"Well?"

"I can't marry you, Carl...Not now."

"Yeah, I figured. Hey listen, it's been a blast. I'll call you if I'm ever back in Dallas."

"Hold on," she cried. "I said I couldn't marry you, but..."

"But what?" He baited.

"I'd be willing to try living together, you know, as a trial, to see how things go."

Jack held his breath.

"In Arizona?"

"Sure. From what you told me last night, it sounds nice. I can get a nursing job there."

"You're making me very happy, Baby."

"I'm scared, Carl. My mother is here. She relies on me. I'm giving up all of my security for a man I just met. It's crazy, I know it. It doesn't make any sense. I feel like I've known you for years instead of days. I lied to my mom. I said I've known you for a long time. She's not happy, but she supports me. Carl, tell me you won't break my heart."

"I'm crazy about you, Baby. If you only knew how happy I am at this very moment. But there's a slight glitz in my plans.

148

I'm going to have to leave tonight. You know that investigation I said I was working on. Well, it just got complicated."

"Tonight! I can't possibly leave tonight. I have to pack. I have to give my notice. I have to take care of my apartment."

"I understand. Do what you have to do and then meet me in Arizona."

"I really want to go with you."

"That's what I want, too."

"You really know how to send a girl in a tailspin. But…I'm going with you, tonight or tomorrow or in two weeks, whenever you leave. I've got no reason to stay. Screw giving my notice. Mom can take care of my apartment. We can pack together. I'll just swing by the bank and close my account. Carl, should I be naughty?"

"That sounds interesting. What do you mean?"

"I'm talking about Sid Michaels's money. The money is as good as mine. I started thinking. Why not take his money? I've earned it just putting up with that family."

Jack laughed aloud.

"That's my girl. Don't take any crap from anyone."

"You know what, Carl? I've had it with this place. I'm clocking out and heading to the apartment. This hospital's seen the last of Rita McDonald."

****

Eager to be on his way and out of Dallas, Jack managed to lure Rita away just after midnight. Lucky for him, she was too preoccupied with love to watch the news or read a newspaper. He knew he couldn't keep this from her forever. He'd find the right time to tell her everything soon. He looked into her sultry eyes that clearly read love.

"It's a shame," he thought, "that I can't love again."

She clutched his arm as the car moved down the dark highway. He put on a Queen CD, their song. She was remembering their first date. Instinctively she ran her hand through his hair and moved over to kiss his cheek and neck. He saw the desire written on her face, even in the moonlight. He drew a wicked grin. Her long mass of hair spread across his shoulder. He pulled off the main road to a side road that led to an obstructed wooded area.

"Don't fall for this woman," he thought. "Enjoy the ride, but never fall in love with her."

****

As Jack drove toward Phoenix, he watched Rita sleep peacefully next to him. Her long hair fell over her face. A tiny heart necklace was tangled within her full locks and he reached over to untangle it. Just before touching it, the moonlight shone down upon the delicate gold locket, causing it to sparkle in the night sky. His first thought was how beautiful she looked, beautiful and innocent. Strangely, he felt compelled to protect her. From what? He wondered. He straightened the locket so that it hung down the full of her blouse. He thumbed the locket and its sheen triggered a memory.

A picture of Red Benning smiling at the two Dallas police officers filled his mind. He heard Benning's shrill laughter echo through the darkness. He was laughing at him. He was laughing at Jack Adams. Jack was suddenly aware of an acidulous reality, so absolute that it slapped him like a biting wind.

Anger consumed him, murderous anger, and he knew that only the feel of his hands around Red Benning's neck would bring release from his anger. He pressed his foot down hard on the accelerator. He felt a stinging in his foot. The speedometer measured his anger, first eighty, then ninety and one hundred. Zipping down the highway, he could feel his heart racing to the beat of the car's speed. The air around him was stifling and he thought he would choke on his own anger.

But then, as suddenly as his anger had surfaced, it faded. He took control of his wits. He let up on the accelerator and resumed a normal speed. He wiped the sweat off his brow. He

150

lit a cigarette and turned to see Rita was still sleeping.

"Sleeping angel," he thought. "My sleeping angel."

He rolled down his window and exhaled the smoke from his cigarette and, in the process, he felt a stirring within his soul. He felt elated, liberated. He let out a cutting laugh.

"I'll be a sonofabitch." He felt drained, but he was in control. "Ah, Benning, you've been damn good. You've been better than good. Almost perfect, I'd say. You've kept me going all of these years. I guess I never put the puzzle together because, until this week, I'd never actually seen you. You and your hideous golden grin—your hideous laugh.

"My hat's off to you, but now I've got the upper hand. Yes, Benning, that was me in the elevator. It was Jack Adams. Did you recognize me? You thought about me anyway. Didn't you, you slimy snake? Oh, I can just imagine what you must be thinking right now.

"You're wondering whether or not I'm a figment of your imagination or if I'm real. And if I'm real, you're thinking, 'I've got to kill that bastard.' Well, guess what I'm thinking? I'm thinking, come and get me. I want you to come and get me. See what happens when you come and get me."

****

Rita twisted in the seat and opened her eyes at half-mast. Jack brushed her cheek gently and she smiled at him. The morning sun peered over the horizon and she glanced up to see a road sign for San Antonio.

"We're going south?" she asked.

"There's been a change of plans. Thought we'd take a detour. You look like a girl who enjoys an exotic beach. How about me and you driving into Mexico and getting away for a while? I made sure you brought your passport."

"What's really going on here, Carl?"

"You're gonna have to trust me, Honey."

"I don't know you well enough to trust you."

151

"You trust me or you wouldn't be with me."

"Stop the car, Carl."

To her surprise, he stopped the car at the next exit. He parked at an Exxon station.

"You want out, here's your chance."

"I want to know what is going on."

He let out a heavy sigh.

"Okay, Rita, you deserve that. To begin with, my name is Jack Adams..."

****

Red Benning sat by the window in row sixteen on American flight 643 to L.A. He had just finished his third martini and decided to take a little snooze. When he closed his eyes, he saw the steely blue eyes of a male corpse staring at him. Red opened his eyes to be rid of the image, but when he closed them again, the corpse's penetrating expression pierced through him. It seemed to be speaking to him through his eyes.

"The gig's up," the corpse said. "I know who you are."

Benning called for the flight attendant to bring him another drink in an effort to calm his uneasiness.

"There's no place in this sport for fear," he said to himself. "Not even a hint of it."

He looked at Bailey Carson's photo. "How terribly inconsiderate of you to go and leave Dallas without telling me. I need you Bailey Carson. I need you to help me with this last hurrah. Help me end this game so I can finally lay my tired bones to rest."

# Chapter 15

Sid drove his rental down the isolated road that led to the Zuni Reservation. He was remembering a time when the Gallup Police had led him down this very road and had shown him the spot where Kate's body had been found. Bailey sat in the back with Mara. Diane and Sammy decided to stay in Taos. Bailey took in the vision of the defined mesas and buttes and the red earth that surrounded them. Though she tried to grasp hold of anything that might induce a memory of that dark night or bond her to a mother who had so brutally been taken from her, she couldn't. This lack of connection left her despondent.

Two weeks had gone by since Sid had told her the truth about her past. She felt as though her old life had been ripped away and that she was now living someone else's life. She tried to imagine the events that led to Kate Michaels's murder and how a couple as seemingly in love as her father and Kate were, could somehow be destroyed by the hands of such a brutal man as Jack Adams. She wondered about Jack Adams. What appeal did he have? What charm? She knew he must have a powerful charisma to be able to persuade a woman to throw away the love of her husband and subject her young daughter to an environment of sin.

Bailey didn't realize it, but Jack Adams was indirectly influencing her. His existence was taking her away from her life with Ron and her dreams of being his wife. In the two weeks, she had been away from Ron, she spoke to him every day. Each time, she felt herself drifting further and further away from him. Last night when she talked with him, she was still telling him lies about her mother being sick. The strain from her lies was growing so intolerable, she feared for her well-being. She decided rather than deceiving him any longer, she would have to end their relationship indefinitely.

He wouldn't hear of it, but she wouldn't back down. She gave him his freedom and told her family if he called to tell him she just couldn't bear to talk to him. Strangely, she felt relieved after it was all over. She would never have to lie to him again. She was doing the right thing for Ron, for herself. The pain in his voice broke her heart. Yet, her own distress was so strong she could do nothing but let him go.

As they neared the Reservation, Bailey felt both protected and isolated. She couldn't explain why she felt a certain calmness as the October winds blew red earth across their windshield. There was a slight rain in the air and the sound of the windshield wipers soothed her somewhat. She leaned against Mara, whose touch had always eased away fear and doubt and confusion. She looked to her for answers.

"Shouldn't I feel something, Mother? I've just said goodbye to my fiancé, the man I love, and I feel nothing."

"It's the stress of everything. A soul can only handle so much."

"I'm afraid, Mother."

"Of Jack Adams? That's understandable."

"It's not just him. There's something else."

"What, Honey?"

"I'm afraid to let myself remember that night."

"Of course, you are. It was a terrible night. Anyone would be."

"Do you think seeing Billy Nehah will help me to remember?"

"You will remember when your heart can no longer keep it hidden and not a moment sooner."

****

Jess Nehah parked near the entrance of the Zuni Reservation. He was anxious to see Bailey again and to meet her family. Several days ago Sid Michaels had contacted him and told him of his daughter's determination to meet with Billy. Jess told Sid of his father's premonitions and Sid was wise to listen. Sid was running out of options and Billy seemed to understand the intense burden Sid had carried all these years. Billy had also carried it. He still did.

Her visit would serve two purposes. She would meet Billy and the issue of her safety would temporarily be addressed. Although Sid had not yet agreed, Billy had suggested that Bailey stay with him and his family. It was the perfect hideout. She would be protected from Jack Adams by the make of the village, and if by chance he did show up, he would stand out. Sid was reluctant because he wouldn't be with her. Out of sight, to Sid, meant out of control. With Bailey's and Sammy's coaxing, Sid was here today, at least willing to listen.

Jess held his jacket closer as the autumn breeze whistled through the cracks of his father's old truck. Too jittery to stay confined to the truck, he got out and leaned against the side. He stood for what seemed like hours until he saw the car come into view. He waved and Sid gave a slight tap on the horn to acknowledge his presence. Bailey set her eyes on Jess and just the sight of him gave her heart hope.

"It's Jess," she told Mara. "He's Billy Nehah's son."

Sid parked his car next to the truck and got out. The two men shook hands and exchanged small talk. Jess found himself looking toward Bailey's car in an effort to catch a glimpse of the woman who had touched not only his father's heart but his, as well. Sid returned to the car and Jess waved as if saying "hello." Soon, he was in his truck and Sid was following him.

Jess led them into a valley that was surrounded by mesas and buttes, and in its very heart was the village of Zuni. The hills that encircled the village were like giant waves of red earth. The horizon reminded Bailey of the jeweled turquoise that so described the Nehah sustenance, the Zunis' sustenance. A gathering of children, brown and eager, assembled as they edged closer to Jess's home. Their bright faces beamed, masked with full rosy cheeks and riveting black eyes that coursed the movement of the strangers who had come to their village. Jess slowed the truck and pulled down a small path that led downhill toward an adobe dwelling. He let out a quick whistle to the dog that had decided to nap where he wanted to park, unconcerned by today's visitors. Sid parked behind Jess and everyone got out of the vehicles at the same time. A small boy around four ran up to Jess.

"Jesseeeee," he said, giving him a hug.

"Pinky," Jess said, hugging him back. He reached into his truck and tossed a sack of candy to Pinky.

"You can have one and share the rest with the other children."

Pinky grabbed the bag and ran to the others excited. The sight of the playful children made Bailey feel some happiness for the first time in weeks. She let out a quick laugh. Sid was quick to note that this was the first time she had laughed since this whole ordeal began for her. Jess turned around to face her. She looked tired and vulnerable. He had an inclination to reach out and hold her but decided it wouldn't be appropriate. His reaction at seeing her was strong. He knew it would be. He took her hand and held it gently.

"Bailey, friend. Welcome to my home."

"Hi, Jess. Thanks for letting us visit. I'd like for you to meet my mother, Mara Carson."

Jess was a gentleman as he took Mara by the hand and led her and Bailey inside his home. Sid followed behind, scoping the vicinity with his keen eyes. Jess led them to the main room, where he offered them a place to sit.

"Come sit, please. Mother has prepared food for your visit. I'll go get her."

Bailey tugged at his arm before he left the room. He leaned in close to her.

"Jess, how is your father?"

He smiled. "He's well and anxious to meet you."

When Jess left, Sid observed his proud stride. He admired

156

Jess Nehah but was also threatened by him. It was clear he cared for Bailey. And, even if Bailey couldn't recognize it, Jess possessed some type of hold on her. He was the kind of man a father would want his daughter to be with, only under different circumstances. Unlike Ron, he knew Jess had no self-serving motives directing him. Jess was a man unimpressed by material things in life, which meant he could never be bought or manipulated. Sid felt unsettled with a man who had both confidence and integrity.

Bailey took in the ambiance of Jess's home. She felt as though she had been taken back in time and placed in one of Dr. Claiborne's history books. It was a simple world of beauty and harmony, where everything and everyone had a purpose. The pueblos were built one upon the other, expressing a society that utilized a small area of land and built upon it a community populated with well over three thousand Zunis. Jess and his family built their pueblo outside the main village, but it was still within the boundaries of the reservation. His home, his family's pueblo, was three stories high, less elevated than the houses in the main village. Jess and his immediate family occupied the lower level of their pueblo.

Jess returned and sat next to Bailey on a wooden bench that was positioned against the wall of the room. Sid and Mara sat opposite them on two wooden rockers. On the floor spread a woven rug, designed with bright hues, made by Sadie. Several shelves hung on the walls, adorned with handmade objects either given to the family or made by the family. Hung on the walls were several of Billy's paintings. Everything in the room was pure and functional, so opposite the lavish lifestyle Bailey had known all of her life. In her eyes, it was far richer than her privileged world. It was almost sacred.

"My mother will be here shortly," Jess told the gathering. He reached to hold Bailey's hand.

Sid was anxious, tapping his foot up and down, jiggling his keys, wondering what the best course of action should be. Mara was quiet. She was studying the body language between Bailey and Jess. They couldn't keep their eyes off each other. They never spoke, but gave subtle hints as to where this relationship might lead. The silence in the room was broken when a small woman dressed in a black woven dress walked into the main room. Her long, braided hair hung down to her waist. Her smile was bright. She moved straight towards Bailey.

"Bailey," she said, brushing her cheek with a kiss, leaving upon her cheek a touch of lipstick. Sadie was a feisty beauty, with the grace and mannerisms of Jess. She turned to Sid and Mara and made her introductions.

"Welcome to our home. Welcome. Come to our kitchen where we have food and drinks for everyone. My husband and daughter will join us there."

****

Sadie guided them down a narrow hallway that led to a cozy room where a warm fire nestled in the corner. Seated at the family table was a beautiful woman just a little younger than Bailey. It was Jess's sister, Nellie. She looked much like Sadie but stood a few inches taller. Next to her sat Soll, a stocky man, probably Jess's age. Bailey recalled Jess telling her that Nellie and Soll would someday marry. At the head of the table, a friendly face smiled warmly at them. He stood to greet them and when he did, Bailey knew it was Billy Nehah. She also knew he had been ill and that he was straining to put on a good front. He wasn't strong and soon sat down, directing everyone to do the same. He looked solely at Bailey and touched the chair next to him. She sat down next to him.

"Welcome, little one. So we meet again."

Bailey studied him. His black hair was peppered with gray, but still thick and coarse. His nose was prominent and when he held his hand out for her, the warmth from his aged hands permeated through her hand. She let out a heavy sigh as if a greater presence had joined them together and was guiding their first encounter after so many years. Everyone in the room was intent on this meeting. Bailey lifted his hand to kiss it.

"I'm so happy to meet you, Mr. Nehah."

Billy smiled.

"Your eyes are filled with life."

"Yes, thanks to you."

"Not me, little one. The spirits have protected you. They have led you to me."

"Yes, I believe this, too."

"It is good that you respect them."

"I feel as though a missing piece of my life has just been found."

"Do you remember me at all?"

"My heart remembers you."

"That is much to remember for a child so young."

Billy noticed the spirit necklace she was wearing.

"A gift from my son?"

She nodded. "He gave it to me when we met in Dallas."

Bailey stroked the necklace gently.

"I think it led me to you."

He touched her head softly, remembering the first time he held her. A memory of his touch filled Bailey's mind. It was the memory of Billy carrying her and putting her in his truck. It was as vivid as if it were happening today. She stared into his black eyes.

"I remember," she whispered.

"What do you remember, child?"

"I remember my guardian spirit."

****

Sid did leave Bailey in the guardianship of Billy Nehah. He knew this would be a cathartic visit as well as a temporary place for her to be safe. It was a time for Bailey to heal and come to terms with her past. It would also allow him time to think of a permanent plan to protect his daughter. Had it not been for Billy's and Jess's encouragement, Bailey could not have said goodbye to Sid. Their departure was tearful and frightening.

"How can I leave you here? At this place? It's all too surreal."

"I'm safe, Daddy. Nothing will happen to me."

"It's so hard to let go."

"For me, too."

"Four weeks. I will come for you in four weeks."

Mara was unusually quiet in their good-bye, almost distant, as if she believed the very mother she had replaced seventeen years ago had replaced her. Bailey kissed her cheek.

"How I love my precious Mother."

Sid and Mara drove away from Bailey, who stood outside Jess's house trying to put on a confident front for them. The mystical surroundings did little to ease Sid's misgivings. Twice he almost stopped the car to return and demand that she come with him. As he moved further from her sight, he stopped the car and sat in a stupor. For a moment, he was stricken with sheer panic, remembering another he had lost to the desert. He couldn't risk losing her. As if sensing his thoughts, Mara touched him slightly.

"She'll be fine, Sid. I believe this with all my heart or I couldn't leave her. It's time to let go."

Sid leaned his head into the steering wheel and began to weep for his daughter's safety and his own inability to assure it. He wept for his beloved Kate, a woman he had loved with all of his heart. Then, a power greater than his love for Bailey overtook his fear and allowed him to let her go. He let go of seventeen years of never knowing what lay behind each day. In this moment of absolute resolution, he was able to release some of the guilt his heart harbored for Kate's death. Without question, he knew Kate was here guiding this moment. She was guiding him away from Bailey and guiding her Rebecca toward her destiny. He turned to face Mara.

"We have done what we can, Mara. The fate of our daughter is in God's hands."

# Chapter 16

The late October sky spewed an early morning snow on Denver, Colorado, covering the ground like a blanket of freshly sprinkled hope to those whose livelihood depended on it. And there was a prediction of more, several days, in fact, lending resort owners and venders an unprecedented flood of customers making reservations and buying up the recent stocks of merchandise. An early snowfall of such proportions was considered a good sign of what was yet to come. It promised to be a profitable year.

John Claiborne watched the snowfall. Strangely, he expressed little emotion at the recent snowfall, even when his solitude was interrupted by his seven-year-old son, Andrew.

"Daddy! Daddy! Do you see the snow? Wanna go out and play in it?"

Little Andrew jumped excitedly into his father's lap. Chelsea Claiborne, John's wife, trailed hurriedly behind her active son, trying to reach him before he had the chance to disturb his father.

"Andrew Claiborne! You know you aren't to bother your father while he is working."

She brushed back a line of blonde hair that had fallen out of place, a slight intrusion on a woman whose outward composure was always intact. She was a tall woman, almost six feet, yet she emitted such grace that her height was rarely considered.

"Leave the boy be. I'm not working right now. I could use a cup of coffee though."

Chelsea nodded and her steel blue eyes shot Andrew a stern glare just before she left the room to fetch John some coffee. Andrew remained perched on his father's lap.

"Mommy said the snow will make you happy."

"The snow will be good for our resort."

"Will you go to Vail?"

John nodded.

"I want to go to Vail, too."

"Not this time, Andy. Maybe next time."

"I bet Tanner gets to go."

John shook his head.

"No, Tanner won't be going either. He has school."

Andy gave a smug grin. At least this time, Tanner wouldn't be getting his father's attention either. Chelsea brought in piping hot coffee for John and sat down in a chair near the window so that she could read the paper in the morning light. She didn't notice John's drawn expression.

"Chelsea," he spoke seriously. "We have to talk."

"Sure," she said without moving her eyes from the paper.

"We have to talk now. It can't wait."

Something about his tone commanded her to look up at him.

"What is it?"

John patted Andy's head.

"Leave Mommy and Daddy to talk for a few minutes. In a little while, I'll take you out in the snow. We'll get that new sled out."

"You mean it?"

"Sure I do."

Andy bounced off his father's lap and ran out the door before his father had time to change his mind. Chelsea stood next to John curious. She repeated her question.

"What is it, John?"

He let out a deep breath.

"Sid Michaels called me yesterday."

Chelsea's mouth flew open. "My God!"

She sat in shock, not believing her own ears.

"I can't believe he has the nerve to call after all of these years and after what he did to you! Did he say what he wanted,

162

John? Has Mara finally come to her senses and left him penniless?"

John gave a short chuckle.

"Sid has plenty of his own money. He doesn't need hers. He said he wanted to talk to me about something vital. He wants to come to Denver."

"When?"

"He just said soon."

"He didn't give a clue what it was about?"

"Not one."

"I don't want you to see him. Every time Sid Michaels is around, you end up being hurt. The man is cold-hearted. I can't believe you're even considering a visit with him."

"People change, Chelsea. I did."

"John, he very nearly ruined us financially."

"Yes, but later, he finally did the right thing and sold me his half of the resort, cheap."

"The resort was yours to begin with! And the only reason he did it was Mara. She made him. Mara's money bought you out. I won't have that man in my house."

"I was feeling the same as you until I talked to Dad."

"Dad? What does he have to do with this?"

"Strangely, when I told him about the call, he said he wants me to talk with Sid."

"I don't believe this."

John looked at Chelsea. His eyes were odd-looking, registering both fear and sadness.

"What is it, John?"

"Dad thinks he's come to talk to me about Katie."

"Why, after all of these years?"

"Remember three or four years back when Dad took that temporary teaching job in Texas and moved in with Seth so he could get his farm in Bailey back on track? And when Seth's farm started prospering, remember how we thought it was strange that Dad turned down the opportunity to excavate in Mexico with some of his cronies? Especially since he lived for that kind of thing."

Chelsea nodded. "Yes, but what's this got to do with Sid?"

"Well, it seems someone very special was keeping him in Texas."

"Who, John?"

"Katie's daughter, his granddaughter, little Rebecca."

"My God, how did he find her? I mean when Sid left Denver, he took every trace of his life and Rebecca's life with him."

"It seems some three years or so ago this young woman came to Bailey, Texas, and was asking all sorts of questions. Said she was trying to find out some information about her birth or something like that. Even though her name was different, Dad knew the moment he saw her she was Rebecca. Said she was the spitting image of Katie."

"This is all so…unbelievable."

"Dad said Rebecca was asking about a Sarah Johnson, a midwife, and the worker at a local store gave him Aunt Millie's number. Evidently, Sid had concocted some story about her being born in Bailey and being delivered by Sarah Johnson. He told her she had been named after the town where she was born. Funny thing, Chelsea, is that Sarah Johnson delivered Katie when Mama couldn't make it to the hospital. You know, I think Sid told her that story in case there ever came a time she wanted to find out who she really was, she could. Either that or to keep Katie's memory alive."

"She doesn't know who she is?"

"Dad says she's known as Bailey Carson, daughter of Sid and Mara Carson."

"And Dad never told her the truth?"

"I guess he understood the urgency not to tell her."

"Because of Jack Adams," Chelsea said flatly. "That's understandable. My God, little Rebecca is living in Dallas. Thank God, Seth moved back to Bailey to farm like his granddaddy. Thank God, Byron followed him. But John, what does this have to do with Sid calling you and wanting to meet

164

with you?"

"Dad thinks that Jack Adams has found Rebecca."

"Well, I'm not surprised. Sid didn't keep her hidden too well."

"He did for seventeen years. She's a woman now, Chelsea. She had to go out on her own. Even Sid couldn't keep her under his thumb forever."

"John, do you think Jack will try to…oh, I can't think it."

John stared at her coldly.

"That's exactly what I think. I'll kill him myself if he tries to hurt her."

"Why would Jack kill her now? Why not seventeen years ago when he had the opportunity?"

"I figured he wanted to back then, but time or bad luck wouldn't let him, so he left her to die. Now he's found her and the sick bastard is after her. Damn it, Sid. Did you forget how dangerous Jack Adams is?"

****

John Claiborne treaded the snow-covered cemetery until he found marker K265. He brushed the snow aside until the entire headstone was visible to his eyes and he could read the inscription on it: *Katherine Marie Michaels – Beloved wife and Mother*. John placed a rose near the headstone.

"Roses aren't easy to come by these days, but you deserve them."

He sat down at the foot of her grave unmindful of the snow and wet earth. He didn't feel the cold wind sweep across his face. He was worn and had been since the day his sister had been murdered. He traced her name with his gloved hand.

"Oh, my sweet Katie. Your daughter is in danger again. But don't worry, my darling. Big brother won't let anything happen to her. I won't fail my duty as I did last time."

He could still hear the desperation in her voice the night she called him from Gallup seventeen years ago.

"Johnny? Johnny, it's me. Katie."

"Katie? My God, where are you?"

"In New Mexico, in a small town called Gallup. Jack's truck broke down and we'll be here a few days. Johnny – I need a favor. I need you to come to Gallup tonight."

"You're coming home! Thank God, Katie. I've been so worried. Sid's been so..."

"Has he Johnny? Has Sid been worried?"

"You have to ask? My God, he's out of his mind. How's Rebecca? She must be so scared. Has Jack hurt you or Rebecca? I'll kill him with my own hands."

"Oh, Johnny, hush and listen to me. I can't talk long, so if I hang up on you, it's because Jack's back. I've made a mess of my life. I want to make sure Rebecca's life isn't ruined because of me. I want you to come to Gallup and take her back to Sid."

"And you? I'm taking you back to Sid, too. I'm not leaving you alone with that animal."

"It's too late, Johnny. Jack would never let me go. He'd hunt me down wherever I went. That wouldn't be fair to Rebecca."

"Sid has resources. He could put you in hiding."

"No, Honey. My place is with Jack. You see – well, I'm carrying Jack's child."

"Katie, no! Not his child."

"It's true. Now can you understand why it would be impossible for me to try to leave him? Anyway, after Rebecca is safe with you, I'll tell him I let her go back to Sid so that there will be no ties left between Sid and me. Jack will be angry, but the baby will make things right."

"I'm afraid for you, Katie."

"Jack would never hurt me, Johnny. He loves me."

"But do you love him?"

"I have to go, Johnny. I think Jack's coming. I'm in a small hotel at the edge of town. It's locally owned I think. It's a Ramada. Check in under the name Joey Black. I'll be in touch with you."

"Come with me, Katie. I'll take care of you and your unborn child – even if Sid won't."

"I can't, but I love you for that. And Johnny, you must promise not to tell Sid where I'm at. It's what I want. You will promise, won't you?"

"I promise, but think about coming home with me."

"Goodbye, Johnny. See you someday. Love my sweet Johnny."

The dial tone on the phone pierced his ears. His heart was filled with an overbearing sense of responsibility and fear that he would fail at returning Rebecca to Sid, just as he had failed to convince his Katie not to leave Denver with Jack. The sharp wind brought John back to the present. Once again, he traced the inscription on her grave.

"Katie, you were always a good mother. How you loved your sweet Rebecca. Loved her till you took your last breath. I know what I have to do. I'm going to do what I should have done seventeen years ago. I'm going to find that bastard and settle the score once and for all. Sweet Katie, I'll fix it so Jack Adams can never hurt our little Rebecca, or anyone else, ever again."

John lent the October night a chilling smile.

"Crazy Johnny will make things right – for Katie – for Rebecca."

# CHAPTER 17

Jess studied Bailey's natural beauty. She had been a part of his family for four weeks. In the time that she had been with them, Jess watched as she healed. The dark mask of worry was fading. She was no longer having nightmares where Sadie or Nellie or even Jess himself had to go to her room and ease away her fears. In the beginning, she was constantly watching for a stranger to appear or for some dark omen to find her hiding and come for her. Rarely, did he hear her crying anymore or see her jump at the slightest sounds. She immersed herself in the goings-on of his family. When Billy talked to her about the Zuni culture and beliefs, she listened intently. She followed Sadie and Nellie around mimicking everything they did in an effort to learn as much as she could in the short time that she was to be with them. She asked question after question and everyone was patient to give her the answers she needed. Everyone had become attached to this tiny bird who had drifted into their world. Today, Sadie was teaching her the art of making bread.

Jess smiled as she fluttered behind Sadie. She was humming and dancing as Sadie directed her. Her long russet hair was braided like his mom's. Her feet were bare. She was wearing one of Jess's old shirts as an apron. She was a mess. She had more flour on her face and her clothing than in the dough. The floor was covered with her prints as she moved about in her bare feet. She tugged at his heart. He thought he'd never seen her look more beautiful. Billy was watching Jess watch Bailey.

"She is like a hummingbird," Billy teased.

Jess turned to face his dad. He smiled.

"She wants to know everything about us."

"You act surprised, Son."

168

He shrugged. "She will be gone soon."

Billy noted the sadness in Jess's eyes.

"She has caught your eye."

"It doesn't matter. It's an impossible situation."

"For now, but later perhaps..."

"At any time, Dad," Jess said adamantly.

Billy touched his shoulder.

"I know you care for her. Anyone can see she cares for you, too."

"She is vulnerable, Dad. She only thinks she cares. She's been through a lot and only a month ago, she was engaged. She's not thinking straight."

Billy watched Bailey as she and Sadie giggled over her futile attempt at baking.

"She is at home here, Son. Never presume what another person feels in their heart."

"Our job is to keep her safe, Dad. Soon, it will be her father's job again."

"Yes," Billy said. "I talked with her father yesterday when I was in Gallup. I convinced him to let her stay two more weeks. When we take our goods to Albuquerque, week after next, we will meet her parents there. Albuquerque will be our last trade show until after the winter."

"I am afraid, Dad. I'm afraid to let her go back to that world."

Billy let out a deep sigh of empathy.

"As I told her father, the spirits have been quiet lately. I have felt no desperate warnings. Perhaps the danger has passed."

Jess gave his dad a skeptical look.

"Is that why you carry a gun, Dad?"

Billy did not apologize for carrying the nine-millimeter gun. Jess put his arm around his dad. Billy Nehah was a man who held not a violent drop of blood within his veins. In his life, he had not once brought a hand upon either of his two children. He could not or would not kill an animal unless it was for sustenance or to protect someone he loved. Yet, he knew the graveness of Bailey's situation. He would protect her at any cost.

"What Bailey can't remember, I cannot forget."

Jess nodded in full understanding. Billy had spared Sadie and Nellie the details of Kate Michaels's murder, but Jess knew every fact. In addition to what Billy had told him, he had read the articles Bailey had shown him. Insurmountable fear kept him on alert at all times. He didn't know what he would do if something happened to her on his watch. He turned to face Bailey once more. Seeing her as she was today, she was like a child. It was hard for him to imagine anyone trying to hurt her. He balled his fist. He would die first before anyone would harm her. She happened to turn around and found him watching her. She gave him a pert smile. His smile was full of sorrow.

"Two weeks," he thought. "Two weeks and she'll be gone."

****

It was almost dark when Soll pulled his truck into the Nehah's drive. Nellie ran from the truck in tears and Soll was quick to follow. Sadie and Billy were reading in the family room. When Nellie brushed passed them without so much as a word, Billy and Sadie both looked at each other confused.

"She's upset," was all that Soll offered, as he trailed Nellie down the hall to her room.

Nellie and Soll had been in Gallup all day. They had gone to take some goods to sell at his family's trading post. Martha, Soll's mother, always said she couldn't keep Sadie's blankets in stock. As soon as she put them out, they sold. Her shop was in the heart of historical Gallup. That's where Nellie's and Soll's relationship first began to blossom. Nellie started working there when she was fifteen, mainly on Saturdays to make a few extra dollars. Soll was a few years older than Nellie and they had known each other from school. From the time they started working together, they were almost inseparable. As the years went by, there was an unspoken understanding between

170

Nellie's family and Soll's family that someday the two would be married.

"Nellie," he soothed. "It's all right. Everything will be all right."

Sadie was behind them. She saw Nellie sitting on the bed weeping. Nellie looked at her mother with eyes filled with regret and concern.

"Soll, please leave. I have to talk to Mom."

He kissed her cheek and left. Sadie sat next to her.

"What is it, Darling? Did you and Soll argue?"

Nellie shook her head.

"Something awful has happened. It's about Bailey."

"What about Bailey?" Sadie asked uneasily.

"You know Paula McPhearson who helps Martha out at the shop sometimes?"

Sadie nodded.

"Well," Nellie continued. "She was working today and was helping me unload the merchandise I had brought to sell. I unpacked the jewelry and she unpacked your blankets from the bag that Bailey let us use. You know, her black duffle bag?"

Nellie blew her nose. It was difficult for her to go on, but she had to tell her mother.

"When Paula pulled out the last blanket, something fell out of the bag. It was a large envelope. The envelope opened up and dozens of newspaper articles scattered on the floor. They were articles about Bailey's mother, you know, the one who was murdered. Paula looked at me strangely and started to read one of the articles. She told me she remembered the murder. She said she was only fourteen or fifteen, but still remembered it. She said it scared everyone in Gallup and that it was big news at the time. I quickly picked up the articles and put them away, but she kept talking about the murder."

Sadie dropped her head and shoulders, wondering what might come of this situation. Nellie proceeded to tell her more about what happened.

"Paula said there was another murder that night. She said a

man named Toby Garcia was murdered outside of his bar. She said the bar was just blocks away from Martha's shop. His murder was never solved, but the police believe that the same person who killed Bailey's mother killed Toby Garcia. Was there a connection, Mom?"

"No one ever really knew. The only thing I know is that Bailey's mother and Jack Adams and Bailey had been at Toby Garcia's bar that night. I know, because your father saw them. Did Paula say anything else?"

"She mentioned Ed Berry's name."

"The ex-police chief?" Sadie asked.

"Yeah. She said that Mr. Berry was Toby Garcia's brother-in-law and that he tried for years to find Toby's killer, but couldn't. She said it broke his heart that he never could. Did you know Ed Berry, Mom?"

"In passing," Sadie said. "I know he took care of his sister, Toby's widow, and her children. Toby Garcia's wife died several years after he was murdered, as I recall. Ed took her kids and moved them to a ranch near Arizona. Said he had to get away from all the memories."

"There's another thing, Mom. Martha happened to glance at a picture of Kate Michaels. You know, from one of the articles. She looked at me strangely, as if she was doing a double-take. She even commented that Kate Michaels looked a little like Jess's friend whom she met at our house a few weeks ago. But then she chuckled realizing that this was just a coincidence. I've never told her about Bailey's mother, but I did tell Soll. I know he has never told her about the murder, but...do you think she could possibly suspect something? Do you think she will put two and two together?"

"Why would she?"

"You know, on account of Dad being the one who found Bailey."

Sadie held onto Nellie.

"Oh, Honey, I don't think so. That was so many years ago. Only those close to the case might possibly make a connection. I think you are just shaken because of what you know."

"Mom, her murder was so awful. No one should die in such a way. I can't bear to speak of the things that happened to that poor woman. She was tortured, Mom. She was so exposed when she died. She was shot and raped and…"

"Shhh, darling, no more talk of the dead. It is bad luck. We must think of Bailey and how we can best protect her. I don't think we have anything to worry about as far as Martha is concerned, but I will talk to your father just the same. Neither she nor Paula would ever say or do anything intentionally to hurt Bailey. But, they don't know who she is. They might unknowingly tell someone something that might tip off the man who is looking for her."

"I'm afraid, Mom. This man could be watching us now. He could just be waiting for the right moment to make his move."

****

Several hours after Soll and Nellie had left for Zuni, Martha put the closed sign in the window but forgot to lock the door to the shop. Paula McPhearson had already gone home for the day. Martha was in the back putting the day's earnings in the safe when a swarthy stranger came through the door. She called out to him.

"I'm sorry but we are closed for the evening. We will open tomorrow at nine."

"I won't take but a moment of your time," he called out.

By this time, Martha had moved to the front of the store. She vaguely wondered if this man was here to rob her. He had an edge to him she did not trust. She kept her eyes intently on his actions that were suspicious and intimidating. She doubted he was a local since she knew practically everyone in Gallup. She had her cell phone in hand ready to call the police. He moved closer to her and held out a picture for her to view. It was a photograph of Bailey Carson.

"I was wondering. Do you know this woman? Have you

ever seen her?"

Martha studied the picture. Her heart was pumping wildly.

"No," Martha said shaking her head. "Should I?"

"I thought maybe you might. See, rumor has it she's a friend of your son."

"My son? I don't know what you are talking about. I've never seen her before and neither has my son. Now, I must ask you to leave."

She was lying. Her body language told him she knew more than what she was telling. His stare fell upon her trembling hands. She dropped the keys to the shop just at his feet. He retrieved them for her.

"Well," he said, handing her the keys. "I guess I was wrong. Thanks for your help."

Even as she watched the man leave, Martha's shaky hand reached for her phone. Instead of the police, she called her husband, Robert, and told him about the visitor. He told her to lock the door and he'd be there shortly. As she locked the door, she searched the area outside for the man, but he was gone. She couldn't shake the strangeness of the moment. Was she just being foolish? Her instincts told her something wasn't right.

For some odd reason, she thought of the envelope that Paula had discovered and the articles about the seventeen-year-old murder that happened near Gallup. She thought of Jess's friend Bailey and how she shared an uncanny resemblance to the murder victim. She also thought it peculiar that on the same day, and out of the clear blue, a stranger would come into her shop asking questions about Bailey. Martha wasn't even sure if Bailey was still in Zuni. She doubted that she was. Until now, she really didn't wonder why Nellie would have articles about something that happened so long ago. She assumed the articles belonged to Billy, since he had been so involved and that for some reason they had resurfaced. Martha wasn't sure what was going on, but she planned to have a long talk with Soll when he got home.

****

Robert Johnson met his wife at the front door of her shop. He wasn't alone. He brought with him Brian Charles, a local police officer. Brian looked over the place and found nothing out of the ordinary. He and Robert took a walk around the outside perimeter and saw no signs of anyone hanging about. They came inside where a shaken Martha waited anxiously. She recapped what happened, word for word, for the officer.

"I guess I let my imagination get carried away with me. You see, just today, Paula and I came across some articles about a woman named Kate Michaels who had been murdered seventeen years ago in Gallup. It was a gruesome murder. Paula and I both remembered it. I remember how scared everyone in Gallup was, afraid the killer would strike again. When the man came in tonight asking if I knew the woman in his photo, well, I was taken back. You see, the woman in the picture could have been a twin to Kate Michaels."

She told Officer Charles that she had seen the girl in the picture several weeks ago. The only thing she didn't offer was the fact that she had seen her at Nellie Nehah's home. Something told her not to tell and he didn't ask her where.

"I don't think this guy meant any harm," Brian said. "Maybe he was looking for a girlfriend or something. Just to be safe, I'll have a car drive by every couple of hours tonight and tomorrow. I seriously don't think you'll have any more trouble."

"Thank you, officer, I appreciate it," Martha said.

Brian Charles escorted Martha and Robert to their cars. He followed them home. When they were safely in the house, he went back to the shop and parked the patrol car in a secluded area in order to keep an eye on things. While he waited, he pulled out his cell phone and made a call. A raspy voice answered.

"Hello."

"Ed Berry?"

"Yeah."

"Mr. Berry, this is Brian Charles. You know, Ben Charles's son. Listen, I hope I didn't catch you at a bad time. You might not remember that I'm a police officer now. I decided to take after you and Dad. Anyway, something happened today that I think you might find interesting. It has to do with the woman who was murdered at the same time that your brother-in-law, Toby Garcia, was killed. I know how hard you and my dad tried to find the murderer. Dad's gone now, rest his soul, but it sure would be nice to finally solve this one, you know, for him and you. The information I have might not mean a thing, but then again, it could mean something."

"I laid all of this to rest, son. I'm tired and weary of chasing false leads. My heart just can't take another setback."

"Just listen to what I have to say. That's all I ask. I really can't talk now, 'cause I'm on duty, but I'd like to meet you for coffee when I get off my shift in the morning. Just coffee and a little chat, I promise. How about seven o'clock at the *Lucky Truck Stop* just outside of Gallup?"

Ed Berry let out a heavy sigh. For his sister, he knew he had to go.

"All right, but I'm a few hours away. Let's make it eight. Oh, and Brian, don't tell anyone about this just yet. Not until we've talked. If it's nothing, I plan to go right back into seclusion. If it's something, this kind of thing has to be handled properly."

"Sure thing, Mr. Berry. See you tomorrow at eight."

****

Darkness filled the night sky and dwelled inside the room where Bailey slept. A soft flow of moonlight managed its way through the window and swept across her face. Jess sat next to her bed and watched her sleep for a while before he had to awaken her.

"I'm sorry my cherished friend," he said to himself. "I have to take you away."

176

He brushed back a fallen strand of her hair and studied her face, so innocent, yet so sensual. His first impulse was to lie next to her, hold her, and declare his feelings for her. He resisted. His heart was breaking. The events of the day were forcing this moment. He had to take her further into hiding. His home was no longer safe. When he took her hand, her eyes opened slightly.

"Jess?"

"I'm here, yes. I hope I didn't frighten you."

"What is it? Was I having another dream?"

Without realizing it, he brought her hand to his mouth and kissed it. She looked at him confused, but even in the darkness, she could see worry on his face. Without thought, she fell into his arms. He held on tightly to her.

"Jess," she whispered. "You're upset, I can tell."

"I'll explain everything later, but we have to leave."

"Leave? Why, Jess? Is Jack Adams here?"

"I don't know. Maybe."

He held her tightly and the two sat silently in the reality of this dark hour. They both knew that this moment had always been a possibility, but prayed it wouldn't happen. Holding Jess, Bailey seized the moment, feeling his warmth, smelling his natural scent. Reluctantly, she moved from his arms to face him. Without reason, she brushed his lips softly.

"I'm so lucky to have you, Jess," she declared. "If this nightmare ends badly, I want you to know that..."

Jess stopped her words by putting his hand on her lips. His anger flared.

"No more such talk, Bailey. We must pack and leave."

His words were strained. He fought for composure. He stood and lit the small lamp next to her bed and reached into a nearby closet for her bags. He began throwing her things inside of them. His emotions and ineptness surfaced. He was literally shaking. Bailey stepped out of bed and took control. Understanding the urgency of the moment, she got dressed and helped him collect her things. It wasn't long before the two were in Jess's truck and driving away from his home. There were no goodbyes from Billy or Sadie or Nellie. She never saw them. He drove down a dark path that led to the back of the reservation and further into the dark desert. The area was so isolated that only someone who really knew it well could follow it without getting lost. She didn't question where they were going or why she felt safe in the keeping of this man who had somehow drifted into her life. She leaned her head against the back of the seat. She felt of the spirit necklace around her neck and in the darkness of the night, she surrendered her heart. She looked at Jess and broke the silence.

"I love you," she said.

Then, it was silent again.

# CHAPTER 18

Sid listened intently as Billy relayed the recent happenings to him and told him that Jess had taken Bailey further into hiding. Billy could sense the fear and hostility in Sid's voice. He understood well his helplessness. He had felt the same emotions.

"Bailey is safe for now, but I don't know for how long. Jess has taken her to my brother, Coyote's, home far into the desert near Arizona. Few people know its whereabouts. Still, I think it's best you come for her. I feel a dire stirring within me and the spirits are calling for her father's powerful hand. I'm not sure that Bailey is Jack Adams's primary target."

"Who then?" Sid asked.

"I believe it is her father. He wants to find Bailey, yes, but he demands a confrontation with you. My heart tells me this."

"Then by all means," Sid's wrathful voice charged. "Let's give the sonofabitch what he wants. I'll be in Gallup before Jack Adams has time to realize he's called for me."

\*\*\*\*

Sid and Mara walked side-by-side, ankle-deep in the freshly fallen New Mexico snow.

"Our plans have changed Mara. I must get Bailey. I know we had planned to get her in a couple of weeks, but a situation has come up. Jack knows where Bailey is, or at least he knows the general area where she is. He is close to her. I'm flying to Gallup today."

"I'm going with you," she insisted.

"No, I'm flying you to Dallas. Sammy will meet you there.

You'll stay with him and Diane."

"But," she cried out. "Bailey is my daughter, too. I love her as much as you do. She needs me! I'm the only mother she's ever known!"

"I know, Darling. Later, I will send her to you, but I can't be worried about you both. Hell, as crazy as Jack is, he's bound to come after you, too."

"I don't believe that. He could have done that a long time ago if that's what he really wanted."

"Things are different now, Mara. He knows his days are numbered and what's scary is he's okay with being taken out. He just wants to go out in glory. He wants to destroy everyone I love. Mara, there's something I need from you. A promise I hope you can keep."

"What is it, Sid?"

He was worn. His voice was cold, void of emotion.

"I've spent the last seventeen years living like a time bomb. I've had to look over my shoulder just waiting for Jack to find us, to find our baby. I've reached the end of the road, Mara. I'm tired and I've made a decision."

"What decision? You're frightening me, Sid."

He continued, unaffected by her obvious distress.

"I'm going to Gallup and I'm going to find Jack Adams. When I do, I'm going to kill him. If I succeed, and I pray I do, I'm certain to go to jail. Or, I will have to go into hiding. I need a promise from you."

She stared at him disbelieving. He continued his oration.

"I need you to be strong for Bailey. She'll need you and Sammy more than ever, especially you. She'll be lost and frightened and angry with me. She'll be filled with questions about her past. I want you to tell her everything.

"I realize what I'm asking is painful for you. I'm just too far spent to consider anything but Bailey's welfare at this point. When this is over, I want you to find Byron Claiborne, Kate's father. Explain why I had to do the things I did. He'll help you with Bailey. He's a good man.

"I've been working with my lawyers and updated our will. Of course, you will receive the bulk of our estate and one hundred percent of my business holdings overseas. As you know, I've already started the paperwork to give Johnny Claiborne my real estate holdings in Colorado and New Mexico. We laid out the plans when I visited him several weeks ago. If truth be known, I should have done this after Kate's death. The remaining assets will be divided equally between Bailey and Sammy, just as we had planned. I'll need your signature to make it legal, so I'm sending it to Dallas. You need to sign it as soon as you arrive. All of this will only happen upon my incarceration, or my sudden disappearance, or my death."

Mara couldn't believe the coldness in his voice. When she spoke to him, her own voice was soft and barely audible.

"What a cold bastard you are. Did you ever once consider the effects this decision will have on Bailey? On me? Do we mean so little to you that you are willing to destroy your family? Isn't it enough what Jack has already done? Sid, it's too late in the game to think you could take him out anyway. You're just not capable."

Sid laughed and his laughter cut through the air.

"You're probably right, Mara, but Jack won't be expecting me to come after him myself. He'll be expecting a hired man. No, Mara, I can't rest until I'm face to face with Jack, even if this means I have to go out with him."

Mara slapped Sid across the face with all of her might. Anger consumed her.

"Damn you, Sid Michaels! I'll kill you myself before I let you go, before I let you do this to us."

Once again, she slapped him. Then, she struck his chest with her fists until she had no energy to do it any longer. She fell to her knees in the frozen snow and sobbed for the fate of her husband, her child, herself. She always knew this day would come, but she wasn't prepared for it. She couldn't bear the thought of never seeing Sid Michaels again. He lifted her up into his arms.

"Darling, Mara."

"Sid, have you ever loved me?"

"What a foolish question. Of course, I love you."

"But never the way you loved Kate. Never with such passion. Never so eternal."

"Mara," he drew her even closer to him. "Let's go inside. We need our time for goodbye."

She fought him for a moment, but only for a moment.

"Sid, I want our farewell to be absent of Kate. I want it to be our time only. Let go of her just this once."

"No ghost," he promised.

He brushed her lips passionately. For the first time in seventeen years, he allowed himself to feel the love he had for Mara. There was no guilt. No haunting memories of a past love. Only irrefutable love for a woman who had loved him with all her heart and soul. She had loved only him – just him– not Jack Adams, too. Mara – unlike Kate – had always been faithful to Sid Michaels.

****

Bailey's nightmare returned. She was four again, hidden in the dark wet ravines of the desert. And like this four-year-old child, an adult Bailey was fear-struck, huddled in a fetal position within the dark compounds of a strange room. As vividly as if she were living her past for the first time, an ominous flash of memory came back to haunt her.

She heard the clamoring of intrusive footsteps on the wet earth and when she peered above the jagged rut where she was hidden, she saw a dark monster, towering over her mommy. Her mommy was still, so very still. By the light of the shallow moon, four-year-old Rebecca sat breathless as she saw the monster abandon her mommy to search for her. She watched him move in and out of the shadows of the night as he made his search and called out to her.

"Rebecca," his strident voice called out. "I know you're out there. Come to me. Don't be afraid. I won't hurt you. I want to help you."

"No," a voice inside of her warned. "Mommy said to stay hidden."

To her, his voice was like a drum's echo, deafening and overpowering. In actuality, his voice whispered to her, not wanting to attract attention. In the course of his search, little Rebecca had grown weary from fear. Shock had left her immobile. She had reached the end of this macabre drama she was forced to act out. Desperate, she wanted her mommy. She wasn't dead. She was just sleeping. Her tiny voice called out, "Mommy," but it was never heard. The assault was over. The dark figure moved once again over her mommy's mangled body kicking it as if she were garbage.

"Well," his cold voice declared. "I guess there's nothing more to do here."

He left little Rebecca to die alongside her mommy. Bailey cried out, stirring from her nightmare. As in long ago, gentle hands rescued her. Jess held her tight.

"Hush, my darling. You're safe. I'm here. I'll always be here."

****

Coyote, Billy's brother, was whittling the roots of a yucca plant and dropping the shavings into a pot of boiling water. Bailey stood at the entrance of the stucco dwelling watching him in amazement. She was weary and worn out. She felt eighty instead of twenty-one. She scoped the land, vaguely remembering coming here in the late of night. Coyote had welcomed them without question and made his home their home. Bailey studied him as he stooped over the fire. He was smaller than Billy, more weathered by the desert sun, but their smiles were the same. He lived alone and rarely left the boundaries of his humble two-room stucco house. Bailey thought Billy and Coyote were much like hidden treasures buried away undiscovered.

When they arrived in the late of night, Jess had made them a pallet on the floor in the main room. He slept next to her, unwilling to let her out of his reach. She wondered when he had awoken and left her side. Again, her eyes coursed the vast desert land. Judging by the direction of the sun, she knew morning had long since passed. Without looking up at her, Coyote spoke to her but continued to whittle.

"I boil this medicine for your headaches."

"My headaches?"

He nodded. "My nephew tells me they happen often."

Bailey actually rubbed her head.

"It's just that sometimes I have trouble sleeping."

"Your spirit is not at rest. You cannot sleep when your spirit is not resting. I do understand. My wife, bless her soul, used to be restless like you. Maybe restlessness comes naturally to the white blood."

"Jess told me your wife was from California."

"Yes," he nodded and then chuckled. "Her name was Linda. Sometimes I think she was more Zuni than me. She understood the heart of my people. Her heart was as wide as the desert, much like yours."

Bailey smiled. "How can you tell what's in my heart? You don't know me."

"I know my nephew. I know my brother. Through them, I know your heart."

Bailey thought of Jess and about the time she had spent with his family. She had not been off the Zuni Reservation for four weeks. In truth, she really had no desire to leave. Each day was a new discovery and she had grown to love the people who had so graciously taken her under their wings. To say that she owed them for everything they had done for her was an understatement. How could she possibly thank them for all they had done? She couldn't. She knew she had put their lives in jeopardy and yet they embraced her, cared for her, and treated her as if she were part of their family. Now she was

184

putting Coyote's life in danger.

She missed her parents desperately and the freedom to live her life as she pleased, but she was reluctant to face her uncertain future. She felt safe in Jess's land. In the time she'd been with the Nehahs' she had escaped her reality temporarily. She was captivated by the dynamics of Sadie's and Billy's relationship, so different from her parents'. Sadie, unlike Mara, was outgoing and playful. She openly expressed her devotion to Billy. He was the center of her world and she wasn't ashamed to show her love. Jess and Nellie were an extension of this love. It was so foreign to Bailey. She tried to remember a time when her parents had shown such affection around her, but couldn't. Not once had she known her mother to be involved in her father's business affairs. Although they had been completely devoted to her, they did so separately. Coyote interrupted her thoughts when he handed her a concoction of milk and yucca and flour and lily onion.

"Here, drink this. For your headache."

She drank it without argument. Anything was worth a try to be rid of her headache. Surprisingly, it wasn't bad tasting. She handed the empty cup to Coyote and happened to stare in the direction of a moving truck. Without wondering, she knew it was Jess. Her eyes never veered from him as she watched him get out of his truck and walk in her direction. She was thinking she had never seen anyone so handsome and wondered how she ever thought she had loved Ron. She tried to picture Ron in her mind, his sandy hair and blue eyes, but the image was blurred. When Jess smiled at her, all thoughts of Ron faded. He leaned, kissed the top of his uncle's head, and then reached for Bailey's hand.

"Sleeping Beauty awakes."

His smile made her weak. Jess found a small stool near the side of the house. He led Bailey to Coyote and directed her to sit down. He sat on the dry earth next to her, pouring himself a cup of coffee that Coyote had brewing on the fire. He offered her a cup, but she shook her head.

"My uncle keeps coffee brewing all day long. It's his one vice."

Coyote snorted. "I've many habits my nephew doesn't know about."

Bailey smiled. She squeezed Jess's hand. Her sunken eyes searched his. They held the same worry. Coyote turned to Jess.

"All is quiet?" he asked.

Jess nodded.

"That is good."

Bailey looked at Jess for direction.

"Where do we go from here?"

"We wait," he said. "Dad will come and let us know what to do."

"Waiting is wise," Coyote agreed, "but it can also be foolish without a plan."

Jess studied his uncle. Except for his father, he couldn't think of anyone else whose opinion he valued more.

"What's on your mind, Uncle?"

"My wife, may she rest in peace, loved our simple life. She never asked for much, just what she needed on her back and in her belly. When we had more than we needed, she would give to the community. Sometimes though, she missed the life she left behind. I understood and let her go back to it for a while."

"Are you suggesting I send Bailey back to her world?"

"It could be," he paused to feed the fire with some loose twigs. "Linda and I built a small ranch house just outside of Tucson. That is where she would go from time to time. It has all the comforts of her former life. Sometimes I go there, too. Not so much as when she was alive. So many times, I thought of selling it, but I held on to it. A soul can get lost there."

Jess nodded understanding that his uncle was offering another place to hide Bailey.

"This is a consideration, Uncle."

"I have another idea," Bailey offered.

The two looked in her direction.

"I could go public. I could get help from the police and tell my story. I'm tired of running and hiding as if I've done something wrong."

Coyote studied her demeanor and wondered if she had the strength to face a man like the one Jess had told him about this morning. Outwardly, she looked like a delicate flower, but inside he sensed she was a woman full of strong courage and conviction. He believed she was underestimated.

"It is a good suggestion," Coyote said.

He stood and brushed the earth from his jeans.

"I will leave for Zuni today. I will go to my brother. We will discuss this matter together. I will not come back tonight, but tomorrow. Upon my return, if you are gone, I will know your decision."

He moved his aged hand over Bailey's cheek and kissed it gently.

"Peace, my child. I wish you peace."

Bailey watched Coyote move slowly toward the house. His slumped body appeared worn and haggard. Still, she thought she had never seen anyone nobler. When Coyote disappeared, she turned toward Jess.

"I love your family, Jess."

While she truly adored his family, what she was really saying was that she loved him. She wasn't sure he felt the same. She had spoken the words last night and he had kept silent. Perhaps he only felt toward her the way a friend feels toward a friend. She didn't press the issue. She wasn't sure her heart could take such a disappointment today—maybe on another day, but not right now. So she didn't speak what her heart felt. She did speak about the darkness that held her captive day after day.

"What happens if Jack Adams decides to go into obscurity once more? He might just go into hiding and wait for another opportune time. Will I live my whole life waiting on Jack Adams? I think we should leave for Tucson right now."

Jess stared into the fire. It was difficult to know what Jack Adams's next move would be, but he did know one thing. Jack

Adams would not go into hiding again. Jess also knew that this was the prime time for him to find Bailey, if given the opportunity. He stood up and reached for her. She stood next to him. They held each other for some time, locked in a hopeless dilemma, unable to escape the inevitable or the strong bond between them. Her heart hammered in her chest when she felt his kiss on her head. She wanted to live in this moment forever. He lifted her head and held her face in his hands, kissing her gently. Though it was a soft kiss, she understood its meaning. When Jess broke the spell of this kiss, she laid her head on his chest, finally finding the peace Coyote had wished upon her. If she died tomorrow, she knew her heart would leave this earth full. Each moment of her life from this point on would be a testament to this new found love. He spoke to her in a resolved tone.

"Tomorrow we leave for Tucson. Today we exchange worry for love."

# CHAPTER 19

Sid's plane left for Gallup on time, but Mara had to wait for her flight – and wait – and wait. While she waited, her mind relived her last moments with the man she had loved so deeply, so unconditionally. Still loved. Still needed. She flushed back the tears that began to swell in her eyes. God, this was hard. Letting him go. Could she? She had let him go a million times before. But, this was different. This time was so – well – so final. She might never see him again. Probably, she would never see him again. Her heart stopped on that thought. Sid was no match for Jack Adams. He never had been. Sid never won where Jack Adams was concerned.

Through her thought process, she haphazardly picked up a newspaper that was stuffed in the corner of the seat where she sat and scanned the front page. There, in bold print, the *Albuquerque Sun* presented to her an article on Kate's murder. As if by some mystical channeling, it too seemed to understand her turmoil, knew what was on her mind. She skimmed over the print, unable to focus on its content. Hadn't she read a hundred, a thousand, articles on Kate's murder before? This one was no different. The only new feature that registered in her mind was a recent composite of Jack Adams. He was absent the usual beard and mustache that so defined him in the early years.

The artist tried to convey an older Jack Adams, a man who had aged seventeen years. As she gazed at the sketching of the man who had haunted her life and her family's life for so long, his accursed eyes penetrated her being—those cold calculating eyes. Dear Lord, she thought, he's going to kill Sid. Kill Bailey. Just the way he had killed Kate. She couldn't sit by and let that happen. Not to those she loved the most. She had to think of something to do.

She folded up the newspaper and her thumb rested on the name of the journalist who had written the article. Red Benning? Red Benning? Where had she heard that name before? Then it came to her. He was the journalist who had contacted Bailey in the hospital. She recalled Bailey telling her that he had been following Kate's murder all of these years and the trail of murders that followed hers. Mara grew increasingly fearful. A trail of murders. Would her family someday be part of that trail? Just then, she heard the call for her flight to Dallas. Halfway to the plane, she stopped and ran in the opposite direction.

Remembering that Red Benning worked for the *Los Angeles Times*, she went to a payphone and called information. She stared at the number for the Los Angeles newspaper for some time before she mustered the courage to call. As her adrenaline pumped, she punched in the numbers. Then, she heard her voice ask to speak to Red Benning. After what seemed a lifetime of waiting, a deep, throaty voice said, "Hello."

In all of her life, Mara had never done anything so brave, so impulsive. She clutched the phone. She couldn't speak. What was she doing? How did she think he could help? Just before hanging up, she saw a flash of Jack Adams the last time she had seen him, just a day before he and Kate left Denver together. He was sitting at his desk in the office he and Sid shared, peeling an orange with his pocketknife. She had come to the office looking for Sid, but had found Jack instead.

She'd met him a few times before when she was with Sid. She never liked him and was sure he didn't like her. Still, they served each other well. She was Sid's gal on the side, his mistress. Jack had kept Kate occupied so that she could be with Sid. It was a tidy, unspoken arrangement, but she always felt obligated to him. She remembered him moving toward Sid's desk where he picked up a framed picture of Kate and put it in a duffel bag. Then, he came within inches of her, his left hand holding the pocketknife.

He brought it within a breath of her throat. She stood stone-cold with fear. Then, he did a peculiar thing. He drew her in his arms and kissed her, like a starved animal who had finally found food. He moved his kiss down her bare neck. He lent her a menacing grin. Then, he pushed her away.

"Tell Sid, that's what I'm doing with his wife. Tell him that Kate belongs to Jack Adams now."

Mara could still smell the aroma of orange. Her mind jolted. Somewhere between her past and present, her bedraggled state heard the voice on the phone shout, "Hello, damn it! Is someone there?"

Her meek voice spoke out. "Yes, Mr. Benning?"

"Yeah. Yeah. This is Benning. Who is this?"

She cleared her throat.

"You don't know me. It's crazy of me to be calling you. But…," her voice cracked. "Dear God, I need your help. My family needs your help."

"Who is this?"

His abrupt tone sent her trembling. Once again, she almost hung up. Then, his tone changed.

"Sorry, Ma'am. I've had a bad morning. How can I help you? How can Red Benning help you?"

"I'm not sure you can. I'm hoping you can. I'm so scared, so very scared for my family."

"Do I know your family?"

"In a way, yes. You see, my husband was once married to Kate Michaels. I think you're familiar with her."

Red Benning stopped dead in his tracks. His heart was pumping wildly. He was the one now who couldn't speak. Mara understood his shock. She took control of the conversation.

"I'm Mara Carson. You met my daughter in Dallas - Bailey. Anyway, I know how much interest you have in this case. That's why I'm calling you. I need help from someone who knows the details, knows the danger involved. Dear God, Mr. Benning, he's found my baby. Jack Adams has found my baby. He may even have her by now. Sid, my husband has gone for her, b…b…but…," she bellowed into the phone, losing her composure. Benning was quick to intervene.

"Get control of yourself, Mrs. Carson. I need some information. Things are a bit muddled to me, but I'm starting to get the picture. When I met your daughter, she said she was going off to be with you. She said something about your being extremely ill."

"Oh," she sniffed. "I was never ill. That was our way of taking her into hiding. I'm afraid we didn't do a very good job though."

To himself, he thought: "You did a damn good job." To Mara, he said: "Let's skip forward a little, okay? You say Jack Adams has found your daughter. How do you know this?"

"Does it matter? I just do!" She began to get hysterical again. "And my husband has gone to kill him! And…and…I'm afraid he's going to be…killed!"

A woman standing next to Mara overheard her distress and offered comfort. Mara fell into the stranger's arms. The stranger took the phone and spoke to Red.

"I'm afraid your party is too upset to speak right now. I'm just a person who was using the phone next to her. Has something tragic happened? A death?"

"You might say that. It's very important that I speak with her. Has she calmed down any?"

"A little." The woman asked Mara, "Can you speak yet? How about I get you some coffee?"

Mara nodded. "Thank you." She took the phone and the woman went to get the coffee.

"Mr. Benning," Mara said weakly. "I'm sorry. I'm afraid I'm on the edge."

"I understand that. Where are you?"

"In Santa Fe, New Mexico, but I'm to fly to Dallas today."

"And your husband?"

She whimpered but took control of her outburst. "He's on a plane headed to Gallup, New Mexico."

"Gallup," Benning's voice whispered triumphantly.

"Yes," she continued. "That's where Jack Adams is."

"You're sure?"

"Yes. He's been identified."

Red let out a large sigh. If what she is saying were true, he really had seen a ghost in Dallas. He doubted it was possible, though.

"And Bailey? Is she in Gallup, too?"

"No. Quite frankly, I don't know where she is. She was moved from her last hiding place. My husband doesn't even know where she is."

"Do your husband's men have her?"

"In a way, yes. She's with an Indian family."

Red let out another sigh. "You said you're on your way to Dallas, right?"

"Yes."

"Tell you what. Give me your Dallas number. I'm going to do a few things around here and then I'm heading for Gallup myself. I'll call you when I get there. If there's anything you forgot to tell me, you can tell me then."

Mara gave Red Sammy's Dallas number. For a moment, there was a silent void between them. Then, Mara asked.

"Mr. Benning, do you think we should call the police?"

"Let me handle those details."

"Can you help us, Mr. Benning?"

"Yes, I can. This is the break I needed, Mrs. Carson."

"Don't let him hurt my family, Mr. Benning. Please don't let him hurt my family."

"Rest assured, Mrs. Carson. When I'm finished with Jack Adams, he won't be able to hurt another person again."

Then, Mara heard the phone click. There was a dead silence. The silence made her cringe. She heard Sid's warnings.

"Trust no one. Trust no one. Trust no one."

His presage brought on another outpouring. Behind her stood the woman who had earlier comforted her. She was holding two cups of coffee and wearing a sympathetic face. It was the kind of face that made a person let go of their reserve. It was just the right face that Mara needed to see her through the next hours. Mara reached for the coffee.

"Thanks a bunch. I have change in my purse."

"Forget it."

The tall stranger touched Mara's coat sleeve and nudged her in the direction of two empty seats in the corner of the boarding area marked gate 28B.

"Let's talk," the stranger said.

Mara nodded.

"My name is Claire Brennen. I know you don't know me from Adam, but if you don't mind my saying so, you look like you could use a friend right now."

"You're very kind," Mara said, reluctant to offer Claire her name. Claire didn't press her.

"Look," Claire continued. "I hope you don't think I'm being nosy, but I really couldn't help but to overhear some of your conversation. I'll be truthful with you. What I did hear scared the hell out of me. And I can see it has you pretty shaken, too."

"Oh, I'll be all right."

Mara's words did not convince Claire that she would be all right. Her hands were shaking and her lips bleeding from where she had bitten them. Claire took the coffee from Mara's grip and placed both cups on the floor near the seats. She held onto Mara's hands tightly. Her voice grew assertive and she spoke pointedly to Mara.

"From what I was able to grasp from your conversation, I believe you and your family are in serious trouble. I hope for your sake you have contacted the police and told them your story."

Mara let out a quick chuckle, trying desperately to make light of the situation.

"I'm not certain of what you thought you overheard, but I assure you, I'm just fine. My family is just fine."

Without hesitation, Claire blurted out, "I'm a psychologist. I know distress when I see it. I also know fear. Your face is consumed with it."

194

Mara held her hand over her mouth, "Dear God! Oh, God!"

The outburst she had tried so diligently to suppress came forth and Mara once again fell into the stranger's arms. Claire Brennen eased Mara's agony by rocking her and whispering, "There, there."

Then, she gripped her so tightly, Mara let out a sharp, "Ouch!"

"Listen to me and listen to me good."

Claire held out a badge for Mara to see. It identified her as Officer Claire Brennen. Mara stared at her bewildered and somewhat betrayed.

"I thought you said you were a psychologist."

"I am. I work for the Albuquerque Police Department."

Mara rolled her eyes. Her face went a placid white.

"This conversation is over."

Claire pressed on.

"I work for the police, but my first priority is to my patients. I would never betray a confidence."

"No disrespect, but I'm not your patient."

"Let me help you."

Mara stood up and started to walk away.

"Thanks for the coffee."

Claire called out to her and her words stabbed at Mara's gut.

"My husband was killed ten years ago. I wish to God someone had been there to help me. I wish someone had been there to point out the signs prior to his murder so that I could have prevented it. Now, these signs seem so damn clear. But I didn't have anyone to help me see them. No one was there to tell me the best steps to take. You have that someone. Let me help you."

"I can't," Mara whispered. "I can't."

Mara happened to glance at the Departure signs and noticed that the plane she was to take to Dallas had not departed, but had once again been delayed. Without looking at Claire, she darted toward the information desk. Claire trailed behind her.

"Is it too late for me to catch the plane for Dallas? I've cleared security. I have a boarding pass."

The attendant picked up a phone and in a minute or so answered Mara's question.

"You can still board."

Mara caught a side-glance of Claire Brennen and saw the pity registered on her face. She pleaded to Mara one final time.

"Please let me help you."

Again, Mara heard Sid's voice: "Trust no one. Trust no one. Trust no none."

Mara looked into Claire's eyes and, for a moment, their thoughts connected and Mara knew Claire understood fully her plight. Still, there was no time to place her trust in this stranger. She had to get to Dallas, to Sammy. Sammy would take her to Gallup. Sammy would help her. In the meantime, she had to rely on the wit and experience of an aged reporter from Los Angeles. This thought calmed her. Mara squeezed Claire's hand.

"I'm sorry about your husband. Thank you for caring."

Then she walked speedily down the hallway that led to her plane. Claire watched her small frame carry the weight of her ordeal and the dark horror of her own past flashed before her. Mara was a stranger to Claire, but they walked on familiar ground. Claire couldn't let this matter go without doing everything she possibly could. Hadn't she dedicated the past ten years of her life to helping such victims? Facts and names rushed through her mind as she tried to recall the jest of the woman's conversation. Claire had a sharp memory. She was like a computer when it came to retaining names and numbers.

"Her name is Mara Carson," Claire recalled. "Her husband's name is Sid." She jotted the names down as fast as she was able to remember them. Then, she called her secretary.

"Greg, see what you can dig up on a few names I'm going to throw at you, Sid Carson, Mara Carson, Bailey Carson, Jack Adams, and Kate Michaels. Also, see if you can match a phone number to a name. It's a Dallas area number. It's 555-2323. Oh, I

196

almost forgot. See what you can dig up on a man named Red Benning. I think he must be a reporter or a journalist."

"Not *the* Red Benning?" His voice shrieked in surprise.

"You know him?"

"Gee, Claire, everyone knows him. He used to work here in Albuquerque a hundred years ago. He's pretty renowned, you know."

"Is he? I didn't know. Anyway, see what you can find out about him. You know, his family and stuff like that. I should be back to my office by noon today. Get with it as soon as we hang up, Greg. It's pretty important."

"Sure thing, boss. Oh, Mrs. Lopez came by today. She joined the victims' group."

"Great!" Her strident voice screeched. "That's one more for our side. Bye now. See ya after a bit."

Claire waited until the plane that took Mara Carson to Dallas lifted. When it was completely out of sight, she made her way to her own plane that would take her to Albuquerque. On her flight, she prayed for the safety of Mara Carson and that of her family.

****

Red Benning packed quickly and efficiently, a standard acquired from years of living out of a suitcase and away from home. In his forty-some years as a reporter, he'd lived more than half of them in a strange motel room, feeling more at home in these rooms than he did in his own place. He packed the usual, his laptop, his favorite coffee mug, his outdated blue-wool suit, his Dodger cap, and his 1967 Arnold Palmer putter. He packed a carry-on briefcase that held the many files connected with Kate Michaels's murder and those murders that seemingly matched hers. He threw in a tape recorder and some blank tapes, along with his camera. Another bag held his handgun, its shells, and a bulletproof vest that would have to be registered with the airport security, an inconvenient but necessary precaution he had learned to take after being shot at several times while on assignment.

He called his neighbor and, as usual, the neighbor promised to check in on Red's apartment every couple of days and let the maid in to tidy up the place while he was away. Six hours after receiving Mara Carson's call, Red Benning was boarding a flight from Los Angeles to Albuquerque, New Mexico. On the plane, he ordered a martini. He had his wits about him, but he was cautious, almost to the point of paranoia. The case had taken its toll on his sixty-year-old body. He knew he had to end this soon. He knew he couldn't take much more. His only prayer was to reach Bailey Carson before it was too late.

His hands clutched the martini and began to shake as he thought of Jack Adams. His stomach was a pit of knots and churns. Could he face this resurrected devil, if he did exist, once more? He thought of Kate Michaels and Bailey and the irony of the present setting. The scene was identical, too damn gruesome to be humane. But here it was and here he was. He was heading toward the exact place where Kate Michaels had been killed. There, he would find her daughter.

Jesus, he couldn't make his hands stop shaking, so he conceded to it and put down his drink. He closed his eyes and tried to find rest. A stewardess laid a blanket over him and turned out the overhead light. He happened to glance up at her and she was smiling down at him. He smiled back and once again closed his eyes. He retained the image of her soft brown eyes and silky blonde hair. He thought of Bailey Carson and his intended goal. He would get to her first. Sid Michaels would take care of Jack Adams. With this assurance, he fell asleep with a smile on his face.

# CHAPTER 20

Sid arrived in Albuquerque at six p.m. on the first day of November. When his plane landed, he had an ominous pitted reaction to the familiar surroundings. It was much the way he felt when he had arrived seventeen years ago. He gripped a black leather carry-on in his hand and moved down the walkway, immediately noticing Billy Nehah. Billy looked frayed and worried, but then again, didn't everyone involved? Sid thought of Mara and he suddenly longed for her arms, for her timorous smile. He chuckled to himself at the thought of him drawing strength from Mara, a woman who'd always needed constant care and reassurance.

Sid and Billy shook hands and then moved toward the luggage pick-up, where along the way, Billy filled him in on the details of the last week. Bailey was safe – for now. She and Jess were near Arizona, only fifty or so miles from Gallup, hidden so deeply into the desert, only those who knew the area well could find it. Even upon directions, old Coyote's house could be difficult to find. It was built amid the mesas of the desert, made of the same red earth, blending in as though the same architect who molded the red tundra carved it.

As Billy drove Sid to Gallup, they talked more, deciding not to go to Bailey right away. Sid had other things to tend to first. He elected not to stay at Billy's but chose instead, the same motel in which Jack and Kate had supposedly stayed. It was under a new name and had been completely remodeled. Sid wanted to get into the mind of Jack Adams. Not that he thought Jack would be there. He knew he wouldn't. He was too smart. Sid wanted to understand the mindset of a madman. He wanted to feel the pulse of a murderer.

At the motel, Sid put the key to room 42 in the keyhole and turned the knob. Inside, he found a modest room with a double bed, a small wooden table, and two chairs. There was a nightstand, a TV, a phone and a bathtub stained from years of use. Unlike the usual accommodations he was accustomed to when traveling, Sid felt strangely at home in such surroundings. They seemed to ignite his purpose, bringing him back to a time before he had money. It was a time when all he had to rely on was Sid Michaels and the instincts street life had given him.

He showered and called Sammy. He wanted to hear Mara's voice. There was no answer, so he guessed they were at the airport still or maybe out to eat. He lay on the bed and lit a cigarette, thinking to himself how he really needed to slow down. He drew in a deep drag and for no particular reason, probably his thought processes tonight, he began blowing smoke rings into the air. He counted how many he could make from one drag. He thought of Kate and how she used to beg him to entertain her this way.

When they first met, he always had his cigarettes tucked in the rolled-up sleeve of his t-shirt like Brando or Dean. She couldn't resist moving her hands over the hard muscles of his arms and chest, fondly calling him her Marlboro Man. Sid flexed an arm and the muscles that were once so rigid, now hung loosely from years of neglect. He laughed at himself.

"Look at your Marlboro Man now, Kate." He consoled himself. "Hell, look how Brando aged. Even I look better than that. That's what happens to men when they grow old."

Then, he thought of Jack, always obsessed with his body, the way a mechanic was obsessed with cars. If he knew Jack, he'd be in mint condition, both body and mind. There was never anything soft about Jack Adams. Sid had little reason to believe the years had changed him. Jack Adams was a hard man. Hard body. Hard heart. Hard mind. Sid flinched, catching a glimpse of his slightly protruding middle. He jumped out of bed and stood erect, alert and suddenly aware of his vulnerability. He didn't even have a gun yet to make the odds even. What a fool he was, dashing off half-cocked to be rid of a man, who even in his prime, he couldn't be rid of. Then it occurred to him. He had power over Jack Adams. The ace was in his hand, the ball in his court. He had what Jack wanted. He had Bailey. At least for now, he did.

Sid thought. "Can I really use Bailey for bait? If I do, she stands the chance of being killed. If I don't, she might be able to elude Jack for a time, but knowing Jack, he'd find her and kill her sooner or later."

Sid opened the curtain slightly and peered into the darkened night. Using Bailey as bait was total insanity and he knew he could never do it. He'd have to think of another way to get to Jack. In the bleak darkness, he felt an odd sensation filter through him, a comforting one just the same. He let out a heavy sigh. She was here. Kate was here. Or maybe she wasn't and he had finally gone off the deep end.

He felt a hand touch his thick mass of hair and then gentle fingers massaging it softly. He closed his eyes and smelled rose attar. Kate's smell. His weary heart was now feeling an internal peace and he edged his way to the bed where he could still feel her touch. He dared not to open his eyes for fear she would leave. Just as he was about to drift away, he felt soft lips upon his lips. Tears fell down the sides of his face. Kate was here to help see him through his ordeal. She was here for him when he had not been there for her.

Sid wondered if this was the way it was immediately before a person reached the brink of insanity. Or was he near death and Kate was here to guide him over to the other side? He suddenly longed for blessed death and to be in Kate's hold again. Yet, as the sweet tide of her touch left him, he was left painfully aware of why she had come to him. She had come for a purpose and that purpose was now plain to Sid. Kate had come to protect her daughter. She had come to lead him to the man who had killed her.

**\*\*\*\***

At the downtown Dallas Police Station, a nervous but astute woman around fifty-five, demanded to speak with one of the investigators working on the Celia Johnson murder case.

"I have some information," she said. "Information that might lead you to the man who killed Miss Johnson."

The young officer on duty seemed uninterested

"Listen, lady. All the officers working on that case have gone home. Come back tomorrow."

"I would," she said. Her eyes began to swell with tears. "But my daughter could be dead by tomorrow."

She threw a photograph at the officer. He glanced at it for a moment and then looked at her and asked in an appeasing tone. "What's this picture got to do with your daughter being in danger, or with Celia Johnson?"

"This is a picture of my daughter and her new husband, Carl Woods."

"Yeah, so?" he asked sarcastically. He looked at the clock. Only twenty minutes until his shift was over. He had a date waiting for him. She had steaks and wine ready. Then he looked again at the woman standing in front of him. Something in her eyes told him she wasn't some nut off the street. Something about her commanded him to listen to her grievance.

"All right, Ma'am. Tell me. What does your daughter and her husband have to do with Celia Johnson?"

For a moment, the woman lost her composure, but then she spoke through shaky words.

"I think my daughter's husband is the man who killed Celia Johnson. At least, I think he's the man the police have been looking for."

The officer held up the photo and studied it. He looked at the woman. A lump manifested in his throat. He tried to swallow, but couldn't. He looked at the photo and asked her directly.

"When was your daughter married and where is she now?"

"She was married a few weeks ago. In Phoenix. That's

where she and Carl live. I only arrived back in Dallas a couple of days ago. You see, I was in Phoenix attending the wedding."

The woman sat in a chair by the officer's desk. She pulled a Kleenex from her purse and blew her nose. Then she resumed talking.

"My daughter left with him about a month ago. I thought she was with her friends at first, but she was with this man she had met here in Dallas. She says he took her to Mexico and asked her to marry him. I tried to talk her into coming home, maybe talk some sense into her. She wouldn't listen to me. She said if I wanted to be at her wedding, I needed to get on a plane and fly to Phoenix. So, I did. She's my only child – my only family, since my husband passed away two years ago.

"Anyway, they had a home wedding. My daughter and her husband, Carl, were there, and of course, me. There was also an Indian woman named Maria and her son. Maria's son was a cop, I think. This made me feel better. Carl said they were like family to him. Carl seemed nice at first, charming and all. He seemed to make my baby happy, but there was something about him I couldn't trust.

"I kept asking Rita – Rita's my daughter. I kept asking her, are you sure you're doing the right thing? I mean, you only just met him. Don't you think you should wait? Of course, she was too much in love or too obsessed, or whatever, to listen to me. And she was happy, so I was happy."

"You said you thought he was the man who killed Celia Johnson. No one just thinks something like that. Surely something happened to make you think this."

"It was the piece on channel five tonight. They did a profile of the murder suspect and talked about all of the women he has reportedly murdered. All of this time, I've been reading about Celia Johnson's murder and all the other women but never made the connection. The sketches in the paper of the suspect weren't that distinguishable, not like seeing him on film. When I saw the man on TV tonight, that's when it hit me.

"The station showed the suspect in an old film footage. I

think he was in some kind of commercial, something about land in Colorado. I realize the footage was very old, but when I saw the man on the commercial, walking, talking, and laughing his laugh, well, I knew. I had a sick feeling come over me. Dear God, I knew. The man in the papers and on TV called Jack Adams is Carl Woods. He's my daughter's husband."

"You're absolutely sure about all this?"

"Dear God," her voice registered her fear. "My baby is married to a psychopath, a murderer! I thought all I had to worry about was him taking her for a ride, you know, draining her assets, but this – dear God – a murderer!"

The officer squeezed her hand.

"He might just be a nice guy who happens to resemble a murderer. But I tell you what. I'll make a call to the lead investigator. I'll tell him what you've told me. He'll most likely want to talk to you later. Write down your name and address and a couple other places you can be reached. I'd like to keep this photo, too. If that's all right."

"Sure," she said, smiling through her tear-filled eyes, relieved to have her awful fear told. "I appreciate this so much. Can I wait for the investigator here?"

"You could, but most likely it will be a couple of hours before he will even try to contact you, if that soon. It's up to you, though. I'd wait at home."

"I'll wait here," she said determinedly.

He smiled. "Kind of figured you would. There's a waiting area with coffee and doughnuts down the hall. It will be more comfortable. I'll come get you when I hear from the detective. If I see it won't be tonight, I'll come get you. Don't worry. Your daughter will be fine."

She lent him a less than convincing smile of relief.

"Please hurry and call your investigator."

"I will."

When Rita McDonald's mother made her way to the lounge, Officer Mike Duncan called Captain Louis Steele, who headed up the Celia Johnson investigation.

A strident voice answered. "Steele here."

"Captain, this is Duncan. Sorry to disturb you at home."

"What is it, Duncan?"

"Maybe nothing, Captain, but I think – well – Jesus, Captain, it's the Celia Johnson case. We may have just found our man. I mean, I think I know where Jack Adams is."


****


Lou Steele called Detective Martin Gee, the lead detective in the case and told him about Theresa McDonald. Gee reluctantly made his way to the station, thinking she was probably another crackpot and her story would take him nowhere. However, Steele was adamant and Duncan wasn't the usual run of the mill rookie. He was solid with a head on his shoulders. He was seldom riled by every lead that came his way. As a rule, Duncan's instincts were right on, so Gee would be negligent not to check this out.

Theresa McDonald told Martin Gee about her daughter's whirlwind courtship and her recent marriage to Carl Woods, a man she believed was Jack Adams. He took her testimony step by step, thoroughly investigating her story. They watched the channel five footage six times and each time, Theresa became more convinced of her suspicions. She gave Gee her daughter's new address and phone number. After a tearful and exhausting three-hour interview, Gee sent Theresa McDonald home with the assurance that he and most likely Captain Steele himself would contact the Phoenix Police together. Carl Woods would be checked out.

Gee took Celia Johnson's file home with him hoping he might find some new tangible evidence to nail Jack Adams. There was more than enough probable cause to arrest him, but could he make an arrest stick? There were no prints found, but there was forensic evidence, including semen and blood, hair and skin, and other residue. And, there was that quirky piece of evidence found in Celia Johnson's matted hair when the autopsy was performed. She had knocked out a gold cap from her assailant's mouth, leaving behind a crucial piece of evidence that just might identify her killer.

Yes, her killer had definitely left his signature behind. Gee thought he reeked of sloppy havoc but realized what a cool snake he must really be, or else just incurably vain. Maybe both, he thought, or just plain lucky. Gee prayed to God that Adams was still in Phoenix. This was problematic. Gee noted that Adams's great genius was not in the nature of his assaults, but the damnable way in which he was able to vanish from the law. Gee was confident that once Adams was in custody, the case would fall into place. He knew Adams would be a match to the scientific evidence. Gee was also hoping to find the weapon. A weapon always holds up in court, where sometimes juries were reluctant to convict on scientific evidence. A weapon would clinch a conviction.

Gee scanned the autopsy report. There was nothing there that Dr. Alan Vinson hadn't reported personally. Vinson was the best medical examiner he'd ever known. He was thorough. He went by the book. In addition, when it came to being a witness for the prosecution, he was savvy and dogmatic. He never swayed from the facts. He was a man a lead investigator wanted on his team, a professional all the way.

What Vinson had told him about Celia Johnson spoke volumes. She had put up a hell of a fight, scratching and clawing and punching her assailant before he had the opportunity to bind her. She'd even bitten him, for on her teeth and on her person were blood residue and skin particles that matched her killer. Underneath her nails were more skin particles and on her hands and arms were markings and scratches, all symbols of her courageous fight. Gee silently applauded the spirit of this young and beautiful victim. He looked into her harrowing brown eyes assuring her she hadn't died in vain.

"We have him, Celia. And thanks to you, your killer won't

206

be able to do this to another woman again."

****

Mara lay in bed that night unable to find rest. She hadn't heard from Sid and she was beside herself with worry and self-doubt. Should she contact the police? Should she hire a private investigator? She recanted her options repeatedly until her head was throbbing. She took a sedative, but it was ineffective. She picked up the phone and called the last number on her list of Gallup motels. There was no Sid Carson or Sid Michaels registered. Mara knew this was a long shot. She really didn't believe Sid would be registered under his own name, but she had to at least try to contact him. He didn't answer his cell. As she wrestled about her bed, she all but decided to contact the police tomorrow. She couldn't live another night like this.

She dreamed of Sid and Bailey and her father and of Jack Adams, but the most disturbing part of her dreams was when Kate appeared. In her dreams, Mara was nineteen again and in the arms of her new lover, Sid Michaels. He was telling her he loved her and wanted to leave his wife to marry her. They made love and then her lover was gone. Sid was gone. She went looking for him. She ran down a long hallway with dozens of doors, opening each one, but not finding him. When she opened the last door, she saw him holding a woman's body. As she moved closer to him, she realized the woman's body was Kate's body. Kate was mangled, shelled with bullets, and her eyes were lost in the void of death's hold.

Mara tried to scream, but she couldn't. As her dream continued, Kate moved her sunken eyes and stared directly at her. Kate's mouth that only moments earlier had been covered with the stamp of death moved and her voice whispered to Mara.

"Help me. Help me."

Mara closed the door and ran down the hallway, but Kate ran behind her. Sid was nowhere to be found. Mara kept running from the corpse-like creature she knew to be Kate, but her efforts were in vain. Kate placed a hand on her shoulder and pleaded again to Mara.

"Help me. Help me."

Then – there was silence – darkness. She heard footsteps moving toward her, but couldn't distinguish them. She waited in the dark hallway, waited until the footsteps were at her feet. The darkness was invaded when the person standing next to her lit a match. Through the glow of the small flame, Mara could identify the person. It was Sid, her lover, her knight.

"Sid!" she cried falling into his arms

"Hush, Darling. Everything is all right."

She touched his black hair to feel if he were real or not.

"You're really here. You didn't leave me."

He held her tightly, but when she looked back up at him, it wasn't Sid. It was Jack Adams. He laughed a haunting laugh.

"Sid's gone. Sid and Kate are gone."

Mara screamed and her cries could be heard throughout the house, awakening not only her from her nightmare, but Diane and Sammy, as well. Diane found Mara shouting and beating on her pillow. Diane shook her firmly.

"It's only a dream, Mara. You're only dreaming."

Mara clutched Diane.

"I've lost him. I've lost Sid. I'm so frightened. I'm so very frightened."

"We all are, Darling," Diane soothed. "Slide over."

Diane lay next to Mara and held her. She tried to ease away the memories of her dream. Mara looked at Diane the way a child would look to her mother for assurance. So Diane patronized Mara, assuming the mother-role. Mara had always needed patronizing for as long as Diane had known her. Diane brushed back her wet hair.

"I'm here, Darling. I'm here."

"Diane," Mara said unerring, certain if she didn't speak her confession there would be no hope for her redemption. "I'm responsible for Kate's death. I've never told another living soul this before. I know I have to tell someone. I must speak of it in order to redeem my soul."

"Mara, you're upset. You're worried."

"Yes, I am. I'm also consumed with remorse and this dark cloud of guilt that never lets me find peace."

Mara sat up in the bed and turned on the lamp. Her stare was unsubtle. Diane could see she was relieved to be speaking.

"Two nights before Kate was killed, she called from Gallup and wanted to speak to Sid. I guess you know Sid and I were – well, you know – lovers while Kate and Sid were still married. Well, Sid and I were together that night and that was unusual since I'd never spent the night at his house before. It was always my apartment. So, when he asked me to come over and be with him, I was thinking that maybe he was finally getting Kate out of his mind.

"It had been almost three months since she and Bailey, I mean Rebecca, had left with Jack and the strain had really gotten to Sid. Each day, I watched him grow more and more despondent from worry. He said it was over Rebecca, but I knew he was worried for Kate, too.

"I loved him so much, you see. I would have done anything for him. I agreed to spend the night with him, in the bed he had shared with Kate. Oh, God, I'll never forget that horrible night. Sid was in the shower when the phone rang. I was reluctant to answer it, but it kept ringing, so I did.

"It was Kate. I remember her being surprised to hear my voice instead of Sid's. But then her tone changed and she sounded resigned. At first, her words were rushed. She asked to speak to Sid, but I lied and said he wasn't there. I told her he was working. I remember there was a long silence before she spoke again. When she did, there was a finality to her voice, as if she might be conceding to her fate. At least that's how I read it now. She told me to tell Sid that she was sorry for everything. And then she told me to tell him that she never stopped loving him – not once."

Mara stared computationally at Diane.

"But you see, I never told Sid about her call. How could I? I was just nineteen and very threatened by Kate. I knew if Kate had given Sid any encouragement, he'd go to her in a second. I couldn't let that happen. Don't you see?"

Diane stared numbly at Mara, understanding fully the dire truth behind her words and the consequences of her not telling Sid about the call. Kate Michaels might be alive today had she told Sid about the call, or maybe it wouldn't have made a difference. Diane was too stunned to speak but did what any mother would do when her child had just relayed to them a dark truth about their life. Diane held Mara close, gently brushing back her black hair, coddling her much the way she had before.

"Rest tonight, Mara. Tomorrow we will deal with this. But for now, rest."

Mara began to drift to sleep and Diane held her fragile form in her arms.

"Poor, dear Mara," she thought. "Her only sin was loving a man who didn't love her."

The decision she had made that night had directed her course for the last seventeen years. Mara had been in and out of mental facilities trying to cope with the consequences of her decision, holding the weight of Kate's death completely on her shoulders. It was too much for one human being to have to endure, especially one as frail as Mara.

Diane thought of Sid. He would never forgive Mara for this act of deceit. Mara knew this and that is why she kept it a secret all of these years. Had Diane been Mara, she probably would have done the same thing. Diane looked at Mara. What she needed was absolution from her sin. Diane kissed her forehead and whispered.

"I forgive you, Mara. God forgives you."

# Chapter 21

In the dark hours past midnight, long after Sid had managed to fall asleep, an intruder entered his room. Sid was instantly awakened by the sinister flow of hot breath ebbing down his back, and then, the cold shock of a pistol being lodged next to the back of his skull. He lay immobile, scarcely able to breathe, let alone turn to face his assailant. Once more, he really didn't have to turn and face this animal who had so charged the quiet of his sleep. He already knew who he was, and in his mind, Sid was cursing his own stupidity at leaving himself such easy prey. Even a docile house cat knew when to hide and retreat from its enemy.

"Sid," Jack's ghostly voice whispered in his ear. "Did I not teach you anything? You really are a chump; you know it, a dumb chump. Why don't you just put out an ad and tell the world where you are – where Bailey is?"

For seventeen years, Sid had fantasized what he would do if he should ever confront Jack again. Most of the time his dreams were filled with revenge, of his killing Jack the same way he had murdered Kate. Sometimes he'd dream of watching Jack being tortured by the electric chair, or more deigning, being locked in prison for the rest of his life. This was a fate Sid knew Jack would find more heinous than death. Yet, when he was faced with the reality of actually challenging Jack again, it was as it had always been. Sid was caught off guard, one-step behind his former mentor. Sid remained silent as Jack continued to control the course of his life.

"Listen to me, Sid Michaels and listen to me well. I could kill you right now and wouldn't think twice of it, but I find myself in a situation where I need your sorry ass to help me.

And – if you want to see Bailey alive again, you'd better listen well to what I have to say."

Jack released the pressure of the gun against Sid's skull and with the agility of a panther, he leapt over Sid and stood next to the bed, where he was looking down at him. Darkness covered Sid's face, but Jack could feel his eyes riveting over him. Jack let out a curt chuckle.

"Don't even think you can take me on."

Sid remained silent and in his silence, he heard Jack move away. He came back, placing a chair where he had just been standing. Jack sat down and Sid could smell the musty stench of his leather boots. Sid remained motionless. Jack lit a cigarette and the miniscule glow from it lent Sid an unerring flashback of a man he hated body and soul. Sid sat up in the bed with the spread covering him from the waist down, his chest bare. He felt vulnerable. He felt unsuited. He felt unmanned. Still, he braved questioning Jack.

"Why didn't you kill me while you had the chance?"

Sid's tone was sobering, not realizing that hearing it was affecting Jack as much as Jack's voice had affected him. Yet when Jack cleared his throat, Sid felt the smallest flair of control. That flair was short-lived and once again, Jack dominated.

"I told you. I need you to help me. Besides, I've had many chances. You're really not worth killing."

Sid found his composure. He wanted to jump through the darkness and tear this man apart, limb from limb, but fear and common sense told him to remain calm. Sid had learned from this very man when to take charge of a moment or when to remain passive and listen. This was one of those times he knew he had to remain quiet. Later when the game was more balanced, when he knew Bailey was safe, then he'd speak his peace. He would do this, even if it meant his own death.

Sid's voice was soft, almost conceding. "My only concern is for my daughter."

"Then you'd better change your game plan or you're both dead."

212

Without thinking, Sid moved toward the nightstand and reached for his cigarettes. Jack fairly flinched as he watched Sid light up and blow smoke in his direction. The warm flow of smoke moving down his throat allowed Sid to regain some of his wit and he began to negotiate with his adversary.

"I have money, Jack. A lot of it. You can have it all. Just don't harm Bailey."

"Jesus, after all these years, you're still singing that same song, aren't you? Give it up, Sid. I'm not any more impressed with it today than I was seventeen years ago."

"I don't know what you're talking about."

"Don't you? I'm talking about money, you bastard. You and money. You thinking money is the answer to everything."

"Come on, Jack. It's me. I know how hard you played at getting money and I know what having it meant to you."

"Sure I played hard to get it, but I played hard to get other things, too. I never lived my life thinking that money is all there is. I know it can be taken away."

"You're just a regular altar boy, aren't you, Jack?"

Jack snickered, always amused when the truth somehow managed to expose a hypocrisy, even if that truth exposed him.

"Well – maybe it used to mean a lot to me, but not anymore. Not since..."

There was a long silence between the two men. Sid broke the silence with a chilling accusation.

"Since when, Jack? Since you murdered my wife?"

Sid barely managed to say the words when Jack thrust forward and placed his gun near Sid's right temple. The two men were so close to one another that even in the dark, their contempt was clearly disclosed, through their heavy breathing and the sweat of their bodies. Only one thought kept Sid from losing control and charging at this savage of a man, even though he knew he had no real chance at surviving a contest with him. Only one thought kept Jack sane, demanding that he edge back and remove the pistol from Sid's head. This thought was Bailey.

Jack backed away from Sid and went into the bathroom,

where he turned on a light and filled a glass with water. He brought the glass and drew from his pocket a pill. He handed the pill and the water to Sid.

"Take this."

Sid stared at Jack, staggered.

"Don't worry," Jack said. "It's not going to kill you, although I can't think of anything that would give me greater satisfaction than seeing you dead."

Sid remained silent, stunned by what the light from the bathroom allowed him to see. He was able to view Jack without the cloak of darkness. Sid was amazed at how little he had changed in all these years. But then, he began to notice defects that weren't there before, defects that only a former confrere would be able to detect. His arms and face were scarred, he walked with a limp, and there was a slight stoop in his back. In all though, he was remarkably fit, dapper, too, given the nature of his past. Had Sid not known him so well, he would have thought him just a regular Joe off the street, one who might be just a little pre-occupied with his looks. Again, Jack told Sid to take the pill.

Sid hesitated before he swallowed the pill, but then he really had no other choice. He doubted Jack would choose a merciful death for him, removing any suspicions that he might have of Jack poisoning him. Poison wasn't Jack's style. Bullets and blood and rape were more his standard. Jack took the glass from Sid and sat back down in the chair. It was then that Jack was able to take a good look at Sid, his dark hair still full, but grayed, his thick middle, his lined face. Jack gave a smug grin.

"You're not exactly the fit ace I remember. I see you've let your riches go to more than your head."

"Let's get to the point of your visit tonight, Jack. You say you're not here to kill me, which I'm not completely convinced that you're not. Then, why are you here?"

"The same reason you are. That's to keep Bailey from being killed."

Sid lit another cigarette.

"Jesus, you are really one sick, miserable bastard. Excuse me if I don't find humor in what you are saying. Give me one reason, one damn reason, why I should listen to anything else you have to say?"

"You have no other choice but to listen to me."

"Oh, I have another choice all right. Being shot is looking better by the minute."

"But, you don't have a choice, pal. You see, if I kill you, then you'll die not knowing whether or not Bailey's life will end the same."

Sid lunged toward Jack, but Jack was quick and he pinned Sid down on the bed. He was left flat on his back, weak from desperation. The pill Jack had given him was starting to take effect and he closed his eyes relinquishing himself to the fate of the night and the madman who held him at gunpoint. When Jack realized Sid wouldn't fight him anymore, he released him and moved back toward the chair. Sid's cigarette had fallen on the mattress, so Jack nonchalantly picked it up and handed it to him.

"You're going to listen to me, you thick-headed bastard, if it's the last thing you do."

Once again, Sid sat up in the bed, drawing up the bedspread. Underneath the covers, he balled his fists and damned his own impotence. He stared straight ahead and kept his silence. Visions of Bailey filled his mind and he focused on these visions. When Jack spoke, he spoke in a voice of regret.

"That night – I thought I had lost everything, but then I learned that Rebecca – I mean Bailey had survived. This gave me a reason to continue."

Vaguely, Sid heard Jack's words and the blaspheme they registered, stirring up such contempt, he could only stare at Jack in bitter heresy.

"My God," Sid thought. "He's a madman who has come to eulogize his past. Surely, he isn't seeking a reprieve. Surely he knows I'd rather see us both in hell than to forgive what he has done."

"I didn't kill her," Jack confessed plainly. "I never could have killed her. I loved her. She was everything to me."

"She wasn't yours to love!" Sid heard himself shout. His eyes shot wildly at Jack, cutting through Jack's reserve. This caused Jack to retreat to the chair, realizing Sid was reaching the point of no return. Clawing Jack's face, Sid drew blood and would have continued with his assault, had his body not succumbed to the drug he had been given earlier. Sid fell to the floor, with his face smashed against the rough fibers of the carpet. He believed he had reached the bottom of a pit he had been thrown down seventeen years ago. Jack knew he'd be sleeping soon, knocked cold from the drug. He knew he had to talk fast.

He tried to drag Sid back up to the bed, but Sid was too heavy, so he propped him against the wall. Panting, he sat next to him. Two men, once allies but now enemies, were sitting side by side. Both were emotionally drained as they were reaching the final hours of their linkage. With their backs against the wall, their arms touching one another, their breaths moving with the same beat, they turned to face each other. Sid's dark eyes met Jack's steely blue ones, each man staring at the other as if frozen in time. Together they had been both friends and foes, both confidants and adversaries. Bittersweet memories emptied into the dark night and Sid offered to Jack a befitting plea, realizing he had lost the game to his enemy.

"I always knew I would die at your hand. But, I'm begging you. Please don't kill my baby. If Kate ever meant anything to you at all, please, in memory of her, spare the child she loved so much."

Without moving, without recoil, Jack spoke. His voice was scarcely audible as he conveyed his intent to Sid.

"Christ, you just don't get it, do you? I couldn't kill Bailey anymore than I could have killed Kate. The only reason I'm here is to protect her. Just once, open your mind and listen to what I have to say. When I'm finished, then you can talk."

Sid let out a sigh and closed his eyes and for the first time, he heard the words Jack was saying.

"Imagine for a moment," Jack said as he laid out his scenario. "Imagine I didn't kill Kate. Imagine that someone else killed her. Then, imagine that person thinking he had killed me, too. Imagine him driving bullet after bullet into me and then dropping my body into a desert ravine, thinking I had surely died.

"Now, imagine this person keeping my persona alive, while all the while, knowing I'm dead. It's ingenious if you think about it. I mean, he kills me, but the rest of the world thinks I've done this murder and then somehow managed to disappear into thin air. No one, not even the police believe someone else might have killed Kate, especially not you, and so this 'Cain' is left to roam. He's free to kill again and again, and every time, I'm held accountable."

"Very impressive," Sid said dully. "If I didn't know you so well, I might even consider such a story. But, I do know you. I know your cunning. Let it go, Jack. Save your fantasies for someone who doesn't know your capabilities."

"Did you ever ask why I would kill Kate? I mean, what reason would I have to kill her?"

"That's easy. She saw you for what you are. She was going to leave you. We all know, no one leaves Jack Adams."

Jack snorted. "You'd like to think that's how it was, wouldn't you? That she didn't have feelings for me. That she wasn't carrying my..."

"Your child, Jack? Don't build up your ego thinking Kate was carrying your child. She wasn't with you exclusively before you left Denver."

"I know," Jack choked back the tears. "I know she was with you." Jack stared at Sid loathsomely. "You had everything. You had her. You had Bailey. She never would have come to me if you hadn't..."

"Go on," Sid cut in bitterly. "Go on and get in your digs."

"No!" Jack said sternly. "We aren't going to do this. I'm not here to rehash the past. I'm here to see a promise through. I'm here to give just reward to a woman who never should have been taken so early and so brutally. I'm here to protect someone she loved more than she ever loved me or you."

"Go on. Humor me with the rest of your reverie."

Jack lit a cigarette and offered Sid one. He declined.

"We knew you had a guy trailing us. Kate was getting nervous. She just wanted peace, you know. She figured you'd chosen your life. She wanted you to let her choose hers. After a while, she saw what our running was doing to Bailey. I know it bothered her. She only wanted what was best for her.

"That night," he gulped as tears filled his eyes. "That last night, we were asleep in our room. Something made me wake up. I saw Bailey staring out the window, so I went to her. She was crying. She said he didn't come. I said, who didn't come, Honey? She told me the man who was going to bring her daddy to her. I asked her what man? She said the man with the golden smile.

"I freaked. I thought surely she must have been talking about your man. He'd gotten close to her and I didn't even know it. Then, I heard Kate crying. She said she wanted to take Bailey back to you and she wanted to stay with me, but that Bailey should be with her father. I told her things would be different when we had a home. Bailey would adjust.

"Kate insisted. She said you would never let her be so long as she had Bailey. That's when she told me about the baby. She said we'd have our own family and that you'd be good with Bailey. I still didn't like it. I mean, Sid, you gotta admit. You weren't exactly a model father back then, even though it's to your credit you turned out to be. You've done a hell of a job with Bailey."

"Let me guess. You told Kate you'd never give Bailey to me."

"I told her I'd think about it."

"And we both know what that meant."

"I loved them both so much. I wasn't ready to let either of them go."

218

"Christ," Sid bolted. "They were mine! My family! Kate was my wife! Even if you weren't the man who killed her, it was the same as if you were. You led her to her death. She'd be alive now, if you hadn't taken her away."

"Yeah," he acknowledged. "It's been a relentless hell that I've been living with. But, I'll be damned if I'll spend the rest of my life regretting and mourning Bailey's death. I don't think that's something you want either. And that's what will happen if you don't listen to me."

Pointedly Sid asked. "Okay, if you didn't kill Kate, who did?"

"Oh, he's a clever one. Craftier than I am, and that scares the hell out of me. He's cunning. He has position. And – he's relentless. Another thing. I'm pretty sure he knows that I'm alive. This also makes him desperate."

"If what you are saying is true, then why after all of these years, didn't you tell the police?"

Jack frowned. "Well, we both know my luck with the law. Besides, it wasn't until a month or so ago, when I saw him in person for the first time, did I put two and two together."

"Who, Jack? Who is this notorious murderer you found?"

"He's a man named Red Benning. He's a reporter."

"Benning!" Sid yelped, recalling Bailey's conversation with a Red Benning in Dallas. A sudden chill invaded him and he turned to Jack. "Go on."

"He's been hassling me ever since Kate died. From day one, he's plastered my mug in the papers and printed fabrications about me to cover up his murderous ass. Always, he was there and always he knew things before anyone else. Hell, I thought he was just a damn good reporter. I kept hoping someday he would find the real killer.

"But years went by and I was still the only suspect. Then, I saw the man for the first time in Dallas, just after Bailey was hospitalized. I saw Benning in an elevator…"

"So," Sid interrupted. "You were in Dallas, just like I thought and calling Spain to rub it in." Then he smiled. "Thank

God I got Bailey away from you in time."

"Thank God you got her away," Jack agreed. "But not from me, from him. He'd just done a hell of a job on a Dallas prostitute."

"I read the papers, Jack. I hear you left enough evidence behind to lock you up for the rest of your life."

"If I thought turning myself in and proving my innocence would keep Bailey safe, I'd have done it a month ago. I don't have much faith in the justice system. In the meantime, Kate's murderer is still on the loose and Bailey is his prime suspect."

"Jesus," Sid's voice said slurred. "I think you're starting to believe your own lies. From what I know of Benning, he couldn't possibly have pulled off all of this."

"Catch someone off guard with a gun, anyone can pull it off," Jack reflected. "Besides, what if I'm not lying, Sid? What if everything I've said tonight is true?"

"If I believed you, even remotely, then I'd find a way to go after that bastard. But – I don't believe a damn word you are saying."

"Let's go over the coincidences then. Supposedly, I'm responsible for at least five women's murders. These murders occurred in five different states. Don't you find it a little bit strange that this man Benning just happened to be on the scene of each crime and that he just happened to know every minute detail?"

"Not really. Like you said, he's a hell of a reporter. He's going to follow your trail until he finds you."

"That's just it, Sid. Up until our chance meeting on the elevator, he thought I was dead."

"So you say."

"Even now, he's only speculating I might be alive. I doubt he really believes I am though. He did quite a number on me. When he was sure I was dead, he took my truck and Kate and Bailey and drove to the place where Kate was found dead. That's why my body wasn't found near Kate's.

"It took me a year to recover from what he'd done. I can

show you my wounds. I can introduce you to the Indian woman and her son who nursed me back to health. I'd do anything to convince you that what I'm saying is true. Not that I give a damn what you think of me, but I do care what happens to Bailey."

Sid held up his hand in disgust. "Please spare me, and please, no more lies."

Jack talked quickly, desperate to plead his case.

"Like I said, an Indian woman and her son found me and took me to their home near the Arizona border. She nursed me back to health. It took me three months to learn to sit, talk, and eat again. It took another three months to learn to walk, but only short distances. After a year, I was finally able to start my life over. She knew I couldn't have killed Kate. She knew whoever thought they had killed me, killed her. We sort of adopted each other. She was an outcast widow and had a son to raise. We took care of each other then. We still do. When I learned that Bailey had survived, I looked you up. But you had taken your family into hiding. I was glad. At least she was safe. Like you, I took on a new identity. In my mind, Jack Adams had died when Kate died. But then, the nightmare continued. Benning resurrected me every time he killed another woman and put the blame on Jack Adams."

"You say when you saw him in the elevator, you made the connection. Was he someone you knew?"

"No," Jack laughed. He was laughing at himself for playing the patsy all these years. "I didn't know him. It was his smile that gave him away."

"His smile?"

"Yeah and we can thank Bailey for giving us the one clue that identifies Red Benning as Kate's murderer."

"What clue?"

Jack looked at Sid and when he spoke, these words were the first he had said all night that made Sid realize there might be some truth behind his madness.

"Remember me telling you that Bailey said the man didn't

bring her daddy to her and I asked her what man?"

Sid vaguely remembered, but he nodded his head anyway.

Jack continued. "Bailey said the man with the gold smile."

Sid shrugged. "Yeah, so?"

"Red Benning has a gold-capped smile and he flashed it right in front of me. Later, when I was driving away from Dallas, it hit me. The truth hit me. I felt like a bird just learning to fly."

"Dear Lord," Sid said overpowered by a memory from the past. "Bailey used to have nightmares."

"About what?"

Sid throttled on this new revelation. Tears streamed down his face and he somehow managed to pull himself up, just so he could lie back down on the bed. Jack grabbed him, shaking him firmly, demanding the truth.

"What did she have nightmares about?"

Sid said dully. "About a man with a golden smile."

Jack released him and sat down on the bed next to him. Sid was despondent. How else could he be, discovering after all these years that the man he had so condemned, so hated, was only guilty of betraying a friendship, but not of murder? The question in Sid's mind was what he should do now. He found it difficult to let go of his hate for Jack, but for Bailey, he knew he must. Only a man like Jack could take down a man like Benning. Jack heard Sid's voice. It sounded hollow and distant.

"What motive?" Sid asked wearily. "To kill Kate and the bar owner, Toby Garcia?"

"My guess? Benning needed money. He robbed Garcia. Or maybe not. I don't know."

"And Kate? Why Kate?"

"I figure he had his eye on Kate for a while, being a serial killer. I figure he had seen her and she fit his profile. You know the kind of victim that turns him on. My guess is Kate wasn't his first, and we both know she wasn't his last."

"It's a hard story to swallow. I mean, that he could pull this off all of these years. Jesus, how do I know you're not pulling a sting on me right now?"

"You know. Would I be here wasting my time with you when I know the police are hot on my trail, probably at the front door as we speak?"

"It would be just like you," Sid remarked candidly.

Jack put his gun in Sid's hand. "Kill me now if you really believe I killed Kate."

Sid laughed outright. His hand was so weak, he could barely grip the gun.

"It's just like you to give me a gun when I'm too incapacitated to aim straight. No, when I aim at you, I want a clear shot. Isn't that what you always said, Jack? If you're going to kill someone, make sure you're in the right position and that you have a clear target?"

"Well," Jack commended as he took the gun from Sid. "At least you remembered something I taught you."

Sid was now lying on his back with his eyes closed. His mouth drooped open slightly. His breathing was hard and irregular. Jack thought he looked like a child – lost. Jack's stomach knotted.

"You stupid fool. Did you really think you could walk into town and kill me?"

Sid fairly moved. "I thought I might get lucky."

Jack sighed. "I always did admire your guts."

He waited for some time before speaking again.

"Sid, there's something I have to know. Who did you hire to follow us? To kill me? I always thought it was Calvin. Please tell me it wasn't Benning."

"Hell no," he said. "It was Calvin. What a blunder he pulled in Albuquerque. What a schmuck. He lost track of you and later stalked the wrong couple." Sid looked at Jack cynically. "You were the only sonofabitch I could ever really count on."

Jack snorted and then turned to Sid somberly. "You can count on this sonofabitch again, Sid. I mean, for Bailey."

Sid stared at him. "Do you know how much I loathe you? Do you know how much I don't want your help?"

"Yes," Jack said truthfully. "But you're too smart to let your emotions cloud your good judgment. You need me."

There was a long silence between the two men. Jack knew Sid would be out soon. When Sid spoke again, his voice was so punchy, so low, Jack had to put his ear to his mouth to hear him. What Sid said bonded these two men together for one final crusade. For Jack, it was a validation that Sid actually believed he was innocent.

"I can't think, Jack. I'm so tired. Help me. Tell me what to do now. How do we get to him before he gets to Bailey?"

"Remember Memphis and how we lured Randolph Greene?"

Though Sid's eyes were closed, his body exhausted, his groggy voice demeaning to Jack.

"Do it. Do what you have to do."

Before Jack could discuss the matter further, the hum from Sid's snoring echoed in the dark room. Sid had surrendered not only his body to this night of truths but also his mind and soul. He had put his fate and Bailey's in the hands of Jack Adams. Not because he hated him less and trusted him more, but because he was wise enough to know he couldn't take Benning on alone. He needed Jack's wit and raw instincts. He and Jack bore a common vendetta against Benning. He had taken from them the woman they had loved and now threatened to take away her daughter. He had duped them both all these years, keeping both their lives in constant upheaval. Jack pulled the spread over Sid and sat down in the chair to wait until he was sure Sid was really out. During his wait, he made another admission.

"About Kate, Sid. You were the one she loved."

In the still of the night, a peace prevailed within Sid Michaels. Kate, his beautiful Kate, had loved only him. A half-hour later, Jack whispered into Sid's ear.

"Forgive me for what I am about to do."

Jack cocked his magnum, aimed it at Sid, and fired twice.

# CHAPTER 22

Detective Gee knocked on Lou Steele's office door and poked his head inside.

"You wanted to see me, Sir?"

"Come in. Come in. Did you bring the files?"

He was referring to Celia Johnson's evidentiary file and her autopsy report.

Gee held up the files and lent him a broad grin. "You ready to go to Arizona and make an arrest."

Lou Steele snorted. "Jack Adams is long gone from Arizona. I'm sure of that. Anyway, this isn't about Adams. Sit down and let me run something by you."

Gee sat down and Steele haphazardly opened up Celia Johnson's file and looked at a photo of her lifeless body. It spoke volumes.

"Celia Johnson gave us the evidence to take down her demon. And what she told us about him is irrefutable, I'd say. God bless you, Celia Johnson. God bless you and your fighting spirit. Jack Adams thanks you, too, I'm sure."

Gee looked at Steel strangely. "Why would Jack Adams thank Celia Johnson?"

"Because," Steele offered. "She has set him free."

"How do you figure?"

"She unveiled the real killer."

"I'm not following you, Sir."

"My dear friend, don't you see? All of this time, we've been chasing the wrong demon."

"You don't think Adams killed Celia Johnson?"

"Pack your bags, Gee. We are headed for New Mexico."

****

Claire Brennen couldn't get Mara Carson out of her mind, even though she'd only known her for thirty minutes in a small Santa Fe airport. Claire worked overtime gathering information about Mara Carson and her family, about her husband's murdered wife, and about Jack Adams, Kate's supposed killer. Claire studied the uncanny resemblances of his victims, their physical features, their assaults. She was fascinated by Adams's profile. She knew him to be a shady fellow, hard to the core. The other players were equally as fascinating. There was Sid Michaels, alias Sid Carson, Kate Michaels, the beautiful wife and girlfriend, Mara Carson, formally Mara Lindsey, and Bailey Carson, Sid's and Kate's Rebecca, most probably the next target of her mother's killer.

The tangled web that wove their lives together was the perfect setting for a crime of passion and Claire would have bought it but for several reasons. Oh, there was no doubt in her mind that Jack Adams was capable of such a crime. Most anything can tick off a man like Adams. And perhaps it was just as Sid Michaels reported when he found his wife dead.

"Kate saw Jack for what he really was. She decided to run. But Jack doesn't let anyone run. If Jack couldn't have her, no one else would either."

Even with all the evidence against Adams, Claire was skeptical. She let out a deep breath. Something just didn't jive here. She picked up Jack's photo and stared into his blue eyes.

"You don't fit the casting of a serial murderer. Sure, you would have killed Kate out of jealousy. That's exactly what you would have done. It's the other women that have me baffled. It's unusual for jealous rage to carry over to other victims, unless of course, you developed an obsession for each one. But Celia Johnson? Did you have time to become obsessed with her? Or, is it that simple for you to transfer your obsessions to someone else? Help me out here, Jack. Did you kill these women? Is this part of your genius, going against the mold? Tell me, Jack. Tell

226

me so everyone concerned can go home safely. Put an end to this game. Convince me you killed these women and if you didn't, convince me of that. Talk to me, Jack. I'm listening."

She already knew a great deal about him and the more she knew, the more intriguing he became. He was born Samuel Jackson Adams. His father left him and his baby sister, Nancy, in the care of his mother, Velma Adams. Jack was a devoted son and brother, working odd jobs in downtown New Orleans to help put food on the table. He learned from the best street thugs. He learned when to pay the piper or when to take the money and run.

He became somewhat infamous in his small niche of the world. Not only two-bit felons, but also those who were the heart of New Orleans's cesspool feared him. The reason he was so feared was plain. Jack Adams was a man who could sense a deal before it happened and he had no qualms about taking down whoever he had to in order for the deal to go his way. It was rumored that before Jack Adams joined the Marines, he'd killed several men. It was a rumor he'd always denied.

He moved his mother and sister out of New Orleans giving most of his pay to them. He kept them well hidden, protecting them from his former enemies. It seems he was able to keep them as hidden from the world as he did himself. In the Marines, he got an honorable discharge, always receiving exemplary evaluations. Of course, there was an isolated incident where he got in a scuffle with a man and the man was killed. Jack was vindicated when the military acquitted him citing self-defense.

Adams never married and Claire noted he had few romantic attachments, although she also noted how women were attracted to him. So much so, they would give their last dime, their last breath to please him. They would leave a good husband to be with him. She vaguely wondered if she hadn't somehow mystically been entrapped within his trellis. A chill invaded her.

"Am I your prey, as well as the others? Am I less vulnerable than they were? You certainly have me captivated. And – I've never even seen you."

From what Claire could assess, other than his mother and sister, Adams was only loyal to two women. Kate Michaels was one and the other was an earlier sweetheart of his, one he had met while on duty at Camp Quantico in Virginia. According to those acquainted with Adams in those days, he was completely dedicated to Jean Bellwood, but after his tour of duty was up, he broke it off with her. On the rebound, she married Benny Harmon. That marriage lasted only a year but gave her a son. When her marriage ended, Jack went to comfort her. He brought with him a Marine buddy of his named Sid Michaels. Jean and Sid hit it off from the very beginning. Two months later, they were married, with Jack as their best man. When that marriage ended two years later, all three remained close.

From what Claire could tell, Jack had the same unbending loyalty toward Sid as he had for Jean and his mother and sister. Jack and Sid were partners for a small investment company in Denver. They began taking steps to branch out into real estate. Because Jack was loyal to Sid, he was equally loyal to Sid's family, Kate and Rebecca.

"What happened to make you cross the line, Jack? What made you turn on your best friend?"

Claire picked up a photograph of Sid Michaels. His facial features, though rugged, were softer than Jack's were. He was handsome, with his dark hair and dark eyes. Like Jack, he was drawn to power, maybe it was even more important to him. Unlike Jack, he had never really controlled anything. At least not until he became rich. With wealth, Sid finally acquired power, making him as dangerous as Jack Adams. Sid became wealthy when he married Mara Lindsey and was made equal partners in her father's, Daniel Lindsey's, real estate company. His hard business dealings and rigid "no surrender" attitude made Sid Michaels a tyrant within the corporate world, which Daniel Lindsey once attested to his board of directors.

"My son-in-law is a sonofabitch, but he's turned the

228

company into a multi-million dollar conglomeration. How can we be dissatisfied with such domination?"

Daniel Lindsey worshipped Sid and when he retired, he turned the company over to him. Sid ate, slept and breathed his work, leaving Mara lonely. Often she would run into her daddy's arms disclosing her loneliness. His standard response was always the same.

"He's what you wanted and Daddy got him for you. Now, you must sleep in the bed you made."

And so Mara made the most of her marriage and devoted her loyalties to Sid's daughter, pampering and loving her as if she had been born of her own blood.

Claire rubbed her eyes. The evening was setting in and she realized she hadn't eaten a bite since breakfast. She looked for something to cook for dinner and as she puttered around the kitchen, she continued to think of Sid Michaels.

"How does a man like Sid react when his wife leaves him for a man like Jack? Was he really so preoccupied with work and Mara not to realize what was going on in his wife's life?"

Claire cracked two eggs into a frying pan and popped some bread in the toaster.

"Money, affairs, murder," she mused. "It was all so intriguing. But was it really? Wasn't it as plain and simple as any murder case?"

She had to wonder. She thought of Kate Michaels.

"Kate, tell me why you left Sid? Did you fall in love with Jack? Was it revenge? Or, was it survival? Just who were you, Kate Michaels?"

The toast popped up and she buttered it, slapping grape jelly on top. The eggs were done. She sat down at the kitchen table and began to realize very little had been written about Kate or the other victims. Most of the articles focused on their murderer, Jack Adams. Claire found this disturbing. She ate in a daze, pausing off and on to scan the many articles written about Jack Adams's trail of vengeance. A peculiar chill overpowered her. From Kate's murder to the murder of Celia Johnson, there had been one constant that she wondered if anyone else had noticed. This constant was a particular reporter who had been a part of each scene—a man named Red Benning.

"That's not too peculiar," she rethought. "Hadn't she followed her husband's murderer until he was caught?"

She wondered what drove Red Benning. She finished her eggs and took her plate to the sink. Then, she went to her computer and began to sort out details of Red Benning's career. He was a man who had devoted his life to his work. He never married and kept much to himself. He was a candid writer, focusing on the gruesome details of a murder, so opposite of her focus, which was the human aspect. She knew he had followed Kate's murder and those after. What she became captivated with was his reporting before that.

Before Kate's death, he had been following another serial killer named Sandy Reed. Reed had been responsible for the deaths of six or more coeds. He would knock them over the head with an object like a bat and then he would bind their feet and hands while they were unconscious. When they awoke into a semi-conscious state, he would leave his trademark by biting them all over their bodies. After that, he would strangle them.

Claire read an interview by a survivor of one of Reed's attacks. She reported that before he began strangling her, he made her beg for her life. Each time she did, he would lay his bite into her. Claire shuddered at such a sadistic act. Then, she read on. A heinous fact bolted out of the pages of the articles she read. After strangling his victims, Sandy Reed got his jollies by having sex with them.

"Sandy Reed," Claire searched. "I remember something about him. But, whatever happened to him?"

She drew up Reed's status on the computer. He was still at large, last seen in Denver over twenty years ago. Something about Reed's string of murders struck Claire as familiar to Adams's. She brushed through the many articles until she found one about Kate's death. Red Benning wrote it.

"Dear Lord," she cried. "Kate's remains were violated, too!"

Rashly, she scanned the details of the other murders by Adams. She covered her mouth in horror. All were victims of necrophagous acts, or so it was reported. Rather than strangling his victims as Sandy Reed had done, Adams shot them in the back. Yet, there were similarities. Claire vaguely wondered if Reed and Adams were the same man. She shook her head.

"No, Jack was in Virginia when Reed was sweeping the Midwest."

A dominant fact prevailed in the scope of her short investigation.

"You were there for all of them, weren't you Red Benning?"

Claire wasn't sure what her speculations were leading to, but she knew she couldn't stop now. She had to continue the investigation, maybe even talk to this Benning guy himself. She stretched her worn body. She was exhausted. She left everything scattered about her office and turned off her computer. She ran a bubble bath and within minutes of emerging herself into the lather, all thoughts of Jack Adams and Red Benning escaped her mind. Lost in relaxation, she heard the phone ring. It was Greg Mitchell, her secretary.

"Claire. Claire, are you home? Can you hear me? I've got some news. It's about Mara Carson. I'm pretty sure her husband's been shot."

Claire jumped from her bath and ran naked into her bedroom. Dripping on the carpet, she answered the phone.

"Greg," she said shivering. "What were you saying about Mara Carson's husband?"

"Well," Greg's voice atoned in a high pitch. "A little while ago Judy, you know the cute little reporter I've been dating? Well, anyway, she told me she was handed a story to investigate. She had helped me gather the information you asked for earlier and she knew I'd be interested in her recent story. It seems this guy named Sid Carson was shot in his Gallup motel room."

"You say he was shot, Greg. Did he die?"

"He's not dead, but he'll be incapacitated for a while.

There's more, Claire."

"What?"

"Well, it appears the same guy who killed his wife years ago has come back to finish off the family."

Claire reached for her heart and whispered, "Jack."

Greg continued. "After he was shot and put in the hospital, it seems this Carson guy phoned all the local papers and TV stations. He's making a public appeal to the world to help his family."

"Fax me everything you know about this recent incident, Greg."

"Sure thing, Claire."

"Oh, and Greg. Cancel my appointments for tomorrow and the rest of the week. I'm driving to Gallup tomorrow morning."

"Claire," he protested. "Why do you have to do this? You don't know these people."

"I can't sit here and not do anything. Not after what I've learned."

"What do you know, Claire?"

"I know Sid Carson is in danger and so is his family. I know a cold-blooded murderer is just waiting for his day. If I can help one family, Greg, I'll feel like I've helped myself."

"Just be careful."

"That's a promise. I intend on being very careful."

Claire hung up the phone and sat despondently for some time before starting to pack. She happened to glance into the mirror over her dresser. She stood for some time studying the image. Dark circles shadowed her deep brown eyes. She swept a hand through her damp blonde hair. Then, it suddenly struck her. Although she faced murder cases before, this one had caught her attention like no other. She had become obsessed with it. It occupied her every moment. Once again, she looked into the mirror and studied her reflection. Her resemblance to Kate Michaels was unquestionable.

"I could be Kate, seventeen years older."

She ran to her office and drew from the pile of articles a

picture of Kate Michaels.

"Kate, I feel this kindred draw to you – and Celia - and the others, but mostly you. I can't say why except that we look like one another. Also, I know the regret of loving a madman and then realizing it wasn't love at all but only an attempt to fill a void in your heart. When I told him our affair was over, he stalked my husband and me for two years. My husband lost his life by this madman. Then, he came after me. He assaulted me and I lost the child I was carrying. So, I do know the insufferable fear of realizing the next moment might be your last. I promise you, Kate. I will find your murderer, for me as much as for you. I will do everything I can to protect your child."

Claire thought about the child she had once carried and then lost do to an attack by her former lover. She batted back the tears and straightened her shoulders so that she stood tall in the face of fear.

"My baby died, Kate, but yours will live. Maybe by saving your daughter, I can make peace with my weary spirit. I must try anyway. Oh, my darling husband and my darling baby, forgiveness comes in the strangest fashion."

****

When Coyote returned home, Billy was with him. Jess had parked his truck in the back of Coyote's house, far from the view of anyone who might happen upon the dwelling. Although it was a rare occurrence for anyone to travel near Coyote's home, it did happen. If it did, it was usually someone who had made a wrong turn or who had gotten lost on the desert roads. Still, it was smart for Jess to be on the defense knowing that if someone should happen by Coyote's house looking for Bailey, he would have the upper hand.

When Billy and Coyote entered Coyote's house, Bailey and Jess were nowhere to be found. They noticed some dirty dishes on the table with leftover eggs and bacon. There were two coffee mugs, one half-full and the other empty. What little clothing Jess and Bailey had brought with them was still there and Billy found Bailey's cosmetic bag and purse. Their toothbrushes were still near the sink. Both men knew something wasn't right and their concern peaked.

"They've probably taken a morning walk," Coyote said trying to ease Billy's apprehension. "Just the same, I think we should go out back and look around."

Billy nodded. His eyes riveted through the house once more before moving out the back to look around. Coyote followed. Billy looked inside Jess's truck. Nothing looked out of the ordinary. Coyote went to the small shed he had outside near where Jess's truck was parked. There, he stored his paint, brushes, and materials that he used to create the masks for the Shalako, the Zunis' winter solace. Next month it would be upon them. The Zunis bestow this time to the spirits as they make their appearances to the people. The masks represent the Kachinas, the spirits. Since the spirits are invisible, the masks make it easier to believe in their presence. Coyote looked toward the sacred mountains.

"The spirits are restless," he called out to Billy.

"Yes, restless and insistent," Billy agreed. "They are telling us something."

A flash of a woman wearing black jeans and a black t-shirt filled Billy's mind. It was an image of Bailey's mother when he first saw her at Toby's bar. Her blonde hair and dark eyes haunted him and he thought of Bailey. He stared in no apparent direction as if he expected Kate Michaels to walk up behind him. Thoughts of the dead were an omen and Billy's heart raced.

They heard a low moaning sound and saw a mound on the other side of the shed. A lump filled Billy's throat as he willed his body to move toward the lean-to, already knowing what he would find would be grave. His greatest fear was realized when he saw Jess lying face down in the red earth. Billy checked his pulse. He was still alive. It took the strength of both men to drag him into the house where they began to assess what had happened to him. He'd been hit over the head, most likely with the butt of a gun. Billy knew whoever had done this had not intended to kill him. It was only intended to knock him out cold. Terror filled his being. Where was Bailey?

# CHAPTER 23

Groggy as if in a dream, Bailey thought she was riding in Jess's truck. She listened as the motor hummed in her ear. It was soothing and she vaguely wondered if they were on their way to Tucson. That had been their original plan. But then, they had decided to wait until Coyote came back with news from Billy. Had something changed? Why couldn't she remember? She tried to recall getting into the truck. She couldn't. She remembered Jess kissing her at the breakfast table and telling her that he loved her. He heard something out back and went to investigate. That's the last thing she could recall.

She wanted to feel his strong arms around her once again and so she reached for him. She couldn't feel him. She thought to move closer to him, but her body and mind were playing tricks on her and wouldn't cooperate. Just as she felt herself drifting asleep again, she felt a strong hand press over her leg. She smiled, thinking it was Jess. She even whispered his name.

"I'm sorry, Bailey. I'm not Jess."

Something like fear overcame her and she tried to open her eyes, but she couldn't. Once again, she said Jess's name. She heard the strange voice speak again.

"If I could have done this another way, I would have."

This time her eyes opened - ever so slightly. She tried to focus in on the dark figure that sat next to her. The shallow viewing through her eyes at half-mast gave her only a slight glimpse of him. Her eyes closed again. She let out a heavy sigh. She knew she was in danger but was incapable of doing anything about it. She was aware enough to know that she'd probably been drugged. She also knew she was being kidnapped and even before she was able to open her eyes again, she knew who was taking her.

With closed eyes, she could recall from photos that infamous face, those eyes that cut through a soul. Driving her probably to her death was the very man who had taken her mother's life. Even without looking at him, she was able to understand the raw magnitude his presence offered. Amid her fear, he intrigued her, by his cunning and wit. Slowly, her eyes began to work right. As she was able to focus in on him, intrigue was replaced by sheer terror. She contemplated her next move.

"You're Jack," her voice said, barely audible.

When he spoke, his words sounded ominous.

"So, you remember me."

She turned to him and stared at him. She asked him point-blank.

"You're going to kill me aren't you, just like you did my mother? Will you shoot me like you did her, Jack? Or will you leave me to die like before?"

"You know that's not the way it was, Bailey. You know I could never hurt you."

"Are you trying to say that you didn't kill my mother? That you didn't leave me to die?"

"Let me put it to you this way. If I wanted you dead, we wouldn't be having this conversation."

She stared into his haunting eyes, feeling vulnerable at the hands of this man who spoke of murder as if he were discussing the weather. Suddenly, she felt ill, most likely from her ordeal or the ether Jack had used to knock her out.

"I'm going to be sick," she thought. Jack sensed her state. His voice was gentle when he spoke.

"Do I need to stop? Are you going to be sick?"

She defied her nausea. She wouldn't be sick now, come hell or high water. She wouldn't let him do that to her, too.

"I'm fine," she lied. He touched her cheek softly.

Jack could see that at any moment she'd be ill, so he rolled down his window. The cool air slapped her in the face and she felt blessed relief. She sat silently wondering how the last moments of her life would be. Would she suffer like her mom? Or would he be more humane? She thought of her father and Mara, the only mother she had really known. She thought of Ron for some reason and Sammy. But then, she thought of Jess and the promise that would never be realized. Reality kept her sane. Every moment she remained alive was a hope for more. She heard his dark voice through the thick air.

"Go ahead and ask me, Bailey."

She didn't reply.

"Ask me if I killed her."

Now, she did speak.

"I know you killed her."

"How do you know? Because Daddy told you that?"

"Yes, and others."

"I loved your mother, Bailey. I loved her more than life. I loved you. I still do."

Her voice raised and she lent him a warning.

"Never say you love me."

"You'd like to think it was me that killed your mother. It would make it easier to understand, me being the one who killed her. But it wasn't me. Your mother's life, Bailey, was my purpose for living back then. Her death is my purpose for living now. That and your safety."

"Stop. I can't hear your lies. All the evidence points to you."

"Now what evidence would that be?"

"She was killed by a .38. You owned a .38."

"And so did a hell of a lot of people."

"You were the last person to see her alive."

"Not the last, Bailey. Someone else. Your daddy wanted me to be guilty and he made everyone believe I was. He couldn't see beyond this."

"You have a history of violence," she continued.

"I didn't kill her, Bailey. I loved her."

"What about Celia Johnson?"

"I've never met Celia Johnson."

"You're mad! Dear God, you're mad! How could my

238

mother have ever left with you? How could she have left my father?"

"Plain and simple. Daddy was a fool. He had your mom. He had you. He threw you both out to make a blessed buck. So if you're going to throw blame – well – enough said."

She wanted to lash out at him, but soon realized her hands were bound behind her back. And so, she used the only defense she had, her feet. In frustration, she brought her feet onto the seat and began kicking him. They were feeble attempts, given the state of her body. She continued anyway. It made her feel like she had some control. One kick turned into two and three and so forth. He allowed her semiconscious assault on him until she was too weak to hurl at him any longer. She was crazed, crazed with fear and betrayal. He stopped the truck and moved to the middle next to her. He wrapped his strong arms around her.

"There, there, darling. Cry all you want."

"Oh," she bellowed, forgetting that the man who held her had long ago held her mother. "Why are you doing this to me? Why don't you just kill me and get it over with?"

"I couldn't hurt you, Bailey. You know I couldn't. You know the truth about that night. Face it, Honey. Face it and you'll know it wasn't me who killed her. It wasn't me who left you to die."

"No!" she screamed. "I don't know! I don't know you didn't kill her! I can't remember that night! I…I…can't re…re…remember anything. N…not…not even what she looked like."

Jack held her weeping face within his large hands.

"If you want to remember what your mother looked like, just look into a mirror. You are her image. Jesus, you look just like her. If only your hair were blonde…"

"Stop," she moaned. "I'm so tired. If it's your intention to kill me, do it now. I'm so tired of living in this nightmare."

"It's not my intention to kill you, Bailey. It's my intention to keep you alive. I'll tell you everything later. But now, we've got to get out of here. Jess will soon be waking up and discovering you're gone. He'll be looking for you. Someone might follow him."

"Jess," she called out. She turned to beg of Jack. "Please don't kill him."

Jack let out a disgusted grumble. "I won't kill Jess."

He moved to his side of the truck and pulled onto the desert road slowly. She kept her stretched legs on the seat because she was still feeling sick and this helped. As she relaxed somewhat, she unconsciously put her feet on his lap. In her daze, she felt his hand drape over them and rest there. She fairly moved at his touch and closed her eyes. A memory of Jack rocking her came to mind. She vaguely wondered how she could feel safe in the arms of a murderer.

"Jack," her soft voice sailed through the stillness. "Did you kill my mother? Did you leave me to die?"

"No," was his truthful reply.

****

Coyote watched as Jess slept. Billy looked around for more clues about where Bailey might have been taken. Some fresh tire tracks showed a vehicle moving northwest toward the Arizona border. He figured by the size of the tracks it was made by a truck of some type. He didn't think she'd been gone too long because the markings were fairly new. He went back into the house to tell Coyote he was going to follow the tracks. When he went inside, Coyote was holding a kachina doll that represented the dark kachina the Zunis know as Esteban. Coyote looked at Billy.

"I found this under Bailey's pillow."

Billy took the doll and nodded. He seemed relieved. Coyote was confused.

"Esteban was an intruder on the village of Hawikuh. Later, he was put to death. He brought lies to the village and troops of the Spanish soldiers. What does this have to do with Bailey? I

240

can see that you know something."

Jess stirred calling out Bailey's name. Billy took the doll from Coyote.

"It is a sign, Coyote. The person who took Bailey is working with her father. The Esteban kachina is the sign that she is with her father's men. That is why whoever took her did not kill Jess. It is not her mother's murderer who has her."

"Who has her, my brother?"

"Jack Adams," Billy said.

"I don't understand."

Billy sat next to Coyote and watched Jess as he moaned in his sleep.

"I know you don't and so I will explain."

****

Bailey had fallen back to sleep and awoke several hours later still in her nightmare. Yet, it was profoundly real. The bright sun stung her eyes and when she was finally able to adjust them, the only thing she could see was the face of Jack Adams. He looked at her. His deep voice remarked.

"We are almost there."

"Where?" she asked.

"A place where no one will find us."

She looked around for some type of landmarks or signs that looked familiar. In the distance, she thought she recognized the outline of Corn Mountain, but she knew she must have been imagining this. He wouldn't take her back to the reservation. He would be taking her away from familiar grounds. She cleared her throat. She was so thirsty and only the taste of water would quench her thirst. He read her mind and offered her some water. Because her hands were tied, she was at his mercy.

"Come sit next to me, so I can help you drink."

She shook her head. "I'm not thirsty."

"Drink it. I won't kill you, but the desert sun might."

Reluctantly she complied. He made a sudden turn down

another isolated pathway and it led into a large ravine. As they ascended down the ravine, she noticed the markings of some type of structure. It looked almost like a house. Next to it was a smaller structure, not completely closed in. Jack drove his truck inside this second structure and turned off the ignition.

"We're here."

She was unsteady. She looked at him and the house and then back at him.

To herself she thought, "This is where I'm going to die."

Before she realized it, he was out his door and opening hers. He took out a knife and cut the binding around her hands.

"Better?"

She refused to speak, but couldn't resist rubbing away the aches in her arms and hands. He took her hand gently and led her inside the small dwelling. She was surprised to find that the inside looked like any normal house. It was plain, but well-kempt. From what she could see, there were three rooms, a living area, a kitchen, and a room to the side. She guessed it was a bedroom. He offered her a seat on the sofa. The pillows on it were brightly patterned and reminded her of Sadie's pillows. This made her think of Jess. Silently, she cried for him.

Jack sat on a chair next to a wooden table opposite her. On the table was a pitcher of water and a bowl of fruit. He reached for an apple and took a bite. Then, he poured some water. She actually licked her lips. He handed her the glass.

"The desert is a vicious animal. You must drink."

She was so thirsty she gulped it down.

"Slow down or you'll end up sick again."

She let out a mocking laugh. He laughed, too. Then, he went into the other room leaving her alone. She sat in this alone state. The front door was wide open and she considered running but realized she had no place to run. She didn't know where she was. From what she saw as they drove, she was surrounded by nothing but desert. If she ran, she would surely die from exposure. He had come back into the room and was watching her now, wearing fresh clothes and holding a .22 in his hand.

She drew back cautiously and actually felt her heart throbbing in her chest. She closed her eyes and waited for the impact of a bullet to penetrate her body, wondering what it would feel like to be shot. Instead, she felt the touch of his hand as it swept over her cheek.

"My God," he said. "It's like seeing Kate again."

She opened her eyes, filled with fear and fascination. Her breathing was labored. She let out a cry. The nausea that had somewhat dissipated returned at full force.

"The bathroom?" she bolted.

He understood, pointing to the room she guessed was the bedroom. She ran, slamming the door behind her. There was a small bathroom connected to the bedroom and she was grateful to find it functioning, with running water and a latrine. The trauma from her recent ordeal at being held captive by the same man who had killed her mother had taken its toll on her. Her nightmare was now her reality. She regurgitated repeatedly until her stomach burned. When the illness passed, she fell to the floor and wept. She wept for her murdered mother, for Mara's arms, for her father, for Jess, for the life she would never have. She looked into a small mirror that hung above the sink. Jack's words stung at her heart.

"Kate," she said. "He says I look like you."

At the thought of her murdered mother, her stomach churned once again. She must never forget that the man who took her mother's life stood in the next room. He was confusing her with his talk of innocence and love. He was reeling her in, the way he had her mother. All hope was gone. She had reached the end of her short life, she knew, but she'd be damned if she would go out quietly. She would leave a trail of evidence to put her mother's murderer away for a long time. She felt of the spirit necklace that Jess had given her. Also around her neck was a cross that Mara had bought her for her graduation. She would gain strength through Jess's love and God's mercy. She knew she couldn't do it alone. She held the cross in her hands and prayed.

"God, help me. Help me to live to see my mother's murderer punished. Help me to be strong for her sake as much as mine. I need you, God. I need you."

She cleaned herself up and straightened her attire. She would maintain her dignity and not allow Jack Adams to reach her soul. She moved from the bedroom and saw him waiting for her on the sofa. His .22 was tucked inside a leather holster that he had strapped to his chest. He was wearing a black bulletproof vest and Bailey thought he fit the perfect profile of a gangster.

"Jack," she said, standing in the doorway. "Before you kill me, I want you to tell me everything you know about my mother."

He studied her face. He knew she still held onto the belief that he had killed Kate. What would it take to convince her otherwise? He could give her his gun as a symbol of trust, but feeling the way she did about him, she'd probably shoot him. He let out a heavy sigh. He figured the truth was the only hand he had left to play. She'd been told so many lies though; he doubted it would do much good. Still, that's where he began.

"I didn't kill your mother, Bailey, but I know who did. When we are finished talking, I'm going to hunt him down and kill him. And, you're going to help me. First, sit down and tell me what you know about a reporter named Red Benning."

**\*\*\*\***

They came in the dark of the night. Bailey watched as Jack and three other men unloaded equipment from two vans and brought it inside. It was an orchestrated effort and each man had a job to do. One man set up what she thought was a radio of some sort, something like the old Ham radios she used to play with when she visited her friend Mary Brady in England. Jack was talking to the youngest of the men and they were discussing codes of some kind. In the midst of their conversation, she heard her name and her father's name. There

244

was something about her father being in a hospital and the man would make a visit to him. At these words, Bailey moved closer to them so she could better hear what they were saying. They stopped talking and Jack introduced her first to the man who stood next to him.

"Hi, Bailey. This is Culmer Sanchez. His code name is Bald Eagle."

Bald Eagle was a stout man, standing about five-ten. He was Indian, Hopi she would learn later, and his hair was like Jess's hair, but his skin was darker. He was around Jess's age, maybe a little older. He was dressed like Jack, wearing blue jeans, a t-shirt, and a bulletproof vest. He wore a gun belt that held some kind of handgun.

She looked around the room that earlier had been a plain living area. In a matter of minutes, the room had been transformed into an elaborate communications center. Bailey looked at Jack and she had the inclination that he was so much more than just a thug and a man who had led a life of crime and deceit.

Jack led Bailey to an older gentleman, around fifty-five. He was dressed more conservatively, with a starched shirt and dress pants. He had loosened his tie that hung unevenly down the front of his shirt. He was standing near a wall map that covered the entire east wall above the wooden table. She noted the bold print on the top of the map. It was titled "Operation Esteban."

"The old guy, Bailey, is known as Mud Man," Jack said. "His real name is Donald Reeder. He's a Dallas operative."

He waved to Bailey. "Nice to meet you."

Mud Man offered her a chair and because she was so dumbfounded by what was going on, she sat down. She looked at Jack as he was conferring with Bald Eagle. It was clear that he was in control of this operation. Everyone seemed to be looking to him for direction. She was stunned. Who was this man named Jack Adams? Was he a cold-blooded murderer as she'd been led to believe? Right now, she didn't think so. Once again he turned to face her. His smile was dangerous. She let out a slight giggle and shrugged her shoulders. His smile grew. He moved toward her and took her hand, kneeling so that they were eye-level.

"These men are here to help us, Bailey. All of them have had their eyes on Benning for some time. We decided to put our heads together and finally get the bastard once and for all."

Bailey looked at the fourth man in the room. He was helping Bald Eagle with some surveillance equipment. He had with him some sort of screens like a TV screen and within minutes had one connected to a security station. The other screens remained dark. Bailey, still holding Jack's hand asked him about Sid.

"I thought I heard something about Daddy being in a hospital. What's this all about?"

"He's been shot, Honey."

"Oh my God! By who? Benning?"

Jack gave her a half-grin. "Not exactly. Listen, he's going to be fine. I promise. You'll see in a few minutes."

She looked at him overwhelmed. Her father had been shot and Jack didn't seem the least bit concerned. Jack squeezed her hand.

"You'll understand everything soon. We are going to hook a monitor up to his hospital room."

Jack motioned to the fourth man. "Meet Clown Boy. He's our communication's genius. His name is Alex Smith from Phoenix. He's helped me out on more than one occasion."

Bailey could barely offer a greeting to him. She was too worried about Sid.

"Daddy?" she questioned Jack. "If Benning didn't shoot him, who did?"

"I did," he said flatly.

Before she could question his motives, a fifth figure came into the room and Bailey ran to him immediately, falling into Billy Nehah's arms. He held her tightly. For the first time since Jack had abducted her, she realized that she wasn't going to die at his hand. Billy's gentle voice calmed her and she caught a side-glance of Jack watching her. She asked about Jess and Billy said he was fine. Her relief at feeling safe again and knowing that Jess was safe was short-lived when she thought of Jack shooting her father. She was about to question Jack further when she saw that the monitor to Sid's hospital room had been hooked up. There was her father lying immobilized.

"Why did you have to shoot him?" she asked regretfully.

"We had to reel in our fish, Bailey. Sid is our bait. Don't worry. He looks a lot worse than he actually is. His sorry ass will be wreaking havoc for everyone before you know it."

Bailey almost laughed at Jack's remark. That was something her father would say. For the first time, she was able to see that Jack and Sid had similar personality traits. It was clear they had once been close, almost family. While she knew they could never be what they once were, they had set aside their history to help catch the man who killed her mother. She also knew that both men had loved Kate Michaels deeply, anything less couldn't have torn through their friendship.

"Can I talk to him?"

Jack shook his head. "We can only see and hear him. He can't hear us unless he calls us."

"Can we call him?"

"Not yet. I don't want to risk it."

She didn't question him. Just knowing her father was going to be all right was enough. She turned to Billy.

"The code names, the operation name, they are like the kachinas Coyote paints. Why use code names?"

"To protect our cover and our spirits," Billy stated.

"All covert operations have code names, Bailey," Jack explained. "Since we don't have time to recruit the help of law enforcement through proper channels and because some of us don't exactly trust the law, we are going rogue. We know we have this window of opportunity and we can't chance waiting. We want to elude parties on both sides of the law, even though we are helping the law by doing what we are doing. When the time is right, we will call in the authorities. We have a few on our side as it is. We just don't know who we can trust at this point.

"Billy came up with the idea of using the names of the kachinas. He said it was the perfect cover-up since this was the season when the spirits visited the people. We also have some Zuni men working with us and they feel that the spirits will bring good fortune to them. Hey, what's to say they won't? Throughout my time with the Zuni and the Hopi, I've seen a lot of miracles. I'm one of them. I say we take help from whatever sources we can."

"Jess? Is he involved?"

Billy nodded. "He's taking care of things in Gallup, working with your father's men. He's getting them acquainted with the area and showing them some back roads and hideouts. If all goes as planned, he will be here by morning. Then, his job will be to keep you here, safe and sound."

"Are you sure he's all right?"

"I've got my best man with Jess," Jack said. "Try not to worry."

She sat down on the sofa and Billy sat next to her. Her legs were weak and her heart fearful. She didn't like Jess being out there with – him.

"Oh, this is all too much."

She happened to notice that another monitor connected to what looked like a security station.

"I thought you said the police weren't involved yet," she said.

"I said they weren't officially involved. However, I do know a few officers willing to throw the rule book out to catch this guy."

"Are you in law enforcement, Jack?"

He laughed. "Not quite. He pointed to Bald Eagle. "Meet Mr. Law Enforcement."

"Oh, this is all so...surreal."

"I know," Mud Man said. "Like Jack said, we've suspected our man for some time. I just didn't have any real evidence until

248

Celia Johnson's murder. When Bald Eagle called me and told me Jack's theory, I made some calls and got the go-ahead. The pieces all fell together."

Jack took her hand.

"I know this is a lot to absorb. I mean, just a few hours ago you thought I was the one who had killed your mother. Red Benning is known as Code Esteban. We're leading him here. That's why I had to put your dad in the hospital. Sid is shot. He makes public the fact that Jack Adams has shot him and is after his daughter. He reminds the press of Kate's murder and that you are in fact, *Desert Baby*. Benning will come, cause he still thinks Sid is on his side. Benning will offer Sid help. Sid will lead him to us."

Bailey sighed at Jack's oration. "I still can't believe he's capable of committing such crimes. I mean, he's...well, he's not exactly spry."

"You don't have to be too spry with a gun in your hand. Besides, he's had the perfect cover," Mud Man said. "I've known him for ten or more years. He's capable all right. And he's been smart, but we've recently found evidence in L.A. to connect him to your mother's death and some of the other women. Once we catch him, he won't see the light of day."

"Jack, when I saw him in the hospital in Dallas, why didn't I remember him?"

"You were only four, Bailey. You can't be expected to remember."

"Still," she sighed. "You would think that I would have found something familiar about him."

"It was dark," Jack wheezed.

Bailey gave no indication of remembering Benning but turned once again to the board with his pictures laid out. Her voice was distant and drawn.

"I don't remember Benning, but I do remember that you were shot that night."

Bailey turned calculatingly toward Jack.

"Forgive me, Jack. You couldn't have killed my mother. He

shot you, too."

"Dear God," Jack said. "You remember."

Bailey stared into the distance as if it held the secrets of her past.

"I was in her lap. She was holding me tight. Someone was driving, but it wasn't you, Jack. She cried for you. I cried for my daddy. He took us to a dark place."

Bailey held out her arms and Jack was quickly by her side. She fell softly into his arms and he stroked her hair. In his embrace, she relived the terror of that night. It was lodged somewhere between her mind and the fear that had manifested in her blood. It flowed both hot and cold. Pain swelled in her chest and she looked at Jack remorseful.

"You didn't kill her. He killed her. Mommy pushed me out of the truck. She told me to run and hide. I cried for her, but she kept pushing me away. She told me not to leave my hiding place. I heard the bangs over and over."

Bailey cried in Jack's arms. She cried in the same strong hold in which her mother had cried. Jack was now crying, too. He kissed her forehead. His chest contracted his own pain. Together, the survivors of that black night cried for the one who didn't survive. Each knew the horror she had faced, for they had faced it, too. And both remembered his harrowing laughter, the cracks of gunfire, the smell of fear, her cries, and the silence of her death. In each other's arms, they mourned her loss – a mother, a lover. Then, Jack pushed her gently out of his arms. Anger and determination replaced his sorrow. He had a sonofabitch to catch. Jack looked at Billy.

"Take her to lie down."

"No," she cried. "Let me stay. Let me help you find him. I'm all right. Really I am."

Jack brushed back her hair. "You've been through a lot just now, Bailey. I need you strong for later. Right now, you need to rest."

She leaned on his broad chest. Her body shook as she beseeched Jack to let her remain.

"Please," she whispered. "She was my mother."

"Well then," he said, brushing her cheek. "I'd say that you've more than earned the right to help."

Her eyes were filled with certainty, but her lips shook unsettled. Just then, Clown Boy motioned for Jack to talk with him privately.

"There's a roadblock in our plan. Hand Runner, our man with Jess and Coyote, isn't answering his calls. Jess isn't answering his. I sent a man to see what's going on. He found Coyote at his home shot to death."

"And Jess?"

"There's no sign of him or Hand Runner. I don't like it, Jack. Something just doesn't smell right here."

# Chapter 24

He took off his wig and rubbed the make-up off his face. It was easier for him to disguise himself when he was younger. Also, he had more drive then. The reward seemed more worth the risks in the earlier years, worth the climactic moment. He was tired. Yet even in his spent state, he was still able to visualize the sweet unerring moment that made everything worth the risks. At the very moment when the obsession takes over, the darkness becomes such a high and the adrenaline kicks in with such a vengeance, nothing can contain it. It was like gaining a seventh sense. The brain starts working overtime, working out the smallest details, so no mistakes will be made. The details were going crazy in his mind right now. He couldn't stop them if he wanted to. He was thinking of Bailey.

"Katie's little girl," he thought. "She'll be worth the risks."

He showered, shaved, and dressed for the hunt. The one-bedroom house he rented was the perfect hideaway. It was within walking distance of the hospital and downtown. He'd flown into Albuquerque and bought an old Ford Granada he'd seen advertised in the paper. He paid cash so as not to leave a trail and drove it to Gallup. He figured luck was with him when he found the small house. He rented it under the assumed name of Maybelle Smallwood, using the façade of a woman recently widowed. She wanted to move closer to town because she couldn't get around as well as she used to. Mr. and Mrs. Dillon, the elderly couple who owned the house were pleased to have someone like Maybelle Smallwood living there, especially after their last tenants.

"It sure is nice to have someone responsible living in the house. The young couple who lived here before you just tore the place up. They had wild parties and carried on like they didn't have respect for other folks' property."

Maybelle assured them there would be no wild parties.

"No indeed," she promised. "You'll hardly know I'm here."

He parked his car in the garage and never took it out except at night. That's when he went hunting. He did his best work at night. His friends said he was nocturnal and he liked the analogy of comparing himself to the creatures of the night. It was gratifying to know that most people slept at night. He hadn't slept at night in over fifty years.

He turned on the small black and white TV. It was almost ten and time for the local news update. For several days, Sid Carson's shooting had been the top local story. He'd made a public appeal from his hospital room. His appeal was for the public to help him find the man who shot him. That man he claimed was Jack Adams. Tonight, he was pleading for Jack Adams to surrender his daughter, whom he had taken from her refuge earlier.

Red Benning sat his worn body on a chair. He was thinking what his course of action should be right now. The game was different now that Jack was alive and had Bailey. His plan to lure her away from the Indian family she had been staying with was less complicated. He thought of going to Sid Carson and enlisting his help. He didn't rule this out, but something inside said this would be a mistake. Something about the whole situation didn't sit well with him. He thought of Jack Adams having his hands on Bailey.

"Bailey belongs to me, Jack Adams. She's mine. Just like Katie was mine. I killed you once, Jack Adams and I'll do it again. I don't know what power resurrected you to haunt me in my latter years, but upon our next meeting, I'll make damn sure you won't be as fortunate."

A memory of Kate Michaels the first time he saw her filled his thoughts. He had to remind himself that he'd been justified in what he'd done. She had rejected him for that low life scum. She turned to Jack for help instead of him and he couldn't forgive her for that. He still loved her, but couldn't forgive her. Even after he hunted her down and she understood the completeness of his love, she turned his help down. She chose to be with Jack and so he had no choice but to right the wrong she had created.

She was so beautiful. He had fallen in love with her the first time he had seen her. He was having lunch with a fellow journalist who worked at the Denver Post. She worked there part-time and just happened to be walking in the main door as they were walking out. She was young and pert and had a body that made a man stop and stare. He was no different. Red remembered his friend speaking to her and later telling him her name. The thing that Red recalled vividly was the way she smiled at him. She had noticed him, too. From that moment on, Kate Michaels was his.

She became his obsession. He followed her to and from work. He watched her take her little girl to dance lessons and to the park in the afternoons. He followed her to the grocery store and to the dry cleaners, knew where she banked and where she had her hair done. At night, before Sid came home from work, he watched her from his car, watched her from the windows in her house. In the dark, he could view her long, firm body as she slipped out of her day clothes and into her nightclothes. He watched her wait for a husband who didn't deserve her. He watched her long into the nights and when Sid finally came home, he watched in torment as she gave herself to this self-serving man. It was agony, but he knew he needed to be patient. His reward would be later. Katie was his. She was worth the hunt and she proved to be his longest and most challenging prey. That was until Bailey.

Red heard on his scanner where a Zuni man had been shot to death twenty or so miles northwest of Gallup near the Arizona border. Mara Carson had given him the name of Billy Nehah as the Zuni man who was protecting Bailey. Red let out a vile sneer recalling his frustration at finally finding Billy Nehah's house and later realizing that Bailey had been taken to another hiding place. It was an obstacle, but certainly not the end of his search. Hell, if he gave up that easily, he'd never be where he is today.

After talking with some locals about Billy Nehah and his family connections, namely a recluse brother named Jimmy Coyote, Red was able to narrow his search for Bailey. Amateurs were so predictable. Finding the place was a little tricky, but the directions a waitress at a local diner had given him led him straight to the place. When he arrived, Jimmy Coyote was there, but his nephew, Jess Nehah, was nowhere to be found.

He had to kill Jimmy Coyote because he had seen his face. The old man was an easy kill. After he killed him, he went through the house and found some of Bailey's things. He went through the clothes she had left, the articles about her mother's murder, and her journal. Red learned from reading her journal that Jess was her lover. She wrote of her love for him, of him touching her. After finding this information out, he decided he had to hunt him down and kill him. That would be another time. Now, he had to get rid of Jack. He knew taking Jack down wouldn't be as easy. He was hoping the police or Sid would do this for him. Red snapped off the TV.

"Time to go to work," he said, snubbing the small-time journalists. "They can't give justice to a story."

He loaded his thermos with piping hot coffee and packed some sandwiches along with a package of honey buns for his sweet tooth. He brought along his briefcase, filled with the tools of his trade. Inside it were his camera, his recorder, and his.38. He set up his scanner to hear the local police and emergency reports. Before the eleven o'clock hour, he was driving down the dark road toward the Zuni Reservation. He parked his car near the entrance of the reservation. He didn't know where tonight's hunt might lead, but he knew Billy Nehah had most likely been informed of his brother's death. This was a place to start. He knew Billy would eventually lead him to his girl.

****

Claire Brennen slipped by the nurses' station near Sid Carson's hospital room. When she entered his room, he was sleeping. She knew she should leave and come back tomorrow. She knew how late the hour was, very late, but she hadn't found rest that night. In her mind, things seemed too important to wait for the morning, especially after she had watched Sid Carson's appeal to Jack Adams.

"Who has Bailey?" she wondered. "I've got to help this man find her. I can't let this wait for morning."

She sat in a chair next to the bed for several minutes before she mustered the courage to nudge him slightly. He let out a gruff moan, but never really woke up completely. She nudged him again, calling out his name.

"Sid," she whispered and then raised her voice. "Sid Michaels, wake up."

It was the name Michaels that caught his attention and he barely had the presence of mind to realize he hadn't been called that name in years. He turned slowly toward the direction of her voice.

"Mr. Michaels," she asked. "Can you hear me?"

"Who are you?" he managed to say. His voice was so low, so jumbled, Claire had to move in closer to hear. He repeated his question. "Who are you?"

"My name is Claire Brennen. I'm a psychologist."

"Christ," he moaned. "You're working a little late tonight, aren't you?"

She smiled through the darkness. Already she was drawn to him, but hadn't she been drawn to him from the beginning? She touched his arm slightly.

"I know you're not up to visitors and I wouldn't be here except I have this unexplained urgency to help you and your family."

"Who are you really?"

"I told you. I'm Claire Brennen. I'm a psychologist"

"Turn on the light, Claire Brennen."

256

She complied. The small overhead lamp unveiled a haunting image and Sid Michaels could do nothing but stare at the woman sitting next to him. Her long blonde hair fell slightly in her face and her dark eyes were riveting over him as if they were awaiting his next move, his next words. On her face was clearly written the seriousness of her visit. For a moment, he thought perhaps the drugs the doctors had given him were causing him to hallucinate and that's why she looked so much like Kate. He shook his head and felt the weight of her hand on his arm.

"Jesus," he said. "Is this some sick joke?"

"I can imagine your confusion, Mr. Michaels, but I assure you, I can explain everything."

He swallowed hard. Again, he asked. "I'll ask you one last time. Who the hell are you?"

She drew in closer to him. "The man who killed your wife, the one who hunts your daughter, I know him, Sid Michaels."

"How?" his voice shook. "How do you know him?"

"I know his mind. I've been in his head a hundred times, a thousand times."

"Give me one reason why I shouldn't push this button and have you thrown out of my room? Are you some kind of a lunatic who's come to haunt me, to play a pathetic game on me?"

"I'm not, I promise. I'm here to help you."

She drew from her purse her badge and showed it to him.

"I thought you were a psychologist?"

"I am. I work for the Albuquerque Police Department."

Sid let out a heavy sigh. "I think you better leave."

Claire spoke quickly. "I met your wife."

"Kate?"

"No," she said, thinking it odd he should still think of Kate as his wife when he'd been married to Mara for so long. "I met Mara at the airport in Santa Fe. She was waiting for her plane and she decided the pressures of her situation were too much. She called someone to help her to help you. I was using the phone next to her and I overheard her distress. I offered her my help, but she refused.

"Well, I'm not one who can turn my back on someone like Mara. It's part of my character, part of who I am and what I do. Anyway, I used my position at the department and started my own investigation. Mr. Michaels, I have my own theories about what happened to Kate. I think they're pertinent, almost vital to your daughter's fate."

He looked at her disbelieving. He attempted to sit up, but only managed to lift his head slightly. She squeezed his arm gently and he looked into her eyes that were firm and steady and sane.

"You're serious, aren't you?"

"Yes, I am. We share a common bond, you and I. Both of us had a spouse who was murdered. I know exactly what you've been through. I know your loneliness. I know your guilt. I know the sleepless nights of reliving the last moments of someone's life and thinking how you could have somehow prevented their death. But you and I are not responsible for the acts of a madman. Sid, I mean Mr. Michaels, this won't bring Kate back. And it sure as hell won't protect Bailey."

"I know this, but really there's nothing you can do."

"I think you're wrong."

"How? How can you help?"

"I want to help you to clear your mind and possibly move your thoughts into another direction."

"What do you mean?"

"You're so set on Jack Adams being responsible for Kate's death. I'm not so sure he killed her."

"Christ," he sat up slowly. "Who...?"

"Who?" she asked intuitively. "I think you've asked yourself this same question. Who besides Jack Adams might have killed Kate?"

"No," he barked. "I know Jack killed her."

"What if he didn't? What if someone else did?"

"Tell me, Ms. Psychologist. If Jack Adams didn't kill her,

who did?"

"I'm not sure, but I'm working on a few leads."

"Like who?"

"Well – a serial killer by the name of Sandy Reed."

"Never heard of him."

"He's incognito."

"Huh?"

"I mean, no one's heard of him in years. And when his murderous streak stopped, that's when Jack Adams's began."

"You think Adams and Reed are the same?"

"No. I think Reed took over Adams's identity."

"What's the connection between Reed and Adams?"

"Their murder victims. They all look like Kate – like me."

Sid studied her face. It was gnarled with pain, but there was something else.

"Like you?"

She nodded. "He likes blondes with brown eyes."

"Claire, Ms. Brennen. I have to know. Were you one of Reed's victims?"

She shook her head.

"No, I wasn't, but I was a victim of someone who could have been Reed. They're all the same when you think about it. They prey on the innocent, on the helpless. Anyway, I'm not really the issue here. What I'm trying to tell you is this. I think maybe this Reed guy killed Kate. Then, when all the hoopla about Jack Adams came into the picture, Reed saw an easy escape. He'd kill his women and the blame would be put on Adams."

"Look, I appreciate your theory and all your hard work, but you're wrong. Jack Adams killed Kate."

"You might be right," she shrugged. "Mr. Michaels, I'm curious about something."

"What?" he asked.

"I told you that your wife was talking to someone on the phone and that she asked him for help. You haven't asked me who that someone was."

"Who was it? Do you know?"

Claire watched his face closely as she disclosed who Mara had called.

"She was talking to a reporter. His name is Red Benning."

Sid clutched the blanket and let out an insufferable cry.

"No...dear God, no...tell me no! Tell me she didn't lead him to her!"

Claire stood next to him now, cupping his head within her slender hands.

"Who, Sid? Benning? Reed?"

She caught the confirmation within Sid's eyes. At that very moment, she knew the truth.

"Benning is Reed," she whispered in his ear. "Benning killed Kate and intends to kill Bailey."

"I know," he whispered back. "Trust me when I say I've got help and we're on his trail."

"I can help," she said.

"How?"

"Let me be his next target."

"Claire, go back to Albuquerque. It's being taken care of as we speak."

A tear fell down her face.

"I carried a child. I had a husband. I'm trained to understand what is going on in his head."

For some compelling reason, Sid held her hand.

"I do understand your need to help, but my daughter's life is at stake here. Tangents can't mislead me, no matter how justified they are. If I need you, I'll contact you. For Bailey's sake, please go home. Go back to your life."

Her admiration for him grew and she conceded to his request.

"All right, but I want you to realize something."

"What?"

"Benning is in his twilight years. He's on his last run and in his mind, he can't fail. He's almost desperate and nothing will stop him, except to be caught or be killed. To possess the

260

daughter of a past victim is almost too sweet for even him to comprehend. He sees Bailey as a gift, if you will. She's his encore to this macabre he's been living. In his mind, he has no other choice. Bailey will be his victim, unless he can be caught first. And Sid – he's a genius at manipulation."

She was sitting on the bed next to him now. They were holding hands. He confided in her his deepest fear.

"If he succeeds, if he takes her, too – oh, God, I'll die. I can't live without her, too."

"Don't," she said, brushing his cheek. "We'll get him."

"We?" he quizzed. "Remember? You promised to go home."

She nodded. "Sure I will."

But in her mind, she was thinking, "I can't go home now, Sid. I have to see this man caught. I have to see Kate's child safely back to her father. I have to see the good guy win for once."

She squeezed his hand. "Kate knew. She knew how much you loved her."

"How do you know?"

"I'm a woman. A woman knows when she's been loved deeply. Kate knew. She didn't forget it."

"I guess you learned that in your psychology books, huh?"

"No," she said, edging off the bed. "I learned that from being loved by my husband so deeply."

Claire tucked a card inside Sid's hand before she made her way to the door. She stood at the door for some time before she told him goodbye.

"Be careful, Sid Michaels. Call me if you need me."

When she left, Sid glanced at the card. He flipped it over and on the back there was a handwritten message. It read, "Call Mara."

He knew the advice was good, but he couldn't call her now. He'd wait until everything was over. He wanted to call her. He wanted to hear her voice.

"When this is all over, Mara, we'll go on a honeymoon.

We'll begin our marriage again. I know I haven't been much of a husband, but when this is all over..."

****

Jack was the only witness to Claire Brennen's visit to Sid. He didn't know what to make of her visit, but he certainly didn't need some self-righteous crusader screwing things up for him, for Bailey. He was amazed at how she had been right on about Benning. He hadn't heard of Sandy Reed, but that was also an intriguing theory. Claire's physical appearance took him aback, just as they had taken Sid aback. He wondered what else could happen to alter what he thought was a tight plan at luring Benning. First, there was the unexpected murder of Coyote, and now this Claire woman shows up out of nowhere. Jack was thinking about how to best handle Claire and how to tell Bailey about Coyote when Bald Eagle came inside. He'd been out double-checking the equipment in the van.

"Listen," Jack said. "I've been thinking. It doesn't look like Benning is going to go to Sid. I'm not sure he's going to take our bait. Thought I'd go do some scouting and check things out. Talk to a few people. Maybe go see Sid."

"You think that's wise? Someone might recognize you. I mean, even though we know the truth, in the public's eyes, you are a cold-blooded killer."

Jack knew this was a possibility, but he couldn't let Benning slip through his hands. It was now or never. He turned to Bald Eagle.

"Has Mud Man reported back since he took Billy to Zuni?"

"Not yet. Man, losing his brother will kill him."

"I've got to find Jess and Hand Man. If something has happened..."

"Clown Boy is already out searching. I still don't know how Benning got past Hand Runner. He's the best tracker I know. He couldn't have been more than a mile from Jimmy Coyote's house. Damn shame."

262

"The desert is like a web in the day, let alone at night."

"Yeah but Hand Runner knows it better than anyone."

"Benning is a cockroach, a damn lucky cockroach. Well – his luck is coming to an end. And when it does…"

"Jack, we have to stay focused. We can't play into his hands."

"Yeah, but all these years, if I had known his name, known who he was. Man, I could have gone after him years ago. All the time, I thought he was one of Sid's guys."

Jack knew his emotions were running high. Culmer had never seen Jack so unraveled. He wasn't sure Jack was in the right frame of mind to see this through.

"Hold yourself together, Jack. You can't rehash the past. Not now! We have to make sure this bastard doesn't live to see the light of day."

"You're right. I'm going to go check in on Bailey. Then, I'm going to Sid. After that, I'm going to scout around the Zuni Reservation. It's the most logical place for Benning to be looking for Bailey. "

She was asleep in the bedroom, exhausted from the day's happenings. When Mud Man took Billy to Zuni to tell him about Jess and Coyote, Jack told her it was part of their plan. He said Billy and Mud Man were going to Zuni so Billy could make an appearance and put Benning off track. They were also going to look for new leads. Jack didn't have the heart to tell Bailey about Jess just yet. He figured news like this could wait. He sat down in a small chair next to her and listened to her soft breathing. He was too possessive of her, he knew. But these were uncertain times. He wondered what kind of relationship they might have when this was all over, if any.

He thought about how different his life would be when Benning was held accountable. There would be no reason to hide. He'd literally be a free man. He also wondered if Rita would be waiting for him like she said she would. He couldn't blame her if she wasn't. Things were hairy the last time they were together, but she hung with him and never showed any signs that she believed him to be the animal everyone said he was. She even warned him that her mother had been to the Dallas Police. She was back in Dallas now, pretending things were over between them. At least, he hoped she was pretending.

"Rita," he thought, "Now you were someone I never expected to meet. You were indeed an unexpected pleasure."

He heard Bald Eagle moving about in the other room. He kissed Bailey's cheek and went to talk with him. Bald Eagle looked concerned.

"What is it?"

"Jack, I think you're right. I can't help thinking that things are going south fast. We need to act now. I just tried to call Mud Man. He's not answering his radio or his cell. It's not like him not to answer or at least report back. First Hand Runner and now Mud Man."

"Maybe he's out of radio and cell range."

"Maybe, but my gut tells me differently. Go, Jack. Go to Sid. Find out what he wants to do. I would go myself, but I'm the only one who knows how to get to our next base in the dark. I can have the equipment loaded in minutes if we need to move out."

"And Bailey?"

"You have to ask, Jack? I'll guard her with my life. You know that. Besides, we probably are just being overly cautious. Just find Mud Man or word of him. I'll hold things together here."

Jack thought for a while.

"Okay, I'm outta here. Give Mud Man one more call first."

Already Jack was putting on his vest and coat. He checked the bullets in his gun. He looked at Bald Eagle.

"Don't try to contact me. I'll be in touch with you."

Bald Eagle gripped Jack's arm.

"Be careful, man."

"Don't you worry about me. You just take care of Bailey. Oh, and don't let her know about Coyote and that Jess is missing. I think Billy or Sid should tell her. This news is going

264

to blow her away. We need her alert and functioning as normally as possible. We don't need her giving up. No need to wait to go to our next base. Pack up now and leave. We probably should have moved hours ago. The way things are looking, our guy is getting impatient."

Bald Eagle lent Jack a broad smile.

"Isn't that what we are hoping for?"

**\*\*\*\***

Bailey heard Jack drive away. She was awake when he came to her, when he watched her, and when he kissed her cheek. She overheard Bald Eagle talking to Jack about Mud Man and Billy and being careful. She also overheard Jack saying something about Jess and Coyote and how such bad news would blow her away.

"Something has happened to Jess," she knew. "I can feel it. Billy never would have left me if something more important had not taken him away. Jess, where are you?"

She slipped out of bed and looked out of the crack in the door. She saw Bald Eagle at a desk in the next room. Her first inclination was to question him, but she knew he wouldn't tell her anything he didn't want her to know. She wondered what made Jack storm out so late at night. And Jack, like Billy, would not have left her alone, unless there was a break in the case or unless something was terribly wrong. A chilling sensation swept over her. She had a peculiar sensation that Benning had something to do with Jess.

"He's found Benning and he's gone after him. Dear, God, does Benning have Jess? Did he…? No! I refuse to believe such a thing. Jess is safe and probably with Billy now."

Still, her heart sank. She had to know. She noticed that Bald Eagle had moved outside. She heard him in the van. She edged to the main room and saw on the monitor that her father was asleep in his room. With that worry gone, she looked at the monitor to the Security Station. It was dark. She noticed the monitor to the outer perimeters was also dark. She thought this strange, but didn't really think about it much further. Her eyes scanned the notes that Bald Eagle had left on the desk. It was coded, so she couldn't figure most of it out, but she did see Jess's name and Coyote's name. And there in bold letters was the word "SHOT." Her mind started playing tricks on her. What was going on? She had to know. At that moment, she decided she had to run. She had to go find Jess, even though she knew her own safety depended on her staying here with Bald Eagle. Something told her she had to go to Jess because he couldn't come to her.

"How can I get past Bald Eagle?"

She crept slowly to the window. He was near the only vehicle left. How would she get the keys? No doubt, Bald Eagle had them in his pocket. Somehow, in her state of rational panic, she went back to the bedroom, slipped on a pair of jeans, a t-shirt, and her shoes. She heard him move into the house and saw him standing over the desk. He was talking to someone on the phone. Again, she heard him say something about someone being shot and killed. Again, she heard Jess's name. She saw him look toward the bedroom and was sure he had heard her up and about. But then, he started packing up some more of the equipment.

"He's taking me somewhere else," she said. "I can't go with him, not if I want to find Jess."

She had studied well the operational map and Billy had told her the exact location of the hideout. It wasn't far from Billy's house and the reservation. She knew if she could get a hold of the van, she could find Jess. Peeking through the cracked door, she saw Bald Eagle messing with some equipment on the floor. His back was turned toward her and he was in a vulnerable position. There was a chair next to him. If she could reach the chair, she could use it to knock him out. She tiptoed out of the room and took the chair into her hands. He made it easy for her and she felt bad for what she was about to do. She brought the chair high up over her head and slammed it on his

266

back. He slumped sideways but was far from down. She brought the chair up one more time, thrusting it over his powerful chest. This time he fell on his back and lay in a semi-conscious state. She saw him staring at her in pain and regret, and something else she couldn't identify. This something was fear.

"Don't," he pleaded, just before he passed out. She felt his pulse and it was still strong. She had done well. He was out but uninjured. She would contact Mud Man when she reached Gallup and tell them what she had done.

"I'm sorry, Bald Eagle. I had to do it. I couldn't leave with you. I have to find Jess."

Quickly, she reached inside his pocket for his keys. They weren't there. Could it be that he had left them in the van for a quick getaway? She ran outside. They were in the ignition. She got inside the van and realized she was sitting on something hard...a gun. No doubt, Bald Eagle had left it there in his haste to leave quickly. She held the powerful piece in her hands. She'd never held a gun before, let alone used one. She would probably shoot herself if she tried. Then, she thought of her mother and Benning. The feel of the gun gave her a false sense of power and security. She tucked it under her seat, turned on the ignition, and drove away in the dark of night. Her only thoughts were of Jess, and she had no concept of the evil that awaited her arrival.

# Chapter 25

Jack got to Sid's room after midnight.

"Christ," Sid said. "Do you always have to sneak up on me while I'm sleeping?"

"There are a couple of glitches in our plans, Sid."

"What? Bailey's all right, isn't she?"

"She's fine, Sid. Bald Eagle is guarding her. We decided to move to the next base. It's more secluded and further from here. She'll be safer. Right now, I'm concerned about the woman who came to see you."

Sid let out a deep sigh. "I've been thinking about her, too. Where in the hell did she come from? I mean to know so much, too."

"She knows just enough to blow away our front. I'm going to go to her. Did she leave you a number where she could be reached?'

"It's written on her business card. I have it in my wallet. It's in the drawer next to the bed. Get it for me."

Jack handed him the wallet.

"Here, you find the number."

He sat on the chair next to Sid's bed.

"So, looks like you're healing nicely. Are you very sore?"

"Like you really give a damn. One shot would have gotten the job done."

Jack grinned. "I had to make it look convincing."

Sid almost laughed, but then he remembered he was talking to Jack.

"You know, I still have plenty of reasons to take you down, Jack. Believe me, nothing would please me more than to see you pay."

"Maybe you have reasons, but you'll never bring me down. You're out of your league. Always have been."

Sid frowned at the truth in Jack's words. He changed the subject.

"You said there were other problems. What are they?"

"It's Jess and Billy's brother, Coyote. Jess and Hand Runner are missing. Coyote was shot to death at his home."

"Benning?"

Jack nodded. "Who else? Bailey doesn't know yet. I thought you should tell her. Or, maybe Billy."

"Is it safe for me to go to her?"

"I figure news like this can wait until it is."

Sid closed his eyes and thought of Bailey. "She's in love with Jess, you know. Christ, will this madness never end?"

"Damn right it will, Sid. We're this close."

Jack positioned his fingers so they fairly touched to show Sid how close they were.

"If Benning doesn't bite tomorrow, Jack, I'm outta here. Then, what do we do?"

"We get Bailey as far away as possible. It's getting too risky keeping her so near. This business with Jess – well, let's just say Benning got too close for comfort."

"Why don't we just go find the bastard right now and take him out of his misery?"

Jack smiled. "Sounds good to me, except for one reason. I don't know where the hell he is. He's close, I know that much. I can smell him."

"Damn," Sid said. "Can anything else go wrong?"

"Mud Man isn't answering his calls. I'm not too worried, but he took Billy back to Zuni hours ago to tell his wife and sister about Coyote and Jess. He should have reported in by now."

"You don't think Benning got to them, do you?"

"I really don't. But that's why I'm here, to check things out. When I leave here, I'm going to talk to this Claire woman and then go to the reservation."

"Jack, you go find Mud Man. I'll handle Claire Brennen. I'll give her a call first thing tomorrow. She's not going to do anything tonight."

"Be careful what you say. We don't know who is listening in on your conversations."

"I know what's at risk here, Jack."

Jack stood up and looked down at his once best friend.

"You do realize we just had our first civil conversation in years."

Sid's stare was cold.

"When this is all over, don't ever expect me to speak to you again."

Jack walked toward the door and Sid followed his form that stopped before opening it. Jack stood there for some time before turning to look at Sid. Sid couldn't see Jack's face in the shadows, but his tone and words were remorseful.

"I guess I have this coming to me. If I could, I'd change everything. God, I wish I could – but I can't."

****

When Jack left, Sid was restless. He couldn't stew in bed one moment longer. He had to do something. Jack's sudden redemption weighed heavily on his mind. It was easier to hate him than to accept he'd changed. Sid picked up the phone and called Claire Brennen's motel room.

"Yeah," her groggy voice answered.

"Sleeping?" Sid asked.

"Sid Michaels? Is this you?"

"Yeah," he whispered. "I need to talk to you."

"When?"

"Is now too soon?"

"They won't let me back in your room tonight, Sid."

"Meet me at the main entrance in twenty minutes. I'm outta this place. But, I'll have to bunk in your room tonight. Hope you don't mind."

270

"Make it thirty minutes," she said and hung up.

****

Jack easily left the hospital without being noticed and walked a couple of blocks down a side street where he had parked his truck. He got inside and the first thing he did was to call Mud Man. There was no answer.

"Damn," he said and felt on the dash for his cigarettes. He lit one and then started the engine. Before he could put his truck into drive, he was greeted by the barrel of a Beretta. Jack looked into his rearview mirror and saw a figure seated in the back seat, wearing dark clothing and a black ski mask.

"Hello, Jack. It's been a long time."

Somewhere in his memory, Jack knew he'd heard this man's voice before. His first intuition was that it was Benning, but the voice was too high, almost squeaky. Jack turned around cautiously to face his attacker.

"Who are you?" Jack asked boldly.

"What were you doing in Sid's room? Are you planning to finish the job off and kill him like you did Katie?"

"Katie?" Jack said. "No one ever called her Katie but her father and her brother, Johnny."

"That's right, Jack. It's me. Crazy Johnny."

"Johnny, you're wrong. I didn't kill her. But, I know who did and he's in Gallup right now. He plans to kill Bailey. Sid knows all about it. Go ask him."

"Always lies with you, Jack. Always thinking of ways to save your own sorry ass. I'm not listening, Jack. I'm going to do what I should have done years ago when I found out Katie had succumbed to your charms. It's payday, Jack."

"So you plan on killing me, is that it?"

"Why else would I be here?"

"Before you do, hear what I have to say."

****

Sid was waiting for Claire at the main entrance of the hospital with his suitcase in hand. They were quiet on the ride to her motel. She didn't ask how he'd managed to leave the hospital. Her guess was he'd just walked out. She pulled into a Best Western and parked in front of room 108. Sid turned to face her. His stare was drawn.

"Claire, you know so much about Benning. Tell me. What's he thinking now? Am I ally or foe?"

"The way I figure it, he doesn't trust anyone. This includes you. I don't think he will come to you. I'd have to say he sees you as foe."

Sid frowned and made no move to get out of the car. She propped her elbow against her door and rested her head on her hand. She brought her leg up and braced her foot on the seat in such a way, it caused her jacket to draw up. This unveiled a woman in remarkable physical condition. The fitted leggings she was wearing captured the long line of her muscular legs and he could tell she took pride in her shape. She probably worked out daily. He noted the way she had her blonde hair twisted in a bun and held up with a silver clasp. She looked delicate, but he knew she was tough, tougher than most men he knew. Her brown-eyed stare penetrated through him and he found himself almost aroused, even at a time like this.

"Do you want to go inside?" she asked.

"I want to get the bastard who's after my daughter."

"Aren't you confident with the people protecting her?"

"I am, but I feel so helpless. I feel like I should be doing something."

"Well," she smiled. "You were shot. What can we do that's not being done?"

"We? Not we, Claire, just me. Tell me. What's your game?"

"I don't play games, Sid. But he does. He likes games and he's made all of us a part of his game. He's out there right now, waiting for our next move. He might be watching us right now."

Sid repositioned himself slightly. Pain shot through his shoulder and his face grimaced.

"Do you think I don't know this?"

She moved from her side of the car to his and leaned so close to him that her mouth almost touched his. She whispered to him and he could feel her hot whisper brush across his lips. The minty smell of her mouthwash filled his nostrils.

"If your plan to take him down doesn't work, Sid, let me help. Benning will never stop unless he's killed. He's an animal, Sid. One I'm not sure you've ever unearthed before. I know his kind. I bear the wounds given to me by a madman just like him. I know what makes him tick."

Sid touched her cheek gently.

"This isn't your fight, Claire."

She took his hand and led it to a knife wound she bore just below her waistline. She held his hand there.

"Like Kate, I had an unborn child taken from me."

Intuitively he caressed her wound. He brought his other hand up over her shoulder and felt his heart race from her touch. So much so, he pulled from her embrace.

"Claire," he asked askance, "Why are you really involved in this case?"

"Kate drew me in with her eyes. It's as if she's been guiding me here. Sounds strange, huh? Truthfully, I can't explain it to you, because I don't understand it myself. This is very frustrating. You see, I'm a woman of logic, and there's no logic in my being here. Except, well, except for the fact that I know Benning's mind so well."

"What exactly is going on in his mind?"

"He knows by now that the police are on to him. He knows his public days are over. He's getting old and he's thinking that this is his last chance. He wants to make a grand finale. He has three plans, the way I figure.

"Plan A, of course, is to kill Bailey now. If he can't, he'll go to Plan B. Plan B is more risky for him, so I doubt he'll try it. Still – he might. He might go into hiding and attempt to get to Bailey later. I doubt he does this though. You see, he's turned on by the idea that he could kill Bailey in the same place he killed Kate.

This is a big advantage for us and it's the only predictable thing he's going to do. That – and the fact that he intends to kill Bailey.

"If Plans A and B fail, he'll go to Plan C. This is a last resort for him because he values himself higher than he values anyone else and he's rationalized everything he's ever done. In his eyes, he's justified. Plan C is a desperate plan and I'm fearful that our Mr. Benning is desperate. He might set Bailey up to kill him. In his tortured mind, she's the only one worthy of killing him and then after she does, he envisions her mourning his death. In many ways, she will, too. She'll certainly be haunted by it. I know I was when I killed the man..."

Claire's voice trailed off and she got a faraway look in her eyes.

"I'm not important now. Bailey's safety is the most important thing."

Sid lifted her chin and in the same moment, her clip snapped open, causing her hair to fall in her face. He drew her closer to him and she responded by wrapping her arms around his neck. Then, she brought her mouth over his and kissed him recklessly. She swept one hand through his thick hair, while the other hand moved over his chest. When she broke the kiss, they were both panting.

"This is a little unorthodox therapy, isn't it, Claire? Do you indulge everyone you help with such intensity?"

"Oh," she moaned. "I'm so, so sorry."

Abruptly, she scooted herself back to her side of the car. In all her life, she'd never reacted so unprofessionally. She didn't dare to look at him, but could hear his breathing, could almost feel his breath. She felt of her lips, still wet from their kiss. She heard him rustling next to her, pulling out his cigarettes and lighting one. The scent of smoke filled her nostrils, reminding her of his strong magnetism — as if she needed reminding.

He smiled at her. Her kiss had been a sweet diversion from the hell he'd been living, even if for the slightest moment. He called to her through the silence.

274

"Claire, what happened was just one of those things. Don't beat yourself up over it."

He flicked his cigarette out the window and then reached to turn the keys that were still in the ignition and started the car. As the engine idled, she stared at him curiously.

"I guess we're collaborators now, Claire. First thing we do is go to Bailey."

"What if Benning follows us?"

Sid lent a sardonic smile. "Yeah, what if he does?"

# CHAPTER 26

Bailey drove the dark road, trying desperately to retain the memory of the path that led to Jess's house. Everything looked so different at night – and so alike. The moon was pale, illuminating little light, and the night was fog-filled, sweeping over the desert like an ominous plague. Bailey was living off adrenaline. She hadn't really rested for a day or so, not since Jack took her from Coyote's house. She turned on the van's secure channel radio to keep alert and to distract herself from the possible danger. She also wanted it on so she could call for help if needed.

She gripped the wheel tightly. The drive was cumbersome and it was getting to her nerves. She thought she should go back. Then, she heard what she thought was Bald Eagle's voice calling for Mud Man on the radio. The dialogue exchanged between the two men gave her a start. They were talking of Billy and Coyote and Jess. She heard them discussing death – Jess's death? There was something about Benning leaving Gallup and Bailey escaping. Bailey couldn't register anymore. That was why Billy had left with Mud Man. Could it be true? With talk of Jess's death, her life seemed to end at that very moment on that dark road. She thought about her murdered mother. Her lover had been killed, too, or at least she thought he had. But Jack hadn't died. Jess, she knew, didn't have Jack's grit. Kate had her child to fight for that night. What was there left for Bailey to fight for now that Jess was gone?

Bailey pulled to the side of the road leaving the motor idling. She searched the dash and glove compartment for a cigarette, even though she'd never smoked a day in her life. Somehow she remembered that Kate had also smoked that night. The spirit of her mother was everywhere, as was the haunting presence of a cold-blooded murderer. Bailey, suddenly reliving her mother's past, looked in the seat behind hers to make sure her daughter was all right. Snapping back, Bailey let out a short laugh, but it was really a cry of mourning.

"God," she cried aloud, "Why did you have to take Jess, too?"

She thought she saw a flash of light streak behind her, but she was too numb to connect it with any danger. She was slipping into a state of darkness and there in that darkness, she thought of Jess and Kate.

Shaking, Bailey forced herself to focus on the two people she had loved so dearly. Their spirits would keep her from falling apart. She held back the tears that had surfaced, realizing this was not the time to break down. Later, she would mourn their deaths. Now, she had to keep sane. She had to do this to honor them.

She steered the van from the side road and drove toward the main road, no longer heading toward Zuni, but toward Gallup where Sid was. Surrounded by darkness, the only sign of human existence was debris spread across the deserted land. Through the open window, the lone cry of a coyote severed her being and she let out a soft cry in response. Once again, she looked to the seat behind her, half expecting to see a frightened child.

"Mommy," she heard her tiny voice call for help.

Disoriented, she looked ahead as if she were searching for something familiar, something in which to focus.

"The truck stop," she thought. "I remember a small truck stop being some ten miles or so from the main road. It has to be near."

She happened to look into her rearview mirror and noticed a light of some sort, probably headlights, coming into range. Suddenly jolted, she steadied her nerves by gripping the wheel and keeping her eyes directed on the road ahead. She was eased somewhat when the light seemed to drop further into the distance. She let out a heavy sigh.

"Keep your wits about you, Bailey."

She spotted a cellular phone on the console of the car and almost yelped for joy. She wasn't alone after all.

"Daddy," she said. "I'm coming to you."

She called his cell but got his voice mail. A combination of numbers registered in her mind and when she punched them, she did get the hospital. The night operator wouldn't let her call go through, even after she said it was an emergency. She suggested she call 911. Frustrated, Bailey hung up and reached for the radio. She called for Jack, but there was no answer. She called for Bald Eagle, but he didn't answer. Bailey vaguely wondered if he had been hurt more than she realized.

She tried Sid's cell one more time. Still no answer. She thought of calling Sammy, but what could he do in Dallas? A set of headlights beamed behind her and she placed the phone in her lap, along with the handgun of Bald Eagle. She draped her coat over them. She watched through her mirror as the car moved directly behind her. When it got within a car's length of hers, she looked ahead to see the lights of the truck stop come into view. As she neared the truck stop, the car trailing her sped up and passed her. She tried to recognize its make and driver but she couldn't. As she watched it move out of sight, she was certain her heart had stopped.

By then the truck stop was in plain view and there were a few cars in the parking lot, mainly 18-wheelers. Bailey calmed down somewhat at the sight of the truck stop. She was connected to living beings. She thought about going inside to have some coffee, regroup and maybe ask around about a Zuni man being murdered. When she parked the van, she swore that a man walking into the truck stop was Red Benning. She knew he was too smart to go into a public place, but she panicked and turned on the van's engine. She decided to keep driving. She knew Gallup was only five or so miles up the road. Just five miles until she'd be in her Daddy's arms.

A mile or so up the road, she saw a detour sign. It led her

down an unmarked dirt road that seemed to parallel with the highway. She knew she was backtracking. When she saw distant lights behind her once again, she instinctively thought to turn the van around and go back the way she came. As the lights neared, her instincts kicked in and she cut her lights, edging the van to the side of the road. She parked it behind a mound of rocks, where she killed the engine. She prayed that her mind was only playing tricks on her and that the car coming in her direction wasn't Red Benning.

She tried once more to radio Jack, but he still didn't answer her calls. She called his cell even though he told her never to call it, because it could be traced. She called the hospital once more and they let her through this time, but Sid wasn't answering. She held the phone in her hand, ready to call 911 if necessary. Then, she sat and waited – waited for fate to catch up with her.

****

Bailey thought she heard footsteps next to the van, even though she had not seen or heard a car. She positioned her coat in her lap so that the gun was well within her reach. She locked all of the doors and shut the windows, except for the one next to her, which she left slightly cracked. She waited – waited for Benning to come for her. She felt the intensity of every one of her heartbeats. The beats drummed in her head like a ticking bomb. She knew this night would end in one of two ways. Either Benning would get her or she would get him. After waiting for some time, she guessed the footsteps had been her imagination. Or, it could have been an animal of some sort. Still, her fear mounted.

And then, from out of nowhere, a car parked next to her. She watched intently as Benning got out of his car and tried to open the passenger's door of the van. She turned on the ignition and made the plan to bolt. She called 911. As she waited for the operator to answer, Benning tapped on her window. She noticed his gun and dropped to the floor between the driver and passenger's seat. Her gun was safe within her clutches. She heard a shot and knew he had shot one of her tires out. The 911 operator still hadn't answered. She hung up and tried again. Through the crack in her window, he was able to manipulate the driver's lock.

Benning was cool as he opened the door and sat in the driver's seat. She was huddled in the opposite corner of the back seat. He smiled as if they were old friends meeting after a long separation. His gold smile gleamed in the darkness and she could feel the blood rushing out of her body. She gripped the leg of the seat to steady her nerves. He was pleased with himself. He'd been planning this moment for seventeen years.

"Hello, Rebecca, I mean, Bailey," he said elatedly. "You've put me on one hell of a chase these past couple of days."

He had a flashlight in his hand and turned it on, moving its light up and down her body. She saw him lick his lips. She swallowed hard. Even in the dark, she could see his hands were shaking but knew his eyes were fixed on her. If he suspected she held the gun, he didn't let on. He told her to move closer to him, but she sat frozen. He told her again. This time his voice was more commanding. He pointed the gun at her. She edged slightly toward the center of the back seat.

"We are going to take a drive, Bailey. I know a place where we'll both be safe. Very slowly, we are going to get out of the van and get into my car. But first, let me see what is under your coat."

Panic filled her. Should she make her move and shoot him now? He might be watching for such a move. One thing she knew for certain, she wasn't going to get into his car. She felt for the phone. Slowly, she drew it out from under her coat and handed it to him. He let out a short laugh, taking the phone and throwing it out the window.

"You won't be needing that."

He nudged her arm with the point of his gun and suggested that she sit in the middle next to the driver's seat. The need to survive kept her alert and sane. She followed his instructions and sat next to him, hiding her gun under her leg. He was breathing heavily as he got a better look at her. As she got closer to him, she could tell he was nervous now and this fact eased her fear somewhat. He looked old and haggard, almost resigned. Was he capable of doing the things she had read about? Right now it didn't seem possible, but she guessed maybe that was part of his lure, no one expected such violence from someone like him.

Then she remembered what Jack had told her. He's an expert shot. That's his skill. He's had years of experience. And...he breeds fear. She assessed her situation and her location. She knew if she could get away from him, she could outrun him. The problem was she didn't know where she was. Could she hide in a dark corner like she had before or was he expecting such a move?

"I knew you'd be an angel," he said. "Just like your mama. So beautiful. So perfect."

He moved his hand down her back and around to her breasts. The touch of his rough hand severed her nerve, but she remained cool and detached. She knew she had to be one step ahead of him if she were to survive. He took her hand and kissed it. She felt the vile taste of vomit reach her throat, but she remained steady.

"You know, Bailey. This place suits me just fine. How about you? I'm really not in the mood for a drive anymore, not just yet anyway."

"Where are we?" she asked timidly.

"The Indians call this spot the *Land of the Dead*," he said.

"Corn Mountain," she whispered. Something like courage began to edge inside of her. If they were truly near Corn Mountain, she might be able to see something familiar. It was so close to Jess's house. Still, the desert played tricks on a mind at night. She stared into the dark night. Through the open window, the residue of an intrusive cloud of smoke caused her eyes to swelter. She rubbed them. She actually coughed.

"Damn Indians," he continued, "are having a ritual. They

are mourning their dead. No matter. It's of no concern to us."

Bailey's head snapped in his direction. Was he speaking of Jess? She knew he was playing with her sanity and emotions. Still, her anger flared. She looked at the face of this animal. He was a wild beast watching his prey, knowing fully well he would have her. The question was when. Bailey thought Benning would hold out until the very last minute. She thought he would want to savor his kill. Now she wasn't so sure. He seemed anxious and impatient. She thought to keep him talking, keep him calm. Maybe, just maybe, help would come for her. She clutched her spirit necklace and the gold cross that Mara had given her. She prayed for divine help.

"I remember you," she said softly. "You talked to me about my daddy. You said you were going to take me to him. You said you loved my mommy."

"I did love your mommy, Bailey. Just like I love you."

"Is that why you killed her?"

Without a reply, Benning abruptly reached for her, drew her near him, and pressed his mouth over hers. His kiss was turbulent and she could taste her own blood because he had bitten her lip. Then, he threw her back down on the floor of the van like a rag doll. He was on fire. Fear enveloped her. No, he wasn't waiting. He was ready for the kill. He held his gun against her head.

"Take off your clothes," he ordered. "Let me see all of you."

"Mommy didn't take off her clothes," she thought. "Mommy ran from him. She ran and he shot her in the back. I must do what he says. I must be smarter than he is. If you fight him, you won't live through the night. He wants you to fight him."

She started to undress, skillfully moving her gun so that it was still positioned under her thigh. She took off her blouse first, but then he stopped her. He took the blouse and tore it in half. She had read enough about him to know what he was going to do next. He was going to tie her hands behind her back. She couldn't let that happen. She noticed the hand that held his gun was slightly open and that the gun was barely in his grip. She heard him asking her something like did she like his game so far. In his moment of hesitation, he had forgotten she was his victim instead of a willing player. She used this to her advantage. This was her moment of reckoning.

"Now!" she cried to herself. "God, give me strength!"

Without hesitation, she took advantage of his weakness and pushed him against the driver's door with all of her strength. Then, she reached for her gun and shot him in the chest. She jumped on the passenger's seat, unlocked the door and started running. With his gun still in his hand, he managed to get one shot out, hitting Bailey in her shoulder. She knew she was hit, but also knew she had to keep running. As she ran, she heard a round of gunshots being fired and she half expected to feel bullets in her back. She ran for what seemed like a lifetime, holding on to her shoulder and praying that God would lead her to safety.

As she ran, she smelled the pungent air of smoke and heard drums getting closer and louder. Something inside of her told her to follow the sound of the drums. She ran as fast and steadily as her feet would take her. The smoke was suffocating and she could no longer catch her breath. When she couldn't run anymore, she fell to the ground. Moving in and out of consciousness, she knew she would die on the desert floor just as her mother had seventeen years ago.

Weak and dazed, she saw a spectral light. She heard humming and what she thought were drums beating, but she couldn't be certain. As she lay on the cold earth, her body seemed to leave its state of reality and it began to float into a new state of being. She was no longer afraid of what she might face. She was crawling now, crawling closer to the light and the peaceful chanting. A smoky haze enveloped her and she felt the heat of the fire burning her body. Or was it her body? She didn't know. She was in a whirling daze, turning around and around as if she had no control of her destiny. For one faint moment, she thought she saw her mother standing in front of her. She heard her voice call out, "Rebecca."

Bailey closed her eyes to assure herself that what she was seeing was only an illusion, a weakness derived from her ordeal. When she opened them again, she was surrounded by a mass of people. They were like floating spirits calling her by name. Perhaps she had died and this was the afterlife. They were summoning her. Somewhere in her mind, she recalled their faces.

She recalled reading about them in Dr. Claiborne's research. She'd seen them in Billy's paintings. Coyote had painted their faces for the Shalako. Their names were used in a covert operation to protect her. These spirits were now brightly dressed and glazed by the light of the bright fire. They were the kachinas who lived in alliance with nature. More gathered and they danced around her like a powerful force of nature, singing and chanting and celebrating.

Strong arms lifted her and she barely had the strength to open her eyes to see a masked spirit peering down at her. Strangely, she didn't fear his touch or his intentions. She knew without being told who he was. He was her guardian spirit. She felt her body being placed into other arms. When she opened her eyes, she saw Jess's face. She heard Billy's voice, and then Jess was speaking to her. At the thought of Jess, she cried out. The arms that held her drew her nearer. She gripped them possessively. She gazed down at the hands that held her. These hands had held her before, had touched her during lovemaking. She felt warm lips brush over her cheek.

"Jess?" she whispered.

"I'm here."

"But, you're dead...you died."

"I'm alive."

"Oh," was the last thing she said before she passed out completely.

"Don't die," Jess whispered. "Don't leave me, Bailey. I love you."

284

# CHAPTER 27

Many weeks after Benning's death, the fellowship of the Zunis and those who lived in Gallup began preparing for their winter solace. This year's celebration would represent a rebirth as such and a healing time. For years, Kate Michaels's brutal killing had overshadowed the land. Now, with the mystery of her death solved and her murderer taken down, they would begin the process of healing.

Sid had rented a house outside of Gallup so that he could be near Bailey while she recovered from her gunshot wound. When she was released from the hospital, it was the perfect place for her to heal and grow strong. He teased her and said they had matching battle wounds. The ranch was large enough to accommodate the many well-wishers who came and went on their behalf. Mara had come the day after Bailey had been shot and hadn't left her side. Sammy and Diane flew in a week later. Sid was overcome with changing emotions, but he was glad Mara was there. She had been there through everything and she knew what he had been through all of these years.

In her arms, there was no need to explain his changing moods. They would begin anew. When they made love for the first time, he considered her a passionate partner as well as a loyal confidant. Had she always been this beautiful? During this time, he noticed she had grown stronger, more confident. He welcomed this change, but was unprepared for dealing with the facets that came with a confident woman.

"Sid, I saw Jack in Gallup yesterday. He wants to come and see Bailey before he leaves. I told him it would be all right."

Sid nodded. He'd been careful not to run into Jack while Bailey was in the hospital. Mara had always made certain their paths didn't cross. She'd done this mainly for Bailey's sake. She didn't need a public or private confrontation between the two.

"I guess after what he did for Bailey," Sid admitted. "He should be allowed to come here and visit. I've got some business in Gallup today. We can go together. Jack can have the day with Bailey. Diane and Sammy can host him."

"I think you should see him, Sid. I think it's time."

"Time for what?"

"Time to face the past. Time to bring things out in the open."

"What's to face?"

"The real reasons you hate Jack. You have to stop blaming him solely for Kate's death. We're guilty, too. Maybe more than Jack."

"Jesus, Mara. He took my wife. He took my child. If Kate hadn't been killed, that would be reason enough to hate him."

"Yes, but — well," she reminded him. "You did take a lover first. You opened the door for him."

He darted toward the door.

"You can come with me or not. I don't have to listen to this."

"Yes, you do," she said in such a way he turned around to give his undivided attention. "There's something else you need to know, too. It's about Kate and what happened before she died. But before I tell you, I want you to know how much I loved you then – still love you. That's why I must tell you this now."

"What?" he shot back impatiently.

"Sit down," she said shaking. "This won't be easy for you – and it may take a while."

****

When Jack arrived later that day, Sid was hardly compliant, well into a fifth of scotch. His mood bordered on disdain, toward both Jack and Mara. Mara was pale but gracious as she

286

offered Jack a drink. He declined. Bailey broke through the heavy cloud that filled the room when she moved toward Jack and gave him a hug and kiss. Sid clenched his teeth and because he couldn't stomach the scene any longer, he left the room. Mara followed him. Bailey's eyes remained on Jack.

"I'm glad you're here."

"I came to say goodbye, Bailey. Now that I know you are going to be all right, I'm leaving Gallup."

"Where will you go?"

"I'm going home. I've got a small farm near Mexico City."

"You've been exonerated, Jack. You don't have to hide out in a foreign country."

Jack smiled at her innocence.

"It's my home, Bailey. I've lived there for years. My mother is there and my wife. It's really a lovely place. Peaceful, you know."

"I didn't know you were married. I'd like to meet your wife, and of course, your mother someday."

Again, he smiled. He wondered if she would be so eager if she knew his wife was Rita.

"Well," he said. "Maybe someday you will."

Jack reached for her hands and squeezed them. When their eyes met, she saw finality in them as if she might never see him again. She also saw his deep love for her. She squeezed his hands and whispered to him.

"How can I thank you? What does a person say to someone who's done so much for her?"

He drew her in his arms. He held her for some time before he spoke.

"Be happy, Bailey. That is thanks enough. Think about me every once in a while and know that I'll be thinking of you always. If you should ever need me, I'm only a phone call away."

"Jack," she cried, still clinging on to him.

He fought back his own tears.

"No more tears, Bailey. Too many have been shed already."

"Oh, Jack. He took so much when he took her."

Jack could only nod in agreement. A lump manifested in his throat. Then, he found his voice.

"Yeah, but he didn't take everything. He didn't take you."

"No, he didn't," she agreed. "You and I were brought together. I found Jess and Billy and my grandfather. I have a family I never knew existed. Did you ever meet my grandfather?"

"No, I never did. Your mother talked about him a lot. They were estranged. He didn't approve of Sid. I do know that before she met Sid, she and her father were inseparable. His life must have been pure hell when she married Sid and more so when she died. You were taken from him. There were so many unspoken words."

"Stay, Jack. You must know what you mean to me."

He looked at her hopeful, but then resigned.

"I can't. You know I can't."

"Daddy will come around, Jack. I know he will."

"It's a lot to ask of him, Bailey."

"Won't you at least talk to him before you leave?"

"Why, Bailey? It would serve no purpose."

"Do it for me, please."

He pinched her cheek. She had his heart in her hand.

"For you? Anything."

"There's something else, Jack. It's about Jess. We're getting married. Daddy thinks we should wait. He thinks we need to sort out our feeling and not rush into anything. He reminded me that not too long ago I was engaged to Ron."

Jack gave her a concerned look.

"He has a point."

"I know he does, but being with Jess has changed me. I know what it's like to be loved by someone who loves me for what I am. Jess is the most gentle and unselfish man I know. He will honor me, Jack. Besides..."

He studied her face so filled with hope.

"What is it?"

"I'm pretty sure I'm going to have a baby."

"A baby? Oh, Bailey…,"  his voice drifted.

"You're thinking of the child my mother lost, your child."

He smiled sadly.  "No, honey. I was thinking of how happy I am for you."

"I hope Daddy will be as understanding."

"Listen, don't let Sid or anyone else steal your happiness away."

"I'm kind of hoping the news of the baby will somehow bring us all together. You know, you and Daddy — Daddy and grandfather."

"Can't you see? Some hurts may never be healed. If I stay, to your father, it would seem like he'd lost you, the way he lost Kate. It just can't be, Honey. Not the way you want it. But don't worry. You and I will always have a connection."

He pointed to her heart.

"Here."

She held him close.

"I'll miss you. Despite what you believe, I'll never forget you. Mommy saw and knew the real Jack Adams and she loved you for what she knew. So do I."

He was losing ground on his emotions. He knew it. He drew her away and kissed her forehead.

"You make sure Jess takes good care of you."

Bailey smiled and brushed his cheek.

"Will you come back for the wedding?"

Jack winked.

"We'll see."

"I love you, Jack Adams."

"I love you," he choked.

Then – he was gone.

****

Jack found Sid crouched in a dark corner of the den, nursing the last of his scotch. He didn't move from his spot when Jack approached him. However, his eyes coursed him until he sat down in a chair directly in front of him.

"I came to say goodbye and to ask a favor of you."

"A goodbye I can give you. A favor...?" He shrugged his shoulders.

"Don't do to Bailey and Jess what Byron did to you and Kate. Jess is a good man. He'll be a good husband to Bailey. They love each other."

"Let me handle Bailey. I've done okay so far without your advice. She's turned out all right."

"Will you hate me the rest of your life, Sid?"

"That's exactly what I intend to do. It's one of the few pleasures I've got left in life."

"Why waste your time hating me? You've got Bailey and Sammy. You have Mara. She loves you, Sid. She can't help it that she's not Kate."

Sid started laughing. His laughter echoed throughout the room. To those who didn't know these two men well, had they heard his laughter, they might think they were celebrating. There was bitterness behind his laughter. As abruptly as his laughter started, it ended. He stared pointedly at Jack and told him of Mara's confession.

"Two nights before Kate died, she called me. I never knew it. Mara answered the phone. If I had talked to Kate, she might still be alive."

"Jesus," Jack said shaking his head. He was thinking of Johnny Claiborne and his indirect connection to the days before Kate was killed. "Will this cycle of guilt ever end?"

"What are you talking about?" Sid shot back harshly.

"She must have called Johnny the same night and told him she was in Gallup. She wanted him to come get Bailey and take her back to you. Johnny was going to be her hero – and yours. Not only was he going to go to Gallup to get Bailey, but he was also going to bring Kate back to you. At least that's what he thought he was going to do."

Sid was suddenly sober. He sat up alerted.

290

"Johnny would have called me."

Jack shook his head.

"You weren't that approachable in those days, Sid. Besides, Kate told him not to tell you. She knew you'd come after her. He wanted to look good in your eyes. He was always trying to look good in your eyes."

"Idiot," Sid retorted.

"Yeah," Jack said. "And that idiot has paid a high price for his actions. More than you'll ever realize."

"He should pay."

Jack continued. "The day before he was to drive to Gallup, he was feeling sure of himself. He was finally going to be someone in your eyes. When he brought Kate back to you, you'd have to realize his worth. Before he left Denver, he was so high on what was going to happen, he decided to have a little fun. You know how Johnny had fun. He'd find a poker game and some booze. When Johnny drinks, Johnny talks more than usual. He brags even more. Well, guess who was playing poker with Johnny that day?"

"Benning?" Sid asked numbly.

"Yeah," Jack said. "Benning must have drugged Johnny or something after learning Kate was in Gallup, cause he woke up a day later thinking he'd come off a hard drunk. That's when he heard the news about Kate. Johnny never made it out of Denver. Like you, he thought I was the one who killed her. But had you really thought about it, you would have known I could never kill Kate."

"How do you know all of this about Johnny?"

"The night Bailey shot Benning, just after I left your room at the hospital, Johnny was waiting for me in my truck. He had some unfinished business with me. I believe he would have killed me had we not seen all the police cars headed for Zuni. I told Johnny that something was going down and that he'd have to wait to kill me. Sometime in our conversation, I must have mentioned Benning's name. Johnny got quiet. The truth hit him like a ton of bricks."

"Where's Johnny now?"

"In a hospital room in Denver."

"Did you shoot him?"

Jack let out a short laugh of irony.

"No. When he realized the truth, he went back to Denver. He tried to do away with himself. He couldn't even do that."

Sid ran a hand through his hair. His eyes were wild with fury, wild with remorse.

"I could kill him myself."

"Will that bring Kate back?"

Sid dropped his head into his hands and sobbed, forgetting that his most hated enemy sat before him.

"Kate," he cried. "I didn't protect you."

Sid's eyes were weary and red when he looked at Jack.

"I let her down. I'm as guilty as Johnny, as Mara, as you. She must have been so scared. You know what the FBI found in Benning's storage in LA?"

"Don't, Sid."

"They found her clothing and strands of her hair. How he had photos of her autopsy, I don't know. But he did, along with pictures of his other victims. He kept them in a book or something. I wish I'd been the one to kill him."

Sid was sobbing openly. Jack gripped his shoulder.

"The way I see it, Benning had his eyes on Kate for a long time. They both worked at the paper and that's where he saw her. He would have gotten to her even if I'd never taken her. Even if Mara had told you about Kate's call. Even if crazy Johnny hadn't told him where Kate was. Even if he hadn't thought he had killed me. He was that determined."

Sid leaned back in his chair. His tears had subsided, but Jack's hand still rested on his shoulder. He spoke dazed.

"Lou Steele, a Dallas police officer, told me they found your old truck. It was in a rented storage in Denver. Seems like Benning had rented storages all over the country. They found your suitcases, Bailey's bunny, and Kate's wedding ring. They even found a ring Toby Garcia had bought from Billy that night

292

for his wife, Sue. It had her inscription on it."

"I know," Jack said. "At least if there were any speculations about my killing Garcia, they've been laid to rest. Ed Berry, Toby's brother-in-law, feels as though justice has been served, with Toby and Kate's murders being solved."

"There are so many things I don't understand. I mean, why did Benning kill Toby Garcia? And how did Benning get out to where you and Kate had parked? No cars were left abandoned. No witnesses saw him there."

"I figure he killed Garcia because maybe he knew him or was suspicious of him. Or maybe he just needed some money. Hell, maybe he looked at him wrong. I don't know what drove that madman. As far as no trace of a car, he probably conned some fool into driving him out there. People will do anything for a few bucks. We're learning that Benning used accomplices for many of his crimes. He was a master manipulator."

"Your guy almost botched this, Jack. He led Bailey straight to Benning. He knew she would go look for Jess."

"She was never out of his sight, Sid, nor the other operatives. There was a tracker on the van. He did what you and I didn't have the courage to do. Deep down we knew it, but wouldn't take the risk. Bailey was the only person Benning would let down his guard for and risk being caught or killed. She was his obsession."

"It was still a hell of a risk."

Jack leaned down to face Sid directly.

"Sid, she's safe. It's over."

Sid stood up and walked toward the window, staring out aimlessly.

"We've all been wrong about so many things, Jack. But one person wasn't wrong – Claire Brennen. She was so right, so damn right about everything. Benning was Sandy Reed. Not only did they find your truck in that storage, but also thirty years of tangible evidence that connected Benning to over twenty killings, most were blonde women like Kate. Some were young boys. Who knows what else they will find."

"Strange how Claire Brennen appeared out of the clear blue and then went back to her world just as quickly," Jack said.

Sid snapped his jaw. "She said Kate drew her in. She said she was a victim like Kate, except she survived."

"Like Bailey," Jack mused. "I guess we're all victims, Sid. We're all survivors."

Sid looked at Jack. His tone was placid. His face was free from its earlier contempt.

"Where will you go now, Jack?"

"To Mexico, to see Mother – and Rita."

Sid couldn't help but to appreciate Jack's bravado.

"Well, you've never been one not to have a beautiful woman by your side."

"She's a hell of a woman, Sid. I'm crazy about her. I'm going to do my best to make this relationship work. You know me, Sid. I've played women, yes, but when it comes to love, I'm a one-woman man."

Sid's contempt almost surfaced, but he was able to control it. He sat back down and leaned back against the overstuffed chair.

"Well, for Rita's sake, I hope it works. I always liked her."

Jack stood tall in front of him. Sid felt his gaze, but didn't look up. Jack held out his hand for Sid to shake. He refused it.

"I'm not quite ready to forgive, Jack."

Jack pulled his hand away. Sid heard his footsteps move toward the door. Jack paused and then spoke sincerely.

"Well, you know where I'm at when you are."

Just as Jack was about to walk out of the door, Sid called out to him.

"I know it was you, Jack."

"What are you talking about?"

"I know you killed Benning."

"Bailey killed Benning, Sid."

"Oh, she got the initial shot, but someone else finished him off."

"You read the police report, Sid. You saw the autopsy.

They matched up. Bailey killed Benning in self-defense. All the bullets came from her gun."

"Did they? I keep remembering what Bailey told me about that night. She only remembers firing one shot and then hearing other shots as she was running away."

"You and I both know what a state she was in that night. She told me everything was a blur and that she couldn't be sure of anything."

"Guess there is no way of really knowing the accuracy of the police report. I mean, since Benning was cremated shortly after his autopsy. Something about the wishes of a nephew he had in Los Angeles."

"Let it go, Sid. The official report states Bailey killed him in self-defense. Besides, it would have been impossible for me to kill him. I was with Johnny when Bailey met up with Benning. Remember?"

"Impossible for other men, Jack, but you forget how well I know you."

Jack opened the door to leave and then paused. He owed this to Sid.

"Officially, Bailey killed Benning. Unofficially, well...," Jack shrugged, giving Sid the answer he already knew. Then, he was gone. Sid stared at the closed door and let out an appreciative laugh. He lifted his glass of scotch to Jack.

"Like I always said, Jack. You were the only S.O.B. I could ever really depend on."

****

Jack was almost to his truck when Sammy waved at him. He'd been on a walk and was just getting back. He walked toward Jack. His dark hair shown blue in the afternoon sun. His gray eyes struck a chord in Jack's heart. He hadn't seen Sammy close up since he was nine years old. Then, he was a pudgy, smart-mouthed brat that Jack barely tolerated. Now, he was a man, a handsome one, Jack observed. He was also aware that

Sammy had the same eyes he saw whenever he looked into a mirror. He wondered if Sammy noticed the resemblance.

"Sammy," Jack said, shaking his hand.

"Jack, I'd like to thank you for what you did for Bailey. I have to say, you surprised me. You surprised us all. Well – all except Mom. She said she knew you never killed Kate all along. She said you didn't have it in you."

"I appreciate her saying so."

Sammy shuffled his boots in the dirt.

"Can you believe our Bailey? She's something, isn't she? I didn't know she had it in her to do what she did."

"She has her mother's blood — and Sid's."

"Yeah, blood means a lot, huh?"

Jack studied him seriously. Could it be he knew?

"I think so, yeah," Jack said. "What do you think?"

"I guess I never really thought about it. I mean, Sid is the only father I've ever known. In that respect, blood doesn't mean a thing. I mean, he was more of a father to me than my own father was. Did you know my father, Jack?"

"I met Benny Harmon once or twice. I didn't like him much. But then, Sid was the only husband of Jean's that I liked."

"Did you love my mother, Jack?"

"Still do. Once I love, Sammy, I don't stop."

Sammy got restless.

"So, where you headed?"

"Mexico."

"Mexico? Why there?"

"That's my home. I left my address with your mom, you know, in case she ever wants to visit or get in contact with me."

"Why would she do that?"

Jack turned his head. In a few minutes, he'd be out of here. Even if Sammy suspected he might be his father, even if he knew, he hadn't made known his thoughts. Why open up something that's of no consequence now? Sammy, by all rights, was Sid's son. Sid deserved that honor. By the time Jean had told him he was Sammy's biological father, Sid had raised him

296

and loved him like his own. Jack turned to face his son. Why was it so easy for him to love Bailey and not so easy to love Sammy? Maybe it's because he loved Kate so much. Maybe it's because Bailey wasn't really his. Jack answered Sammy's question coolly.

"Your mother and I have been friends a long time. We've shared good times together."

"Sure," Sammy said just as casually. "I guess so. Will you be coming back? I mean, to see Bailey?"

"Might be," Jack said.

"Well, then, maybe we'll see each other again."

"Maybe so."

"Well," Sammy said, slapping Jack awkwardly on the back. "Thanks again for what you did for Bailey."

"I'd have done as much for anyone I love."

Sammy's gaze shot directly toward Jack's heart. Jack moved closer to him and called out his name. Sammy stepped back defensively.

"You'd best be going, Jack."

Jack retreated.

"I guess you're right."

Jack opened the door to his truck. Sammy called out to him one more time.

"If Mom were to come visit you in Mexico, would she be welcome?"

Jack wiped his wet eyes.

"Damn right she would."

Sammy lifted his hand to wave goodbye.

"I'm glad. She'll be happy to know that."

Jack moved his truck slowly from Sammy's view and that of the ranch. He was leaving two of the most important people of his life behind. No, three, he rethought. When he thought of Sid, he smiled.

"You've been a hell of a father, Sid. You were a hell of a friend. Looks like I fell short at both. Someday, maybe..."

Jack thought of Rita. He felt like a damn soldier coming

home from war.

"Hold on, Baby. Daddy's coming home."

**** 

Mara was packing when Sid went into the bedroom.

"You're leaving?"

"Bailey's well enough now and she has Jess to care for her. I'm leaving with Sammy and Diane today. I've taken an apartment in Dallas. I think it's best we separate for a while. You have some serious things you need to resolve before we can begin to rebuild our marriage. I'm not blaming you, Sid, or me. I'm just stating facts."

"Mara, I know I've said things. I know I've done things. I was distraught. I was confused."

"I know, Sid. But I can't take you back into my arms, into my bed, until I'm certain."

"Certain of what?"

"Until I'm certain it's my arms, my bed, you want to be in. Do you think it's been easy living in the shadow of Kate all these years? I can't do it anymore, Sid. I won't do it anymore."

Sid laid on the bed and covered his face with his arms.

"Mara, don't go. Don't you know what I've been through?"

"Yes, I do. Do you know what I've been through?"

She moved toward the bed and sat down next to Sid.

"My address and new phone number are written on a tablet on the dresser. Call me when you're ready to make this marriage a real marriage."

"I'll be lost if you leave me, Mara."

She kissed him softly.

"I'm lost with you."

**** 

He laid in bed for hours after Mara left with Sammy and Diane. The silence in the room tore at his heart. He felt as though he'd been kicked in the gut. He heard voices and movement in the house, but his mind was lost in the many goodbyes he'd said today. Yet, the most important goodbye he had to say was still left unspoken. He darted off the bed and down the stairs as if he were running from a fire. He grabbed his coat and keys and told the kids he'd be back later. He drove down the road until he reached another road that led to Zuni. There on that obscure path, he saw the outline of Corn Mountain. He pulled up within a few feet of it and parked his car. It was time, time he said goodbye to Kate.

It was near evening by now and the air was cutting. The horizon blazed in colors of deep azure and orange. It was a spectacular sight and he thought if he had to be laid to rest somewhere, it would be at a place as splendid as this. He got out of his car and had the inclination to sit in the very spot he knew Kate must have awakened. He felt of the earth, sifting it through his fingers as if it were Kate, herself. Tears filled his eyes and he was suddenly overpowered by her presence.

"Kate," he called out. "I've been so lost without you. I've been so lonely. Help me. Help me get on with my life before I lose everyone I love."

A gentle breeze swept over him and at first fear, but then peace overcame him. As if she had brushed his face, he felt free. He stood tall and drew from his pocket the ring she had placed on his finger over twenty years ago. He rubbed the entire circumference of the ring and a picture of Kate placing it on his finger played in his mind.

"You were so filled with hope and wonder, Kate. We both were. How I loved you."

Once more, he placed the ring on his finger. Then, he brought it to his mouth and kissed it, as if he were kissing Kate. He took the ring off his finger and in an instant, threw it in the direction of the setting sun.

"Goodbye, my love. May we both find peace."

He walked slowly back to the car and glanced one more time toward the beauty of his surroundings. That he could see only the beauty after all the horror was amazing to him and he didn't think this was by chance. He looked up to heaven.

"Where do I go from here?"

A vision of a beautiful woman came to mind, but it wasn't Kate or Mara.

"Claire," he whispered.

He smiled as he pulled away from Kate's resting place. He knew she was directing him toward Claire.

"Claire was right. You brought us together."

He pulled out his wallet and found Claire's card. He remembered their kiss. He couldn't wait to call her. As he drove back toward the ranch, he noticed that Jess's truck was still there. He thought of Jess and Bailey, feeling a happiness that he hadn't felt in years. He parked the car and ran inside. He found Bailey and Jess holding each other in the quiet of the den. He edged away as not to disturb them. Later, he'd tell his daughter about her parents' separation. No one deserved happiness more than these two people did. Inside the bedroom, he picked up the phone and called Claire.

"Claire, it's me. Sid Carson – Sid Michaels. Listen, I'm going to be in Albuquerque in a couple of days. I was wondering if we could get together. Maybe have some coffee or dinner. Yeah, Claire, I'm fine. Yeah, I look forward to seeing you, too."

****

A few nights later, when everyone was gone, Bailey sat on the front porch and watched the starlit night. A peace surrounded her, one she had never known. She had always been a restless soul. She had always known that something in her life wasn't quite right. Then, everything was brought to light and the pieces began to fall into place. There were still some that were missing though. The doctors told her she might remember more details about the night her mother was murdered, but that she might not. She was only four years old and the mind can only remember small details in the best of worlds, let alone a

300

world of trauma. She knew some things didn't connect and that the police were finding out new information about Red Benning each day. She wouldn't dwell on the details she couldn't remember. Instead, she would focus on the blessings in her life...Jess and the baby. Soon, they would travel together, where Jess would be performing with Jimmy Lee and his band. Life was good now and she would not take it for granted.

She thought of Jess's family. Soon they would be her family. She loved them as deeply as she loved her father and mother and Sammy. She was connected to them through both love and tragedy. Billy Nehah would be more than a father to her, he was her spiritual connection to a woman taken so young in life...her mommy. In the weeks that followed the death of Red Benning, Bailey had little time to reflect on things. There was always someone around, hovering over her. Tonight, she was alone. Sid had gone to Albuquerque and Jess was busy getting things ready for his tour. He would be over later tonight. As she sat alone on the porch, she looked in the direction of Corn Mountain. She was feeling a strong connection to her birth mother as she sat only miles away from the place she had died. Billy had always told her to embrace the spirits. Tonight, she beckoned her mother.

Bailey closed her eyes and could instantly sense her mother's presence. She embraced the moment, praying it would not end too soon. The air smelled of rose-attar and in her mind, she could hear her voice calling out her name...Rebecca. A warm breeze swept over Bailey. She actually called out "Mommy." And then, the most remarkable thing happened. For the first time in her memory, she could see her mother's face. She was beautiful. Her brown eyes were dancing merrily at the sight of her little girl. She was smiling and Bailey felt as though her smile was singing from love.

What registered most in Bailey's heart was the serenity that flowed over her mother's face. Bailey understood that her mother was giving her a gift tonight. Always in the past when she tried, she could never remember her mother's face. Tonight she saw it clearly as if she were sitting in front of her. The image remained only for a short while, but it was ingrained in Bailey's memory forever. She would never wonder what her mother looked like or smelled like or sounded like. She would never wonder if her mother was still suffering. Bailey wiped away the tears that fell profusely down her face. Tonight was a night of surrender and love. She knew she was the last person to hold onto her mother's spirit. Tonight she knew she must love her enough to let her go. Knowing her mommy was finally at peace, Bailey opened her eyes to her new reality. She touched her tummy and embraced the life inside of her. Billy Nehah wasn't her only guardian spirit.

"Mommy, I do understand the love between a mother and her child. Nothing, not even death, can break through it."